Praise for Sarah Maine

'A gripping page-turner'
Woman

'Its portrayal of life in a gold-rush town is vivid,
and Rose's story is absorbing'
The Times

'Maine reworks the conventions of historical romance
in a narrative that regularly undercuts expectations
of what is to come'
Sunday Times

'An echo of Daphne du Maurier'
Independent

'Maine's gift of setting the mood shines'
RT Reviews

About the Author

Sarah Maine is the author of *The House Between Tides*, *Beyond the Wild River* and *Women of the Dunes*. She was born in England but grew up partly in Canada before returning to the United Kingdom, where she now lives.

For more information visit sarahmainebooks.com

Also by Sarah Maine

The House Between Tides
Beyond the Wild River
Women of the Dunes

ALCHEMY

AND

ROSE

SARAH MAINE

HODDER

In memory of E.R.M.

First published in Great Britain in 2021 by Hodder & Stoughton
An Hachette UK company

This paperback edition published in 2021

1

A CIP catalogue record for this title is available from the British Library

Waterstones exclusive paperback ISBN 978 1 529 39444 3
Paperback ISBN 978 1 529 38502 1
eBook ISBN 978 1 529 38500 7

Typeset in Adobe Caslon Pro by Palimpsest Book Production Limited,
Falkirk, Stirlingshire

Printed and bound in Great Britain by Clays Ltd, Elcograf S.p.A.

Hodder & Stoughton policy is to use papers that are natural, renewable
and recyclable products and made from wood grown in sustainable forests.
The logging and manufacturing processes are expected to conform to
the environmental regulations of the country of origin.

Hodder & Stoughton Ltd
Carmelite House
50 Victoria Embankment
London EC4Y 0DZ

www.hodder.co.uk

Prologue

For a week he slept in an old sheep shelter, bedding down in straw lately used for lambing, whiling away the days watching – and waiting. On the seventh day he woke early, rose and stretched, then consumed the last of his bread and cheese, taking a moment to steady his nerve. This was it. He picked up the bottle of kerosene he had brought with him and set off, keeping low, and worked his way back to where he could see the little huddle of turf-roofed croft houses set around a small loch. He crouched in the heather to watch for Armstrong starting his rounds.

The wind was getting up and it stroked the silken grasses on the pasture below, shaking the gorse bushes by the walls. He smiled a little: it was on his side, blowing gustily from the east, so there was no chance the fire would endanger the houses. The heather was dry and it would burn quickly and well. And this was the best place to set it alight, not too close but not too far to run from, and where the blaze could not be missed. He had already timed how long it would take him to get into the factor's house and out again, devising places to hide in case he was seen leaving. It was a desperate undertaking, he knew that, but the anger was still strong in him and his head was clear so it must be now while his courage held.

Then he saw the factor emerge from his house to start his rounds, going from tenant to tenant, hammering on each door;

1

a pattern he knew all too well. He cursed both Kinnloss and his factor as he watched, crouched down in the heather, until he saw the man emerge from the last house and make his way back to his own larger dwelling, which stood a little apart.

The moment had come. He rose, glanced down at the houses one last time, and then doused the heather with the kerosene, lit a match and ran.

He sprinted for the trees, reached them and took cover in the little valley, panting hard, listening as the sound of crackling grew. The smoke wafted down to him and he heard a shout, and then another, and he looked back, seeing the hillside well ablaze. Stealthily he made his way through the trees in the valley bottom, having known which way they would come, the factor surely with them, and then he circled back and hid behind a field wall and watched as the houses emptied.

Everyone would turn out to beat the flames, they were that sort of folk.

The rest was easy. He had expected to need to force entry but the factor had left the door unlocked in his haste and so it was straight into the room where he had lately been spurned. He prised the desk drawer open, lifted the lid of the box and tipped the money into his leather bag. That was it! His pulse was thumping and his legs felt weak but he had done it. He turned to leave—

—and his heart stopped. A figure was standing in the doorway, watching him. The factor's son, his father's stamp on his features. 'Put that money back.'

Damn the lad! 'Stand aside, Jamie.'

The youth stood his ground. 'You'll have to kill me first.' His eyes were fierce and angry.

'Stand aside, I tell you, and I'll be away.' He saw then that the boy was gripping a bar of iron by his side, his knuckles white, and the man's heart sank. The last thing he wanted was a fight with a stripling but it was urgent now that he was gone.

The lad lifted the bar and held it across his body in readiness and the man allowed his shoulders to droop. He lifted the bag as if to place it on the table in defeat but then swung it towards young Armstrong instead. He grabbed the iron bar as he ducked, and twisted it from his grip, shoving him out of the doorway. The boy staggered but recovered fast, snatching at the bag and leaving the man with no option but to punch him low and hard as he made for the door.

He was almost through it when he turned, just too late to dodge the iron bar as it came hurtling towards him. It caught him a glancing blow, splitting the skin above his eyebrow, and he stumbled, dazed and blinded by the blood, and the lad was straight onto him, kicking and biting, untried muscle against a full-grown man. All pluck and folly. He thrust him aside and the boy fell hard, hitting his head against the wall, and lay still.

Oh God. He dashed the blood from his eyes and went to him, sick now with dread, and bent to feel for a pulse. It was there, good and strong, and the boy moved a little, and then groaned. The man turned him onto his back and propped him up against the wall, then stood looking down at him, desperate to leave but now unable to go.

Then the boy's eyes opened to a slit.

'You'll hang for this, McAuley,' he said.

Chapter 1

Will thought at first it was the storm.

He heard a shout, and then another, and a roar that grew in strength and passion. He went to the window and saw people running down the street, shouting and pointing, pelting towards the shore. 'Something's up,' he said.

'What?' Robbie mumbled from the narrow bed they had shared that night.

'God knows.' More figures ran past, heads down against the wind, and Will leant from the window to shout, 'What is it?'

'A ship,' came back the answer.

A ship. His heart went cold.

Pinned to a leeward shore no ship would have a chance. 'I'm going down there,' he said, pulling on his boots. He wrenched open the door and took the stairs in leaps, then stumbled into the street.

A crowd was gathering above the beach. Will recognised diggers, store men, cooks, whores, and ragged souls who knew only too well the fury of the western winds. Surf boomed relentlessly, throwing spray high into the air to drift in a grey veil over the roofs of the town, enshrouding the gold diggers' shacks along the shoreline.

Dawn streaked the sky and the silent watchers stood in the cold light, some reliving their own arrival across the unforgiving Tasman Sea. Tossed like a plaything the ship struggled, lurching and powerless, sails shredded, engine swamped, and Will imagined the poor devils hunkered below deck, helpless, praying for a salvation they must know would be denied them. Listing now, the doomed ship lay broadside to waves, water pouring off in sheets as she attempted to right herself. Not a soul was in sight.

'She'll hit at any moment,' a voice said beside him, 'and then break.'

'May sweet Christ deliver them,' said another, crossing himself.

The first man laughed. 'Aye! He'll deliver all right, it's kegs I'm waiting for.'

Will turned and saw avarice in the man's eyes. He wanted to punch the light from them, but then a groan went through the crowd and he swung back to see the ship had struck the deadly bar of sand that ceaselessly formed and shifted at the river mouth. The vessel came to a shuddering halt and its main mast snapped, falling amidst a tangle of spars and rigging.

Just two hundred yards from the shore.

Boiling surf hid the stricken vessel for a moment, and when the waves sucked back, Will saw that she had already split in two and goods were spilling from the hold. Anticipation rippled along the shore. And then a figure appeared on the angled bow, a hand raised in entreaty, only to be swept away by the next wave.

Moments later the first pieces of cargo appeared, borne on wave crests like appeasement from a careless god. The crowd shifted, necks craned forward. Crates, boxes and barrels multiplied and Will sensed the growing tension; no one in authority had arrived and the goods would vanish the instant they hit shore, a precious bounty. His eye was caught then by a figure further down the beach, stooped over a tripod, wrestling with a dark cloth that writhed around his shoulders. The photographer. Will had seen him in the streets, but for pity's sake, this was no peep show! He turned back to the unfolding drama and his gaze sharpened, fixing on a shape that was riding the waves. It was a pallet of some sort, surfing in, raft-like, and there, clinging to it, was a figure.

'Look!' he shouted.

But no one heard, or no one cared.

Blinded by spray he lost sight of the crude craft, then it reappeared, riding the next wave, the figure hanging on, arms stretched across it. 'There!' he shouted again, but still no one heeded him. He pushed his way to the front, deaf to the curses, and stood on the shingled beach.

The raft had vanished.

Miraculously, it resurfaced a moment later but even as he watched, the purple curl of a huge wave formed behind it, its crest blown back in a mane of spray. 'Hang on!' he yelled into the wind.

The wave broke over the pallet, and the figure was gone.

A murmur behind him signalled that other eyes were watching and Will was filled with a great fury. Would they do *nothing*? He began pulling off his boots in sudden desperation. The pallet was only fifty yards from the shore now, surfing towards the shallow waves, and behind it Will could see a dark bundle. One soul, still quick with life. Casting the boots aside, he plunged into the spume, the shingle sharp on his soles. Someone shouted out but he pressed on, gasping at the killing cold.

The beach abruptly shelved and he lost his footing, pulled under to be rolled like flotsam in the pitiless sea. He was sucked deeper, his ears roared and he swallowed salt water, then he surfaced spluttering and gagging, cursing and helpless, and had just taken a breath when something arrived beside him, relinquished by the wave, and he reached for it. The bundle. Long hair streaming behind. He grasped icy flesh as the next wave hit and they were tumbled forward together. His feet touched the shelf of the beach and he had braced himself for the pull-back when he felt hands grabbing him, holding him there, and he tightened his grip on his prize. Voices shouted above the surf as he was dragged out of it and unceremoniously dumped onto the beach. 'Stupid bugger,' someone said.

'The woman!' Will cried. 'Get the woman.'

'We've got her. She's dead, man, and thanks to Big Sven, you ain't.'

Scrambling to his feet, he saw the sodden bundle on the shingle a few yards away. He went and stood over the woman's still form, seeing limbs askew and wanton, her small feet bare and bloodless. A slight figure, a girl, torn clothes exposing milky flesh, her face masked by streaks of hair.

A moment ago she had clung to the pallet as if to life itself, and now she lay there, a broken thing.

Denial exploded in his head and he grabbed her body, turning her onto her side, forcing her mouth open with his fingers. Water dribbled from her lips and he rolled her onto her back, straddling her, and began pressing on her chest.

'She's gone, you fool.'

'Leave the poor lass.'

Will ignored them, feeling for a pulse, making himself believe that he felt a flutter. One soul, quick not dead. It was the closest he had been to prayer since boyhood. Hair falling forward, he went on pressing on her chest as he had seen a fisherman do once when a survivor had been brought ashore at Srath an loin from a storm-tossed wreck.

'For God's sake, man, leave her be!'

Quick not dead. The words repeated in his head, desperate now. He stopped, feeling again for a pulse. That man, of course, had died. He shut out the thought, but if there was a pulse it was faint, and he bent to the girl, closing his mouth over hers.

Ignoring reproaches from the onlookers he breathed once, twice and stopped. Again. Had her chest risen? He pulled back and watched . . . and . . . yes!

Twice more he mingled his breath with hers and felt a slow reawakening in the form beneath him, and then the girl convulsed, drew a shuddering breath, spluttered, and her eyelids flickered. Will straightened, and looked down into eyes that were the colour of the grey sea from which he had plucked her.

As grey, and as cold. Perhaps the waves had, after all, entered the soul of her. She stared back up at him, her eyes filled with anguish, and gave a great keening cry, curled onto her side like a hurt creature, and retched.

Then Robbie was there, standing over him, and smirking. 'Some got kegs, some got crates,' he said, 'and Will Stewart got himself a girl.'

Chapter 2

The crowd parted and Moll O'Shea appeared, elbowing her way through the spectators – Irish Moll, Black Moll, Big Moll, with her dark hair and ample figure. She bent to cover the girl with a blanket. 'Will you just stand then, and gawp?' she asked, turning on the onlookers. 'One of you lift the lass and bring her to my place.' Then, addressing Will: 'And you, you fool, get yourself dry.'

Robbie stripped off his jacket and draped it over Will's shoulders before bending down to scoop up the girl. 'I'll take her, Will. Stand aside, my friends, and let me through.'

Back in their bare lodgings, Will felt the aftershock of cold as he peeled off his wet clothes, casting about for something dry. He grabbed Robbie's spare shirt and pulled it over his head before climbing into the bed, shuddering uncontrollably. He was still there when Robbie returned a while later, a bottle in his hand, and the glint in his eye suggested he had supped from it.

'How's the girl?' Will asked.

'Well now, I'd say she's quite lovely! Young and slender and fair. A real prize.'

Will snorted. 'Will she live?'

'Oh aye. Doing fine, she was, then she started moaning and groaning and clutching her stomach. Moll threw me out, but sent this for you.' He raised the bottle. 'Said you'd done well.'

A commendation from Black Moll! But he took it anyway

and drank, feeling the raw spirit set his guts aflame. 'Did she say anything?' He passed it back to Robbie. 'The girl . . .'

'Just that her name was Rose. No ring, so she's maybe a Miss Rose.' He paused. 'Miss Flotsam Rose, now there's a grand name for a lovely girl. You're in luck, me friend.'

Will took the bottle again and his mind went back to the ship, laying broken on the shifting bar, and to the bodies that must now be coming ashore. 'Were there other survivors?'

'A couple of dozen, perhaps, and over a hundred on board,' one of them said, packed like pilchards in a rotting ship. Came across from Melbourne. Pickings were good, so folk say.'

Will ignored the last. 'Was she travelling alone? Rose . . .'

Robbie's eyes gleamed as he took back the bottle. 'Now that, me boy, you must ask her yourself.'

———

The storm had blown itself out later that day when Will crunched along the shingle on the shore. The big ocean swells were still rolling in, remorseless, and boxes were now piled high above the tide line. Official-looking folk were down there now, issuing instructions as remnants of the cargo came in on the surf. Too late for that, he thought.

Above the high tide line of dry seaweed and driftwood the dead had been laid in grim rows. God, what an unforgiving place this was. Someone had fashioned a stretcher of sorts and men were lifting the cadavers onto a mule cart just ahead of him. Was there one amongst them for whom Rose would weep? The churches, Free and Roman, were being used as makeshift morgues, so it was the luck of the draw whose heaven or hell their poor souls reached.

And then Will saw him again, the photographer, further down the shore, his camera pointed towards the wreck. But even as he watched, the man began shifting his gear and setting up where he could photograph the cart and its macabre load. Will changed course and went towards him. 'For God's sake, man! Leave them with a little dignity.'

The man swung round and waited for Will to join him. He was a tall, angular sort of a man. 'I take nothing from them,' he said, but quietly.

Will dragged a sodden blanket over the bodies and scowled at him. 'And if it was your kin, would you want them gawped at?'

The man regarded him, evenly. 'No, I wouldn't. Nor would I wish them to be here, drowned and dead.'

Will grunted. 'Then take your pictures somewhere else. Shift yourself!'

The man stood his ground. 'I record only what we see, you and I. I neither add nor remove from the situation, I simply preserve the moment. Wherein the disrespect, sir?'

Fancy words, on an educated tongue. A fellow Scot, but one who spoke like a minister, a class of men for whom Will had little time. He glanced at the cart where limbs protruded from sodden clothing, seeing the pale flesh of a naked foot, a hand stiffened in unanswered appeal, and looked away again. This, at least, he had spared that poor girl.

'You can't bear to look,' the man remarked. 'Out here, in the wind and cold, with death hanging in the air, it's too dreadful, is it not, too hard to confront and accept, and so we look away. A photograph permits a little distance, a safer context, and allows us to dwell on the scene at a later time, to linger there, revisit the moment and consider, and maybe measure the human cost.'

'And you make a living from the gawping.'

The man shrugged. 'You wish to shame me, sir, but you fail. What is the difference, after all, between printed words or the grey tones of a photograph. Both are simply marks on paper, both record and report. But while words engage the intellect, photographs use another language; they have a more visceral appeal, that punch in the gut.' The man was watching Will's face, as if gauging his reaction, and added, unapologetically: 'I'm neither voyeur nor predator, sir, and I can withstand any amount of your derision if I can awaken in others an understanding of this raw place and the true price of gold. It's little enough, perhaps, but some small contribution, to set in the balance.' Will turned away, unconvinced, but the photographer was not done. 'Yesterday a man swam out into that killing sea, and rescued a woman – a mad act but one of selfless courage, something I could not have done. But I can do this. So now, sir, if *you* will shift yourself, I'll . . .' he paused, his eye caught by something over Will's shoulder, and his tone changed. 'Oh God, now cometh the custodian of souls.'

Will turned to see the Free Church minister striding towards them, flanked by others, their outrage radiating before them. 'What, in heaven's name, d'ye think you're doing?' The man's anger swept over Will, including him in condemnation. 'Have you no respect?'

Will looked across at the photographer, an eyebrow raised, ready to enjoy the encounter, but then saw that one of the men was staring at him, plucking at the minister's sleeve, and he heard the word 'rescue' and drew back, having no wish for attention. 'You'll be served hell and damnation now, so best sharpen your defence,' Will said, in sudden sympathy with the accused, and continued into town.

Hokitika. Grog shops, hotels and dance halls, low weatherboard buildings with flaking paint, or sun-bleached to a silver-grey, aligned along a grid of rutted streets beside general stores, smithies, bakeries, bootmakers and, of course, the banks, recently rebuilt

in brick: solid, square and confident. The town, barely a decade
old, was still raw but vibrant, its fortunes locked on to a balance
beam that measured the price of gold.

He reached Big Moll's place and stared up at it, wondering
how Rose was faring there. It too had started life as a grog shop,
but now its false façade proclaimed it to be a hotel, and a dance
hall had recently been added. It was at the seedy end of town, a
haunt of the less lucky diggers, and its real business, as everyone
knew, went on in the rooms at the back. Moll herself, it was
loudly claimed by an extended clan of Erin's sons, had a heart of
gold but, if so, it needed steam-driven stampers to release it from
its stony cortex. Moll's status, and her view of the world, was
promoted by the ready fists of these Fenians, and the town's
purveyors of morality wisely left her alone. She was amassing a
fortune, and Will knew to his cost how fast a week's takings
could vanish in the hard liquor and soft flesh offered by Black
Moll's establishment.

And Rose had been taken there.

———

It was ridiculous that he should worry, he had told himself as he
washed dirt through the cradle and looked for colour in his pans
through the following week. Just because he had pulled her from
the sea and breathed life into her did not make the girl his
responsibility, and yet he had seen desperation in her eyes when
she had looked into his, and had read there an anguished appeal.

It was that look that brought him back to town at the end
of the week, arriving as the light was fading and gulls were gathering on the low-tide sand bars, their beaks set seaward. He made
his way down the back streets, avoiding a figure that lurched
towards him swearing in a foreign tongue, feeling anxious about
her. She was young and Robbie had said she was pretty. Will

recalled fine features and milky flesh, and such women were a scarce commodity here.

And now Black Moll had her.

He pushed open the door to be confronted by Moll herself, seated at a round table playing cards with an old timer. She chuckled when she recognised him. 'Come to claim your booty, Will Stewart? Well, she's not fit.' So Moll had learnt his name, had she? From Robbie, presumably. An Irishman himself, he regularly sank a week's earnings here.

'I came to see how she's doing.'

'She'll mend, but she's lost her baby.'

Will stared. 'She was pregnant?'

'Aye.'

'So was her husband on board the ship?'

The woman smiled, considering him, and echoed Robbie's words. 'Ask her yourself, Will Stewart.'

'I will,' he replied, daunted, though, by the prospect of such grief.

Moll got to her feet, tossing a losing hand in her partner's face, and led him down a rear passage, past cribs with which he was, shamefully, familiar. Drunk and lonely he had sometimes sought oblivion there, departing unsatisfied and broke, and with no clear recollection of which girl's company he had paid for.

The room Moll led him to was the furthest from the bar, and had a proper door rather than a curtain. Greater privacy at a greater cost, and the loss of income from it would soon add up. His concern intensified. What was Moll up to? She glanced at him, as if reading his mind, and gave a wry smile as she tapped on the door.

───────

It seemed to Rose that she had been lying there for an eternity, staring at a triangle of light reflected on the wall, floating still in wave-tossed limbo, leaving fate to determine her future. She turned her head as the door opened and saw Moll, and behind her, a man.

She frowned, recognising him as the one who had thwarted fate's intentions, and looked away again. 'Now, Rose.' Moll's tone was almost maternal. 'Here's Will Stewart come to see you, so you can thank him for saving you.' The woman peered into the bowl beside the bed and frowned. 'You've not touched a drop!'

'I'm sorry.' Her voice came as barely a whisper.

'I'll warm it again and eat it you will, my girl. Five minutes, Will Stewart.' Sweeping up the bowl, Moll left them, pulling the door closed behind her.

Rose regarded her saviour and could find no word of thanks.

He stood there, looking uncomfortable, but then he smiled. 'You'll mend, Moll said.' She made no reply, and turned her head away, fixing again on the shaft of light from the window, resolved to play no part in fate's next steps. 'I heard about the baby. I'm sorry.'

'Are you?' She kept her face averted. On board the ship she had contemplated throwing herself overboard but later, when their peril was clear, some primitive force had awoken in her and she had been driven to save herself and the child. How strange it was. But now that drive was gone.

As was the child.

Impossible to grieve for, and yet . . .

She hoped her response would silence him, but no: 'Is there someone . . . was there someone with you? There are survivors, I'm not sure how many . . . Is there anyone you want me to look for?'

'No.'

He frowned. 'You came alone? From Melbourne?'

'I was sent. Alone. From Melbourne.' And those who sent

her would not have thanked him either, preferring her to have drowned.

'Where were you heading? Can I send for someone to come to you?'

'I was sent *here*.' She turned and looked steadily back at him, her tone flat. How would Tommy have felt if she had died, she wondered. But then, he would never have known.

The man continued to look puzzled. 'Why?' he asked.

'To find work, and to vanish, and I would have. But for you.' It would have been so much simpler. If it had not been for this man's crazy action, the space she occupied in this bleak room would be a void now, a vacancy.

He looked bewildered, but had no time to respond before Moll swept in bearing the bowl, its contents steaming. 'Make yourself useful, Will Stewart, and see that she eats this.' She jabbed a thick finger in Rose's face. 'I saw you clinging to that pallet, young Rose, so don't you be giving up now.' She thrust the bowl into the man's hand and left.

He looked down at it, then at her, and smiled a slow smile. 'Moll has a lovely way with her,' he said. 'Can you sit up a bit more?'

All she wanted was to embrace the void and vanish, and she wanted this man to go now, and take his concern and his kindly eyes away with him, so she shuffled up, pulling a shawl around her shoulders, and reached for the bowl. 'I'll eat it. You don't have to stay.'

He shook his head. 'Too risky.'

She raised the spoon and looked across at him. 'You're not afraid of the Tasman Sea but you're afraid of a woman.'

'Of that woman, aye.'

She examined him more closely. He had a good face, regular features but for a scar that pulled at the skin above his left eye.

Brown hair and very dark eyes. When he smiled the puckered eyebrow lowered to become a wink and she glimpsed a warmth there and, despite the emptiness inside her, she felt herself responding and dropped her eyes to the bowl, resisting him. 'You're a Scot,' she said presently.

'Yes.'

'My mother was a Scot, or at least her mother was.' Transported for thievery many years ago, she had given birth to Rose's mother on the passage over. Did that make her a Scot? Or a nobody . . .

She contemplated him over the spoon where he stood like a dog on guard. 'Why did you risk your life to get me?' she asked.

'Because you clung on so bravely, and got so close.'

She supped in silence, and felt the broth begin to warm her. 'I clung from instinct. I'd no reason to live.'

'That's not true.' She glanced at him, but said nothing. 'The baby?'

'The baby wasn't wanted.' If she shocked him, maybe he would leave, and she handed him the empty bowl to emphasise that he should go. But first she had a question: 'Moll tells me this is a hotel, her hotel.'

'Aye, it is,' he replied, then added, 'and a bar and dance hall.'

'And a brothel?'

He hesitated. 'Yes.'

'I thought so. I heard noises next door.' Rhythmical grunts and cries and drunken laughter. Blatant and raw. Not like Tommy's inexpert love-making, which had been furtive and fumbling, but in all essentials no different. But here, at least, a more honest transaction.

The man looked concerned again. 'Look, there are other places you could go, better hotels. They might give you work when you're well again. I can tell you which ones. And if you need money—'

She gave a hard little laugh. 'I don't. I've five sovereigns stitched into the hem of my dress, and thanks to you, Will Stewart, I have them still. So I'm all set up, you see. Just like they said.'

He seemed about to say more but the door opened and Moll returned, her face brightening at the sight of the empty bowl. 'Off you go now, Will. What Rose needs is rest and food, and then she'll blossom for us all, eh? Away with you.'

Rose saw the man glance at her, uncertain again, and she looked steadily back at him. He left without another word and she returned to her contemplation of the sharp triangle of light reflected on the wall.

Chapter 3

Will went out through the bar, raising a hand to those who greeted him, refusing gestured invitations, in no mood to be sociable. What a strange and bitter girl she was, he thought as he pushed open the door, with her sea-grey eyes and her sorrow. And how pale; her skin stretched tight, her eyes ringed by dark hollows, fair hair lank on the dirty pillow. And yet that mole, high on her cheekbone, gave her an oddly raffish air. He stood a moment, disturbed by the encounter.

Rose.

The name suited her and he imagined that, beneath the strain, she was lovely. But Moll's was no place for the vulnerable and friendless. Half her clientele would soon be drunk, slipping dead-eyed under the tables or ejected, staggering, into the street, pockets emptied. The rest would soon be pounding the wooden floors to the tune of fiddle and accordion, swinging each other wildly around, the lucky ones clasping girls who even now would be stretching and yawning, fastening buttons on dresses whose button holes were wide and worn, preparing for the night's work ahead; the less fortunate making do with their digging partners. Robbie too would be heading into town to join the endless round of drink, dance and noisy competition for female flesh.

But it would not do for Will, not tonight.

He lingered a moment on the boardwalk and looked to the end of the muddy street where the ocean's swells still rode high into the estuary, lifting the vessels moored along Gibson's Quay.

These ships had made it across the sand bar before the storm, catching keels perhaps but piloted to safety by skippers who could better judge the tides and the currents. Melbourne to Hokitika was a regular route, supplies brought as fast as from Dunedin round the coast, and with those supplies came a diminishing stream of hopefuls. Talk was that the west coast was finished, and that the noble quest would take its followers elsewhere. But where next?

It was the quest itself, Will had come to understand, not the golden grail, that kept men on the move – the eternal hopefulness, the never-ending maybe. The diggers had sloughed off their old lives, they were masterless men now recognising no obligation other than to their partners, or to their consciences if they had left families behind. And they liked it that way; this freedom kept them questing even as the dream eluded them. Old timers spoke of times past when fortunes were made in weeks and men could be homeward bound with their futures secured, or might choose to stay and open a business, buy a farm, take a wife, raise a family.

And it was this that Will craved. Land he could call his own.

His quest was simple.

The gold was just a means to an end for him, but the days of easy fortunes were gone. Pickings were thinner on the crowded goldfields and a greater investment was needed to extract what lay buried deep. The likes of Moll might be richer by morning, and her girls would have coins in their pockets, maybe saving a few shillings towards an uncertain future, but most diggers were standing still, treading water. Sly-grog or cheap spirits might assuage the deprivations of hard living but, having danced the night away, the men could only shamble back to tents or shacks, milked of their week's takings, rising next morning, foul of breath and bleary-eyed but with the dream still lingering. Fleetingly remorseful perhaps, before they were consumed again by an unquenchable thirst for riches.

And no amount of grog and the flesh of fair nymphs could slake that sort of lust.

The surface gold was all but gone now, and the efforts of small-time diggers were poorly rewarded. Companies were forming or moving in from elsewhere, and men were forfeiting their cherished independence for paid employment and it was the company bosses who grew fat. Grumbling spread as dreams crumbled, but the old timers just smiled and said nothing. Their crazy nomadic lives had buffeted them from California to Victoria, down to Otago and back to Victoria, and now they were here on this rain-drenched coast, shadowed by the Southern Alps, biding their time, ears to the ground and ready at a moment's notice to rise like a flock of migrant birds, hitch up their swag bags and move on.

There was talk. There always was. Always the next great goldfield over the horizon, and rumours came and went like the ocean swells. 'South Africa,' someone said, huddled with his cronies around a beer-stained table. 'I was talking to a fella who—' He was brushed aside. 'I'm headin' back to Queensland, better winnings there.' A small man with a wooden leg shook his head. 'Canada. West coast. That'll be next. North of the line . . .'

'Nah. We're not done here.'

And Will had seen how Robbie listened, his cool blue eyes flicking from face to face while smoke rings rose from the briar-wood pipes of wiry sages who picked food from grey beards, their faces like windfallen apples, cheeks hollowed over toothless jaws. Did Robbie not see the irony? Big talk of big yields and yet here they were, still chasing the mother lode, as shiftless as when they started out. No, it was the eternal adventure that kept these diggers going. Half of them could no longer remember where home was and had no wish to return if they could, wanting nothing more than this – jawing over a drink with like-minded souls, the future vague and undefined, still beckoning.

But it was not the life for him, Will thought, kicking a stone down the road. Nor did he think it was for Robbie. Robbie Malloy dreamt big and talked big, and there was a ruthless streak in him. For all that their meagre takings slipped through his fingers at the end of the week, faster than muddy run-off through a digger's cradle, Robbie had grand ambitions. 'I've a mind to become a gentleman,' he told his company, sweeping aside their mockery. 'And when I return to Ireland, I'll go with gold weighing my pockets down to my boots.' Will had laughed with the others, but he wanted more than that. Or different, anyway, and he knew that one day they would part company. For now though, they worked well together, pulling each other out of fights, buoying each other up. Keeping going. Partners.

From the top of the beach, Will considered the sprawl of the gold-seekers' town where grey smoke drifted over grey roofs silhouetted against a backdrop of grey mountains, and wondered a little where this adventure might lead. Somewhere a dog barked, setting off a chorus of other strays, and he raised his eyes to where, high above the town, the last of the light caught the shine of the great glaciers. An awesome but forbidding sight.

Dropping his gaze, he turned up his collar against the wind, and sniffed: woodsmoke and sea spray, and the smell of rotting refuse. How long could he stick at this? May now and colder by the day, in a world turned upside down. Winter was not far off; mighty storms, rain and cold to come, the old men said – snow, too. Empty shacks stood abandoned as numbers, like the gold, began to thin. It was almost two years since he and Robbie had disembarked at Dunedin, on the east coast, and then followed the gold trail down through Otago before coming here but, hard as it was to accept, the best was over. They had come too late.

Hunching against the cold, he went down to the edge of the sea and watched the swells roll over the wreck, indifferently lifting and dropping the hull. A few boxes were still coming ashore and a few ragged figures still waited for them. What a world was this where half the town was quaffing champagne with whores while others waited in the darkness for dead men's booty?

And suddenly Will longed for another west coast where the days would be growing long now, the mornings crisp and the evenings sweet with the buttery scent of gorse, fragrant with bluebells. Lambs would be dotting the lower slopes of The Saddle and calves in the in-fields would be staggering to their feet. And above them always the persistent jangle of laverocks would be filling the air with joyful sound, hovering above the lush daisy-strewn pasture, which made sweet fodder for the kine.

But he had burnt his boats, and there could be no going back. He had taken the leap and must set his face to the future. Just as soon as he had gold enough he would get a patch of land of his own, and find a woman who would work beside him, raise a family, start afresh. And this would become his home.

Chapter 4

Curiosity, and a lingering sense of responsibility, drew Will back to Moll's establishment a week later. Recent rains had reduced the street to quagmire and he crossed on wooden duckboards, pushing open the door to be greeted by a tobacco haze and the smell of spilt liquor. A fiddler had started up and already there was dancing. He spotted Rose at once, taking a turn on the dance floor with a short, wiry digger whom Will knew by sight. Spanish, he thought, or Portuguese. They made an incongruous pair; Rose was a full head taller and the man's eyes were fixed unwaveringly on her breasts.

The girl had recovered then, had she, and taken Moll's employment? Will felt a stab of conscience and turned back to the bar, glad that she had not noticed him. But when the fiddler stopped, she drew up alongside and while the poor sot bought drinks, she gave Will a slanting look. 'So, Will Stewart. You never came back.'

He rested his forearms on the bar and stared ahead. 'Should I have done?' She was hot from the dancing and he could smell the musk of her.

'I thought you might.'

Her partner handed her a glass of champagne and slipped an arm around her waist, his face flushed, eyes bright, breathing fast. 'You're managing nicely just the same,' Will said, glancing at him.

'Moll has been kind.'

Will took a drink. 'She's a saint, that woman.'

Not unreasonably, Rose's partner believed he had purchased Rose's full attention and began nuzzling her neck. Rose pulled away. 'I said dancing,' she told him, 'just dancing.' When he persisted, she put her palm to his chest. 'I'm glad of the drink, thank you, but I'm dancing with this man next.'

Will turned back to her and met a challenging look. 'I'm drinking, not dancing,' he said.

'But you were about to ask.' She smiled at her erstwhile partner. 'We'll have another dance, I promise.' The man seemed inclined to take issue but, having assessed Will's size, moved off with a shrug.

'So you take a man's money, his drink and then ditch him,' said Will, suddenly furious with the girl. Gone was the listless figure he had left staring at the wall; there was life in her now, but was this how she planned to use it?

'I took his drink. The dance was free.'

'He expected more, and you knew it.'

She frowned at him. 'No. I just dance and get the men to buy drinks. Nothing else, Moll said that's all I have to do. And I can leave when I'm tired.'

'Moll's a shrewd hag, I'll give her that.'

'I earn my keep, nothing more.' Her cheeks reddened but she held his look.

Will leant his back against the bar and contemplated her. She was decorative, that was for sure. Slim-waisted and tall, but not too tall, and fine-featured, her fair hair swept up into a soft knot at the nape of her neck. And that mole – a definite asset. A draw. The pallor had gone from her face now and her eyes had a spark in them. He was well aware of the other diggers watching them; he sensed their envy, their appetite, and it seemed to him that the other girls were trying harder, laughing more loudly. Had she any idea of the impression she was making?

But that spark would soon dim in this rough place, he thought, looking about him. For all that Moll was playing motherly now, flesh as fair as Rose's was rare, and living here, under Moll's protection, she was already branded a whore. Moll was neither saint nor fool and by placing Rose out of bounds, her value was rising.

From the corner of his eye, he saw a group of men looking in their direction, urging one of their number forward, and he straightened. 'Let's have that dance then,' he said, his hand on her waist, 'since there's no charge.'

She allowed him to propel her forward. 'Rescuing me again, Will Stewart?'

The fiddler struck up a jig. 'I expect no more gratitude than last time.'

There was a great deal of stomping and whooping but little grace to the dancing in Moll's place. It was the same in any of the establishments in this part of town where men linked arms and swung their partners in a jig or a polka, or in a parody of a waltz. Dancing loosened tired muscles, music offered an escape, and the physical contact met a gnawing need. Will whirled Rose around to a cacophony of whistles and cheers, and they finished up again at the bar, breathless and hot. 'Now you buy me a drink,' said Rose.

'Wait to be asked.'

She looked around the room anxiously. 'But that's how it works.'

'You're telling *me* how it works?' He pulled her back to face him, angry again. 'So you ask for champagne, maybe a bottle, and dazzled by your charms I pay a crazy price and we sit and we talk and I put my hand in your lap, testing my luck, and you smile and start calculating a price and then . . .'

She pushed his hand away. 'I just dance, I tell you.'

Moll was watching them from across the room, a fact that fuelled Will's anger. 'If you value your independence, you'll leave this place tomorrow and find work elsewhere, if anywhere will have you. Otherwise, Flotsam Rose, I might as well have left you to drown.' Robbie's name for her had risen unbidden to his lips.

She glared back at him. 'I never asked you to save me.'

'You wish I hadn't?'

'Yes.'

And there, he sensed, was honesty. So it had been an act then, the flirting and the boldness. The stricken look was back in her eyes, that utter desolation he had read there on that chill dawn, and it triggered the same protective response. 'Then I'm sorry,' he said.

'You put the burden back on me.' Her grey eyes were sorrowful, and the anger drained from him. Life should be more than a burden, for one so young.

And lovely.

'Since I did, you might as well live better than this,' he said, but more gently.

'What makes you think I know how, Will Stewart? I was carrying a child, unwed. Perhaps I'm already a whore.'

Not wanted, she had said of the lost child. But Rose was no toughened and resilient whore, that much was obvious; she was barely more than a child herself with no notion of what course she was set upon. 'You're not,' he said, and her eyes fell before his. 'Tell me about the bairn.'

She was silent, staring down at the table, circling with her finger the overlapping rings of countless bottles. 'It's no concern of yours.' But then she lifted her head and looked at him. 'I was in service to a rich man and his family. His son said he loved me, promised me the world, and the stars and the moon and the skies, as soon as he was of age. He would defy them all, he said, and marry me – granddaughter of a convict, raised in an institution. What a fool I was! He'd persuade them, he said, and I believed him and his promises and we became lovers, secretly. But I fell pregnant, being ignorant and stupid, and then the world exploded. It was all lies, you see.' She paused and her expression hardened. 'He went crawling to his father once I'd told him – full of remorse, no doubt, desperate to find a way out – and so I was packed off here to find work, given five sovereigns on condition I didn't return to Melbourne, and my fine lover was sent back to England.'

Will considered her, but believed her words. 'I see.'

'Do you, I wonder,' she replied, with a coolness. 'Being a man . . .'

Will looked at her, then over her shoulder he saw that Moll was still watching them, frowning. The fiddler had started up again and he turned to look as the dance floor filled, but when he looked back Rose had gone, swept off on the arm of Big Sven, the Swede, who was grinning down at her in delight.

He felt a touch on his shoulder. 'Careless of you, old son,' said Robbie. 'She got away.'

Will grunted. 'I thought you were at Ah Luan's. Did you make your fortune?'

'Not this time. They're better at it than me.'

'At playing, or cheating?'

Robbie grinned briefly, then leant his back against the bar, his eyes following Rose and her partner. 'Now that,' he said, gesturing towards them, 'wouldn't have happened to me. And young Rose is a rare one, I'd say, and worth a bit of trouble. Get some drinks in, Will, there's a mate.'

Will signalled to the man behind the bar. 'But he doesn't mark any more of his to my slate. Got that?'

Robbie cursed him briefly and downed it. 'Watch and learn,'

he said, and heading into the dancing he neatly tripped the Swede, causing him to stumble and, a moment later, he swung past with Rose on his arm, and gave Will a brazen salute.

Robbie Malloy was a volatile man. A gambler, he won more often than he lost, a fact that raised eyebrows, but Robbie was smart enough not to be caught cheating outright. Smart enough to learn new tricks as well, and Will reckoned this was why he spent time with the Chinese storekeeper; Ah Luan had something of a reputation in that regard. Will had long since refused to play with Robbie for stakes higher than pennies, which had earned him his partner's scorn. 'It's true then, what they say about the Scots?'

He was a ladies' man, a handsome charmer, and the sight of his dark head bent to Rose's fair one made Will frown. Robbie made a good digging partner all right, but he could not be trusted to behave well. He was resourceful and as ready with his fists as his charm, and had employed both in equal measure to get them from Dunedin down through Otago and over the pass to the west coast. And Will had learnt that he too was escaping the law. One night, somewhere in the steaming tropics during their passage over, sitting drinking on deck, backs to the bulwark, Robbie had asked about the scar and Will had told him how he came by it. The Irishman had lifted a bottle to his lips, his eyes laughing at him. 'Well, it gives you a devilish look, I'll say that, and the ladies sure do love a rogue, but it's not much to hang for, is it?' He wiped his mouth with the back of his hand. 'I'd half the Dublin constabulary after me the night we took on the lads behind Weaver's Court. Six dead, and one of them a constable.' Robbie had not explained his own part in the episode, and Will had not asked, not wanting to know.

Enough for now that they shared a common dream. They had agreed to become partners while on board, and home these last few months had been a half tent, half shack out on the Kaniere goldfield – a canvas roof, timber walls clad with strips of corrugated iron, and a chimney tacked on to the front. Permanently damp, and never comforting. Feet rotted in sodden boots; their clothes were never dry. Takings were modest at best and the week's earnings usually went on supplies, getting drunk and, if they could afford it, getting laid. Lodgings and drink in town were cheap but clean women were costly, and moderation too soon forgotten.

It was no life, when all was said and done, and as Will made his way back down the street, he wondered again why they stayed. Winter storms were on their way, with downpours that would overflow the rivers, uprooting trees and causing mud slides, while gales at sea drove the tides over the sand bar flooding banks and brothels alike. And there were months of it to come. Wind, rain and starvation. May, June and July – seasons that conjured up light, warmth and a sense of ease – were mocked by what was promised here. He buttoned his jacket and headed back to their lodgings. Robbie was right, they should move on.

And then, as if to echo this resolve, it was that same night that Robbie stumbled into their lodgings late, stinking of drink and cheap perfume, beyond drunk and sobering fast. He shook Will's shoulder. 'Wake up! Wake up, damn you, and listen!' he said. 'We're away, Will. Payable gold's been found in the Taramakau, out Kumara way. We're sorted, me boy. This is it.'

Chapter 5

Kumara. The word whipped around street corners and in through the doors of bars and banks, snaking out to the goldfields and into the shanties of disillusioned diggers. And as Will made his way along Beach Street the next day, he could sense that every man and woman was calculating what the news meant for them. Established businesses would stay, providing goods and services, but enterprises like Moll's might struggle if the newcomers were simply passing through. Several hotels had already put their shutters up as the rush slackened, their owners having vanished, leaving debts, while the remainder competed for a diminishing trade. Hokitika's quay would continue to be a vital link with the world and a flood of hopefuls would need supplies, sure enough, but would this alone restore the town's fortunes? Businesses would follow the gold.

One abandoned shop had recently reopened, advertising *cartes de visite*, portraitures and commercial work, and the name Fraser Urquhart was painted above the door, obliterating that of the former occupant. Will paused and looked through the newly cleaned window at photographs of the wreck that had been posted there, seeing again the pale light of dawn and the row of dark silhouettes, their gaze fixed on the stricken vessel, a grey shape on a silvered sea. In that captured moment the whole tragedy was exposed, raw and dreadful.

And the man was right: words would not have been enough. He rounded the corner and there was the photographer himself, surrounded by a group of diggers, Robbie amongst them. Will drew back to watch as, with good humour and determination, the man arranged them along the boardwalk. 'Shorter ones in front, if you will, and the very tallest of you seated on the bench.' Will grinned. Daft as schoolboys they were, trying the limits of the man's patience. 'Gentlemen! I will make you immortal, so look, and act, like the gods you are!' And so thumbs were hooked into waistcoats and belts, felt hats set at rakish angles while Robbie, at the end of the back row, chose to slouch against the weatherboard building. One youth stood with his arms akimbo until required not to, and a seated man stretched out his legs and crossed his booted ankles, arranging a crimson sash, the emblem of a veteran digger. Preening themselves like whores, they were! Then one of them spotted Will and called out to him to join them. Will shook his head but the photographer swung round and recognition lit his face. 'Yes indeed! The hero of the Tasman. Quick, man! Stand at the other end and balance the numbers.' Two diggers broke rank and dragged him forward. It seemed easier to comply, so he took his place, pulling his hat brim over his left eye.

'Excellent. Now, gentlemen,' the photographer called out, 'relax and stand *still* otherwise your handsome features will blur and be a disappointment to all.' His cultured tones rang out, incongruous in this raw setting, but they obeyed him. 'If you look solemn, then solemn you will remain for eternity. Smile by all means but fix me a rictus grin. Breathe if you must.'

The seconds ticked by in silence then he reappeared from under his hood and straightened. 'Splendid! I'll display the photograph in the studio window tomorrow for all to see, and you can place orders with me if you wish. Good morning, gentlemen, and good fortune.'

The group dispersed and the watchers fell away, one or two lingering to speak to the photographer as he packed up his gear. 'The image gets fixed when the plate is exposed to light,' Will heard him say. 'Controlling the *amount* of light is key . . .' The man moved off, and the photographer folded the legs of his tripod, looking up as Will passed. 'You must forgive me for the other day, sir. I had no idea.' He glanced out beyond the estuary to the sea. 'There aren't many I'd leap into that for, let alone a stranger.' Will raised a dismissive hand and went to move on but the man called him back. 'Look, could you give me a hand with this stuff?' Will shrugged, picked up the tripod and they set off down the street together. 'Much obliged. My name is Urquhart, Fraser Urquhart, and I'm from Roxburghshire. And you, sir, where do you hail from?'

'Scotland.' Will was not inclined to be civil.

'Of course, but where?'

'Argyll.' That much was true.

'Argyll! Where exactly?' Will mentioned a small place to the north of Kinnloss and Urquhart shook his head. 'I don't know it. I photographed a number of country houses in the area, for my sins – rank flattery and conceit, of course. Connel Castle, Reid Hall, Kinnloss House. Do you know them?'

Will schooled his face to remain blank as his heart lurched. 'Hardly my circle, Mr Urquhart.'

'Fraser, please! And may I have your name?'

'Will Stewart.'

'Pleased to meet you, Will – if you allow. I delight in the informality here, the levelling of social norms.'

'Oh, aye.'

The man stopped abruptly in the middle of the street. 'I mean, look at those men just now, one could feel the very pulse of their energy. Answerable to no one, making their fortunes by the sweat of their brows. There's a wild romance to it all, is there not?'

Will thought of the mining companies, and the investors who funded the shafts and the flumes and the sluices, paying miserable wages to men whose own dreams had foundered. What did they know of sweat? Or was the man blind? 'Rank flattery, you said. Your work.'

Urquhart turned back to him. 'Yes. Sold my soul I did.'

'Why?'

'For the money,' he replied, cheerfully, moving forward. 'I needed it.'

Will raised a sceptical eyebrow and followed him down the street. Urquhart fumbled for the keys to his establishment and unlocked it. 'Set the stuff on the floor if you will.' He dug a hand into his pocket and proffered a coin. 'Thank you. I'm much obliged.'

Will looked down at the coin, then up at the man. 'Keep it, Mr Urquhart,' he said, and pulled open the door. 'Since you're short.'

'No! Look, I didn't . . .' but Will strode off down the street, tossing a coin of his own to a ragged man crouched in a doorway. Wild romance, my arse. He had no need of the man's charity, nor his condescension, and the reference to Kinnloss House had him rattled.

He went looking for Robbie but around the next corner he ran into Rose, who was walking quickly, head down and preoccupied, carrying a bundle of clothes in her arms. He stepped out to block her path. 'Good morning.' She looked up, and then aside, giving a tight little smile, not seeming pleased to see him.

'Mendings?' he asked, falling into step beside her, looking down at the bundle in her arms which appeared to be dresses, the sort of finery the dance girls wore. 'I've trodden on a few skirts in my time.'

'Aye, mendings,' Rose nodded, her head turned away from him.

Will put out a hand. 'What's wrong?'

'Nothing. Except a need to make haste. Good morning, Will Stewart,' and she whisked past him into the seamstress's shop.

Puzzled, Will retired to the opposite corner of the street and stood in the shadows. And waited. Rose was inside longer than it should have taken her to dump a pile of dresses, and longer than might be expected for a good gossip, and besides, the seamstress was a German lass whose English was poor. Eventually she re-emerged, empty-handed, and crossed the street, heading back towards Moll's place.

Will followed her progress from under the brim of his hat, then went across to the shop. The woman looked up as he entered. There were the dresses, in a pile on a side table. Fancy, tawdry gowns, low-cut, stained under armpits and bodice. Whores' clothes. 'The woman who brought these . . .'

'Gone.' The seamstress gestured down the street.

'Are they for mending?' She looked blank. 'To mend? Torn?'

She shook her head. 'Not mend. Make fit.' She gestured to her own waist.

'For her? For that woman. To make them fit her?'

The woman nodded, pleased to be understood. 'Yes, to make fit for her.' She pointed to a crimson silk gown with a low-cut, lace-trimmed bodice and a nipped-in waist. 'This for today, rest for tomorrow. Make smaller.'

Will left.

Outrage grew in him as he strode down the street. So the star of Moll O'Shea's was about to become available, was she?

The woman's plan was obvious and now, with men slathering like dogs, the time was right. Rose would boost the hotel's fortunes, drawing diggers from other establishments, and was about to learn that debts must be repaid.

He headed for Moll's place with no real plan in mind, heedless of the growing numbers gathering on the street corners and the undercurrent of energy, until he heard Robbie call out to him and he found himself pulled into a crowd of voluble Irishmen. 'Have you heard?'

'I've guessed,' he said, his mind still on Rose.

'Guessed?' Robbie looked at him oddly, then waved the distraction aside. 'It's true! The rumours. Someone saw outwash in the river and tracked it back to a creek where these two diggers had built a dam, got sluices all set up, piles of tailing already and they're finding colour in every pan, nuggety gold too, in the old river gravels.' Robbie was fair pulsing with excitement. This was what they had been waiting for – the next big strike. 'They claim they went to set up a still and struck lucky and they've been at it for months, the sly bastards. Tried to deny it at first but now there's a boundary dispute between claims and some folk have already staked out theirs so we need to get out there, Will me boy, quick before the swarm hits. These lads'll work with us—'

And so Will was caught up in a whirl of handshakes and backslapping as Robbie introduced the men. There would be six or eight of them, they could work a bigger claim that way, he explained, more hands to dig and sluice. Will looked round at the grinning faces, all Irish, cousins he was told, and wild lads from what he knew of them. Dan McGrath he recognised, a thick-set man whose passion was for drink and women and whose reputation was as large as his fists, which he readily used in defence of his half-witted brother, Ted. Jim Kelly was a slight, silent man and while Callum Butler Will already knew a little, and was a decent enough lad, the others were strangers. Pointless now for Will to remark that he had not been consulted, that they had agreed to work together, he and Robbie, just the two of them; he sensed that Robbie would go with these lads whether Will did or not, and few could survive here alone. He had seen those who tried, half-crazy old timers, hatters they called them, who were occasionally driven out of the forest by the sand flies and mosquitoes, and who would sit for hours in the bars rambling on to anyone who would listen before collecting supplies and returning as silently as they had come.

Better the devil you know than strangers.

Maybe.

They bore Will off to the nearest bar and drinks flowed as they discussed what they would need, the cash they had, the credit they might get and how they would transport materials into the virgin rainforest. Someone produced the stub of a pencil, another a scrap of card, and passed them to Will who made lists and soon found himself caught up in the excitement. Three of them, including McGrath and Robbie, would head off at once to work out the lay of the land and peg their claim while the others would stay behind to pack up their belongings and order supplies, ready to move as soon as the others returned. The essentials of goldfield life – canvas, picks, pans, shovels and flour – would soon be in short supply.

The group dispersed, speeding to their allotted tasks, and Will was left standing in the street, deflected from his original purpose. And what, after all, could he do for Rose? Kumara might be only a few miles away but it might as well be a hundred. Dense forest, with barely a track through it, and land to be stripped, shelter to be built before work could begin, and all before the winter began to bite.

He walked back out to their claim, angry still at the thought of Rose in Moll's clutches, and spent the rest of the day packing up while all around him men were doing the same, driven hard by their dreams. He razed their shelter, salvaging the worn canvas roof, and dismantled the simple cots on which they slept, taking only the best planks of timber and leaving the rest to the elements; there would be no shortage of wood once the forest was cleared. After the grog shops, it was the sawmills that would thrive. He paid a Chinaman with a packhorse to carry their meagre belongings back into town where he arranged storage, then returned to their lodgings, sat on the bed and considered his options.

Chapter 6

Darkness had fallen by the time Will got to Black Moll's that evening and he found it full of diggers fair drunk with excitement. Kumara! The quest was on again, the new field of fortune. Men leant across tables talking intently, faces alive, eyes glinting, tobacco smoke rising to the rafters in a thick haze of optimism. Will ordered himself a drink and glanced around. Rose was nowhere to be seen but Moll materialised at his shoulder and signalled to the barman not to make a charge. 'So, Will Stewart, you're off with the rest of them.'

'Aye.'

'Mad fools.' Her face was grim. 'It'll come to nothing, you'll see, and you'll come crawling back like whipped puppies.' Will shrugged. 'You and that handsome partner of yours have linked up with some of our lads, I hear. Fine lads they are too, hard-working and honest.'

'Like your good self, Moll.' He raised his glass and drank.

She eyed him suspiciously, then chuckled. 'When are you away, Will?'

'Soon. Bit of business here first.'

'You've come to say goodbye to Rose?' Her eyes were on him, shrewd as ever. 'Keep it brief, Will Stewart, or make it pay, she's a working girl,' and off she sailed like a queen, and he watched her go.

Fiddle and accordion then struck up, heralding the arrival of the girls, and the din abated briefly as the groups at the

tables sat back in order to assess the nymphs who spread themselves around the dance hall, giving old friends a peck on the
cheek while surveying the company for newcomers and easy
pickings. Rose was last down. She was wearing the crimson
silk and lace gown Will had seen at the seamstress's shop. Face
painted, dressed for slaughter. Catcalls and table thumping
greeted her arrival and Will felt the anger surge in him as he
watched her, hanging back, eyes wide, her smile fixed, a hand
fluttering at her stomach, looking around the hall, not seeing
him.

He had started towards her when a digger grabbed at his arm.
'Are you off too, Will? I heard you were.'

'Aye, but . . .' Damn, his chance was lost. Rose had been
whisked away and was already dancing. Her partner, he saw, was
the photographer, and Will watched them as they circled the
floor with a grace that Moll's place seldom witnessed. Urquhart
had been taught the finer things of life, it seemed, and Will
watched resentfully as Rose matched her steps to his confident
lead. Others were watching too, appreciation wrestling with envy,
the same thought on every mind. Would the lordly Urquhart
be the first to pluck her petals?

Damned if he would.

The dance brought them close to Will and he stepped forward
and gripped the photographer's arm, finding it more muscled
than he had expected. 'I'll cut in here, Urquhart,' he said and the
man turned, his haughty expression vanishing as he recognised
his assailant.

'To you, Will Stewart, but to no other.' A bow to Will and
a smile to Rose. 'We'll meet later, my dear. And you, sir, if I
offended—' But Will swept Rose away, grasping her hand as hard
as he had gripped Urquhart's arm.

'You're crushing my fingers!'

'Has she got you to sign anything?' he asked, speaking low into her ear. 'Moll. Has she produced a contract?'

Rose's face paled. 'How do you know?'

Will gritted his teeth. He had heard tell of these contracts, cast-iron shackles that bound girls to provide 'services', paid them a pittance, their keep and clothing deducted. 'I guessed. Have you signed?'

'Not yet—'

'Don't. It'll tie you to . . .' He broke off to jab an elbow into the guts of a competitor attempting his own manoeuvre.

'Will, I've no choice! I owe her money for food and board.'

Will scowled at her. 'What about your sovereigns?'

'It's not enough, she says.'

Five bloody sovereigns! He looked out over her head to where Moll was standing at the bar, hands on her wide hips, and swore. 'And tonight? What happens tonight?'

Rose flushed. 'I'm to make promises. Flirt and so forth. And see . . .' Moll was looking back at him, a detestable smile on her face.

The dance took them past the bar and he pulled Rose aside and slammed a coin onto the counter. 'Champagne,' he said to the barman, loud enough for the old cow to hear. 'A bottle.' And he steered Rose to an empty table in the corner. 'Right then. I've bought your time, so you listen. I'm heading off into the bush, to Kumara, with Robbie and a group of Irish cousins, God help me. We might make our fortunes or it might be a duffer and then I'll have nothing but the clothes I'm wearing . . .'

'You're leaving?'

'In the next day or so.'

'And Robbie too?'

What had Robbie to do with anything? 'Yes.'

Her eyes fell and she began plucking at the lace on her dress.

The champagne arrived and the sound of the cork was greeted with applause from the neighbouring table. 'So you're celebrating,' she said, with a false bar-room smile, raising the glass he had filled.

'That, Rose,' he said, touching his glass to the rim of hers, 'depends on you.'

'How so?' she asked.

The moment hung there, below the haze of blue, dizzying and chancy, and then he seized it. 'Marry me, Rose. Now. Tomorrow. Before I go.'

Chapter 7

Moll was furious.

Rose quailed as the woman glared at Will. 'She's not leaving here 'til she's paid her debts. Board and lodging for three weeks. Aye, and let's not forget the nursing, too.'

'What about her wages for the dancing?' Will asked. Moll snorted but Rose saw that Will's jaw was set firm. 'Show me an account of what you say she owes, set against her earnings. I'll look at it and we'll come to terms, but she leaves here with me now.'

Moll's eyes narrowed, almost disappearing above her fleshy cheeks. 'Do you think because you saved her, you've rights of possession?' It had not occurred to Rose that he might and she glanced at him, struck by the thought, but Will was facing Moll down.

'No. I don't.'

The woman's eyes flashed dangerously but, in the end, Will paid less than half the figure she demanded, which astonished Rose and perhaps earned Will Moll's grudging respect. She watched silently as he paid the money over and then went upstairs and removed the hated crimson dress, pulling on the one that she had almost drowned in, now repaired and decent. She was breathless, hurrying, desperately fumbling with the buttons, terrified lest Will Stewart should come to his senses.

Whatever had possessed him?

She stared at herself in the mirror and wiped the vile colour from her lips, rubbing her sleeve against her rouged cheeks. What mad impulse . . . ? Would he wake to regret it? Or did he, as Moll implied, believe himself to have rights? Even now the woman might be persuading him to retract, or threatening him; Moll had supporters, ugly types. Smoothing down her hair, she took a deep breath, steadying herself, and descended the stairs again.

And he was there, waiting at the bottom.

He looked up at her and smiled, and she smiled back. And breathed again. They left to a roar of good wishes which Moll, tight-lipped, was obliged to endorse, but once out in the street he stopped and turned her to face him. 'You're sure?' he asked.

'I'm sure.' It felt as if her very survival depended on him.

'Then that's all right.' He gave her wry smile. 'It's been an odd sort of courtship, by any measure.'

'And are *you* sure, Will Stewart?' she dared herself to ask. 'Or is rescuing me just becoming a habit?'

He took her hand and squeezed her fingers. 'I'm sure.'

———

'Tomorrow? *Tomorrow!*' Robbie's face darkened as he stared back at Will. The mud of Kumara was still on his boots and he had returned bursting with energy and optimism, but Will's news seemed to stop him in his tracks.

'I've got a licence and the minister agrees.' Will patted his pocket. 'So, will you stand up with me?'

'You barely know the girl.'

'Soon remedied.'

'You can't afford a wife.'

Will laughed. 'You just said our fortunes were made, my friend.'

'She's a whore.' Robbie's eyes had a way of turning an icy blue.

A strange response . . . 'She's not. And she won't be.'

'But why *marry* her?'

'Why does any man marry?'

'You're crazy, saddling yourself with a woman.'

Did he reckon Rose would be a burden? 'You've not answered me.'

'What?'

'Will you stand with me?'

———

Almost the last of Will's money went on lodgings for Rose, and he left the boarding house counting his loose change. The rest would doubtless go on liquor at the wedding, but somehow they would have to manage until the claim began to pay.

He spotted the lanky figure of Urquhart ahead of him and dropped his head, still unreasonably annoyed with the man, but the photographer saw him and raised a hand. 'I offended you that other day, Will Stewart, and I'm sorry,' he said, without preamble. 'Behaved like an ass. It's my appalling upbringing, I'm afraid; I was taught to be superior and it detached me from reality.' He was watching Will's face carefully. 'Forgive me, if you will, because I'm going to ask another favour of you.' Will raised an eyebrow. 'So you are to marry Rose. How very fitting! And an exceptional girl in every way. I've spoken to her several times, light on her feet and so pleasing on the eye. You must have wished me to the devil the other night, I'd no idea she was spoken for.' He paused, then grinned. 'We got off to a *very* bad start, Will Stewart.'

Will found himself answering the smile. 'And the favour?'

'Allow me to take your wedding photograph. No cost. And I'll tell your story. We can put the picture in the studio window and I'll . . .'

'Get more business?'

'Exactly.' Will found his hand being clasped, the deal agreed, and Urquhart fell into step beside him. 'You're off to Kumara, I understand. I've never seen a rush right from the beginning, I always seem to come along when the initial excitement has passed and drudgery sets in, but this time I'll be right there to see the forest felled and the flumes built. Do you imagine it will be a big rush?'

Will shrugged. 'Might be a complete duffer.'

'As in poor returns?'

'Aye.'

'Or it might make your fortune, and your good lady wife's! Let's assume that it will. It's tomorrow, the wedding, I gather? I'll be waiting there when you come out of the church and I'd like a picture of you both with all these splendid diggers about you, throwing their hats in the air and cheering, or whatever it is you do for weddings here.' Will laughed, shook his head at the man, and went on his way.

When he next saw Robbie he was told that his new associates had fixed to have a 'bit of a do' after the wedding, at Moll's. 'Special rates, my friend,' he said with a grin. Will had hoped to put that place behind them but Robbie was deaf to his protests, and there was an unsettling glint in his eye. 'We'll make a night of it, eh?' he said.

And so it was that next day the bride and groom were escorted from the white-painted wooden Free Church straight to Black Moll's where they were thrust onto the centre of the dance floor to the inevitable accompaniment of whistles and whoops, stamping and table banging. Outside the church they had paused just long enough for Fraser Urquhart to take a photograph, together with Robbie, and more would be taken, he assured them, in the calm of the studio the following day.

Moll's place that night was anything but calm. 'We'll leave as soon as we can,' said Will, bending close to be heard above the din. But a bride, he soon discovered, was considered fair game and every man felt entitled to a dance, and every man bought Will a drink. Colourful shirts and velvet trousers had been donned for the occasion by those diggers who had them; others sported sashes or scarfs of silk and high spirits fuelled a mad cacophony of sound. Moll, with jet-hard eyes, kept setting drinks before Will and once she leant across and hissed in his ear: 'Steal my best girl, will you, Will Stewart?'

'How was she yours, Moll?'

'She'd have died after that miscarriage, but for me. And I loved her like my own.' The woman rolled her eyes to heaven.

Will stifled a snort, then relented. 'You were good to her, Moll, and we're very grateful.'

'Hark at him!' Moll put her hands on her hips and guffawed. 'Married five minutes and already talking like a prig.'

And yet the wedding night cast a shadow. Getting Will drunk was the clear intention of his new partners, who replaced every empty glass with a full one, but Will quietly disposed of them, either passing them on or filling others' empty ones, and everyone was soon too drunk to notice while he remained sober, watching the swirling figures in a room filled with noise and movement – seeing only Rose. She had furbished up her dress with scraps of lace given by Moll's girls and in Will's eyes she looked so very lovely. Slim and lithe, and full of grace. His wife. He thought his heart would burst and he struggled to keep his temper in check as he watched diggers swing her around, claiming outrageous kisses and bawdy fondles. Robbie took her onto the floor twice, dancing wildly even for him, one minute bringing her close, holding her tight to him, and then flinging her away at arm's length as the music quickened before giving her a mocking bow and handing her to the next man.

Will watched Rose's every move and saw when her shoulders began to droop and the smile on her face became fixed and glassy. He went to her then and cut into the dance. 'Peace, friend,' he said, catching her partner's raised fist. 'Marital rights.' The fist was lowered and the man swayed away. 'Shall we leave them to it?'

They left, escorted out of the door by a hard core of drunken diggers who flanked them all the way down the street, stumbling through shadows cast by lanterns in doorways, ignoring oaths and threats from the houses on either side. Eventually they reached their lodgings and it was only by the swiftness with which Will slammed and then bolted the door that he prevented their unruly escort from following them in and fulfilling an intention to strip the newlyweds and put them to bed.

'Thank God,' he said, his back against the door, listening as their bawling receded back up the road. 'And where was Robbie when I needed him?' He sat on the only chair and tugged off a boot. 'He might have stood by me!'

'He left earlier, I think. I saw him go.'

Something in her tone made him pause and look across at her, the second boot half off. She was standing, pressed up against the edge of the bed, her hair tumbling down, a hand at her throat and her eyes wide. 'Rose?' She tucked an escaping lock of hair behind her ear and forced a smile, but he could almost smell her fear. Marital rights, he had said. Good God, what did she expect him to do? He left the second boot on. 'I'll not touch you, Rose, except that you want me to.'

And this was the girl prepared to sell herself to any digger willing to pay.

She looked back at him, and then away. Disappointment rose in him like bile, and soured into resentment. She knew what to expect of married life – for Christ's sake, she had carried another man's child! He picked up the discarded boot and slowly pushed his foot back into it. She had, of course, only accepted him in desperation, grabbing a lifeline thrown to her, a reprise of her rescue from the waves. He must remember this. It would take time. But he would do his best by her, he would love her and he wanted to tell her so, and a wedding night was surely the right occasion for such assurances.

Yet he sensed that this one was not.

Booted once more, he stood and forced a smile. 'I'll go and take the air for a bit. You're worn out, all that dancing. Get yourself into bed, you're shivering!' He hesitated. 'Now, do I lock the door, or will you? Which makes you feel most safe?' The answer became suddenly vital.

'Will . . .' she began, but he put up a hand.

'Bed, Rose. Go to sleep, you look done in.' He held up the key. 'You or me?'

'Take it, Will, and lock me in.'

He left, turned the key in the lock and stood for a moment on the step, the fan of light and shadow shifting in the breeze. Good God. Rejected, on his wedding night. What a fool he must appear! He turned down the side of the building and strode quickly towards the sea.

Dawn was already streaking the night sky when he reached the shore, and the ocean was every shade of grey. Spectral driftwood lay in piles on the tide line, tangled with rusting hoops from broken casks, and the surf pounded endlessly. Ragged fronds hung limp on stunted tree trunks, clattering in the wind, and the bitter tang of seaweed hung in the air. What was the tally of ships wrecked along this fatal shore, he wondered; the price of shattered dreams? And he thought of Rose the day he had saved her, a broken thing, the child inside her dying.

What did that do to a woman?

He stood, watching the dark waves break and vanish into spray, and thought again of the white shell-sand beaches of home where seabirds skimmed the wave crests of a blue-green sea, flashing white in the sunlight. By now there would be primroses in the hedgerows and cushions of pink sea thrift spreading in a thick carpet above the tidal reach. Some day he would take Rose there and show her. He stood a while and watched the sky lighten, lifting his head to watch the seabirds heading for the horizon with the dawn on their wings.

After half an hour he turned back, fingering the key in his trouser pocket. How best to reach her, and reassure her? A group of revellers swayed down the street towards him and he stepped into the shadows. They passed him close, not seeing him, but as he slipped along the side of the building one of them looked back over his shoulder.

Robbie.

Damn. But if he had seen Will moving like a thief under the eaves-drips he gave no sign and Will soon reached their lodgings. He stood a moment outside the door, then turned the key and entered silently. A shaft of light struck the narrow bed illuminating the bundle that was Rose, her hair dark on the pillow. She was awake, he could tell. Carefully, he pulled off one boot and then set the other beside it, stripped off down to his drawers, eased the blanket aside and slipped in beside her.

Chapter 8

Almost as soon as Will left, Rose came to her senses and went to the door. Too late – already locked! She ran to the window, flung it open and leant out, but the street was empty except for a couple embracing in the shadows and three diggers who staggered, arm in arm, down the middle of it. 'Will!' she called, and her breath hung in the misty lantern light.

The diggers' drunken insolence was her only response.

Why on earth had she asked to be locked in? She closed the window, turned back to the room and slowly unhooked the scraps of lace from the collar of her dress, frowning. What a wretched mess to have made of things! Bed was clearly part of the contract, for why else had he married her?

After all the wild dancing, her hair was cascading down and she removed the remaining pins, stretching her neck to ease the tension. If only he had waited a moment longer, she would have been all right, the shyness would have gone, but the sudden realisation that this stranger was now her husband had paralysed her.

If only he had stayed, and held her.

She so wanted to be held.

Her dress slipped to the floor and she stepped out of it, shivering in the cold room. Where had he gone, she wondered. Not back to Moll's, she was certain of that. Oh, if only she could go after him! And if they had walked a while, just the two of them, in the darkness, it would not have seemed so odd. Will was a good man, she was certain of that, with his scarred forehead and his strange intensity. An honest man, a kind man. He had saved her twice, and instead of showing gratitude, she had rejected him.

Why had she not kept the key?

She washed quickly and slipped into bed, pulling the blanket around her, longing for the warmth of company, for the reassurance of his presence. And she lay there, staring up at the ceiling where light from the street lantern slipped through a gap in the curtains and wondered if even now he was regretting their reckless marriage. How long would he stay away? Not all night, surely? She wanted to explain, to tell him that it was no more than a fleeting echo of the fear she had felt that other evening at Moll's. Her debut, the woman had called it, chuckling at her dismay. No matter how much the other girls had tried to reassure her, telling her that she would learn to cope, when the moment had come and she had looked down on a sea of wolfish faces with hungry eyes, she had been terrified. Only the firm grasp of the photographer had stopped her from turning and running back upstairs in panic. And then Will had cut in, and made his extraordinary offer. She had accepted him without hesitation, without thought, a lifeline seized, her instinct for survival as strong as on the day of the wrecking. She wanted to make him understand all this, and tell him that her fear of him had been a passing thing, and that she would strive in every way to be a good wife.

But then again what did she know of men, and what they expected of their women? Tommy Gilbert had been a boy, barely a year older than herself, and all she had learnt from that encounter was that she was naïve – and worthless. Less than worthless, his father had told her; she was a creature, brazen and depraved. Taken into service out of charity, he had reminded her, given a roof and a position, and this was how she repaid them. Shameless behaviour, ungrateful and wicked! Five sovereigns and a passage to Hokitika had been thrust at her with contempt that was hardly less painful than the whipping his wife's pleading had spared her. 'Thomas shares the blame,' she had heard Mrs Gilbert say, 'and we cannot allow the girl to starve.' But Rose had been taken to the docks that same day, escorted by the tight-lipped housekeeper and put aboard the ship, and the woman had stood there on the granite dock until the vessel slipped her cables and headed down the Yarra River.

Ice had entered her soul already that day, and later the sight of New Zealand, shrouded in cloud, had brought a cold reality. She had been a fool and was paying the price, and as the coast came too swiftly close it was clear that the price would be high. The terror of it all stalked her nights and she still woke, crying out as her dreams returned her to the punishing seas.

What mad impulse had propelled Will into the waves to save her, she wondered as she wrapped herself tighter in the thin blanket, and now to rescue her again? She could have been anybody clinging to that pallet, and she was as much a stranger to him now as she had been then. She lay there, puzzling the matter, and watched the light move over the ceiling as the lantern outside swayed in the wind and a new day began to lift the darkness. It was a shaky foundation on which to build, and she must prove to him her resolve to prosper.

So she would never tell him that his extraordinary offer had not been the only one she had received. Robbie Malloy came regularly to Moll's and sought her out, slipping an arm around her waist and murmuring nonsense in her ear. Will would never learn from her how persistent his partner had been, forever trying to get her on her own, promising that he would set her up in style one day, confident that she would agree. 'Are you playing coy with me, sweetheart? All right then, I know that game.' They would go to Melbourne, he told her, and make their fortunes. Each time the plan became more elaborate. 'We'll have our own hotel, darlin', and we'll grow rich and fat,' and he had pinched her arm and laughed, showing his white teeth before swirling her out onto the dance floor, clasping her tight. 'And then we'll retire to Ireland and breed horses. The squire and his lady, with dozens of sons.' For all that the other girls might sigh for the charm of Robbie Malloy, she had not taken him seriously and had been astonished at his fury when he learnt that she was to marry Will. 'If it was a wedding band you wanted, girl, I'd have got you one! And I'd have kept you in better style than Will Stewart ever will, ring or no ring. He wants to be a farmer, for God's sake. You should stick with me, I'll see you right.'

'I was never *with* you, Robbie Malloy, except in your head. You *knew* what Moll had planned for me, and yet you did nothing.'

'She'd been feeding you, hadn't she? Putting a roof over your head.' Rose tried to pull her arm away but he gripped tight. 'I'll speak to her, come to some arrangement, so tell Will it's off, tell him you made a mistake.'

'No! Of course I shan't. He's a good man, is Will Stewart, a better man than you'll ever be.'

'Is that so?' He had glared down at her, and then stormed out of the door.

And she had let him go.

No, it was the other offer that had intrigued her, and it was one she might even have considered. Ever since the first time the photographer had come into Moll's establishment he had taken to sitting at a corner table and watching her in a way that was intense, but different to other men. Eventually he had sought her out, bought her a drink and sat staring at her across the table in the same disconcerting manner, exploring her face, saying nothing. Then he had reached across and run his finger lightly over her cheek, lingering on the mole there. 'Just skin and bones,' he had said, tilting her chin with his thumb, turning her head to one side, 'and yet perfection. An Ophelia profile. Come and be my model, child, my muse.' She had laughed, uncertain at the unfamiliar word. 'I would pay you, of course, and keep you if you like.' Seeing that Moll was about to descend on them, he had led her onto the dance floor, holding her a little away from him, his eyes sliding down her form. 'A rare pearl. Come to me, sweet Rose, before this dreadful place crushes you. Say yes! Come, and I'll take good care of you, and I swear I'll make you immortal.' And she had laughed, baffled by him but refusing to take him seriously either. He, at least, had congratulated her when she told him her news. 'How splendid! I am, of course, distraught for my own loss, but you have a good man there, Rose, and I wish you joy.'

And now, with her sudden fear, she had dispelled that joy before it had a chance! She banged her head on the lumpy pillow in vexation and scowled up at the ceiling, hoping that Will would return soon and that she could start to make things right between them. She wanted him here.

It was then that it happened. The wind dropped, the lantern outside her window steadied and on the little strip of ceiling above the curtain, a faint image appeared. She felt the hair lift on the back of her neck as she looked. It was a building with a sloping roof extending over a walkway like the ones in town, just floating on the ceiling, blurred but identifiable. How extraordinary. She sat up and the image vanished. She lay flat again, breathing fast, and it returned, a little sharper now. And she saw then that it was the boot maker's shop opposite their lodgings, but upside down and somehow wrong. There was no mistaking it; there was his cut-out boot sign suddenly clear and distinct, and the wooden duckboards, the upright posts that supported the roof. Not only upside down but the wrong way round. Whatever did this mean? The wind gusted, the lantern swayed and the image vanished. Had she dreamt it? But no, the light steadied again and she saw movement close to the buildings, someone walking.

A figure was crossing the street towards her, upside down.

Will! Or an apparition summoned by her thoughts? She rolled onto her side, bewildered at the magic, and frightened. Whatever had she seen? A moment later she heard boots on the stairs, the floorboards creaked outside the door, and then the key turned quietly in the lock.

She lay still, listening to the sound of him undressing, and then the blanket was lifted and he slipped in beside her. She turned over. 'Will . . .' she began, but he put a finger on her lips.

'Shhh, sleep now,' he said, and he moved her, shifting her so that she was curled into the shape of him, and he wrapped his arms around her and held her.

Chapter 9

Two tents went up on land they stripped that first day. Moll was right about these lads, they were no slackers, and Will collapsed beside them in the makeshift shelters at the end of that day and of each that followed, exhausted, face down on his cot, rousing only to eat and then to carry on. They had pegged out their claim on an old river terrace at the edge of the predicted goldfield, clearing the low manuka shrubs that grew there, quick off the mark, and then slowly, one by one, they felled the great giants of the forest. And even as they stripped the land they began to work it, first the surface deposits, making plans as they worked to dig back against the terrace edge and begin sluicing. Only later would they think of sinking shafts. All the signs were that the area was rich but that the gold was deep, and at uneven levels. They had dammed and diverted a small creek to provide water to wash through their cradles, but more ambitious schemes would be needed. Channels must be dug, and water races and flumes constructed before sluicing on any scale could begin. There was talk of cooperative effort with neighbouring claims and Will spent much time discussing possible routes, exploring upriver, working out how best to take advantage of the contours of the land. But even now, the results of hand digging and cradling were rewarding.

Word of the new goldfield took wing and flew east across the Southern Alps and west over the Tasman Sea, crossing continents, and there was soon a steady flow of new arrivals, staking claims and hacking away the rainforest, stripping the land of its primeval vegetation. Naïve first-timers mingled with hardened veterans returning from Victoria and Queensland, joining forces with diggers from Otago and others who crossed over the pass from Dunedin.

Fortunes would surely be made.

Optimism made for a good atmosphere and Will's concerns about his partners receded. There was colour in every pan, and occasional small nuggets, thimble-sized at best, and all were placed together in a chamois bag and secreted away ready to be taken into town to be weighed, converted into cash and divided between them. Thievery was an ever-present concern but it would be a bold thief who tried robbing these lads, and there was trust between them. Hard workers, big drinkers, sociable types. They enjoyed a fight too, and Dan McGrath's reputation had travelled with him. Their two shelters soon became a place where folk gathered in the evenings bringing sly-grog, strong and vile, and as the light faded a dozen or more diggers would lounge outside the tents, smoking their pipes, aching limbs stretched out, or they would pack themselves inside when it rained. Occasionally one of them brought a fiddle and some of them never went home but slept off their excesses curled up on the earthen floor before disappearing, bleary-eyed and silent, next morning.

By the end of three weeks of close living and endless conviviality, Will's nerves were frayed and every night he dreamt of Rose, of the sweet warmth of her, this woman who was his wife. He hungered for the touch and smell of her, for the intimacy they had still to find. Sometimes he awoke in the fetid tent and thought that he must have dreamt her, that nothing this good had ever happened to him. He learnt that a carter was going back and forth each day, bringing supplies for the diggers and helping to set up stores and, on impulse, he sent a message with the man telling Rose to expect him. She must be lonely, he told his partners, and then had their guffaws and crude jokes to endure; he retired early to avoid them.

As he washed and changed next morning, he reminded himself of his resolve to give her time, to woo her slowly, not to rush her. It seemed that she was more at ease with him when there were other people around so maybe they should go out dancing, let her get used to being with him. She had, after all, only married him to escape from Moll.

———

Rose walked back to her lodgings, tired after a busy day stowing cloth brought from a shipment unloaded that morning at Gibson's Quay. It had been heavy work and she was weary. Before he had left for Kumara, she had agreed with Will that she should get a job to bring in some money until the claim began to pay. 'Not in a bar, though,' he had insisted, and been pleased when she managed to secure a situation in a draper's shop now occupying an old theatre premises. The building's closure as a place of entertainment had been an early sign of the town's faltering fortunes, but the shop was run by a decent enough man who had looked her up and down and employed her on the spot. She had been lucky as everywhere the town was suffering; shopkeepers and publicans might condemn Kumara as just another duffer, but they watched their customers heading up the trail and began making plans to follow them. The strip of shanties along the beach now stood largely abandoned; some had been carried away by a recent high tide and not replaced. Ships still tied up at the quay but it seemed their passengers paused only long enough to gather supplies before heading for Kumara. Rose reminded herself of her good fortune in getting the draper's job as she walked home, but wondered how long they would keep her on.

Just as she arrived at the door of her building, a man with a mule cart hailed her and told her that Will would be coming to see her the very next day and a thrill of excitement pulsed through her. Will! She let herself into their room and stood a moment and surveyed it critically. 'It's not much,' Will had said when they moved her in, 'but the best we can do for now.' And he was right – it had little to commend it. Just a bed, a table and two chairs, and in the corner a washstand, which stood beside a battered chest for their clothes. Its saving grace was the brick chimney which warmed the place when the tiny range was lit. She had done what she could to make it more homely but with pennies so tight she could do little more than beat out the thin rug and keep the place clean.

But at least she could have some food ready when he arrived and the next day, a meaty broth was simmering on the range, filling the room with good smells. She washed her hair too, resolving that tonight things would be different between them, and she was sitting in front of the fire, existing somewhere between excitement and shyness, combing it through when she heard tap at the door.

It opened.

'Will!' She rose and went to him and he bent to kiss her. It was a brief kiss, almost brotherly, and he released her too soon. Hastily she twisted her hair into a knot and pinned it, covering her disappointment.

'Something smells good,' he said as she took his coat. He looked tired, and had brought with him the earthy smell of the goldfields, and he shot her a questioning glance. 'How've you been?'

'I've been fine, Will. The work is mostly easy as the shop's not busy.' He dumped a bag beside the washstand, filled the bowl from the jug she placed there and briskly washed his face and neck. He gestured to the stew pot on the fire as he dried himself. 'Shall we eat that now?' he asked, with a friendly smile. 'And then maybe go out dancing?'

'Dancing!' That was not what she had in mind.

'I thought you might be getting lonely here. Keen for company.'

'And I thought you'd be tired, and as for company . . .' she gave a little smile '. . . I have yours.'

He laughed, and his eyes lit up, but she swung away from him, shy again suddenly, and went to the fire, lifting the lid from the stew pot, thinking that his face altered when he smiled. At times he could look quite stern, almost hard, but a smile seemed to lift his features and there was a warmth there. 'Let's decide when we've eaten,' she said.

As they ate he told her all about the claim, describing how they were clearing the land, the shelters they had built and the madness of his partners with their drinking and their gambling and their opium.

'Opium?'

He drank the beer she had brought for him. 'Oh aye, it helps, they tell me. The Chinese have set up on the edges and seem to supply the whole goldfield.' He told her too that the signs were promising though it was early days, and how a town was already being planned amongst the wreckage of the forest and how more and more people arrived every day. There was an energy to him, an excitement. 'And maybe,' he said, watching her as she ate, 'once things are a bit more settled out there, I could build us a cabin.'

A cabin? She put down her fork. 'You mean just for us?'

'Unless you'd prefer to share it with Dan McGrath.' He laughed at her expression of horror. McGrath was one of those who had terrified her at Moll's with his wild eyes and wandering hands. 'Yes, just for us, Rose. Would you like that? Would you come?'

Her own cabin. She could barely conceive of the idea. 'Of course I would,' she said, reaching out a hand to him. 'I'm your wife, after all.'

A little silence fell.

'About this dancing . . .' he said, pushing his bowl away, his eyes questioning.

The room had grown warm with the fire, and it must be that which made her face feel hot. 'Are you not too tired?' she asked.

He stretched elaborately, his eyes not leaving hers. 'I was, but that broth has set me up grand.'

'So you'd like to go dancing?' she said, sitting back in her chair, having no intention of this happening.

A little smile began to play around his lips. 'Maybe not so much, after all, now I think about it.' His fingers began to tap a tune on the table. 'How about you?'

'I could clear away and we could stay here instead, and talk some more . . .'

'We could . . .' he agreed, nodding thoughtfully. 'And you know what, Rose? I liked it when it was down – your hair, I mean, when I came in.'

'I was drying it.'

'Were you? Well maybe we could stretch out there for a bit,' he gestured to the narrow bed, 'and talk some more . . .'

'Clear away later, you mean?' she said, not moving.

'Aye. And maybe you could unpin your hair again, let it dry

some more.' He had brown eyes, with such a warmth to them. 'That might be a better plan?'

She raised a hand to the pins that held the knot in place. 'Yes, Will,' she said, with a little smile of her own. 'I think you might be right.'

Chapter 10

Will was back in Hokitika two weeks later, desperate to see Rose again. He had spent the fortnight endlessly reliving every moment, every touch, and what a sweet torment it had been. Good God, how he wanted her! He had gone into town that last time with such misgivings, concerned that things would still be awkward between them, and had been overjoyed at his reception. How lovely she was, just a slender lass, so sweet and with such a softness to her. His own, his wife!

So this time as he strode down the trail he was riding high on optimism, and desire; even more so as there were takings to bring to the bank. Not a fortune, not by any measure, but his share would be enough to take Rose out tonight and leave her some extra, above the rent. Callum, the best of the wild cousins, had come in with him and as they waited in line at the bank to cash in the gold, they joked and laughed.

Life was good.

He had not sent ahead to tell Rose this time, intending to surprise her at the draper's and so, with coins jangling in his pocket and a bounce in his step, he crossed the street only to be turned away. 'I had to let her go,' the owner told him, with a shrug, 'business is slow.' Worried then, he went to their lodgings where the cold hearth and the careless untidiness of the place set his pulse a-thudding. It had an abandoned look . . . God, what had she been doing for money, for food? He went in search of the landlady but failed to find her and so, with deepening concern, he went back onto the streets.

It was in the seventh hotel that he found Rose. She was serving drinks to a clientele that was better than that which frequented Moll's place, but not by much, and she did not see him arrive. He slid into the corner and watched her, feeling a jealous anger growing in him as he watched her smiling at customers, laughing with some of them, lingering to talk. He saw Big Sven, who seemed to be a fixture at the bar and whenever Rose returned with an empty tray, he spoke to her and she responded with a familiarity that made Will itch to throttle the man. He watched her a moment longer then fixed a smile on his face, and approached the bar.

But all anger vanished when she saw him. '*Will!*' Her face lit up, there was no mistaking it. She dumped the tray she was carrying and came from behind the bar and flung her arms around his neck.

———

Seeing Will appear so suddenly gave Rose a jolt of delight and she pulled him over to the bar where Sven shifted himself with good grace and offered to buy him a drink.

He looked leaner, she thought, and weary. And there had been anger in his eyes as he approached her. 'What was I to do, Will? Starve?' she said, pre-empting any rebuke. He had shown her such tenderness, but she did not yet have the full measure of this man. 'None of the businesses need women like me. There's no work other than bars and the hotels, and little enough of that.' She dropped her voice, her eyes on the landlord. 'This is a respectable place, Will, and I'd nothing to live off. I had to survive somehow until you came.' She moved away to serve another customer.

'Just the same, I don't like it,' he said, when she returned a moment later. 'I was watching you, and you . . .'

She raised her chin. 'I what?'

He stopped and their eyes locked and then she saw the tension drain from his face. 'You look wrong here, Rose, too fine for this place, too lovely. And I was worried. I – I thought you'd left me.' She reached out a hand to him, and he took it and kissed her palm. A good man, Fraser Urquhart had said, and she was lost for words. 'I'm sorry I left you short,' he went on, 'but I've money now. The claim is starting to pay.' He glanced at the landlord. 'When can you leave?'

But even as he spoke the door opened and Fraser himself strode up to the bar. Rose tensed. 'Ah, *ma muse*, blooming as ever!' he said, before noticing Will and when he did, without skipping a beat, he clapped him on the back. 'Odysseus! Returned to claim his Penelope. And do you return a rich man, Will Stewart?'

Rose had grown used to Fraser's nonsense, but she saw Will frown and his reply was curt. 'Signs are good.'

'So not a duffer?' Fraser grinned at him. He took a curious pride in learning the language of the diggers, often asking Rose the meaning of words. And he was teaching her some of his own.

Will grunted in reply.

Fraser glanced at her, held her look a moment, then pulled up a stool and sat. 'Well, this is very timely, Will, as I've been having an idea.' Rose stiffened; this was surely not the moment. Fraser flicked another glance in her direction, as if to reassure, and silence her. 'I was waiting until you were next in town to broach it. I've need of an assistant, you see, to help me to print and process. Someone smart but someone careful and precise, as success in my art depends as much on judgement as any other skill.' He paused but Will's face was inscrutable. 'When you came to my studio after the wedding, your wife showed an interest in what I do. You did, I think, did you not, Rose?'

She nodded, watching Will.

'And so?' her husband said.

'And so I thought of Rose. I'd like to employ her. I'd teach her, train her in the dark arts, and pay her well. If you would countenance such an arrangement?'

Will raised an eyebrow. 'Dark arts?'

Fraser waved a dismissive hand. 'A figure of speech. Some claim that photography is simply science and not art at all, but I dispute that position. Optics and chemistry underpin the process, of course, but it is artistic judgement that—'

'And what would she be doing?' Will sat back and Rose noticed that his left eye had become hooded, as it did sometimes. His expression was unreadable.

'Washing the used plates, varnishing, printing out the positives, mounting them. There is a complex set of processes at every—'

'How much would you pay?' Fraser named a figure and Will nodded, then half turned away from him, dismissing the matter. 'We'll discuss it later, Rose and I.'

'Come tomorrow and see for yourself!' Fraser persisted.

'I need to get back to the claim.'

'Half an hour of your time. At most. And you can give me your answer then. That's fair, is it not?' He looked over Will's head to Rose, and gave a little nod.

She returned him a tentative smile.

Every time she went to Fraser's studio she told herself that she had no reason to feel shame. But men, she was learning, were strange creatures and saw such matters in black and white: chaste or wanton, virtuous or shameless. Or worthless . . . Husbands, she imagined, would be even more particular and she feared that if she told Will of the pictures Fraser had made of her, he would take ideas into his head, and she was not sure that she could persuade him that he had no reason for concern. Nor did she think she could find the words to express how she had felt when she had seen the image of herself slowly emerge in the developing dish.

It was something she barely understood herself.

The first time she entered Fraser's studio had been when she and Will had gone to sit for their wedding photograph, and it had been like entering a different world; a theatre, a place of fantasy. Urquhart had offered them three alternative painted screens as a backdrop and Will had chosen a pastoral scene which, he said, reminded him of home, and so they had posed against green rolling hills, framed by European trees in full leaf. Fraser had placed the two of them very precisely: Rose seated, her head against a head rest, Will standing beside her with his hand on her shoulder. 'Now hold that position, if you will. Move not a muscle,' and he had disappeared beneath his hood while the seconds ticked by.

She had sat, waiting for something to happen, but felt nothing. No sharp prick, no pain, no buzz of sensation. She was unchanged. How extraordinary . . . Was all achieved by simply standing still? 'How does it happen?' she asked after he released them, and had gone over to examine the camera.

'Have a look, my dear.' He had placed a small stool for her stand on, pulling the hood over her head. She had looked ahead as instructed and given a little shriek, stepping down at once and freeing herself from the hood. And she had stared at Fraser, quite bewildered. 'It's upside down! And the wrong way round – like the boot-maker's' shop was, on the ceiling!' The two men had exchanged startled looks and Will had pulled forward a chair and sat her on it. Shaking slightly, and with eyes wide, she had tried to explain the strange phenomenon she had seen the night before when the lantern had steadied. 'Will had . . . he had to go out, and then I saw him, crossing the road, but on the ceiling, upside down. It was you, Will, I know it was!' And he had stared back at her as if she had lost her senses.

Fraser, however, had been delighted and beamed at her. 'How splendid! What you saw, my dear, was precisely what you saw just now through the lens. A tiny hole in your curtain must have bent the light and projected an image of the street onto your ceiling. Optics, Rose, not magic. How clever of you to notice. All the lens does is refine the image, and the prepared plate allows me to capture it, and so preserve the moment.' He had gone on to explain the processes that followed and she had wanted to linger and to watch but Will had taken her arm and they had left. And when Fraser had handed them the photograph next day, mounted on card with a fancy framing, she had marvelled again.

It was shortly after Will had first gone out to Kumara that she had next encountered Urquhart. 'Mrs Stewart, good morning!' he had said, with a gentle mockery. 'Married life suits you, I trust? But Will has gone.'

'Yes.'

'The bride already forsaken! Dear me. But I have something I forgot to give you. Come with me now and collect it.' He had offered her his arm as if she was a fine lady and they walked down the street to his studio where he handed her the photograph he had taken outside the church immediately after the wedding. She had looked back at her unsmiling, anxious self and saw that Will's face too was serious. Perhaps it was the commitment they had just made, the great leap in the dark, or simply the require- ment to stand still, although Robbie, on her other side, had managed to maintain a grin as he stood close to Rose. Closer in fact than Will . . . She stared down at it, still grappling with the whole extraordinary process. How strange that a simple box could capture their likeness, shrink them to fit on a piece of card, and all in a matter of moments.

Urquhart was watching her. 'Thank you,' she said. 'Will shall be pleased.' But she would not show it to Robbie. He had been strange with her the odd times she had seen him since the wedding. Mocking her new respectability, insolent when Will was out of earshot. Almost hostile.

Urquhart remained still. 'And you, Rose, are you pleased?'

She looked again at the image. 'Yes . . .'

'But? I sense an unspoken *but*.'

'It still seems like magic.'

He had smiled down at her. 'Would you like to see the alchemy in progress?' He touched her lightly on the arm, sensing her lack of comprehension. 'Come, my dear, and let me show you.' And he had taken her into a second room which had darkened windows and where an array of glass-stoppered bottles, shallow basins and drying frames was set out along a bench. One part of the room was curtained off, its half-drawn folds barely concealing a narrow bed with rumpled covers. He went across and pulled it closed.

'You live here too?' she had asked, before she could stop herself.

'Some of the time,' he replied shortly. 'But come and let me reveal to you the mysteries behind the magic.' And he had shown her the camera, his various lenses, the glass plates, and explained to her the processes involved. She had taken in very little, and he sensed this. 'Allow me to take your portrait now and I will demonstrate.' But she had backed away, shaking her head, thinking that Will would surely not approve. She sensed her husband's ambivalence towards this man, and was mindful too of the offer that Urquhart had made to her. 'It is entirely proper, Rose, m'dear,' he had smiled, as if reading her thoughts. 'I'll not lay a finger on you, I promise. You simply sit and I point the camera at you as I did before. Nothing else. And you can present the portrait to Will with a clear conscience, and I'll have had the pleasure of capturing your delightful features and flawless skin tones which, speaking frankly, I've been longing to do. My interest is purely aesthetic, I assure you. Artistic,' he added, seeing that the word was unfamiliar.

So she had sat for him, holding her head as instructed and looking, not at the camera, but aside. 'For this is not a personal exchange between you and me, Rose,' he explained. 'If you glance aside as I suggest, you have a dreaming faraway look that is frankly quite devastating.' He had brought the equipment close and, although he was true to his word and never touched her, she had felt vaguely wanton.

He removed the plate and together they had gone through the various processes again, and she noticed for the first time how long and slender his fingers were, and how the nails were blackened and his skin pocked with stains. A curiously angular man with his sharp aquiline nose and narrow chin. 'The skill lies in judging exactly when to drop the shutter and decide that the picture is true, or true to your intention. Drop it too late and the result is pale and bland, too soon and you achieve only darkness, and the moment is lost.'

They had bent over the developing dish together. 'See, Rose!' he had said, as the grey tones began to appear. 'Look! And see how beautiful you are. Quite lovely, my dear.' And she had peered down at herself, astonished but enchanted.

Beautiful, he had said. Quite lovely.

Not worthless. Or depraved.

'If I am,' she said, slowly, 'it is your photograph that has made me so.'

'The camera can only draw out what is already there. What

you see is yourself, Rose.' And she had lifted her head and looked back at him. This man intrigued her, he was like no other she had known.

He had persuaded her to return the next day and sit for him again, insisting once more that it was a perfectly respectable thing to do. Fascinated by the process she had agreed, and arrived to find an armchair positioned in front of a classical scene, one wing of it draped with a silken shawl. 'You permit, *ma muse*?' he asked, smiling at her, and arranged it so that it fell in soft folds over her shoulders.

'What did you call me?'

'*Ma muse*, Rose, my inspiration. A muse is a sort of goddess, a nymph who inspires an artist's work. In your case a water nymph, perhaps, plucked by Will from the waves.'

She frowned at him. 'Nymphs of the pave' was how the men referred to the girls in Moll's place. 'I am neither nymph nor goddess.'

Urquhart had disappeared under his hood. 'No?' he had said, his voice muffled. 'A sylph then, a spirit with winged sandals.' She gave up trying to understand him and became conscious instead of the softness of the silk, its warm caress against her skin. So many new and strange sensations.

'Empty your mind, Rose.' He spoke from under the hood. 'Fix your eyes on the floor below the window, drop your chin a little – that's it, and now let your thoughts drift a million miles away. And remain . . . absolutely . . . still.' His disembodied voice had a mesmeric quality and she felt herself relaxing in a way that was unfamiliar. All the bad things receded – Tommy's betrayal, his father's contempt, his mother who had been briefly kind but resolute – she let it all go, together with the shipwreck, and the lost baby. Even Will, her saviour-husband, faded, leaving her with a languid inner peace.

'Ah!' Urquhart said, as he emerged from the hood and looked down on her. 'You are a natural, my dear.' And so she had returned the next day, and the next, and had worn the silken shawl again, loosening her hair when he requested, resting her chin in her cupped hand, looking away from the camera into an unexplored world.

'That other word you used,' she asked him. 'Alchem . . . ?'

'Alchemy. Ah yes – the mystical transformation, the eternal quest to turn base metal into gold. A fitting analogy for our fine diggers, perhaps, as they shift through the mud and rocks! I hadn't thought of that. But who, then, is the alchemist, I wonder?'

'But that's impossible!' she said, fixing on his first remark.

'Is it?' It was then that Fraser had said that he wished she would come and work for him so that he could prove otherwise.

'Will'll never agree.'

'Do you think not?'

Will, she was learning, might be a quiet man but there were depths to him that she had only glimpsed, and she doubted very much that he would even consider Fraser's offer. So she was surprised when he suggested that they should go to the studio next morning and discuss the proposal, before he returned to Kumara. She grew anxious then. If Fraser had not been so hasty with his offer, she might have told Will about her visits to the studio, been open about it, reassured him and gained his approval, but Fraser had made that impossible. And yet, given Will's reaction to finding her working in the bar, perhaps openness was unwise; her mild-mannered husband, it appeared, had a steely side.

Better perhaps that she left Fraser to explain, and so she stood meekly beside Will while Fraser described the tasks that she would learn to undertake. 'There is so much demand for *cartes de visite* that I find myself quite overrun,' he said, although Rose had seen nothing to support this claim, and Fraser was not the only photographer in town. There were at least two others advertising their portrait rooms.

He showed Will the apparatus and her husband bent forward to study the labels on the glass-stoppered bottles. 'Will her hands become blackened like yours?' he asked.

Fraser shook his head. 'Not for the world, I promise you. Rose shall wear gloves, and I'll handle the silver nitrate myself. Women have a nicety of judgement, I find, and that is all I need.' Rose was touched by Will's concern, but also desperate that he would agree. 'And I'll do a portrait of your wife for you, Will, my best work, free of charge,' and Rose felt again a little prick of conscience that so many portraits had already been done. Despite his assertion that their conduct had been entirely respectable, she noticed that Fraser made no mention of these. And she dared not.

Will glanced at her and grunted in a way she was beginning to understand meant that he was uncertain, but in the end, they agreed terms and Rose's spirits soared. She was free now to explore this strange new world with a clearer conscience. While Fraser, the man, she felt offered her no threat, Urquhart, the photographer, was awakening in her something beyond her understanding.

Chapter 11

But he proved to be an exacting master.

True to his word he had given her gloves to wear, carrying out the task of preparing the plates himself. 'I would never forgive myself if any part of you was sullied by this work,' he said, intending perhaps to give her a wider reassurance, and he smiled in a way that confused and yet intrigued her.

Apart from the odd accidental encounter, he also stuck to his promise never to touch her, and they worked together through the processes, side by side, saying little as they produced the ever-popular *cartes de visite*, or more ambitious portraits of prospering townsfolk. He taught Rose how to wash the plates clear after exposure, and she quickly became proficient in all stages of the developing and printing. She learnt how to fix the prints in their card mounts and add his little cipher, a stylised design overlaying F and U. Eyebrows might be raised at her presence in the studio, but she was always quiet and modestly dressed, her hair pulled back and netted in a neat bun, and she would withdraw while Fraser took his photographs. Some of the female customers, however, felt reassured by her presence, and occasionally he would signal for her to stay.

In the mornings, he would take his equipment out into the street, hunting, as he called it, seeking the spontaneous and the unexpected. On these occasions he was assisted by a young Māori lad, known as Harry, who would speed back to the studio with the exposed plates, his face split by a grin, and hand them to Rose. 'Excellent,' Fraser would say, when he returned and viewed the results. 'We capture the unrepeatable, my dear, the unique and the singular.' And Rose began to recognise that besides an intense passion for his work he had an insatiable curiosity and, at the same time, a strange detachment from reality. 'Photographing stout matrons and town worthies keeps me fed, but no one but themselves care a jot for these damned *cartes*. A glance and then forgotten.' He smiled a little wryly. 'As for the diggers, bless them, I can forgive them their preening, but it's the rawness I want to capture, the reality of this mad enterprise.' And he would stand and look over her shoulder as she lifted a print for his inspection, nodding his approval. 'You learn fast, my dear. Next, I'll go out to Kumara and photograph that crop of gold being harvested, and you shall come with me, Rose, and surprise your Will.'

'I should like that.'

And then had come the extraordinary day when he had asked if she would like to take a photograph for herself. 'Do the whole thing, start to finish. What do you say?'

'Would I be able to?'

'But of course! Let's go outside and find a subject.' They carried his equipment into the street and Fraser crossed the road to ask a woman carrying a sleeping child if she would oblige, explaining that there would be a print for her, free of charge, and that Rose would take the photograph. He left Rose to decide on position and framing, bringing out a chair for the woman to sit on, and he stood, leaning against the building offering suggestions but leaving Rose to work things out and ask if she needed help. She frowned, concentrating hard, but found it the most satisfying business, capturing another woman's likeness. They gathered quite a crowd of onlookers and she became self-conscious and nervous but Fraser simply nodded encouragement and she exposed her plate. At Fraser's suggestion, they then stepped into the studio and he took another photograph of the mother and baby himself, which was just as well as Rose's attempt, when developed, was found to be underexposed and dark. But in the days that followed she tried again, and improved, and Fraser devised for her a little cipher of her own – an R placed on the central curve of an over-sized S – and she had been delighted, drawing it for Will to admire when next he came.

Sometimes, though, Fraser shocked her. One plate of his she processed showed a man who had been brought out from Kumara on the back of a mule cart, his leg half-severed by an axe. 'You photographed the poor soul!' she said, staring into the man's agonised face.

'Of course. Who records the pain, if I do not? God knows if he'll survive to speak of it.' She stopped work to stare at him as he inspected the plate. 'A little blurred,' he muttered, 'inevitably, but that provides a sense of urgency. By good fortune I'd a plate already prepared when I saw him being carried on the stretcher, his bandaged leg suitably bloodied.'

'But who will want to look at that?' she asked, repelled.

He looked up at her, his face austere. 'Am I only to photograph the palatable, then, Rose, and the lovely? Only offer to posterity an acceptable past, cleansed of suffering?' She looked at him uneasily, struggling to comprehend and, with a swift gesture he turned a chair and straddled it, leaning his arms on its back. 'How dishonest that would be, and what a waste when photography has such power! Tell me, Rose, if I were to write about a child living in poverty, starving in some slum, or describe its predica-ment to you, you would listen, tut tut a little, shake your head and say "ah dearie me", but if I were to *show* you a child, its filthy hide stretched taut across its bones, hollow eyes looking unblinking into yours, that would take your attention, would it not? The child becomes real, he has entered your drawing room, stirred your conscience. And you might act!' He paused, then added. 'As I know to my cost.'

'How so?'

He rose and fetched a book from a closed cupboard, thumbed through it and passed it to her, open at a photograph of a dark alley, framed on both sides by tall tenement buildings. In the centre of it, the focal point emphasised by converging walls, stood a group of urchins, clothed in filthy rags, staring back at the photographer. 'Glasgow,' he said, 'some five years ago.' Rose looked at it and saw her own early childhood in the backstreets of Melbourne reflected back at her, but she said nothing. He turned the page to a photograph of a house, warm and mellow, bathed in sunshine. Steps led down from a terrace, marked by stone posts topped by black marble urns containing luxurious ferns, to lawns and gardens, clipped and neat. Light reflected off a large conservatory through which more ferns and vines could be seen; wicker chairs had been set out and a table was laid for tea with white linen and fine china. 'Kinnloss House, bought and adorned by Lord Kinnloss using money made at factories where those children's families worked,' Fraser told her. 'The two photographs, set side by side, tell a story, do they not? In fact, once you know the connection, there is no need for further words.'

He turned the next page and she frowned, peering at a confused scene of silhouettes against a darkening sky lit in places by the white light of what she came to see were flames from the burning roofs of houses. Blurred figures occupied the foreground and conveyed a sense of rushing movement, of panic and terror. To one side was the dark shape of a woman with what must be an infant in her arms, standing quite still, transfixed by the scene, clear and stark on the skyline. 'I had been commissioned to photograph that second picture, of Kinnloss's shameful citadel, and that evening I stumbled on this scene on his estate, just a couple of miles from those sunny terraces. I had wandered away from the house enchanted by the light in the evening sky and had my portable equipment with me when I spotted smoke and went to investigate. The light was going and I was forced to prepare in haste and only one plate I made was successful. But it was enough! Ten families were driven from their homes that evening by men who came with cudgels and torches alight, they saw their possessions burnt before their eyes – an eviction, it was, raw and savage.' His eyes glinted with anger at the memory. 'I caused a scandal with that photograph, Rose. I published it, you see, beside the others and there was a court case, which I lost, and thereby engineered my own fall from grace. I cared little for that, though, for I had thereby learnt the astonishing potency of photography, and at the time it was altogether gratifying that it became such a cause célèbre. Though later—' He broke off and looked again at the open page, saying nothing more. Then: 'Mere words could not have conveyed the cruelty and the injustice of that evening, but that photograph did.'

Together they stared down at the image.

'Some of the fishing boats were saved, I was told, but all else was destroyed. And because I published it, together with the other, I showed the man, and his class, in their true lights. Kinnloss claimed, to anyone who would listen, that torching the houses at Srath an loin had been carried out by his factor, without his authority, but he was not believed. He bought as many copies of the publication as he could and destroyed them but enough were circulating to ruin him – and me.' He set the book aside and returned to straddle the chair again.

'He ruined you?'

'Or redeemed me, depending on your view of the matter.' He smiled a little. 'My father was appalled at what I had done, you

see, and so I became a disgrace to my family, and my class.
Kinnloss accused me of trespass and he won his case, so overnight
I became a pariah, a social outcast.' He gave her a twisted smile.
'The liberal press adored me, if only briefly, but my father made
it impossible for me to stay, and paid my passage out here to get
rid of me.' Rose looked back at him, sensing the hurt. 'But I
should thank him, you know, as I believe he provided me with a
purpose. Not only to explore the bounds of beauty as I do with
you, but to chart the unpalatable, record the unseemly and I
challenge anyone, even you, *ma muse*, to prevent me.'

This last was said with his whimsical smile and she began
to understand that there were many facets to this man. He had
an artist's eye and yet an anarchist's passion, and she better
appreciated the hours he spent roaming the streets searching
out intriguing and provoking shots, or cajoling passers-by to
form his little tableaux. And she would watch him bent over
the developing dishes, swearing softly when his efforts failed
to meet his exacting standards, or crowing with pleasure when
a particular effect had been achieved. He was like no other
man she had known and soon she was sharing his quest for
perfection.

For at the end of the working day, when the sign on the door
was changed from *Open* to *Closed*, the atmosphere in the studio
changed. Commerce was abandoned and a more subtle artistry
took over. They became conspirators: Urquhart the innovator, she
his compliant model, trying different exposures, different positions,
different effects of light and shade on her skin tones. 'The female
form has challenged painters down the centuries,' he remarked on
one occasion as he moved the lanterns to a side table, 'and I am
no less seduced by it than the next man.' He smiled and she felt
a small tremor of unease. 'Photography has yet to explore what
contribution it can make beyond replicating the classical or

exploring well-worn themes: desire and pleasure, sin and sexuality. Which will its audience choose to see? Virgin, goddess, harpy or whore?'

And she wondered a little how he saw her.

He asked her once if she would allow him to pay her for sitting for him and she was unsettled by the suggestion. It had echoes of Moll's establishment where the girls took money for all manner of acts done at men's bidding and, in some confusion, she refused his offer. He smiled that amused, distant smile of his. 'I'd no intention to offend, but wouldn't have you think I exploit you. Painters always pay their models, my dear, so I felt I must offer.' They carried on, and no more was said. He worked rapidly but with care, placing her in different poses, some chaste, some more sensuous, but all executed with a professionalism that reassured her. It was at her own suggestion, some days later, that she bared her shoulders that first time, sensing that this was what he might want, and he had nodded and arranged the silk drapery around her, his eyes sharp and intense. Stepping out of her skirt and blouse was simply the next stage and he photographed her with her thin shift unbuttoned, curled into the armchair, her legs bare, the silk shawl swirled around her waist.

'Ah, Rose, how lovely you are,' he said, from beneath the hood. But still he never approached her except to cover her with a blanket when she started to shiver. And together, with a shared eagerness, they would lean over the developing dish and watch as the images appeared. 'Such flawless skin, my dear, and that outrageous mole. Innocence and experience displayed in a single countenance. How perfectly has nature endowed! And mark the gleam of the hair on the shoulder's naked flesh.' The words, although impersonal, rang a sudden alarm in her head and as she looked at the emerging print, she saw how far they had travelled, and into what dangerous territory.

Her reflection rebuked her. 'Will . . .' she began, tentatively, and Fraser swung round to look at her. 'Will . . . Will would . . .'

'Disapprove, I fear.'

And the moment hung there.

'Perhaps we need not tell him?' she said, and he gave her a measured look. She felt herself blushing; he must think her treacherous, but her two worlds seemed suddenly irreconcilable. 'I don't think he would understand.'

'I'm quite sure that he would not,' Fraser replied. 'Will is the salt of the earth, but a man of conventional views, I believe. My conscience is entirely clear as we have not transgressed. I have seen your body largely unclothed, but what of it? You are just another living creature, born naked, and so there can be no sin in that.' Again she felt uneasy, perplexed by him. For a man with strong passions he sometimes struck her as quite devoid of understanding, inhabiting a world where normal rules did not apply. 'But if your conscience is uneasy then we will cease forthwith.'

She moved away from the bench and dried her hands, not answering. What a strange man he was! And yet she felt safe with him, though could not have explained why. When she posed for Fraser her mind was set free, and she followed his instructions in a mesmeric daze, revelling in the extraordinary sensation of being admired, but not desired, being made to feel beautiful and sensuous for herself alone.

Not worthless.

Or depraved.

But she saw that the print told a different story, and would certainly be misunderstood. The thought that Will, or anyone else, might look at it made her face burn with shame.

'Answer me, Rose!' Fraser commanded. 'Do we cease or continue?'

She bit her bottom lip. 'What will you do with the photographs?'

'Why, nothing, my dear! They are simply exercises in technique. I experiment with light and form, texture and emotion, nothing more. What did you imagine I might do with them?'

She hesitated. 'So will you destroy them?'

'Must I?'

'If someone were to find them and . . . and misunderstand?'

'They are safe, I assure you. No one comes here except you and I, and Harry – and he has no interest – and besides, he is much more concerned about other photographs I take, and what his people would say!' She looked up at him then and met a steady look. 'I do other work, you see, long after you have gone home.' He held her look, and then spoke softly.

'You need have no concerns, my dear.'

Chapter 12

At least if Rose was working in Fraser's studio all day she was not sitting lonely in their lodgings, Will thought as he walked back to the goldfield after his latest visit – and nor was she working in a bar prey to drunken diggers and their insults. Urquhart, he sensed, was not interested in women, and seemed to be an honourable man. Even so, the sooner he could bring Rose out to the goldfield to be with him, the happier he would be. He wanted to spend time with her, to get to know the woman he had married, to hold her close to him in the darkness. To love her.

A grid of planned streets was being surveyed at Kumara close to the Taramakau River and one or two weatherboard buildings were under construction along a track, which looked set to become the main street. A gold commissioner's camp was established, and there was talk of a bank being built, so it must be widely held that the Kumara goldfield was no duffer. Official order was being imposed so past mistakes could be avoided; life on earlier goldfields had become disorderly and dangerous with diggers frequently taking the law into their own hands. He moved aside to allow a wagon to pass him on the narrow trail where already there was talk of tram rails being laid to connect the place with other goldfields, and with the coast. Things moved fast with the smell of gold in the air.

A pair of aerobatic fantails flew out of the scrub and flitted before him as he skirted around a swampy patch, smacking at the sand flies which were an ever-present torment. Could he really bring Rose out here?

Various riders passed him and, as evening fell, he hitched a lift on a mule cart hauling supplies for a general store that had set up in a tent. At the end of the trail he emerged from the forest and stood a moment, looking out over the stripped land. It was as if a race of giants had lumbered across it, uprooting trees, leaving a trail of destruction, or as if a battle had been waged there, ravaging the landscape. There was now a wide view across the old river terraces where a calico city had mushroomed into being. Where once mighty rimu and white pine had raised their tops above a tangle of aerial roots and tree ferns, there were now only butchered stumps and piles of brushwood. The trunks and usable branches had been dragged away, leaving trails through the carnage, and half-built shanties stood along tracks destined to become streets. The sounds of cutting and sawing, shouts and cries now filled air once sweetened by the melodies of bellbird and tui amongst the supplejack vines. Large fronded growths, known as widow-makers, would crash down from high branches as trees were felled – the forest's final defence. Seeing the stacks of timber brought him back to earth, and his mind went to considering the task of flume construction that must be undertaken. My God, there was work to be done!

The recent rain had turned the ground to mud and, as the light faded, Will made his way carefully through the encampment, stepping over felled branches as he navigated a route through the tree stumps. A rat ran across the track ahead of him and he kicked at it. On brushwood rafts laid between tents, diggers were hunkered down close to their campfires and some greeted him with a nod or a word as he passed. From somewhere came the sound of a fiddle and of voices raised in song, as if in homage to their humanity.

He felt a brief satisfaction in the sense of common purpose, of muscle and sweat expended in the pursuit of dreams, and his burst of good humour lasted all the way to their claim where he found the nightly drinking session well under way. Ducking to enter the tent, he dumped his gear beside his sagging cot on which three men were seated, side by side. They raised a bottle in acknowledgement of his arrival but showed no sign of moving, so he squeezed himself into the available space and accepted a drink. But the dense tobacco smoke and their drunken nonsense soon drove him back outdoors where a hundred fires now glowed in the darkness, the shambolic army at rest. Woodsmoke mingled with the smell of cooking and a wan moonlight shone through the blue-grey haze. He found himself wondering how this place would look a hundred years from now. Would a city grow here, or would the gold run out and the diggers move on, leaving paddocks to be settled and farmed? Or would the trees take back the violated land and this brief moment of madness be forgotten?

At the edge of their claim a small creek had found a crack in the old terracing and eroded a channel there. It was little more than a run-off for rain, and had only been evident after a heavy downfall on their second night had forced them to shift their tents. Close by there was an area of flat land, which formed a rough square between four tree stumps. It was, strictly speaking, outside the claim, but Will had his eye on it. There was enough space there for a small cabin and, if he could get the others to agree, he would start to build. The tree stumps could serve as corner posts, giving stability to the structure, and no matter if the walls were of uneven length – all that was needed were split logs or rough planks for walls, with shingles or tin sheets for a roof. Will was used to building with stone, and if he put boulders in the foundation it would give the structure strength.

A hand fell on his shoulder. 'And how was the lovely Rose?' It was Robbie, and Will found himself telling him of his plan. 'You'd bring her out here?' His partner stared at him. 'Are you mad?'

'She's lonely in town, and the nights are long.' Robbie laughed. 'She lost her job at the draper's and she's working now for Urquhart—'

'The portrait man?' Robbie frowned. 'What sort of work?'

'Helping with his printing and other processes.'

'In his studio? And you out here . . .' He searched Will's face. 'You trust the man?'

'I do. But even so, I'd like her with me.'

'Sure you would, and then she can keep house for us all – a cooked dinner every night, and clean clothes for everyone.' He gave a grin. 'As you say, the nights are long; we could all do with a woman.' With a laugh he disappeared back inside the tent, and soon the whole group knew of Will's plan. He bore their ribaldry with a shrug and a smile but he got their agreement for his cabin.

Which was all that mattered.

Their mockery continued next evening when he started work, and they sat about smoking and scratching insect bites, content to watch him toil, tossing back their grog while he cleared the low-growing plants, digging trenches for the drystone foundations.

'Sure, it will be a fine place,' one of them remarked. 'But it'll never take the seven of us!'

Will worked on.

'Eight with the missus,' said another.

'This is a partnership, Will, and you remember that,' said Dan McGrath. 'And if you're all night a-fucking, you'll not be up to doing your bit.'

'I will,' Will replied, his foot on his spade.

'Is that the doing or the fucking?' Robbie asked and the others laughed.

'We're willing to share the load,' one of them said, and Will made no reply.

'So will it be strictly turns then, Will, one at a time?'

Will ignored the man, but Dan McGrath answered, his voice soft. 'There were lasses at Moll's who'd take on two . . .'

Fighting the urge to knock the man's teeth down his throat, Will kept digging, head down. Perhaps it was a bad idea to bring her out here, after all, he thought; perhaps she was safer where she was, in Urquhart's care. But he would give it until spring and then, whether luck had favoured them or not, they would be away from here.

A layer of old river cobbles provided stones for the foundations and he transferred them, one by one, to the trenches he had dug, working up a sweat. He had repaired enough walls and sheep fanks in his time on Kinnloss's estate to know what he was doing, and focussed on the job in hand. Eventually his tormentors drifted away, discouraged by the lack of response. He watched them go, then he leant hard on his pick to dislodge one deeply embedded boulder, applying leverage and muscle. Eventually it moved and he lifted it, shifted it – and stopped.

And stared.

At the stuff of dreams.

He dropped to his knees, scrabbling in the old river gravels, shouting out, but his audience had moved out of earshot. Carefully, almost reverently, he picked up one of the little nuggets and held it between thumb and forefinger. It was the size of a broad bean, water worn, and was one of six – no, seven, eight, *nine* – in a clutch beneath the obstinate boulder, caught there in some ancient eddy, laid by a golden goose for him to find. He stood staring at them and a pulse began thudding in his head as he weighed them in his hand. He turned towards the tents from where raucous laughter and the clink of bottles could be heard.

Then he stopped.

He looked down at his palm, and then back at the tents, and even as he thought the unthinkable, he found his fingers had closed over the gold, concealing it in a fist.

Chapter 13

'Working late?' Will remarked. Rose still had her coat on when he arrived two weeks later, unannounced, from Kumara.

She discarded it hastily and smoothed her hair, nodding slightly and giving him a tight little smile. 'I had a lot of prints to prepare for customers to collect tomorrow,' she said. 'I wasn't expecting you, Will! I've little food in, but I can warm you some broth? And there's bread.'

'That'd be grand. But first,' and he pulled her into an embrace and kissed her, wondering briefly if something was wrong. Was Urquhart working her too hard?

Or perhaps it was he who was out of sorts.

Callum had been intending to bring the takings to the bank this time but had injured his foot with a pick so Will had come in his stead, seizing the chance to see Rose – but also keen to get away from his partners. Contempt for them and a bad conscience made an uneasy mixture. He had widened a hole amongst the roots of one of the corner posts of the cabin and hidden the gold pieces there, adding two more small ones he had recovered subsequently, and there they lay, radiating hope well laced with guilt. He had considered bringing them to town and leaving them with Rose but was reluctant to involve her in what was, after all, a monstrous betrayal of trust.

And he did not want her to think the less of him.

He was wrestling with this dilemma when she spoke. 'Was

it Kinnloss, the place you said you came here from?' she asked, presenting him with a steaming bowl of broth and bannock.

He looked up sharply, his spoon half raised. 'Why do you ask?'

'Fraser showed me a book of photographs, and some were taken there. The name sounded familiar.'

He relaxed again and nodded. 'He told me about the book, sold his soul for the money, he said.' Kinnloss was far from his thoughts these days and hearing the name was a shock. 'It was an affront, that place. Could have housed the whole community of Srath an loin in comfort. But instead . . .'

She was shaking her head. 'Not just the big house. There was a photograph of a fire.'

'Of a fire?' He stopped chewing. 'Where?'

'At a place where the tenants lived, that place you just said.'

And he felt the blood drain from his face as he listened to what Urquhart had told her. He put down his knife. 'Is he there now? Urquhart? Will he still be there, at his premises?'

'Why yes, he might be. But—' Will rose, grabbed his hat and left, coatless, ignoring Rose's bewildered questions.

The studio was locked when he arrived and the sign on the door was turned to *Closed* but he hammered at it anyway, got no reply, and hammered again. He heard movement inside and then Urquhart's voice: 'Come back tomorrow.'

Rose caught him up, breathless, a shawl slipping from her shoulder. 'Whatever's wrong, Will?'

He brushed her aside and shouted at the door. 'Open up. It's Will Stewart.'

'Will! Hang on.' A moment later there were sounds of the door unlocking. Urquhart looked startled and had to flatten himself to the wall as Will barged past. 'Good God, what's happened?' he said. There was movement from the corner of the room and a figure slipped from the shadows, past them and out of the door.

Urquhart glanced at Rose, then back to Will. 'What is it?' he repeated.

'A book. Rose said you showed her a book. A picture—'

'What book?'

'The fire,' she explained.

Urquhart seemed to relax. 'You mean the scandalous book? But what—'

'Show me,' said Will.

He looked bewildered. 'Of course. Wait here, and I'll get it.' But Will followed him through to the back room. Urquhart hastily covered some work that was spread out on the bench and pulled a curtain across one corner of the room before lifting a book from the cupboard. He waved Will back into the studio. 'I'll bring it through.' He closed the connecting door and placed the book on the table. 'But whatever brings you in such a stew?'

Will pulled the book towards him, making no reply, and leafed rapidly through it, sensing rather than seeing a look shared between Urquhart and Rose. There was a pattern to the pictures, a repeated order: an image of a great country house was followed by one of poverty and privation, of wretched people in slum houses or rural squalor. There were no words, nothing to identify the houses or the places. Then he came to a photograph of Kinnloss House and he stopped.

There it was in all its complacency, newly extended with its balustraded terrace, the conservatory, the urns overflowing with ferns, the trimmed lawns. He turned the page and the eyes of ragged children stared back at him from a dark space between towering tenements. The latter meant nothing to him, must be in Glasgow, or some other town. Then he turned the pages back and saw what Rose had described.

A chaos of bleached light and contrasting darkness, blurred and indistinct. He jabbed it with his finger. 'Where is that?'

'The mark o'er stepped? My fall from grace.'

'Where, damn you!'

'On Kinnloss's estate. Srath an loin or some such was the name.'

Will swore. 'What happened there?'

'An absolute outrage.' He looked back at Will, his expression puzzled. 'I was out on the estate and I heard shouting and a great tumult, and then I saw smoke and assumed there had been some sort of accident, a fire, and I went to see.' His face became grim. 'No accident, that. It was deliberate – calculated and cruel. I ran back for my equipment – I had it with me, you see, as I'd been trying to capture the extraordinary light on the headland beyond the house. I prepared as best I could and was an unseen witness, arriving as the light faded. There was just enough left for the moment to be preserved.'

Will leant over the page, transfixed, his pulse thudding. That shoulder of land in the background, that dip where it fell away to the little harbour . . . The burning house, that was Donald MacNeil's, a family of eight lived there. The woman and child standing so still on the ridge he could not be certain of, but it might be Flora MacAskill and her little girl. 'When? When did you take it?'

'June, I think it was, early June, in '73 maybe – no, '74.'

Will felt sick. 'Those blurs, are they people?'

Urquhart nodded. 'Aye. People running and screaming and grabbing their children. A dreadful business. Men had come with torches lit and cudgels raised, and they took the community by surprise. They'd no chance to remove their possessions, the poor souls, and it was all flames and confusion. Two houses were ablaze when I arrived and then they all went up, one after the other, without pity or warning.'

Will sank his head into his hands, and Urquhart eyed him with concern. 'You know the place?' Will stayed silent, imagining the scene, a leaden sickness in his stomach. 'Had you kin there?'

'Did everyone get away?' he asked, raising his head slightly.

'A child and an old woman died on the hills in the night, I heard. A late frost, and they'd nowhere to go.' Will shut his eyes. 'Some said it was the factor's son who torched the first—'

'*What*!' His eyes flew open.

'Either him or the factor himself, no one was sure, but it was generally held that Kinnloss ordered it.'

Aye, but surely not like this, not even Kinnloss would order this savagery – this was Armstrong's doing!

Urquhart's next words were a hammer blow.

'I learnt later that rent money had been stolen and the tenants were believed to be in cahoots with the thief. He had set the hillside ablaze as a distraction, you see, and some said this had been in revenge.' Pain clutched at Will's heart and he froze, hardly able to breathe, then slowly he lifted his head and stared at Urquhart. 'I'm so sorry, Will. It was a bad business all round. Had you family there?'

More than family. He had known these people, every one of them by name, all his life. They had *been* his life.

And this was his doing.

'The thief?' He felt compelled to ask.

'Never caught. But he was known, a local man. The factor said he'd left his son for dead and fled with the money.' Will sucked in his breath. No! Young Armstrong had been fine. It was a lie concocted to justify— 'Everyone assumed he'd left the country—' Urquhart stopped and the air seemed to tighten between them. 'He left no trace at all, I was told,' he continued more slowly and Will met his eyes briefly, then looked away. The tick of the clock measured the silence before Urquhart went on:

'I published the photograph, imperfect as it was, to show what had happened there that night, and Kinnloss decided to charge me with trespass. I was found guilty and fined. A paltry business but, in the end, it was Kinnloss who came off worse.' He paused again. 'There was another fire raised, this time at Kinnloss's mills, soon afterwards, and the man went bankrupt.' Urquhart's voice grew strained. 'And blew out his brains in consequence.'

Will's eyes widened. That was surely not on his account. Nor on Urquhart's. But between them . . .

The photographer leant back against the wall, his arms folded, and looked steadily across at Will, saying nothing. And then he continued, in the same measured tone. 'I was outraged by what I saw that night, Will, absolutely sickened. I wanted to expose the crime, pillory the man, but the train of events that followed I could never have imagined. Later I wondered a little at what I'd done, what forces I'd set in motion, but at the time one never truly considers the consequences.'

Will sat motionless, staring at the photograph.

Eventually he rose. 'I'd not grieve for Kinnloss, Urquhart, but the people, that's another matter. And their fate is not on your account. Come, Rose, let's go home.' But then he stopped, remembering, and turned back to Urquhart, his face hardening. 'But first: what was it that you covered up just now? In the other room.'

Was he wrong or had Rose stiffened beside him?

'Private work, Will,' Urquhart answered, evenly. 'Of no concern.'

'Show me.'

Urquhart looked steadily back at him. 'I would rather not.'

'Nevertheless, you will.'

The silence was suddenly dangerous. It lasted for a long moment and then Urquhart went over to the connecting door and held it open. 'Rose, I would ask that you remain here, if you will,' he said. 'And you, sir, since you insist, I ask for your discretion.'

He pulled aside the cloth with which he had covered the bench. Four prints had been laid out there and Will saw what Fraser had been working on, the smooth contours of a half-naked body half in darkness, half in light, of skin wondrously tattooed. It was a beautiful, though unsettling, image, but Will felt a deep relief and turned away. He had been right about this man.

Urquhart gripped his arm. 'Judge me, by all means, Will Stewart,' he hissed in his ear. 'I care not a jot.'

Will looked back at him. 'I'll say nothing.'

Urquhart looked back at him. 'And nor will I, Will of Kinnloss,' he said. 'This evening is best forgotten, don't you think?'

———

Rose and Will walked in silence back from Urquhart's studio and once inside their room he slumped into a chair and stared into the embers of the fire, saying nothing. Rose began quietly clearing away the remains of the abandoned meal, uncertain how to reach him.

'It was me,' he said at last. 'I stole that money.' She nodded, keeping her face carefully blank. She had guessed he had been involved, and she saw how much it pained him. 'I was angry and frustrated, and desperate to get away, but I never imagined—'

'No.' Rose went to him and took the other chair, and they sat in silence.

'I set fire to the hillside – like he said, as a distraction – and then took the money. But the factor's son caught me at it and I had to hit him in order to get away, but as God's my witness, Rose, I did not leave him for dead. He was no more than winded.'

'No, Will I'm sure—'

'Once he'd seen me I had to see it through – they'd have hanged me. But, oh dear God, I never thought . . .' He covered his face with his hands.

She reached a hand out to him. 'You heard what Fraser said, Will: we can't always know where our actions might lead. And he's right. You didn't torch the houses, you weren't responsible for that.'

He gripped her fingers, not looking up. 'It doesn't feel that way.'

'No.' The embers moved and made a hissing sound as gum from the wood boiled in the heat. What could she say to comfort him?

'I was desperate, Rose.' He withdrew his hand. 'I knew my aunt was getting frail but when I asked to take over the tenancy of her croft, Armstrong just laughed in my face. And when she died I was given a week to leave the house, with nothing. *Nothing*, Rose, after all the work I'd put into the land, and the little harbour. Nothing! Even the furniture was taken to pay rent arrears.' She nodded, listening, encouraging him to go on. 'So I made a plan. For years I'd heard talk of New Zealand, you see. When I was young, emigration agents came offering to arrange passage, saying there was free land, and some families went.' He paused. 'Letters back said the climate was good, there was pasture, sheep farms were prospering, but I could only dream; I'd my aunt to consider.' He leant forward, his elbows on his knees, and stared into the fire. 'And then the letters began to tell of gold washing down from the mountains and how a man had only to dip a pan in the rivers there and he was set for life. I must have been about thirteen or fourteen at the time and I remember one letter being passed through so many hands the paper was worn thin and the ink faded. But there was no way I could ever get there.'

He straightened and looked at her and she saw the pain the

memory brought. 'So, years later, once I'd been given orders to leave, I remembered and was determined that somehow I *would*. Thievery seemed my only option, and stealing from Kinnloss could never be a crime.' He shook his head. 'Made a poor job of it, though, getting caught. Had to change my name and even now I'm looking over my shoulder half the time. The place is full of Scots doing what I'm doing, seeing gold as a means of getting land, a new start. Who knows who I might come across. Like Urquhart!' He drew in a deep breath and then shrugged. 'I can't go back to Scotland because of it, you know – at least, not back anywhere near Kinnloss. What with the theft, and the arson, and God knows what other charges they'd level at me.'

She took hold of his hand again. 'We don't *need* to go back, Will. You came here to start afresh and that's what we'll do.' She felt the stirring of a new tenderness for this man, that he too was flawed. How could she tell him that she liked him the better for it? 'And Fraser feels as guilty as you do, I think, and he'll never say anything, I'm sure.'

'So sure?' he said, looking up at her.

'He's a good man, Will. He keeps his word.' She rose to pull a curtain across the window and was conscious of her husband's eyes following her. The photographs he had demanded to see must have been of his other work, but it had been a bad moment.

It might have been other prints that had been laid out to dry.

'Those pictures he showed me.' Will must have picked up on her thought. 'The ones I demanded to see. Do you know about those?'

'I know he works late at night,' she replied carefully, 'but he has never shown me what he does.' He grunted and went back to staring into the embers, and no more was said.

The next day, after Will had set off back to Kumara, Rose made her way slowly to the studio as usual, wrestling with a renewed sense of her own guilt, and when she arrived Fraser asked her quietly if she was happy for their sessions to continue. 'It is entirely acceptable for you to refuse,' he said, smiling at her.

It was hard to express her conflicting thoughts, and she hesitated before replying. 'I don't ever want Will to know,' she said at last. 'If those prints had been of me, and with Will in the state he was in, I hate to think what might have happened.' However could she have made him understand that Fraser was not taking liberties, and that she was acquiescent?

And how would she explain how much what they did together meant to her?

'He won't know, I promise you.'

'I . . . I don't wish to stop.'

'And why is that?'

How hard it was to frame the words. 'Because . . . because of how it makes me feel.' He nodded, watching her, accepting what she said, seeming to understand.

Chapter 14

Kumara continued to grow, and with it grew Will's cabin. The sound of chopping and sawing and shouts as felled trees crashed through the canopy provided the backdrop to his endeavours. So too did his partners' coarse jibes, but Will doggedly pressed on, swiftly checking under each cobble before placing it in his foundations, and when this task was complete he set about shifting other stones, in order, he explained to his partners, to construct a little channel to divert the stream away from the cabin. 'Remember that first night we had, when the rain poured through the tent?' They listened without interest, and that suited Will just fine.

He existed in a state of constant tension now lest any of them suspect him, knowing that their justice would be swift and brutal. No finding came close to that of the first extraordinary day but he had added a few more small gold pieces to his tree stump cache. By itself it was not enough to leave with, but if the claim also continued to yield through the winter, then they would have enough to buy a decent bit of land by spring.

The first hotel in Kumara opened its doors with the paint on its faux façade still drying and the back rooms half built and on its opening night, Will went with his partners, half dead with exhaustion, to wet the threshold. He would as happily have stayed away, begrudging every spare second now, but the half-built cabin was driving a wedge between him and the partnership and he was anxious that the gap did not widen. His conscience served to make him cautious and he was careful to work on the little channel only when some of the group were around, explaining his activities if any approached.

Cutting Robbie out troubled him only a little more than cutting out the others, for Robbie, he had come to see, had switched allegiances. Had it been otherwise Will might have felt differently, but his old partner treated him with the same derision as the rest of the group, ever ready with crude quips about cold nights and warm women, and he would sometimes catch him considering him with a strange, calculating expression.

Two walls of the cabin were built now and Will had borrowed a saw to cut trusses for roof supports and a frame for a door. Callum occasionally gave him a hand but the others preferred to sit and smoke, and sneer. Keeping up his share of work at the claim as well as labouring on the cabin was taking its toll and at the end of the day he was bleary with exhaustion, barely able to stay awake long enough to eat. Dirt and sweat glued his clothes to his body, his hair became matted and his face remained unshaven. The nightly revelries at least had ceased now that the hotel had opened its doors and after that first night, Will invariably stayed behind while the others went off to drink, past caring what they thought.

But he was careful to stay away from his stash in case one of them returned.

And all around them Kumara expanded. A shaft had been sunk to the east of the original claim and coarse gold found there, confirming that this was going to be a major goldfield; already, a secondary encampment, Dillmanstown, was growing up. Hopeful diggers continued to arrive and peg out their claims but it was becoming increasingly clear that big investment would be needed to sink the necessary deep shafts and remove the tailings once the surface gold was worked out. His partners were negotiating terms with adjacent claims, committing to the long term even as Will grew more anxious to be gone. Belatedly, as the nights grew colder, they too began erecting a hut, close to Will's, and he could only hope that they did not find another old stream bed with gold in it to give them reason for suspicion about his overly complex construction.

Once a bank became established in Kumara there would be no need for any of them to go into town, but until then a regular trek back into Hokitika was required if they were to get a decent price for their winnings. Next time he went into town he promised himself he would bring Rose back even if the roof was only planks and calico. But it had been the turn of Robbie and the McGrath brothers to go and they had headed into Hokitika a couple of days ago.

Before they left Will had asked Robbie to call in and see Rose and check that all was well. 'And tell her about the cabin, will you? Tell her it's almost done.'

'I'll tell her.'

'We'll take care of young Rose, Will, make no mistake,' Dan McGrath had said, and his brother Ted had sniggered. Will had glanced at the lad, thinking that what slender powers of reasoning he possessed had diminished as his opium use increased. He watched the three men, their swags on their shoulders, jostling each other and larking about until they disappeared along the trail.

———

Since their brief discussion of the matter, things between Rose and Fraser had continued as before, with her staying on at the studio later and later each day after the last client had gone. She often brought food with her, knowing how long she was likely to be there, and sometimes she persuaded Fraser to share it with her – otherwise, he simply forgot to eat. He was lean to the point of gauntness and she urged him to take better care of himself. Meekly, he promised that he would.

The incident with Will soon faded and her reservations about their activities were forgotten, too. Such was her enchantment with this other-life, and so complete her trust in Fraser, that she grew bolder. The sense of liberation was entirely new, and it consumed her. She had no feeling of being misused, but was immersed in the pleasure of self-discovery, existing in a strange, contradictory world of calm and euphoria. Sometimes she tried to express this to Fraser but still struggled to find the words. He smiled, though, and nodded in understanding. 'We explore the boundaries, my dear, a sensual meandering between the marches of dignity and exhibition, and we will never stray beyond. For me it is the allure of your exquisite skin and the lovely harmony of your features, and the fact that you allow me to travel this path with you. If I were a different sort of man . . .' he paused a moment, 'if I were, I would say it was a form of love-making. No! Don't move, Rose. A chaste form, my dear, I promise you, an homage and a delight – an artistic consideration of desire, which is, after all, the most sublime force of life—' The way he spoke, the words he used, words she had never heard and often failed to understand, added to this feeling of un-reality, opening up another world. 'Beauty and seduction go hand in hand, my dear,' he said, as he arranged her again on the chaise, 'but such matters must always be understated in imagery, there must be space for the imagination, for the emotions to explore. I've seen photographs of French whores so crude and blatant, their anatomy exposed in hideous detail for the eyes of the soulless, and ask myself: where is the loveliness in that?'

'And what would the soulless make of your work?' she asked, curious.

'We will never know. But be assured, sweet Rose, I pay you homage. We explore the concept of allure through grace and beauty, far beyond mere lust.'

And so the adventure continued.

On one such night Rose undressed behind a screen that Fraser had provided for her and he waited, then positioned her on a chaise longue, curled up with her waist and lap covered only by the swirls of the silken shawl, her hair loose over her breasts. 'Ah, Rose,' he said. 'You can no longer deny that you are a goddess. I feel—'

A loud knock came at the door to the street and Rose froze, her eyes flying open, wide in horror.

'Don't move,' Urquhart murmured. 'Door's locked.' He straightened and let the hood fall over the camera. The knock came again, louder this time, and Rose glanced across to the window, at a gap below an ill-fitting shutter. It was not large enough for anyone to look through, but sufficient to show that the room inside was lit. Fraser followed her gaze and shrugged, gesturing to her to remain still. The knock came a third time and the handle was tried, the door shaken.

They must have made a strange tableau: Fraser immobile beside his camera, Rose naked and rigid on the chaise longue, terrified, her flesh goose-pimpled with fear. Tears sprang into her eyes and she winced as the door was kicked, but again Fraser signalled for her to be still. They stayed frozen for what felt like an eternity until at last they heard footsteps retreating along the wooden sidewalk, and she breathed again. Then lightly, and silently, she jumped to her feet and disappeared behind the screen, pulling on her clothes with shaking hands.

'Wait,' Fraser commanded in a low voice as she came from behind it, twisting her hair into a hasty knot.

She dashed a hand across her eyes. 'I must get home.'

'Wait.'

'What if it was Will!'

Fraser's face was grim. 'He'd have shouted out like he did that other night.'

'Then who?'

He made no reply but swiftly dismantled his equipment and took it through to the back room. When he returned, he was wearing his coat and his hat was in his hand. 'I'll take a look outside, and if the coast is clear you slip out, my dear. Cross the street where there are deeper shadows.' He came over and gripped her shoulder. '*Courage, ma muse.* I'll follow you home, and make sure no one else does.'

She nodded, grasping his meaning. For if it *had* been Will and he now saw them leaving, having not answered to the knock . . . After waiting a further five minutes Fraser unlocked the door and stepped outside. Rose closed her eyes, expecting him to be jumped upon or for a voice to accuse, but heard only silence. He stepped back in and beckoned. 'Straight across the street now, and stay in the shadows. I'll be right behind you. Put a light in the window when you get home to let me know all is well.'

She slipped past him and went swiftly across the muddy street to where a row of abandoned businesses was in darkness, the lanterns above the doors unlit. She reached the shadow of the overhang and paused, imagining movement at the corner opposite, watched a moment and saw nothing. Next, she saw Fraser come out of the studio, turn to lock the door, and then look both ways before pulling his hat brim low and crossing over to her.

'Go!' he hissed. 'And quickly. I'll be with you all the way.'

With a pounding heart she sped silently along the boardwalk, head down, and slipped down the alley between two buildings, a shortcut back to her lodging house two streets away. What if it *had* been Will? The thought terrified her. Would he be waiting for her, and how could she ever explain? There were people in the street, grey anonymous figures, and a drunken man loomed out of the darkness. He was easily evaded and she reached her door, fumbling for the key. She did not turn around, but was conscious of Fraser in the darkness behind her.

The door was locked, a relief in itself, and once she was in, there was no sign that Will had been there. She hurried across to the lamp, lit it and placed it in the window and watched a moment, still breathing fast. A familiar figure stepped out into a pool of light, looked up and nodded briefly, and then disappeared down the street.

It was some time, that night, before she slept.

Chapter 15

The next day, Rose did not go back to the studio and Fraser sent Harry to check that she was all right. She sent him back with a message that she would not be coming in and sat in her rooms wondering who it might have been, sick with dread at the thought that Will might come to hear of it.

Consequences.

Her other world had shattered. How reckless she had been, she thought as she roused herself to clean the ash from the hearth that evening, allowing herself to be caught up in such folly, putting so much at risk. Too late now to recognise how far she had allowed Fraser to take her into that world that he inhabited.

Then, as if to compound her qualms, a loud knock came at her own door and she froze, brush in hand, and stared at it. Was it Fraser? Surely not – he would not come here, he never had, and she credited him with more sense. The knock came again, louder still, and then she heard the shuffling of feet and supressed laughter and knew that this time she must open it.

Robbie Malloy stood there, grinning at her, with Dan McGrath and his brother behind him. 'Will told us to look you up, Rose darlin',' he said, 'and take you dancing. Not sure we'd find you in, though . . .' She looked sharply at him and caught a glint in his eye, and McGrath's wandering gaze was insolent.

Oh God. Had it been them last night? The thought horrified

her. 'Tell Will I'm just fine. I'm tired, though, and—' She made to close the door.

Robbie stuck his boot out, preventing her. 'No excuses, we promised the man. Wash your face, tidy yourself and we'll wait just here for you.' She tried again to refuse but Robbie was having none of it. 'We're not moving, macushla, so be quick about it. Unless you've had a better offer . . . ?' He grinned and McGrath's brother giggled. 'You're keeping good men from their drink, girl, and that's a dangerous thing to do.' He removed his foot and pulled the door closed, repeating his instruction for haste and she stood there, listening to their laughter outside. It was most unlikely that Will had told them to take her dancing, but if it *had* been them last night and if she now refused the invitation, goodness knows what Robbie might tell him.

It was perhaps inevitable that they would take her to Moll's, and the place was once again pulsing with energy, the atmosphere thick and raucous. Rose hesitated at the door as panic overwhelmed her but Robbie steered her firmly in with a hand on the small of her back, tossed her shawl aside and led her straight onto the dance floor, holding her too close. She saw that Moll was watching, poker-faced, from behind the bar. When the dance was finished Robbie bought her a drink and passed her onto Dan McGrath and he too held her tight, hands wandering until the music changed to a jig and he unclasped her.

From the corner of her eye she saw Fraser come through the door and saw him glance at her, and then away, and he did not approach. And as the evening progressed, the men from Kumara got more and more drunk, passing her from one to the other, giving her no rest until she insisted that she would drop and then they sat her down and bought her drinks. An undercurrent of mischief flickered between them, and Rose looked around for an excuse to leave.

Fraser, she noticed, had moved closer and was sitting next to the bar.

'Now isn't that your boss, young Rose,' McGrath said, nodding in his direction. 'He's a fine man on the dance floor, is he not! Very nimble, as I recall. Will you not have a dance with him? Sure, the man looks lonely.' Rose said nothing and turned to find that Robbie had bought her another drink, and was watching her. 'Come on, now,' Dan growled. 'Don't be coy. You've surely not forgotten so soon how to get a man out there dancing.' He turned and called across the bar. 'Hey, Mr Portrait Man, there's a lady here pining for a dance with you but she's too shy to ask.'

Fraser glanced across at them. 'I doubt that very much, since she works for me.' He came over, looking down his nose at McGrath who narrowed his eyes in amusement. 'But will you dance, Rose? I'd be honoured.' And as he took her onto the dance floor, she felt the men's eyes burning into her back.

'I think it was them last night,' she said, as the music carried them out of earshot. 'At the studio.'

'There was only one lot of footsteps.'

'Then one of them. Robbie. Come looking for me.'

'Smile, Rose. You appear anxious. And if it was, he saw nothing.'

Unless he had waited in the shadows and seen her leave, seen Fraser follow her home, and drawn his own conclusions. Rose bit her lip. 'We must stop, Fraser. The photographs. I've thought of nothing else all day. I wish now I'd never—'

'Hush, *ma muse*. Never regret, it's a wasted emotion. And of course we'll stop if you wish, not for the world would I want you to continue unwillingly.' He swept her round, his hand on her waist. 'And I too have been thinking. Time I went out to Kumara and saw things for myself. I thought I might go tomorrow, perhaps for a couple of days, and set myself up for a longer stay. I'll close up the studio for now but I'll let you know when I'm back.' She nodded, noting that he had not offered to take her – not that she would have gone with him; gossip bubbled as freely as champagne around Hokitika's bars and needed no such encouragement.

But had he, too, been rattled?

A roar of laughter rose from the table where McGrath and the others were seated and Rose looked over to see that Robbie had one of the girls bent backwards in his arms and was attempting to pour champagne straight from the bottle down her throat. 'Trust me, girl, trust me!' he was bawling, but at the last moment, with cool deliberation, he poured the liquid down her cleavage and bent over her to lick it. To the audience's delight the girl straightened and smacked his grinning face, while Moll looked on, and smiled.

'Dear me,' Fraser remarked. 'Are they being troublesome?'

'They say Will told them to take me dancing, but I doubt that he did. There's something brewing between them.' Was it her imagination or did the girls seated on McGrath's ample knees keep looking at them as they danced? McGrath was whispering in their ears now, his eyes fixed on her, alive and impudent. What was he telling them?

'I'd not worry,' Fraser said. 'They're far too drunk to be artful. Keep smiling, Rose. Shall I take you home?'

'No! But I saw Big Sven earlier. Find him, will you, tell him I'll dance with him and then he can take me home.'

'I'll take you—'

'No! Find him, Fraser, and explain. They won't argue with Sven.'

The music ended with a flourish. Fraser took her back to the men who were now sprawled at a table, shirts unbuttoned and disorderly, their drinks spilt and their pipes spewing ash. Robbie looked up from his game of two-up with another digger, glanced at Fraser, and then back to Rose, and Dan's eyes followed the photographer as he left. 'Aye, you make a lovely couple,' he remarked. 'Now which of us will have the pleasure next, boys?'

But Big Sven hove into view. 'Come, Rose, now *we* will dance.'

She went with him with no small measure of relief and explained the situation as they danced. He nodded in understanding and, at the end of the dance, he picked up her shawl and placed it around her shoulders. 'I am tired, boys,' she said. 'Sven will take me home.'

McGrath's brother hooted and Robbie's eyes narrowed. 'Now, he's a married man, young Rose,' said Dan, leaning forward, and taking hold of her arm, 'and he tells us often enough that he's a wife and family waiting for him in Gotland, and so we can't have you leading the poor man astray.'

Rose released her arm from his grip. 'And I, Dan McGrath, am a married woman.'

Dan nodded sagely and pulled out a seat beside him. 'That's just my point, girl, so you sit yourself down. We told Will we'd take care of you, and we will. You're a sacred trust for us and we'll see you home safe all in good time.' His brother snorted.

'I'm going now.' Rose lifted her chin and took Sven's arm. Something in the Swede's expression must have warned Dan, who sat back and swore under his breath. And from the corner of her eye as she left, Rose saw that Fraser Urquhart was dancing again.

Chapter 16

The higher up the creek Will went the less gold he was finding, and it was becoming hard to justify any further elaborations to his channels. Time to stop. Better to be cautious, and besides, he was bone weary.

A day off would be good.

Robbie and the others would be back soon. Had they been to see Rose, he wondered, as he made his way through the growing townsite where shanties were springing up like weeds along what was beginning to resemble a street, and he dwelt a moment on the thought of her being here; the joy of it, and the concerns. Would she be safe? At the end of the track he saw a mule cart was unloading. More new arrivals, no doubt. Too late, my friends, he thought – the best claims are gone. He was continuing towards the hotel when he heard his name called and turned to see Fraser Urquhart, staggering towards him under a load of equipment.

Will walked back to meet him. 'Looks like you need another favour.'

'You've been sent by the gods, Will,' the man panted. He set a bag down and shook Will's hand in that oddly formal way he had, taking in his appearance. 'I recognised the hat, if not the man. Do folk not wash in Kumara?'

'Not often. Why are you here? Is Rose all right?'

Urquhart smiled. 'I'm here because I needed to see all this for myself.' His gaze swept the half-built street and the goldfield beyond, his eyes sparkling. 'And Rose is fine. I saw her just last night. Your mates took her to Moll's place, dancing.'

'To Moll's?'

Urquhart pulled a wry face at his expression. 'Big Sven saw her safely home, don't you worry. I'd offered to take her myself but she reckoned more to Sven's clout than mine. Sensible woman, your wife.'

Will frowned. 'Were they drunk?'

'As lords. But they were still at the playful stage. I had my eye on her.' Will grunted, and wondered again at the wisdom of bringing Rose out here. Urquhart picked up on the thought. 'I understand she'll soon be joining you?'

'Soon as the cabin's built.'

'Then perhaps when I come to stay longer, she can assist me again. With your permission, of course.' Their eyes met, each man remembering their last encounter, then Urquhart turned away and surveyed again the scene before him. 'Behold, the kingdom of gold. What a sight! Truly a forge of endeavour. Those great timber structures going up over the rooflines, are they to be water races?' Will nodded, watching him taking it in, the squalor and the enterprise, the drive and the determination, and wondered what this man really knew of endeavour, for all his fancy phrases.

Urquhart turned back to him, his eyes alight. 'And you, my friend, have you struck it rich?'

'Give us time. Where will you stay?'

'I was told there was a hotel. The Bendigo . . .' Fraser replied, looking around rather more sceptically. 'Main Street, the man said.'

Will smiled. 'Well this Only Street, so you're in the right place. And there's your hotel.' He pointed to the newly built structure with a high frontage on which the letters *BENDI* had been painted before the last deluge hit. 'You wanted to be in at the beginning, you said.'

The man grinned back at him. 'And so I am. Come and have a drink with me, Will.' He picked up the bag again. 'Does it always rain so much?'

'Always.'

The hotel boasted only bare boards and bare walls in the public rooms, a table or two and simple benches, but Urquhart was able to secure himself a room which had been built on at the back. Together they heaved his gear into the small space and Will went to wait in the bar. Urquhart joined him a moment later and ordered drinks. 'And whatever there is to eat.'

They found a table and sat down at it. 'So! Tell me all.' And Will told him about the promising results, what he knew of the plans for the town, the businesses that were coming in, the growing need to bring water from the Taramakau and halfway through, his companion pulled out a notebook and a pencil and started scribbling. 'First-hand accounts and all that,' he murmured. 'Context and insights. I won't remember the detail otherwise.'

'Things change by the day.'

'All the more reason for me to be here, to capture for posterity the fleeting moment.'

'And what will posterity do with it?'

'Gain understanding.'

Which hardly answered the question, Will thought, as he lifted his glass. 'And is this a business proposition, or simply for your own entertainment?'

Urquhart glanced at him and took a drink before replying. 'I'll look for a publisher in due course. In the meantime, I'll continue to keep myself as before – with portraiture, social events, commercial photography.'

'So you'll set up here?'

Urquhart shook his head. 'I'll keep my main business in town, and just keep coming here when I can. I can leave basic kit here so I'm not carting it backwards and forwards. And so Rose can still assist—'

'Rose'll be staying put. Here.'

'Yes, yes. I quite imagined so.'

The food arrived and they ate. Bannock and meat of some sort; it was best not to ask. 'And where are you living until the cabin's built?' the man asked, between mouthfuls. 'In one of those tents we saw?'

'Aye.'

'And how does Rose view the prospect of goldfield life through the winter?'

Will stopped, mid-chew. 'Has she said something?'

'Not to me. Except that she's looking forward to joining you.'

Will grunted, concealing his pleasure. 'Well, it'll not be for too long, I hope.'

Urquhart raised an eyebrow. 'It's that promising, is it?' Will shrugged and hacked at the unknown meat. 'Playing your cards close, eh? I expect you already have a fortune stashed under your floorboards.'

Will continued to chew. 'No floorboards.'

'Will you show me?'

And so, when they had eaten, Will took Urquhart across the encampment and the visitor admired his handiwork, first walking around the outside of the cabin and nodding his approval. 'How very practical, using the tree stumps. Stone foundations too! A true Scot.'

'Just needs a roof. I'm waiting to buy a sheet of tin.'

'Why, when there's all this wood? Shingles, my friend. And clay or moss in between.' Will considered him, a little surprised, and Urquhart met him look for look. 'You've a poor opinion of me, I think, Will Stewart. A wastrel with a camera and time on his hands. Give me an axe.' And so together they stripped the bark off some of the wood that was lying about and fashioned a dozen or so shingles. Urquhart was surprisingly efficient. Will then went back to the tent where his companions lay sleeping to fetch some nails he had been saving.

Urquhart followed him and stood at the entrance, surveying the sordid scene. The air inside the tent was fetid with the smell of unwashed clothing, sweat and worse. Jim Kelly was asleep, curled up in a cot in the corner, an empty gin bottle beside his head and a filthy foot protruding from underneath a thin blanket. Callum was in the other cot sleeping off a heavy drinking session, mouth open and drooling, dirt etched into the creases of his skin, his hair lanky and long. 'This is the reality, isn't it,' Urquhart said, quietly. 'This is where the dream has brought them. I wish I had my camera.' Jim stirred, rolled over and, opening a bleary eye, swore at him.

'Aye,' said Will. 'Rat shit and cold. What will posterity make of that, do you think?'

'It will marvel at men's fortitude.' Urquhart looked across at him: 'Your cabin will be an improvement.' They went back and together they hammered their few shingles onto the trusses. 'I'll give you a hand again tomorrow if you like. And might I come and watch you and your partners at the workings in return, do you think? I need to use every hour of daylight.' Will nodded, thinking that Urquhart would get context and insights aplenty, but then again they were a vain lot, these wild cousins, and would delight in posturing.

His visitor seemed in no hurry to be away and he sat on another stump and regarded the channels that Will had dug. 'Hero, miner, builder, engineer – is there no end to your talents? What is the purpose of all this construction?' Will told him. 'And did you find gold there too? They say it accumulates along stream courses, settling in the eddies.'

Will shrugged, cursing the man's sharp mind, and then saw that Callum had woken and emerged from the tent and was standing there stretching and yawning, scratching bites on his arse. 'If he has,' he remarked, 'he's kept quiet about it.'

'I stash it down by the river,' Will said. 'Nuggets the size of your fist. Great pile of them.'

Callum yawned again. 'So why're you still here?'

'Greedy.'

The man laughed and Urquhart made his request about bringing his camera to the workings the next day. 'Please yourself,' Callum said with a shrug, but it seemed to Will that his gaze went back to the little walls and channels, and lingered there.

When Urquhart had gone Will confronted the issue head on. 'Do you think the man might be right?' he said. 'We could widen the stream bed, and maybe put a box there when it rains. It might be worth it.'

'Outside the claim,' said Callum.

Will shrugged. 'True, but overnight, who would know?'

The others returned soon after and, once the money from the traded gold had been divided between them, Will saw Callum talking to Robbie and Dan McGrath, pointing to the channel and Will's construction, their expressions serious. Will went over to them, schooling his features. 'I was suggesting to Callum that I widen the channel,' he said, 'as long as it doesn't flood the cabin. And who's to know if we put a box in the stream after a downpour?'

Dan McGrath was eyeing him. 'If there's gold higher up it'll have been washing down. But you found nothing?'

'I'll put a cradle there tonight, after dark, and see. It's worth a try.' He turned to Robbie. 'You saw Rose, then. Urquhart said you took her dancing.'

Will saw an exchange of glances. 'She's doing grand, isn't she, boys?' Robbie said. 'Flotsam Rose is blooming, every petal in place, and we treated her like royalty, we did.' The others smirked. 'She's in fine fettle, Will.'

'Took her dancing, like your man said,' Dan added. 'Fair cheered her up. Like having brothers there, she said. Eh, Teddy boy?'

'Brothers,' the lad agreed, and smirked.

'Did you tell her about the cabin?' Will asked, keeping a grip on his temper.

'We did, Will, we did.' It was Dan who answered. 'And she's that excited to come out here and join our little family. All the talk is of Kumara, Kumara, Kumara, and life's a little slow in town now. Plenty of work soon for dancing girls in Kumara.'

'Rose'll not be working—' He saw the trap just too late.

Dan's eye sparked, then he stuck his pipe between his teeth and focussed his attention on lighting it. 'That's exactly what we said to her. You're a respectable married lady now, young Rose, no time for dancing and fun, you'll need to be keeping that cabin clean for your husband and it'll be a full-time job. All twelve foot of it.' Will smiled at the laughter, silently cursing the man. 'In fact,' Dan continued, his pipe now lit, 'and we said we'd discuss this with you, but we wondered about sharing Rose between us. She was fine with it, wasn't she? For a price, of course, agreed in advance.' His brother stifled another snort. Will said nothing, refusing the bait, and Dan looked up at him, and then started in mock astonishment. 'For the washing and cooking, I meant! Whatever else were you thinking?'

'Leave it, Dan,' said Robbie. 'We're partners.'

'Aye, and that's just what I'm getting at – partners share stuff, don't they?'

Chapter 17

A week later Rose stood framed in the doorway of the tiny cabin, and behind her Will held his breath. He had done what he could to make it look half decent, and even found time for a wash and shave himself, nicking his chin in his haste, but he was quaking now. Had she expected something better? What if she refused to stay? He focussed on the little curl of hair at the nape of her neck, and held his nerve.

She stood there a long, painful moment but when she turned to him her face was radiant. 'Will, it's *lovely!*'

He breathed again. 'It's a start. We'll do better soon.'

He followed her in, leant against one tree stump corner and watched her as she examined the cot against one wall, the bench along the other and the two rough stools he had fashioned. There was little room for more. The chimney, of stone and tin, was finished and he had lit a fire; basic utensils bought from the general store stood in the hearth. He had covered the earthen floor with simple planks, secured, as far as he was able, to the four corner stumps, having first dug a central channel to serve as a drain. Inevitably it would be damp, and already the planks were bowing. 'There's no windows, because of the cold,' he explained.

'It's cosy this way.'

'And there's still a patch where the roof leaks a bit.' Half shingle, half tin, it was hardly ideal.

'We can fix that.'

'I'll get more stuffing for the mattress. What I wouldn't give for heather!'

'Will.'

'What?'

'It's grand.' And she swung around, threw her arms around his neck and kissed him. 'Our very own place!' He lifted her from her feet, jubilant, and stepped towards the bed but she wriggled away from him, laughing. 'No, Will Stewart! *No*! There's no lock on the door and it's the middle of the day and Fraser said he'd drop by to see how we were getting—'

'To hell with Fraser,' he said, pulling her back as she continued to laugh and to squirm. Reluctantly he released her. 'You're right about a lock, though. I'll make a sliding bar this afternoon. Then we're all set.' He was beaming foolishly as she went over and inspected the hearth, tapping the base of the cheap pans he had bought, and instantly he wished he had spent more on them. Then she took the fastenings off the baggage she had brought with her and began to set out their possessions: a small mirror, their framed wedding photograph, two chipped cups and saucers, a jar of Holloway's ointment and a comb. Little enough.

Should he tell her about the gold? He wanted to, so very much, but should he tell her now and risk spoiling the moment, or leave it for later? Knowing that a better future lay just around the corner might make it easier for her to contemplate the privations ahead and for all that she was excited now, the bleakness of winter here would soon bite.

The other parcel she had brought contained flour and salt, a stained tablecloth, a little packet of tea and a screw of sugar. 'So will it be bannock tonight?' she asked, as she arranged it on the bench.

'No. Wait.' He went outside and returned with the plucked carcasses of two partridges he had snared and left hanging under the eaves. Rose's eyes lit up and she tied an apron around her waist and took them from him. 'We'll make it a feast,' Will said, and set off across the encampment to fetch beer from the hotel.

On the way he encountered Fraser coming up through the camp. It was he who had accompanied Rose along the trail from town, bringing her on the back of a mule cart hired to bring his own gear out, waving aside Will's offer to pay half the costs. 'Enough for me that Rose will continue to work for me when I'm here,' he had said, and now he raised an arm in greeting. 'I was on my way to see you!'

'I'm going for beer. Carry on, Rose is there.'

'And is she impressed with the evidence of your devotion?' Fraser asked as he reached Will, his face lit by his attractive smile. It was that smile, more than anything, that had persuaded Will to trust him.

'It'll do.'

'Oh come on, man! She said more than that! Did she like it?'

'She says she does.' Will felt as pleased as a schoolboy and Fraser thumped him on the back. Will waved him on and continued to the hotel.

———

A place of their own. A place built especially for her by her blunt and taciturn husband; that alone made it special. A deep sense of wellbeing crept over her as she looked around at the uneven walls and odd tree stump corners. She smiled. Rooted to the earth, like the man himself. Beneath his reserve she recognised something in Will that was solid and lasting, as steady as the stone foundations he had so carefully laid. And perhaps from now on she need never feel vulnerable in the same way again, never allow others to shape her view of herself. Perhaps it was that in gradual shedding of her clothes for Fraser's lens she had cast off the person that others had judged her to be, and with this unfolding self-awareness had come an unfamiliar assurance. A rebirth? A second chance. She and Will were bound together now, exploring in a different way, learning to know each other, and they would build a future together, and that thought made her proud. The adventure with Fraser was behind her, finished and done, and although she woke sometimes cold with fear at the risks they had taken, she knew that she owed a great deal of her new-found confidence to him. He had taught her to believe in herself.

But she was here now beside Will and they would strive together, and make their way in the world. And, if her suspicions were correct, by March they would truly become a family, but she would wait a while before telling him, just to be sure.

She continued to smile as she lit the fire and found that the chimney drew well, and once it was going she set the two plump birds on spits beside the flames. The proximity of Will's partners was regrettable, of course, but Will had hinted that they would not need to remain here long, and they would surely respect her because of him. She went outside to fill the water jug from the little stream and stood for a moment admiring the elaborate channels and the pool that Will had created. Fresh water, right outside the door. How perfect.

She had turned back to the cabin when a familiar voice hailed her. 'Ah, *muse* turned water nymph, I see.' Fraser removed his hat and bowed.

Rose looked quickly around. 'We agreed—'

'We did indeed. Strictly business from now on, Mrs Stewart. *Cartes postales, cartes de visite*, advertising and commercial work. No more *ma muse*, although the pleasure will remain with me always.'

He smiled down at her and she frowned back. 'Will must never know—'

'I've promised you he won't.' He continued to smile, in that way of his. 'Now, is that jug being filled for a purpose?'

She led the way inside and he admired the completed cabin. 'All very snug and practical, I must say. He's a fine man, that husband of yours. I encountered him on my way up. You will—' He broke off and turned with an expectant smile as the door opened.

But it was Robbie Malloy whose figure filled the doorway and he stood there, his eyes sharpening as he recognised Fraser. 'I'd have knocked, but I expected Will.' His gaze flicked towards Rose. 'You've arrived, I see.'

'Will's gone for beer.'

'Good man. I'll come back later then.' He gave Fraser a crooked sort of smile. 'It's a grand place, is it not? Just big enough for two, but three makes it awkward, don't you think? So I'll be leaving you.'

He gave Rose a brief nod and withdrew, and she glanced across at Fraser who simply shrugged. Then she heard Will outside, trying to persuade Robbie to come in and share a drink, but a moment later he entered alone.

Fraser said a few more words in admiration of the cabin, then rose to go.

'Stay, man, and eat with us. There's plenty,' Will said.

'On your first evening? No, I . . .'

But Will waved away his protest, gestured to one of the stools and then sat, cross-legged, on the bed. 'So, you're all set up at the hotel?'

'Just about. There's the room at the back where I can sleep and a sort of lean-to where I can do my wizardry. I've no work for you yet, Rose, but you'll be busy setting up house, anyway.'

'Yes indeed.' Rose looked about her at the tiny cabin and her laughter joined theirs.

Nonetheless, in the days to come she found that there was plenty to do. Will's clothes needed a good deal of attention and she found little ways to improve their comfort. She plugged the gaps in the walls where the wind whistled through and together she and Will fixed the leaking roof. And as they went about these tasks she was aware of his eyes following her with a warm look, a look that was quite different from Fraser's detached observation, and she would find him smiling for no reason.

She felt safe in that smile. Not worthless. No longer a creature.

And at the end of each day that followed when Will sank, stiff and exhausted, onto their tiny bed she would rub his shoulders until she felt his muscles relax. And then, if he had energy left, he would pull her down beside him and his hands would start to explore and under his caresses she would grow warm and loving. Something akin to how Fraser's photographs had made her feel would start to build in her, but so much stronger, so much more immediate and so entirely focussed on this man who was *her* man, who had made himself the centre of her world. His hands might be rough and dry from his labours but they awakened in her such joy, a joy where they met in fierce delight and when, at length, he gave a deep groan of pleasure and fell asleep she would lie there, in his arms, and think again how far she had come.

Chapter 18

It was, perhaps, inevitable that Rose's presence would widen the gulf between Will and his partners. Few women lived on the goldfield or in the mushrooming town, and there were none of Rose's grace and beauty. His greater physical comforts, in every sense of the word, seemed to fuel the others' resentment, and his worry about her sharpened. And yet he became aware over those first few days that his wife seemed to have developed a new confidence, a sense of her own worth, and she let their remarks go by her with so little concern that they soon diminished; perhaps this indifference contributed to the ill will. 'They're envious,' he reassured her when she remarked on their hostility, 'and by God I would be too, in their shoes. But they mean no harm.'

He hoped that he was right.

No longer was there an incentive for him to go into town, so it was Robbie and the McGrath brothers who took the gold to the bank the next time, announcing their intention to stay away two nights. 'Shake the shite of this place off us,' as Robbie put it, a surly bottom lip stuck out. There was a growing disillusionment amongst the group; they complained that this was turning out to be a poor claim and it was certainly taking longer now to accumulate enough gold to make the trip to the bank worthwhile. Shafts would soon need to be dug, they agreed, and they spoke of sluicing on a bigger scale. Will watched the three men leave, relieved at the respite, and could only trust that the division of the gold would be fair, and that the cash would not have dissolved in liquor or card play before they got back.

But then again, who was he to talk of trust?

The thought did not sit well.

He had promised to take Fraser upriver to where men were working to lay cables that were intended to carry a caged contraption across the Taramakau, for use in transporting goods headed north or south. An ambitious project, they agreed, but it would save miles travelling to where the river was fordable.

They set off together early next morning and followed it upstream towards its source in the snowy heights of the Southern Alps. The river was wide and shallow in these lower reaches, milky jade in colour, and it followed a braided course, with channels divided by ever-shifting banks of shingle and boulders. Old timers spoke of spring meltwaters that transformed it into a swollen monster, and some had already had a taste of its power following heavy rain when the turbulent water overflowed the riverbanks, charging down to the coast, carrying with it cradles and half-built races, sweeping away the tents of diggers whose claims sat close to its flow. Will had seen in town how, when downpours coincided with high tides, the swollen Hokitika River reduced weatherboard houses to matchwood and turned the streets to mud.

An unpredictable place.

He and Fraser stood and watched the men working on the riverbank, sinking uprights to support the cable. 'Extraordinary! Such enterprise!' Fraser said, looking around. 'But I need a better vantage point, somewhere I can get a sense of scale.' He squinted at the rocks and boulders further upriver where the gradient began to rise. 'Up there, I think, then I can get the bend in the river in the picture, as well as that cable support.' They carried on, clambering up onto the giant boulders. 'Bit of a slog to get all the kit up here,' he panted, 'but it'll be worth it.'

They reached the top of the largest boulder and Will watched as Fraser paced about framing the view between the angles of his finger and thumb, trying it from different places. Perhaps that was how Fraser saw the world, he thought, a segment of reality removed from the whole, a two-dimensional cut-out he could capture and preserve. It would account for the man's odd detachment, his otherworldliness, what folk back home would call fey. It was as if his self-appointed role of onlooker allowed him to exclude himself from his surroundings, to play no part *other* than that of observer, or recorder, or however he saw himself. He stood there now, the wind blowing his unruly hair across his brow, his eyes screwed up against the sun, conscious of nothing other than the question as to which bit of the scene should be selected for posterity.

He turned and smiled at Will, satisfied at last. 'Excellent. It'll do just fine.' Then he went to the edge of the boulder and looked down into the swirling water. 'Tried fishing?' he asked.

'No time for that.'

'Can't see the blighters, the water's too opaque. I wonder what they catch.'

'Trout, I'm told, higher up, and the odd salmon on the lower reaches. And no bloody water bailiffs dragging you off for poaching,' he said, remembering narrow escapes on Kinnloss's estate.

A pair of fantails danced out of the forest snatching at the sand flies, as light and silent as the damsel flies that flittered over the rivers back home. 'Will you go back to Scotland one day?' Urquhart asked, glancing sideways at him, perhaps guessing where his thoughts had gone.

Will shrugged. 'Too risky,' he said, dropping any pretence,

and Urquhart nodded in understanding. How strange it was that knowledge of each other's transgressions, and a shared remorse at unforeseen consequences, had brought them closer.

'But one day, maybe? Sins are forgotten in time.'

Will snorted. 'Not in Kinnloss! So many people suffered one way or another because of what I did.'

'What *we* did, between us.'

'Perhaps.'

They were silent, watching as the current brought a branch past them, twisting and turning it on the eddies. The river moved majestically between the boulders, a blue-green pastel, like frosted glass, but it was narrower and deeper here.

'Leaves a lot of Scotland to return to, just the same,' Fraser remarked.

'I think we'll settle here.'

'I saw gorse everywhere in Otago,' Fraser continued a moment later, 'and broom. They told me it was the Scots who planted it, bringing Scotland with them, so to speak, along with the sparrows and the blackbirds they shipped over. Yearning's a powerful emotion, is it not, but ultimately futile.' He paused, then when Will said nothing, went on. 'They came for a better life and yet they yearn, christening their settlements and rivers for places left behind – Glencoe, Clyde, Berwick, the list goes on. Is it nostalgia or the appropriation of new territory, I ask myself. Yearning or simply the transference of affection? Some fled terribly hard lives and yet they still look over their shoulders.' He fell silent again, musing on the question. '"The old identities" was a phrase I heard. An emotional transition, as if identity were a half-shed skin.'

The man was perceptive, Will thought, and nodded. 'It feels like that sometimes. I was so desperate to leave, and yet sometimes I long for the smell of home.'

'The immigrant's lot. One carries the old identity through

life, I imagine, a foot in each camp, straddling the gulf. And yet distance can distort the realities. Memory, over time, becomes selective.'

Sometimes, Will thought, he actually made sense. 'What about you?' he asked. 'Will you go back?'

'Not until my father dies. And he'll die before *he* forgives me my sins.' He was silent again and Will wondered how much he minded. 'My mother would have me back tomorrow, and for her sake I would go as she is unwell, but what weight does a woman's word carry in the world of self-made men?' Then the reflective moment passed and Fraser straightened. 'And in the meantime, the adventure continues. Do we go forward from here, Will Stewart, or back?'

They went back, and on the way Urquhart announced that he would return to Hokitika to close up his business there for a while, and arrange for a longer stay in Kumara. 'I'll return in a week, my friend. There's work to be done here.'

———

He was, in fact, back much sooner than that and Will was surprised to see him heading up towards the cabin just two days later. He saw at once that something was wrong. 'What is it, man?'

Urquhart pulled him off the track behind a pile of timber awaiting flume construction. Rain was coming down, blown by a gusting wind. 'Someone broke into my premises while I was away.' His face was drawn and pale.

Will made sympathetic noises. 'Much taken?'

He shook his head. 'They left a mess, but little was taken, and I'd left much of my equipment up here.' He began pulling at the bark on the stack, his brow wrinkled in distress. 'I imagine they were looking for money, though there was precious little of that either.'

'But they took what there was?'

'Yes, but it's not that, Will—' He broke off, his eyes not quite meeting Will's and his agitation seemed to increase. 'They went through my stuff, you see, and . . .' he seemed unable to continue, turning his attention back to the bark.

Will was puzzled and then it came to him: of course, the photographs he had glimpsed that night, the half-naked man with the tattooed skin. 'Ah. I see. Did they take them?'

Urquhart looked up quickly. 'Them?'

'The tattooed man.'

Again he looked away. 'Truth is I'm not sure. I had them hidden but they found where I kept them, the package was opened, you see, though I'm not certain how many there were in the first place. I'd hardly miss a print or two.'

Will nodded. 'I'd not worry. They'll be sniggered over and passed round, I expect, but soon forgotten.' He wondered a little at Fraser's reaction. Perhaps in his circles these matters were judged more harshly, and the fall from grace was from a greater height. 'They're a broad-minded lot out here, you know. Men work together, dance together, and sometimes they bed together.' Carefully, he added, 'No one will mind very much, you know. I'd forget it.'

Urquhart gave a weak smile. 'You're a good man, Will Stewart.' Again he seemed to struggle for words, his eyes shifting to Will's face and away again. 'But if ever things are said to you, or shown to you, don't think the worst. I *promise* you that things are not what they seem and—'

Will put up his hand. 'I count you my friend, whatever's said. Forget it, man! Come and eat with us. Rose'll be pleased to see you.' He made to start off but Fraser did not move.

'Will you tell Rose?'

Will turned back, and frowned a little. 'Is there a reason why I shouldn't?'

Fraser said nothing, and their attention was taken by the sight of the McGrath brothers and Robbie passing by on the track, just returned from their spree. Hidden as they were in the shadows of the timber stack the men failed to see Will and Fraser. 'And if it should be that I have to leave town, Will, in haste,' Fraser said, watching their retreating backs, 'I . . . I wouldn't wish you in any way to misunderstand, or to imagine, or to leap to judgement.' And then he turned and walked quickly away, leaving Will staring after him.

'Meaning what, for God's sake?' he shouted after him, but the photographer either did not hear, or chose not to, and Will was left standing there.

———

The fact that Fraser's taste ran to men rather than women troubled Will not at all – in fact, it had given him reassurance regarding Rose. But why had he showed such acute alarm? Will watched the man's gaunt figure diminish as he wove in and out of the piles of brushwood, avoiding tree stumps and tents as he hurried away.

He shrugged and headed back up to the cabin and, as he approached he saw that Rose was on her hands and knees at the small pool where he had dammed the creek. Dan McGrath and his brother were sitting outside their tent smoking, and Dan, he noticed, had his eye fixed on Rose's backside. He felt his hackles rise. Were they giving her a hard time? But she turned and saw him and, to his surprise, spoke tartly, loud enough for the men to hear. 'So *there* you are, Will Stewart. You said you'd fetch me water before you left.' Somewhere there was a false note.

'So I did,' he said, but slowly.

'Ah, she's becoming a shrew already,' Dan McGrath remarked. 'Always the same once they've a band on their finger.'

Rose flicked him a scornful look but addressed Will in the same sharp tone. 'I told you that big jar is too heavy for me.'

'She wants schooling, that one does.' Dan blew smoke into the air above him.

Will came and stood beside her. 'Right, move over then,' he said, and Rose shifted slightly, moving the earthenware jar a little to the right.

And then he understood.

It was almost the size of McGrath's fist, its edges crinkled, the centre smooth and water-worn, and it dwarfed anything that Will had ever found. Quickly he moved the jar back to cover it. 'How can I fill it, woman, with you right there?'

McGrath tutted and turned to his brother. 'It'll be pans and broom handles next, just like it was with Mam. You can come to us though, young Rose, when he starts beating you.'

Rose straightened and stood between Will and Dan, hands on her hips, and replied in a bantering tone. 'You think I can't look after myself, Dan McGrath?'

The Irishman laughed, his eyes alight. 'Now me, I like a lass with a sharp tongue, but if I'd the bedding of you—'

'Well, you haven't.'

They kept it up while Will filled the jar, his mind racing, and he took time to grin over his shoulder at them while he rearranged the cobbles at the base of the pool, covering the yellow glow. Hardly a solution, but it would do until nightfall. He straightened, holding the jar by its handle. 'Right, shrew, where do you want it?'

'Inside,' she said, tossing her head at Dan McGrath.

As soon as they were inside the cabin Will raised a finger to his lips and asked loudly where to put the water. 'Not a word,' he mouthed at her.

Rose nodded, tight-lipped. 'Over there, by the hearth,' she replied.

It was not until the light was going and Will heard the men departing for the hotel that he went outside again. 'Are you and the missus coming?' Callum called back to him.

Will pretended to consider. 'Later, maybe,' he said, and watched them all go. Then he took the jug back to the stream, looking around as he filled it, and reached into the pool. The nugget was heavy in his hand and too large for his pocket, so he pulled out a rag, blew his nose, and then balled the cloth over the nugget and returned to the cabin, barring the door.

Rose was waiting for him, her eyes alight. 'I just shifted some stones in the bottom of the pool and there it was. I didn't know what to do!' she whispered. 'And with Dan McGrath sitting there, and his eyes everywhere. I should have told them, I know, but he'd made me angry, and you had said the stream was not on our claim and so I—'

'You did just fine.'

'Do we tell them?'

'No,' he said, and their eyes met.

Then Will went over to the tree stump and crouched, scraping away the clay that covered his cache and pulled out a little chamois bag. He poured the contents onto the bench in front of Rose and they lay beside the one he had just retrieved. Fifteen of them there were, guilty golden goslings around the new-found golden goose.

———

Plans were whispered in the dark, masked by heavy rain drumming on the roof. 'I didn't dare tell you,' Will said. 'I didn't want you to think the less of me.'

She lifted her hand to his cheek. 'Do you imagine that Dan McGrath wouldn't have done the same? Or Robbie?'

'Perhaps, but I swore that after stealing that money to get here I'd live an honest life.'

She smiled a little. 'And you chose those men as partners! They don't know the meaning of the word. But finding this means we can leave, doesn't it?'

'Aye, but not straight away. Can't have them a-wondering. We'll need to get to Dunedin or Christchurch to sell that nugget, and quietly. We'll not get its full value.'

'Because it's not from a registered claim?'

He grunted. 'Aye, nothing official about it, and McGrath would slit my throat if he came to hear of it. So we stay a week, maybe two, and invent a reason to go.'

She lay beside him, looking up at the roof rafters, her heart pumping as she digested his words. 'We should quarrel.'

It was his turn to smile. 'If you like. What about?'

'I'll refuse to stay. Say I hate it here.'

'You shouldn't have admired the cabin so much.'

She wriggled closer to him, her head on his chest. 'I'll become the shrew that McGrath called me, and demand to be taken away.'

'Making me the hen-pecked fool who gives in?' He pinched her thigh and she gasped, then closed her hand over his, twining their fingers together.

'You could be worried about me being here, with so few women.'

'I am.'

She lifted her head to look at him. 'Are you? Are you really? I'm tougher than you think, Will Stewart!'

'Is that right?'

'Yes.' In the darkness she could imagine the scar lowering over his eye in that ironic smile of his that she was learning to love, and felt his arousal hard against her. Oh, how much more she wanted to know of this man. She raised their entwined hands and kissed his knuckles. 'As you'll discover.'

'Good to hear,' he replied, twisting his wrist so that he could return the favour. 'There'll still be hard work ahead of us.'

She sighed and lay back, her arms in an arc above her head. 'But on land of our own, Will, think of it!' Was this the moment to reveal her suspicions? Or would he worry, make the wrong decision, move rashly. It was still early days . . .

He pulled aside the blanket, cupping her breast, and looked down at her in the darkness. 'Land of our own, my love, and a future to build.' And the moment passed as he pulled her shift over her head, and she twisted in his embrace, arching as he found the quick of her.

———

He left early next morning. 'Stay where you are, Rose,' he said, pulling on his trousers. 'No need to get up.' He had arranged to meet men from other claims that morning to discuss the water courses. 'Our lot said they'd be there, so I'll have to go.' He dropped a swift kiss on her forehead and left.

In a little while she rose and laid the fire, her mind leaping madly as she thought about the nugget. A little white weather-board house, with an orchard to one side, hens and perhaps pigs, a milk cow . . . a child. And then other children.

She was bent to the hearth, lost in her day dream, when a draft of cool wind made her turn and she saw Robbie standing in the doorway. 'Can I come in?' he asked.

She straightened, wary of him, even more so now, knowing what was hidden. 'Of course,' she said, 'and welcome.'

'Am I?' he gave her a sharp glance as he stooped under the low lintel, then he looked around, taking in the neatness and the order, the wifely touches. 'Well, you're snug here now, aren't you, girl. Will's a lucky man.'

She smiled. 'And I'm a lucky woman.'

He scratched the stubble on his chin as he contemplated her. 'Is that right?' He had an odd expression on his face and fear lurched in her. But he could not possibly know . . . 'And so you love the man, do you?'

The question came out of nowhere, but his expression suggested that it was a serious one. 'Yes, Robbie, I do.' But, even as she said it, she realised that she had never told Will as much, never said the words.

'No regrets, then?' She shook her head, puzzled as he continued to consider her. 'So you'll make a life here, will you? With Will. In this shitty little cabin, in this shitty little gold town.' She said nothing. 'I thought you'd bigger dreams than that.'

'You're the one with the dreams, Robbie.'

'Aye, and they'll take me far from here, I'll tell you that for nothing. And . . . and I'd have taken you with me.' Still he stood there, looking intently at her with bloodshot eyes. Recovering from a night of it down at one of Kumara's drinking holes, no doubt, and made surly by his excesses. 'Still would, if you'd come,' he added softly.

She pretended not to hear. 'There's another hotel opened up, I hear, on Main Street,' she said, turning away from him. 'It won't be a *little* town for long. Someone said there are two thousand folk out on the goldfield now.'

'They'll be building a bloody church next,' he said and she laughed, although he did not. 'And that's enough for you is it?' She was considering how best to start weaving the fiction that she and Will had agreed upon when Will himself appeared at the doorway, stooped and entered, arrested by the sight of his partner. 'I was making a morning call,' Robbie said. 'Neighbourly, I thought.'

'I'm surprised you can stand up, from what I hear of last night.' Will straddled a stool and regarded him. 'Where are the others? I thought we were going to meet up to discuss routes for the flumes with the other claims?'

'We are. We will. Maybe. When they wake up. If the bloody rain's stopped.'

Will snorted. 'And if there's any daylight left. So shall I go with the other men now and report back?'

'You do that, Will. And you can tell us all about it later, at the Bendigo.' He nodded briefly at Rose and left, pulling the door closed behind him.

'What was that about?' Will asked, frowning.

'I'm not sure.'

They looked at each other.

'They went on to Lo Li's last night and stayed 'til God knows when,' Will said. 'Oblivion through opium. Some are hardened to it, but these lads are green, and it'll be the death of Ted McGrath.' Easy prey for the wily Chinese storekeepers, he had said, who, barred from staking claims themselves, had become adroit at extracting gold by other means.

'So will you bother going upriver with the other men now?' Rose asked. 'If we won't be staying?'

He pulled a face and shrugged. 'I'll go anyway and meet up with the others, like I told Robbie. It'd look odd otherwise.'

Chapter 19

Some hours later Will entered the Bendigo Hotel. A strange hush fell as he approached the bar and he looked around, puzzled, as all eyes turned towards him.

A card fell from the bar and landed at his feet.

He stooped to pick it up, and as he straightened and turned it over, the air tightened.

Shock collided with the flashed thought that he had never seen Rose look more lovely and he stared down in stunned disbelief. Christ . . . She sat, curled up on the chaise in Urquhart's studio, a flimsy garment swirled around her waist, her hair loose on her shoulders, barely disguising the fact that she was naked. His hand trembled. She was looking not at the camera but at some point over her shoulder, and her lips were slightly parted, and he went on looking, his brain reeling, incapable of taking in what he was seeing, unable to think— Then a snigger from the bar shattered the moment and he felt a hot rush of fury, and of shame that Rose had been so exposed. Even as his mind staggered, though, his instinct was to protect her, and his anger, stronger than any he had ever felt, was directed not at Rose, nor at his partners, but at the man whose eye had looked through the lens.

Slowly, not looking up, he bent the image in two, creased the fold between his fingers, and put it in his pocket, then he turned and faced the men who had gathered round. Robbie stepped forward. 'God knows, Will, we wanted to keep this from you.'

He laid a hand on his arm and Dan McGrath's brother giggled again.

Will looked down at Robbie's hand; it was dirty, the nails blackened and broken. He shook it off, picked up his hat, surveyed the company from under its wide brim, and departed, leaving silence behind him.

First he went to Urquhart's makeshift studio behind the hotel but was told that the man had gone out, an hour since, carrying his equipment, and had headed upriver, and Will spun on his heel.

He knew where he would find him.

The Taramakau was in spate as he moved fast upstream, taking the route they had gone before. Swollen waters were now scouring mud from the banks of the river, darkening its pastel shade, stopping for nothing, tearing at the overhanging shrubs as they hurtled down towards the ocean. Will scrambled quickly against the flow, the roar of it in his head, making swifter progress along the higher ground, driven by his fury, his breath coming in short gasps. So it was not the theft of the tattooed man's photographs the bastard had been worrying about, prompting that half-arsed plea: *Don't leap to judgement*. Will swore as he stumbled and fell, tearing his trousers and badly grazing a shin, but the pain was absorbed in a greater hurt. By God, there would be judgement aplenty when he caught up with him.

But why? The anguished question pulsed through his fury. Why had she done it? Rose! Was it for love of the man?

Or for money?

Either way he would settle with him, and then he would take Rose and they would leave. Today. Now. They would take the gold and leave this place forever, leave the squalor, the grubbing in the ground, leave the dissolute and desperate.

Should have gone already. Dear God, why had they not?

And maybe then, away from here, she would explain.

Climbing higher, he saw his quarry standing on the large boulder where the two of them had shared that moment of reflection just a few days ago. He cursed him as he stood watching, catching his breath, and saw the man bend over his tripod, absorbed in the task.

And through that same lens he had looked at Rose.

The pain was almost too much to bear.

But whatever the reason, a reckoning was due. Slowly he removed his hat and his jacket, and started climbing, grabbing at low plants rooted in the crevices to pull himself up. And as he did his foot dislodged a stone, which rattled down amongst the rocks and Urquhart, emerging from the camera's hood, turned, straightened and raised a hand. 'Will! Excellent. Perfect timing—'

He got no further. Will was on him, his fist smashing into Urquhart's jaw, and he saw the man's eyes widen in astonishment as he went down. He fell across the tripod which crashed onto the rocks, taking with it the camera box which splintered, and Urquhart roared in dismay. 'For Christ's sake! What—' Will pulled him up by the front of his jacket and hit him again. Urquhart rolled onto his side and away, then staggered to his feet. Somewhere in his past he had learnt to defend himself and when Will came at him again, he was prepared.

'Will! Stop, man!'

But Will was stopping for nothing, and again Urquhart had to defend himself. 'Listen!' Will swung at him, panting, but Urquhart dodged the blow and caught Will's arm. 'Is it . . . Rose?' he asked.

'What else?' Will shook him off and swung again. His blow found its mark and Urquhart went down. Will was onto him, straddling him, his fingers closing around his throat, thinking only of Rose. Of dirty hands passing the photograph around, eyes devouring her, their lust slaked in fantasy. Urquhart tugged at the fingers on his throat, his eyes bulging, their gaze fixed on Will as he struggled to speak. Will's fingers tightened and he felt the photographer's body gather itself in desperation and then give a great heave, and then they rolled over, locked together even as Will lost his grip.

'I swear to God, Will,' Urquhart croaked, 'I never laid a hand on her.' But Will was beyond reason, the blood roaring in his ears as loud as the torrent below, and the two rolled together over the smooth rock, made slick by the ceaseless rain. Urquhart turned his head, and shouted out a warning.

Too late.

And so it was that they fell, still locked together, into the river's fast-flowing waters, separating only when they hit the ice-cold surface.

Chapter 20

Rose stood in line at the general store and waited her turn, running over in her mind what they might need. Will had said not to buy much as they would have to leave most things behind, but enough to look as if they intended to stay. Lamp oil was a necessity, she decided, as was the hard soap required to get the dirt from Will's clothes. Their jar of Holloway's ointment was almost empty too, and Will needed it to ease his aching muscles.

Her mind had drifted off again, contemplating the little white house and the orchard, when she suddenly became aware that two men in the corner were staring at her. And as she looked across at them, one of them struck a pose, putting a hand behind his head, the other on his hip, and pouted. She turned away. Vaguely she recognised them as cronies of Dan McGrath, low life. Most of the men who drank with Will's partners showed her respect but with women a rarity in Kumara she had grown accustomed to remarks and stares, though not usually from men she knew. But the goldfield was a man's world and they made her uneasy.

Another digger joined them and she heard laughter and a low whistle, but it was her turn so she got her goods and made to leave. As she approached, one of the men moved and stood in front of the door, forcing her to brush close to pass him. He gave a mocking moan of ecstasy which was followed by a shout of laughter from his companions. Angry, she pushed past him, lifted her skirt above the mud and crossed the track, heading back to the cabin.

As she approached she saw that Dan McGrath was sitting in front of the diggers' half-cabin-half-tent, sleeves rolled up, darning a sock. 'Rose, m'darling,' he said. 'Why the big frown? Come and sit a while, and tell uncle Dan all your troubles, and you can finish this off while you do. I'm no man with a needle.'

'Darn your own sock, Dan McGrath, and when you're done you can go and tell your mates to mind their manners. That one, with the red hair and the squint, tell him I'll get my Will onto him if he tries that again.'

'And what did the wretched man do?' Dan patted the log beside him. 'Come and tell me, sweetheart. You're all in a fuss.'

'Just tell him. He knows.'

She walked on towards the cabin, and Dan sighed as she passed. 'Ah well, the poor man is likely just confused.'

She stopped. 'Meaning what?'

He lowered his head and looked out at her from under bushy eyebrows. 'Confused like the rest of us, Rose m'dear.' She held his look for a moment, puzzled, but whatever his game was, she would not play along. She made a gesture of dismissal, and Dan chuckled. 'Away with you then, my pretty.'

Back in the cabin she began to prepare food, pushing aside her irritation. She would not tell Will; it would only make for trouble and in any case, they would soon be gone. Unpacking her stores, she decided that she could stretch the remains of the meat from the day before with bannock and make a meal from that. She mixed the flour, checking first for weevils and mould, using some of the fat she had kept back and put the pan on to heat. When that was done she turned the clothes she had hung on a short line beside the hearth, refilled the lamp in readiness, and awaited Will's return. He had said that he would be back long before dusk, so they would eat when he came.

Except he did not come. Will was not a big drinker, nor was he one for card play and gambling, so what was keeping him? She gave up trying to keep the food warm and it sat congealing at the edge of the hearth. As the shadows lengthened she considered whether she should go down to the hotel and meet him there, but the encounter at the store had unsettled her and it would soon be dark. Perhaps he had met Fraser and they had lost track of time? Friendship was deepening between the two men, which pleased her.

She looked at the bannock and the now-unappetising meat and frowned. If Will brought Fraser back to eat then the food would hardly stretch. It was irksome to be just waiting, and not knowing, and if she dithered any longer then the light would be gone and it would be even less safe to venture out. Quickly she gathered up her shawl, wrapped it over her head and shoulders, and stepped outside. No sound came from the shanty next door so either the men were sleeping off the drink and opium, or were out somewhere consuming more. She set off and went rapidly through the encampment, head down, ignoring shouted invitations to join those gathered beside the various campfires. Brushwood crackled beneath her feet as she stepped aside to avoid the swampy areas and stagnant puddles, and she reached the street without incident.

She made for the small hotel to which Fraser had moved having found the Bendigo too rowdy and, not liking to go into the bar alone, she asked someone to check first in his rooms. The man returned a moment later and said they were locked and that no one had answered his knock. He went to look in the bar but came back and gave a shrug. 'He went out earlier, landlord said. Someone else was asking for him.'

They must be drinking at the Bendigo after all, she decided, but as she stepped back out to head there, she saw something of a commotion at the far end of the track. Two men were leading a laden mule towards them and others were gathering, clustering around, and she watched their slow progress towards her.

As they drew closer, she felt her throat tighten. A figure was seated astride the mule, slumped forward with a blanket draped across his shoulder and on each side men were holding on to him to prevent him falling. The men leading the mule were German and were explaining in broken English: '. . . in river . . . came down on water . . . He must be dry . . . must get quickly warm . . .' The man's head had fallen forward, his chin on his chest and, when the mule halted, he half fell into the arms of the men.

It was Fraser.

The men half-carried him into the hotel, his arms draped across their shoulders and Rose followed, aghast, and watched as they lay him on the bed, and she saw that his clothes were wet, hair plastered onto the top of his head, his face bruised.

He looked almost dead.

'We need to get him out of these wet clothes,' one of the other men said and looked across at Rose. 'Are you his wife?'

Rose backed away, shaking her head but not before she heard a stifled laugh and saw two men nudge each other. 'My husband's missing,' she said. 'What happened here?'

'Looks like he went in upriver. These lads pulled him out.'

'Was Will Stewart with him?'

By this time the landlord had appeared. 'Will Stewart was here earlier,' he said. 'Looking for him.' His thumb gestured to Fraser who lay as still as an effigy, his face bloodless.

Another man spoke. 'If he's not got out of those clothes, they might as well have left him where he was. Make space here, and let's get him sorted.'

The landlord hustled Rose out of the room along with other onlookers. 'When? When was Will here?' she demanded, tugging at his sleeve. 'And where did he go?'

'He went after yon fellow in there, I expect. I told him he'd set off upriver with all his gear and your man left.' There was something in the man's expression as he looked down at her, halfway between pity and scorn. 'Seemed in a rush.'

'He's not come back,' she said. The man shrugged, his expression implying that it was no concern of his.

News of Fraser's accident must have spread because a moment later Robbie appeared, with Callum beside him. For once she was pleased to see them and quickly explained the situation. She saw Robbie glance up at the sky where the yellow-grey shades of evening were deepening, and the two men exchanged quick words. 'Go home, Rose,' Robbie said. 'We'll get lanterns and go along the banks, far as we can get. We'll find him, don't you fear. Go on, girl, get home.'

———

All night she waited, drifting occasionally into a troubled sleep before jerking awake again and each time the fear in her tightened. He had not been found. The fire had gone out and she sat wrapped in a blanket beside the dead embers, shivering uncontrollably. As dawn crept under the door she pulled the blanket tight around her and got to her feet, stiff with cold. It was impossible to stay in the cabin even a moment longer and, pushing open the door she stood there, her hand on the bolt, and looked out to where blue-grey smoke was rising from newly lit fires. Men were emerging, stretching and yawning, lighting pipes and scratching bites, just as they did every day.

Except that this day was like no other.

Then she saw them, walking towards her in single file through the awakening camp. Robbie, Callum and the Free Church minister. And Robbie, in the lead, was carrying Will's jacket and hat.

Chapter 21

They had collected the minister on their way, they told her, to help break the news, and they stood there shuffling, uneasy with their task. They had found only smashed equipment, they told her, and, a little further back, Will's hat and jacket. She stared back at them, her brain refusing to take this in, and the minister left to enquire after Fraser and see what he could learn from him, promising to return. Callum and Robbie stayed a moment longer then they too left with the intention of drumming up assistance and continuing the search. They refused to let her join them. 'You'll only slow us up, darlin'. Wait here.'

And so again she waited.

When the minister returned, his mouth was turned down at the edges. 'They fell, Mr Urquhart said, he and your husband. The rocks were wet, perhaps slippery after the rain.' He looked uncomfortable and added, lamely: 'They just fell. Men are out looking again now that it's light. So let us pray together, Mrs Stewart.'

She had barely moved since he had her left earlier. 'Will it help?'

He frowned at her. 'Prayer, Mrs Stewart, always helps. We can pray that he is found, and for forgiveness.'

'Forgiveness?' She looked up sharply. 'There is nothing to forgive. Will was a good man, the very best.'

He looked down his narrow nose at her. 'And is your own conscience clear, Mrs Stewart?'

His disapproval was very evident now and a sickly dread began to creep over her. 'What are you saying?'

'It's hard to find comfort with an uneasy mind.' She sensed a suppressed excitement in the man, a gleeful piety. 'And so I suggest again that we pray, and that you ask for God's forgiveness.'

She rose and gripped tight to the bench. 'What is it you're not telling me?'

Perhaps it was the intensity of her expression, or because the man was in fact a moral coward, but he began edging towards the door. 'I will go now, Mrs Stewart, but we will speak again when you have examined your conscience, and then we will pray.'

She moved to block his way. 'You'll not leave here until you tell me what it is.'

The man looked shocked. 'Even making allowances, this is no way to behave.'

'Tell me, damn you.'

Outraged, he straightened his shoulders and took a moment to reassure himself of his righteousness. 'There's talk of a photograph. Taken, I understand, by Mr Urquhart. Due to its nature, some are questioning whether they simply fell.'

It was all that Rose could do to stay upright. 'And Will saw it? The photograph?'

On surer ground now, the minister allowed himself to scoff. 'So you do not deny it exists! I have not seen it myself, of course, but I understand it was being passed around the bars, and was of a lewd nature. *Not* the sort of photograph that a good man – the very best, you said – might expect to see of his wife. And yes, he did see it. So I imagine they were arguing.'

With a cry Rose whirled around, tugged open the door and ran down through the encampment, her breath coming in gasps as she tripped over tent lines, scattering ash from spent fires, ignoring the startled stares. Oh God! What had she done? Panting, she arrived at Urquhart's hotel, found his rooms, and pulled open the door.

He was sitting on the side of his bed, shoulders drooped, staring at the floor.

'What happened?' she cried. He looked back at her, and said nothing. 'Tell me, Fraser! A fall, you told them, an accident. But that wasn't true, was it?' She was breathless still and a fury was building in her. 'A photograph, the minister said, a *lewd* photograph—'

Fraser looked back at her, his face wretched and contorted. 'We fought, Rose. He came on me like a mad man and we fought, and we fell. There was no time to explain.'

They looked at each other, and neither could find words.

'You *promised* me,' she said, at last. 'You swore—'

'My studio in Hokitika was broken into, and photographs were taken.'

She stared at him. 'And you said nothing!'

Urquhart's face was ashen between bruises that marked his cheek and his jaw. 'I told Will. I tried to warn him, I tried to tell him but I wasn't sure what was missing. And I was hoping, that possibly, just possibly, if they *had* been taken, he'd never see them.' He lifted a shaking hand to his brow. 'I told him some of my work had gone, and he assumed I meant photographs of tattooed men, and I didn't . . . couldn't . . . in the end I simply *couldn't* tell him. I just said that he shouldn't leap to make judgements, should not think badly of me and . . .'

She gasped. 'Of *you*?'

'Rose—'

'And what was he to think of *me*?'

'Rose, I would—'

'Why didn't you warn me, give me the chance to explain?'

He looked back at her. 'He would not have understood.'

She stood in front of him, trembling with grief and rage. 'It was not for you to decide.' She raised an arm to strike him, but let it drop and crumpled, grasping the table for support. Oh God, to think that she might have had a chance, she might have persuaded him, might somehow have found the words . . . 'What did he say? Tell me what he said.'

Urquhart stood and went over to the little window and looked out at a patch of virgin forest behind the hotel which so far had survived the axe. A group of tui flew from a high branch to a lower one, unaware of the imminent destruction of all that was familiar. 'There's little to tell. I was all set up to photograph the place where a cable is being slung across the river, where Will and I went the other day. He just appeared. And I was delighted to see him,' he added, bleakly. 'I'd no idea then, you see, and he gave me no chance to explain.' Tears flooded her eyes. 'I think he came quite specifically to kill me.'

'Oh God, how I wish he had.'

He did not turn. 'Not more than I do myself.'

Her face hardened again. 'Go on.'

'As you know yourself, the instinct for survival is strong so I defended myself. And besides, I *wanted* to explain! But Will seemed set on murdering me, and so we tussled on the ground, his hands on my throat, and we quite simply rolled off the rocks and into the river.' He paused. 'The river was in spate, so I was swept along, very fast, and I never had even so much as a glimpse of him.' She closed her eyes. 'Some hundred yards or so downstream, I caught at an overhanging branch and managed to pull myself ashore. By luck it was close to a claim and some diggers heard me calling out, and brought me back here.'

'So Will might have survived, too?'

'God, I hope so. Could he swim?'

She looked back at him. 'You ask me that?'

He closed his eyes. 'Of course. The wreck. Forgive me.'

The room was still and silent, and his last words hung there.

'Never.'

'Rose—'

'You promised me that Will would not see the photographs, that I was safe, and I believed you.' Her breathing came fast and she saw things suddenly with a dreadful clarity. 'And now I've lost the man I love, and the best chance at life I'll ever get.' She stopped, choked by the thought. 'And you deceived me, Fraser Urquhart, you made me feel that I was not worthless as I had been told, not a creature, not depraved . . . But you were *wrong*. I am all those things. I was given a chance by a good man, and I wrecked it. And you . . . you have *shown* me to be worthless, and . . . and I am more despised than I have ever been.'

'Rose, God knows I—'

'You and your pictures portrayed a shameless woman, displaying herself like a whore, and that was what Will saw. If he's dead, *that* is the picture of me he carried to his death. And if he *is* dead it's because of us . . .' He put out his hand but she drew back. 'Will saved me from drowning, saved me from Black Moll, and I thought that you . . . you had rescued another part of me. And yet, because of you—'

'Rose, I beg you. Nothing I can—'

She put up a hand and squeezed her eyes shut. 'Stop! I can bear no *more* of your words. If you have other photographs of me, destroy them. They are of *me*, and so they are mine as much as yours, and I don't want them to exist in this world that they have poisoned.'

Chapter 22

Chen Lee was always careful not to be seen. His biggest concern was that someone might notice the muddy outwash from his workings staining the translucent river water, so he had devised a way of storing waste water from the cradle behind a little dam. When a pool had collected, he breached the dam and it emptied into the river, but always at night when this discoloration would not be evident, and he would check at dawn that his activities had left no traces. On the whole he felt pretty safe. He was well downstream of the main encampment and on the opposite side of the river, where few came, and a bend in the river meant that he was largely invisible. Whenever he went into town he waited until late in the day when most men were either in the bars or dance halls, and he was content to settle for a lesser price for his gold from the various stores and businesses, taking care to bring only small amounts to each. He heard it said often enough that all Chinamen looked alike and so he had little fear of being recognised. The store of sovereigns he brought back from town he had secreted away and it had grown steadily in the two years he had been working his various unregistered patches. Soon he would return to the Pearl River, collect his wife and children from her parents, buy the farm he dreamt of, grow rice there, and then life could begin.

He never stayed long in any place but over the past two years he had slowly worked his way along old river terraces, always prospecting alone. If the takings were good, he would stay and work the surface gold until it was no longer worth his while and then move on. He spent some money on food, just enough to survive, a little more on opium, which was equally essential – although he was careful to smoke his pipe well away from where he kept his stash of coins. That way if someone came upon him when his senses were disordered, they would find nothing other than his prone body under a roof he had woven for himself from supple vines. His dwelling, where he cooked, ate and slept, was further back from the river, hidden between rocks, and he was careful to have a cooking fire only when it was necessary, and when the wind would blow the smoke away from the new encampment that was growing across the river.

It worried him, this new field of gold. He had seen other prospectors working their way along the riverbank and had known for months that two men had established themselves on the opposite side and, hidden in the willow scrub, he had watched them set up a whisky still and had smiled to himself. So, having been unsuccessful in the goldfields, he thought, they had found a surer way to the gold – other men's gold, hard won and foolishly spent. Chen Lee had tried whisky once but preferred the ease that opium brought to the heavy head and bad stomach he had had from the alcohol.

He had wished the men luck and thought no more about it.

Then suddenly there had been people in the forest, on the other side of the river, and then more and more came, a great flood of them! And then there was the sound of trees being felled, and quickly the land had been transformed, and an encampment had started to grow. Chen Lee had moved downriver, away from this sudden rash of humanity and had, to his gratified surprise, hit a good place where once a tributary of the river had joined the main stream, and so he had stayed and worked it.

That evening, as usual, he went down to the little pool that had risen against his dam and decided that it was time that he let the water out. The heavy rains had caused the level to rise and there was a danger that it would overflow the dam during daylight hours. The two men who had come to make whisky and found gold had been careless, and it was said that their dark outwash had given them away.

He stood a moment beside the willow scrub and looked about him. No one there, almost dark. He proceeded down to the dam and looked again, and then with a spade that he kept handy, he breached the dam wall, letting the water flow away. He paused, and listened. He had heard a sound – a moan. A moment later it came again. He dropped to his hands and knees and crawled forward to look over the bank, then drew back in shock.

A man was lying there, a white man, on his back, on the little delta of silt the outwash had formed beside the river. The sudden rush of water from above must have disturbed him, falling onto his face and chest.

Chen Lee drew back, uncertain.

What to do?

After a moment he crawled forward again and studied the man. A young man with stubble on his chin and an old scar on his forehead. His eyes were closed but he was moving his head from side to side as he tried to escape the flow of muddy water and he continued to moan quietly. His trouser leg was torn, exposing bloodied skin and he saw an ugly cut, puffy now and turning blue. Chen Lee felt bad about the water falling on his face. The man looked half drowned and, having made it ashore, he now had that too to endure. Not good. But what to do, he asked himself again.

It would be easiest to simply heave him back into the river, into the flow of the current, but that seemed unkind. Chen Lee sat on his haunches and considered.

A moment later he reached a decision and scrambled down to the man, and lifted his upper body to one side, apologising, explaining that he had not known he was there and asking how he came to be in the river. The man opened his eyes and looked back at him.

Later, much later, Will came to properly for the first time and lay looking up at a roof of woven twigs. Where the hell was he? This view had not changed for what seemed like days as he had drifted in and out of consciousness; it had become his whole world. He appeared to be inside some sort of tiny tent, no bigger than a coffin, with a blanket draped over him. Was that it? He was dead. Yet somehow, he doubted it. Calico had been draped over the top of the twig roof and it fell on both sides, giving some protection from the rain. A calico coffin? Unlikely.

As awareness slowly returned he saw that he was lying on a carefully made bed of twigs and ferns and that a blanket had been draped over him. He remained puzzled. In the back of his mind he knew that something had happened, something bad, but he was not yet inclined to examine what it was. It could wait.

He slept again.

When he woke next he looked into a pair of almond eyes belonging to a man who was lying close beside him on the brushwood bed. The man said nothing, but nodded slightly before lifting a small pipe to his lips.

Was that it? He was in some strange opium den. But how could that be? He never used the stuff. But perhaps he had and that explained why he felt so bad, why his limbs felt too heavy to lift and there was a strange pulsing sensation in his left calf. Bewildered and too bleary to work it out, he slept again.

Next time his head was clearer and he managed to raise himself on his elbows and look around him. The man had gone but through a gap in his calico coffin he saw that the sun was up and he dragged himself off the brushwood to look out but all he could see was shrubs and trees. And then he saw the same Chinaman approaching, an odd little hat atop hair tied back in a pigtail.

The man looked startled to see Will sprawled, half off the brushwood bed and outside the coffin tent, but then his face broke into a smile and he said something Will could not understand. He turned and disappeared, but returned a moment later with a bowl in his hand. Rice, and some sort of chopped meat. He spoke rapidly, gesturing to it and while Will could not understand a word, he recognised that the man wished him well and wanted him to eat. He nodded his thanks and took the bowl, hungry suddenly, and ate greedily. The man looked satisfied and clapped his hands and then offered Will a cup of rice water.

As Will drank, the man entered into an elaborate pantomime, accompanied by a ceaseless flow of words, and appeared to be explaining how he had found him down by the river and had dragged him back and treated his injuries. He pointed to Will's left leg and frowned, wagging his finger at it and holding his nose.

'Infected?' Damn. But that explained the thrumming. Will sat up a little more and examined it. It was bandaged. How bad? he asked and the man seemed to understand and gestured again, his thumb rocking between the horizontal and vertical, mirroring the movement with his head, side to side, implying that it was improving, or at least was not too bad. Will bowed to him, his palms together in a gesture of thanks. The man grinned, and left.

And slowly, as Will lay there watching the shadows of branches move across the calico, the events which had led up to his immersion gathered like a dark cloud across his mind, and the pieces fell into place.

The photograph. The leering faces.

Rose.

And Urquhart.

They had gone into the river together, that much he could remember. He had been trying to choke the life out of the man and they had gone over, separating as they fell. Had Urquhart survived or had the Taramakau exacted the revenge that should have been his? Will's face darkened and he lay there, wondering.

And what of Rose?

That thought brought him sharply to his senses. She was there, alone, and that damned photograph was being passed from hand to hand and she had no one to protect her, no one to turn to. With him gone and with Urquhart gone she was at the mercy of his partners, and God save her from the likes of Dan McGrath! Whatever she had done she was still his wife. He tried to rise but he was too weak and his leg sent out sharp stabs of pain.

How long had he lain here?

It was a question he asked the Chinaman when he returned some hours later bringing more food. 'How long?' It took a while for the question to be understood, but by pointing up at the sun and making marks in the soil the answer seemed to be three days. Three days! Will cursed and tried again to rise. His saviour looked anxious and tried to stop him, but when he saw that Will was determined, he helped him to stand, which he managed until his legs gave way beneath him and he collapsed, cursing and in pain.

It was two more days before Will could walk more than a few steps. His host fed him, chattering as he changed the dressing on Will's leg. The cut looked better each time he did this and whatever was in the poultice that the man applied seemed to be working. The thought of Rose alone in Kumara was driving Will to distraction and he pushed himself hard to recover. By now he could recognise where he was, downriver and on the other side of the flow, and he also knew that there was no way to cross over here, especially in the river's present turbulent state and so he would have to walk a ways and cross at the beach road, unless there was a crossing of which he knew nothing. Chen Lee – by now they had made their names known to each other – seemed to suggest there was none.

From the beach road he could get onto the trail to Kumara and find Rose. But it was miles, and he could not walk miles. He tried to ask Chen Lee if he would take a message to Kumara but either he failed to make him understand, or else his host was reluctant to do so. The man was furtive in his movements, active early and late but moving little by day so the claim must be unregistered, and however good he had been to Will the man had no intention of compromising his seclusion. And so, for one more day, Will continued to chafe.

Eventually he decided that he had to make the effort. He could rest along the way if necessary and once he had reached the beach road he could find someone who spoke English, get a message to Rose, or hitch a ride on a cart and tell her himself. He made his intentions clear to Chen Lee who, after a long period of head shaking, shrugged and indicated that if Will was going, then he would go with him.

Chapter 23

'Eat, girl. You have to have food.'

If it had not been for Robbie and Callum, Rose would have eaten nothing. They came to the cabin two or three times a day, bringing food and insisting that she ate it. And so she did, to make them go away, to make them leave. The minister had not returned, and nor had she wished him to come, and few others came to offer their condolences.

And why would they? Will had been well liked and so how, in any way, was she deserving of sympathy?

For the first two or three days she had clung to the thought that he, like Urquhart, had survived and that if she waited, he would be found and somehow she would make him understand. She could not pray, she had never done so, but with every fibre of her being she willed him to be found alive, and endlessly rehearsed what she would say to him, what justification she might give. A voice in her head asked why she thought that he would forgive her, and perhaps he never would but at least she would not have to live the rest of her life with this desperate guilt. Knowing that his gold still lay secreted amongst the roots of the tree stump sustained her in the belief that he would come back for it, if not for her, and so she would at least know that he lived. And as long as the searching continued, she would stay at the cabin, and then she would be there when they brought him home.

But the days passed and the searchers found no sign of him.

'There've been men walking the riverbanks almost as far as the coast,' Robbie said when he came to tell her that the search had been called off. 'And nothing found. The river has been fast-flowing for days.'

'But why have they not found his body?'

Robbie shrugged. 'Washed out to sea?' and she gave a cry at the thought and the pain of it consumed her. Had he saved her from the ocean only to meet his own fate there? She contemplated taking her own life, but she grew more and more certain that there was a child growing within her and unlike Tommy's, this child of Will's was wanted. It was all she had of him.

And so, for the child's sake, she ate.

Next day Robbie was back. 'Only me,' he called out as he drummed his knuckles on the door. She went to open it and he stepped inside. 'I brought you this. We'd more than we could eat ourselves.' He set a bowl of steaming broth on the table. 'Eat it whilst its hot.'

'Later,' she said, glancing at it. 'I'll eat it later.'

But Robbie pulled up a stool and sat. 'I'm going to sit here and watch you, girl, because I've a hunch you've not eaten since yesterday.' He handed her a spoon. 'Sit, and eat.' She sat and pulled the bowl towards her.

He watched her as she made an effort to eat. 'What will you do, Rose?' he asked, softly, after a few minutes had passed. But she had no answer.

What did it matter what became of her, and what could she do, after all? Back in Hokitika the only occupation open to her was the one that Will had saved her from. Robbie continued to study her, awaiting a response. 'I'm not sure,' she said.

But she did have Will's gold, and that extraordinary nugget from the bed of the pool. Riches indeed.

Had she any interest in living.

'It's not safe for you, staying here alone.' Robbie's words brought her back to the moment. 'Will and I were partners and so I'll see that you're all right, see that you're looked after. I'll do that for him, and for you.' He paused and she made no reply. 'It's a bad business, but I want you to know this.'

She nodded.

The words were kind and his tone rang with sincerity but she was wary, trusting Robbie Malloy only a little more than she trusted Dan McGrath, whose intentions were blatant and crude. 'You'd be better moving into one of the hotels back in town,' he went on. 'More company for you there, safer. And you could find work.' She looked sharply at him, and he pulled a wry face. 'Not that sort of work, girl. I'd not be letting that happen.'

What was he saying? Then she looked away, knowing the answer.

He rose and lay a hand on her shoulder. 'I'm running ahead of myself, but it's a thought, and you should at least consider it, Rose. You can't be on your own. You need someone keeping an eye out for you.'

———

Exhausted, she slept, and woke to hear rain drumming on the roof. She rose slowly and then saw that something had been slipped under the door of the cabin during the night. She bent to pick it up. A letter. The handwriting was elegant, the letters well formed.

She opened it with reluctance and read.

My dear Rose, I would have come and spoken to you but I doubt that you would have received me, and by the time you read this I will be gone from Kumara, and from Hokitika, and will trouble you no more. Other photographs, you can imagine which I mean, were also stolen and it seems these have come to the attention of the local worthies. They have small minds and will, no doubt, see them as morally reprehensible and indecent, when what I saw was exquisite beauty and an intriguing grace. If I stay, I may well be taken up for offences against morality and so like a thief in the night, I will leave. My equipment has been sent on ahead by a trusted carrier, and I will flit at dawn.

Rose, my dear. What can I possibly say? I can hardly bear the thought of the troubles I have brought to you. In Scotland my attempts to expose a wrong led to a man's suicide, and here my desire to create beauty has caused a friend's death and your own incalculable woes. I don't expect you to forgive me, for I can never forgive myself. The camera is a more potent weapon than even I imagined . . . All I can do is tell you that if you are in need, or want, or if in any way I can help you then I can be contacted through Colin McIntyre, the landlord at the Glen Etive Hotel, Princes Street, Dunedin. He will know my whereabouts and I will go to him now. Contact me there, and I will do whatever you ask of me.

If, despite all evidence to the contrary, God does exist, then he will watch over you.

Fraser Urquhart

She read the letter twice, stumbling over unfamiliar words, and when she reached the end, she tore it into a hundred pieces with a cry of anguish, and cast them into the hearth. Rather would she starve than accept Fraser Urquhart's help!

The letter did, however, have the effect of galvanising her into action. If he could flit, then so could she. If she too could reach Dunedin then there would be other choices open to her there. The city was growing, she was told, flushed with gold but no longer dependent on it; the place had a life and purpose of its own and, in a city of over ten thousand souls, she could surely find somewhere to live and keep herself going until the child was born.

It was either that, or accept Robbie Malloy's offer.

Robbie himself came round again later, bringing more food. 'Ah! You are looking better, darlin', there's a spark in your eye and colour in your cheek. If you promise to eat this then I'll leave it with you.' And yet he lingered, exploring her face, his cool blue eyes searching hers. 'And there's news you'll not have heard. Urquhart, it appears, did a runner in the night, left with a carter at dawn. He'll be back to Hokitika by now, though I doubt he'll find a welcome there.'

Rose schooled her expression. 'Why is that?'

'Seems you were not his only victim. Pictures of black men, all tattoos and not much else, got passed round and the churchy folk are up in arms. Mr Fine Portrait Man could be charged with unlawful behaviour, so he would do well to vanish.'

Rose looked aside. Fraser had always been careful to remove evidence of the other work he did so she had never seen them, except one that he had overlooked. He had come up behind her and looked over her shoulder. 'Ah. Careless of me,' but he had not taken it from her. '"Who told thee that thou wast naked?"' he had murmured. 'Is he not exquisite? Or does it shock you?' She had shaken her head, seeing beauty in the velvety smoothness of the man's skin and the wondrous tattoos. And yet— '"Hast thou eaten of the tree, whereof I commanded thee that thou shouldst not eat?"' Fraser continued, taking the print from her and picking up on her thought. 'I can assure you, my dear, that my interests are aesthetic – I taught you that word, do you remember?' He smiled. 'And I've not eaten of that tree, no matter how alluring the fruit. But what a fine culture it is that makes of their own skin a canvas.'

If Fraser was as fastidious regarding these models as he had been about not touching her, then he was to be believed although, as ever, he had failed to consider what it was he was doing and what damage might result from it. Why had Harry vanished, after all, if not for shame, or fear? Fleetingly, she wondered where he had gone.

She became aware that Robbie was still watching her, perhaps awaiting a further response, but when she made none he shrugged, and took his leave. 'Make sure you eat that, macushla.' She did as he said, but she ate slowly. Making plans, pushing the pain aside, forcing herself to be practical. Her baby's life might depend upon it.

And later, when she was certain no one else would call, she slid the bolt across the door, retrieved Will's gold from the root of the tree and took out her work box. In the hem of her skirt where once she had hidden five sovereigns, she now carefully stitched fifteen small pieces of gold. When she had finished she stood and tried walking, tried lifting her skirt, finding it heavier but not too heavy. She sat, arranging it carefully, and decided that no one could possibly suspect.

The question of the big nugget was more difficult. It had been too large to fit in the tree root hole, so Will had brought home an old Chinese ginger jar and knocked the base out of it and the nugget was sitting under that, amongst their other utensils, hidden in plain sight at the back of a makeshift shelf, covered in flour.

Carefully she lifted it down, dusting her hands, questioning bleakly for the hundredth time why they had not simply thrown caution to the wind and left the day they had found it. How different things would have been! Regret is a wasted emotion, Fraser had said, but the bitterness remained. Wasted it might be, but nevertheless it gnawed and gnawed, and was like to cripple her. She dashed a hand across her face, pushed the thought aside, straightened and decided that the only thing she could do was to put the nugget in her bag and take care that nobody offered to carry it for her. Size was not a problem but it was heavy and would cause suspicion.

She would leave Kumara in the morning, she decided, before her courage failed her. These days there were plenty of carts going backwards and forwards to Hokitika and if she could get a ride back there, she could then take the stagecoach over the pass, and on to Dunedin. She could use one of the smaller gold pieces to pay her expenses for the journey, sell the large nugget when she arrived. The plan blossomed in her mind. She would leave as if to go down to the general store, wearing as many items of clothing as she could, pushing others into the bag she used for shopping, disguising the nugget with their bulk. The rest, including all of Will's clothes, she would leave.

Along with her dreams.

She slept little that night, but lay there looking up at the roof of the cabin where spiders had woven lacy webs in the tree trunk corners. Could she possibly do this? Leave this solid place that Will had built for her, with its foundations of stone on which they had planned to build . . . By her own actions she had brought all to ruin, and Will to his death. Leaving would be to lose him again, but she must, having forfeited not only her own future but the solace of grieving free from the gall of guilt and regret. When at last she had no more tears she lay, dry-eyed and drained until morning came. She rose, heavy-hearted and weary, prepared food and made herself eat. There was the child to think of, that must be the drive in her.

So then she sat and she waited. She would make no attempt to leave until the men had started work and the route through the encampment was clear; if no one saw her, she would not be stopped. But the waiting was hard . . .

The minutes passed slowly until mid-morning came and she decided that she would go. She rose and straightened, breathing in deeply. She must be strong and go quickly, no second glances, no turning back. The small pieces of gold in her skirt hem knocked around her ankles but served to give her courage. Carefully, she rolled the large nugget in her spare shift and then wrapped this in her second shawl, placing it in the bottom of the bag. By alternating arms as she went along it would not feel so heavy and once on whatever cart would take her, she could rest it on her knee, and clutch it close. She opened the door then, and stepped out, bag in hand, willing herself not to look back – but at the last minute, she weakened, and turned at the door remembering that first day when Will had stood behind her, his chin nicked from shaving, holding his breath—

'Forgotten something?'

She swung around to see Robbie, coming towards her. He raised his eyebrows at her expression. 'Why darlin', it's only me.'

'You're not at the workings.'

'I'm not. Since you looked so much brighter last night I decided it was time you came out of that cabin of yours, and so I've come to take you down to the hotel, and see about getting rooms there. Timed it just right, it seems.' He smiled his handsome smile. 'Were you running low on supplies?'

'No! That is . . . yes.'

'I'll walk with you then.' He reached for the bag but she clung onto it, her heart pounding. 'No?'

'No,' she said, thinking desperately, her pulse thudding. 'I've changed my mind. I can't face folk yet, and I've enough food to keep me going. I'm not ready to go out.' She turned back to the cabin but Robbie jammed his boot against the door.

'Courage, girl, you've survived worse! No one will bother you if you're with me. Here, give me that bag and take my arm. We'll go together.' He pulled the bag from her grasp before she could stop him. 'Why, it's full before you set off! Whatever's in it?'

She stood, helpless, as he peered inside.

'Clothes?' He looked across at her then, his eyes suddenly shrewd. 'Why Rose, darlin', were you doing a flit as well?'

'And if I was?' she said, grabbing at the bag, but he swung it away from her.

'Heading where?'

She bit her lip. 'Hokitika, then on from there. I'm not sure. Just let me go, Robbie.' She reached for her bag but he kept it behind him.

'Dunedin, perhaps?' His expression hardened. 'Meeting up with your fancy man, eh? Will barely cold and now you're away to him.'

'No!'

'Dunedin's where they say he'll head for,' he said, considering her. 'But you knew that, I think.'

'I never want to see Fraser Urquhart again.' She lifted her chin but his eyes had narrowed in disbelief.

'You knew he was leaving though, didn't you? You weren't surprised when I told you.'

'He wrote me a letter.'

'With an address in it, eh?'

She gestured to the hearth where scraps of papers had escaped the fire. 'That's what I did with it. Now give me my bag.'

'And let you go alone to Dunedin? You'd not last there two minutes.' He turned his attention back to the bag. 'Not much to flit with, but it's heavy. Whatever have you got in there?' He peered inside and Rose shut her eyes, sick now with fear. She opened them again to see him reach in, and pull out what she had tried so hard to conceal. His eyes widened and for once he was bereft of words, then he glanced swiftly around, let the nugget fall back and gripped her arm, pushing her roughly back into the cabin where she half stumbled, saving herself by grabbing the bench.

He shut the door and rammed the bolt home.

'Jesus.' Carefully, almost reverently, he took the nugget from the bag and held it up as if it were an offering. He gave a low whistle. 'Oh Rose, girl,' he said, not taking his eyes of it. 'Rose, Rose, *Rose*! Wherever did this come from?' The softness of his tone made it all the more menacing, and his eyes stayed locked on the gold. She said nothing, her heart hammering. 'So, while you were busy cheating Will, Will was cheating us, eh? Oh Rose.' He set it down and turned to look at her where she stood, frozen beside the bench, his expression dark and unreadable. 'Have you nothing at all to say?'

'*I* found it. Not Will. And it's not from the claim.'

He raised an eyebrow. 'Is it not? And that made it all right, did it? You thought you'd to keep it for yourself eh, girl? And Will didn't know. Is that what you're telling me?'

'He didn't. I found it in the pool.'

He looked at her, long and hard, and then laughed. 'Are you after saving a dead man's reputation?' She said nothing, ready to be sick. 'But all right, let's agree that Will never knew. Doesn't alter the fact that *you* did, though, does it? You found it and you kept it and you told no one. Or did Mr Fancypants Urquhart come to hear of it?' She shook her head, terrified by him. 'Were you taking it to him, Rose? Is that it? Set the two of you up nicely in Dunedin, that would.' She tried to say no but could only mouth the word and he continued looking at her with eyes of blue ice, deciding whether or not to believe her. Then he grunted and picked up the gold again, weighing it in his hand, assessing its worth. 'At best, it's from an unregistered claim, at worst it's plain theft. And if I was to hand you over to the law which do you think they'd say? Eh, girl? Given that you'd hidden it in your drawers while you tried to flit?' He paused. 'And you with your reputation just a little tarnished right now.' There was no humour in the smile he gave her.

Better to call his bluff. 'Hand me over to the law then, Robbie Malloy, and be done with it.' Robbie's encounters with justice were always rancorous and she doubted that he would, but nonetheless she began to tremble.

He considered her as he scratched his chin, his eyes glinting at her, but not in any way that gave comfort. 'I think you'd better beg me to do that, young Rose, as I don't care to think what Dan McGrath would do if he got wind of this little beauty.' He paused to let the words sink in. 'He's a nasty man when roused.' His pretence at concern repelled her and she gripped tight to the bench to stop herself from falling. 'Whatever fairy story you told him he'd only grasp that you've robbed us, see? Because this little charmer would have made us *all* rich, not just you. And Will.' He continued to weigh the gold in his hand. 'Or Urquhart.' He watched her face for clues. 'A man was strung up by his mates, I heard tell, for stealing from them a fraction of the worth of that. And there's worse things can happen to a woman first.'

He set the nugget back on the table, though his gaze lingered on it.

'Take it,' she said, desperate now to leave. She still had the gold hidden in her skirt hems. It would be enough to get to Dunedin, and to live on for a while. More than enough. 'Have it, and let me go. Tell whatever story you like. I'll say nothing. I'll just go and you'll never see me again.'

He raised his eyebrows. 'Well now, that would be a shame.' He regarded her a moment longer then hooked his foot around a stool and pulled it towards him, blocking her way to the door.

'Just let me go, Robbie.'

She tried to get past him but he reached out an arm and looped it around her waist. 'No, no, not so fast. You just sit yourself down, macushla, and let's see if we can come up with a plan.'

Chapter 24

Will and Chen Lee made slow progress. This was due in part to Will's leg but his escort seemed over-cautious as they made their way downstream, staying a little inland from the riverbank. Several times he held up his hand, and signalled to Will to drop down, clearly anxious to avoid contact. Twice they saw movement and twice it turned out be a weka pecking its way through the undergrowth, and once they heard voices and the distant sound of chopping. Other Chinese diggers had illegal claims at the point where the Hohonu River joined the Taramakau and Chen Lee took what Will considered an unnecessarily wide diversion to avoid them. And it was slow going anyway through the swampy land, their clothes snagged by the vicious bush lawyer spikes, legs lassoed by vines and creepers.

And always the sand flies, in their eyes, in their nostrils and deep in the roots of their hair, enough to drive a man insane.

The sun was sinking as they finally reached the track that ran parallel to the coast and there they stopped, ate some of the rice that Chen Lee had brought, and rested. It was now just a matter of waiting for some form of transport to pass. Will was exhausted and he sank to the ground, resting his back against the trunk of a giant rimu with Chen Lee squatted companionably beside him. With his thumb Chen Lee indicated south and said a word that Will understood to be Hokitika, he then reversed his thumb and said 'Greymouth.' It was clearly a question and Will pointed south. In fact, all he wanted to do was get to the other side of the river and then retrace his steps east to Kumara, and find Rose. He tried to explain this to Chen Lee: 'Kumara,' he said. 'Just Kumara.' And, as if in mockery, a cart appeared along the track, heading north rather than south. Chen Lee pulled him back into the trees as it passed and then, to Will's dismay, the man indicated that he would leave him here. He had done enough, his gestures made clear; he had brought him to a place where, sooner or later, there would be a cart or a wagon heading south. He would say goodbye.

Will nodded to show that he understood and tried to convey his thanks for all that the man had done. Chen Lee rose and dismissed this, indicating that Will should keep the rest of the rice, and then he slipped his hand into his clothing and drew out a small leather bag, which he handed to Will. He bowed with a formality that was wholly incongruous with this wild setting, spoke words that sounded almost like a blessing, and disappeared.

Will called his thanks into the dark forest. He had not even had the chance to shake the man's hand. The little bag he found contained a brown cake of opium, a highly polished greenstone pendant and a screw of rice paper that contained gold – not much more than an ounce, but enough that Will was not destitute – and he returned the blessing into the silent forest.

No more carts passed that evening and, as darkness fell, Will bedded down under the trees, listening to the sounds of the night creatures, curled up as best he could, shivering from cold and perhaps a resurgent fever. He slept a little and, a couple of hours after dawn had lightened the skies, he woke to see that a man on a mule was approaching, leading another mule, and he told Will that he was heading for Kumara.

Will traded him half the opium cake for a ride.

It felt as if he had been away for weeks rather than days as he sighted the familiar gold-seekers' encampment sprawled behind the emergent town. Men were stirring as he limped towards it, his heart in his mouth, dreading what he might find. Some diggers glanced indifferently up at him as he passed them huddled over smoky fires, and one or two muttered a greeting but none showed recognition, taking him for some crazed hatter, perhaps, with his ragged clothes and matted beard, his face swollen with bites.

It was all he could do just to keep going.

The cabin was there, he could see it, just as he had left it, and joy oh joy there was smoke rising from the chimney! Rose— He hurried forward, stumbling in his haste, and pushed open the door to see a girl, crouched over a pot by the hearth, and his heart sang. 'Rose!' The girl turned and shrieked at the sight of Will, who stood staring back at her without comprehension.

A slattern, her hair lank and greasy, her face unwashed, a dirty blouse slipping from her shoulder.

Not Rose. Not his wife.

'Holy Mother and all the saints!' Dan McGrath sat up in the bed that Will had built and his eyes widened in disbelief. 'Are you for real, Will Stewart, or a púca come back to haunt us? Christ, man, will you look at yourself.'

A swift glance took in the plundered tree root and the empty ginger jar laying on its side beneath the bench. 'Rose. Where's Rose?' McGrath recovered quickly, pulled himself up scratching his chest through a filthy vest, and yawned. 'Tell me, for God's sake,' Will demanded, his heart pounding, for if McGrath had found the gold, God knows what he had done to Rose. His face broke out with sweat and he clutched at the bench, hanging on by sheer force of will, his infected leg throbbing.

'She's gone, son.'

'Where?'

McGrath shrugged. 'She never said. But she didn't go alone, so no need to fret.' The man was enjoying himself and Will grabbed a spade which lay on the ground beside him and thrust the blade of it under the Irishman's chin.

'I'll take your head off.'

McGrath swore, and then chuckled and pushed the blade away. 'Such heat, Will, me boy, such passion! But save your threats for that spalpeen Robbie Malloy, if you ever catch up with him. He'd been paying court to the lass since your death and yesterday they vanished together, him and your lovely wife, with never a goodbye to any of us. And it's my reckoning he took gold that wasn't his to take so he's dead meat if ever I see him again.'

With Robbie? His head was spinning and a dark fog was beginning to descend, but he needed to establish the facts. 'What gold?'

'Let's just say that the bag we're taking to the bank today weighs less than it did yesterday.'

Will's eyes flitted again to the empty ginger jar. So McGrath knew nothing of his illicit hoard, or of the nugget. But had Robbie found it? Or had Rose given it to him? He gripped the bench hard, his mind reeling at these catastrophes and the sound of Dan cursing the girl, ordering her to make haste with food, was the last thing he heard before his world went black.

Chapter 25

Rose stood beside Robbie on the grey shore and watched as the schooner drew close, dropped its sails and anchored beyond the surf. Every fleck of colour drained from the sky as night drew over the horizon, and the chorus of birdsong fell slowly silent. A cutter was lowered overboard and she saw casks being loaded onto it and then two men began rowing towards them, coming in fast on the surf.

She and Robbie had been brought to this place by a great bear of a man who waited with them now, another Irishman who spoke to Robbie in a language used by Will's partners at the goldfields. Her demands to know what was happening were answered by a flick on the cheek, a grin and: 'You're in good hands, Rose, never fear.'

'Are we not going to Hokitika?'

'I'd have thought you'd seen enough of that place.'

She frowned at him. 'We agreed. Hokitika, and then Dunedin.'

'Business first,' he replied, and would say no more.

The light had already been fading when, two hours ago, the cart they were in reached the point where the track to Kumara met the one that ran parallel to the coast. They had turned north and gone just a little way along it, passing a Chinaman and a wretch of a man who had limped off into the bush as they approached and a little further on Robbie had told the carter to set them down, and the cart had continued on to Greymouth. They would wait for another one heading south, she assumed, or simply walk the remaining miles to Hokitika but no, they had set off on foot into the strip of forest along the shore and come to a small beach at the top of which a shanty stood, a place with which Robbie, apparently, was familiar.

'Wait here,' he had told her, gesturing to a driftwood log, and he went inside, leaving her to sit there clutching her bag. Not that there was any point to her clutching it so tight now as the nugget had been transferred into Robbie's keeping before they had left Will's cabin, and she had been powerless to oppose him. His plan, such as it was, had been that they would leave at once, nothing said to his erstwhile partners, take the nugget and sell it in Dunedin and divide the money between then. She had agreed, recognising that she had no choice, and accepting that there was little chance of her seeing her full share of its worth.

But then again, she had had her own salvation sewn into the hem of her skirt.

Will's gold.

Travelling with Robbie would make the journey less hazardous than travelling alone, she told herself, and once in Dunedin she would leave him.

She had waited on the log outside the shanty, shivering a little in the cold, until Robbie re-emerged, together with the big Irishman, and the three of them had tramped a mile or so up the coast to a cove, and it was then that she saw the schooner rounding the headland. 'What's happening? Tell me!' she insisted, but Robbie simply squeezed her arm.

'Wait, girl.'

The wind caught at her hair as they stood there and she heard their companion mutter something and look up at the sky. Up until now it had been a light southerly breeze, blowing along the length of the shore, but it was shifting and if it swung

round and began to blow onshore then the schooner would have
to hoist sails and make a run for it, and this, she observed, was
making the man anxious. But the approaching boat was almost
through the surf now and a moment later the rowers leapt out,
dragging it through the spume, and shouting for assistance.
Robbie and their companion went down to the water's edge
and rapidly the casks were unloaded, together with boxes
wrapped in oiled canvas, and payment was made. Robbie too
seemed to be handing the man money. Had he shares in this
contraband delivery, she wondered, for surely it was that.
Anxious looks were again cast up at the sky, and Robbie beckoned to her. 'Quick now, Rose.' And only then did the obvious
strike her; they were not here simply to take delivery but to
leave on the schooner.

'No!' He came up the beach as she backed away, his face set
hard. 'This is not what we agreed.'

'Is it not?' He grabbed at her arm.

She tried to pull it away. 'Is the ship going to Dunedin?'

'I hope not,' he replied, tightening his grip.

'Then where?'

'Melbourne.' And without another word he picked her up and
strode with her down the beach, her protests ignored, passed her
to a sailor waiting in the surf who tossed her aboard as if she
was just another cask to be stowed. Then Robbie helped to run
the boat back into the waves before jumping aboard, leaving the
large Irishman ashore, wheeling the casks up the beach. Ahead
of them the schooner was raising its sails even as the boat cut
its way towards it, taking on spray.

They were drenched by the time they reached the vessel
and once again Rose was tossed from man to man until she
landed on the sloping deck where she was pushed aside as they
hoisted the cutter on board, heaving hard against a rising sea.

And a moment later the ship heeled sharply as the skipper took her bow away from the shore and set a westerly course.

Robbie turned to her then. 'Skipper says we can have his cabin,' he said. 'Come on, girl, let's get you below.' He steered her before him towards the companionway and she descended the narrow ladder into the fetid lower deck. At once her head began to swim and she put a hand to her stomach. 'You'll be better lying down,' Robbie said, opening a cabin door.

They were met by the rank smell of unwashed humanity and bilge water and she began to heave. Robbie grabbed a bowl and held it while she vomited, pulling her hair to one side and grinning. 'Running off with you is no picnic,' he remarked as she collapsed onto the squalid bunk, clutching her stomach. 'Take off your wet things and wrap yourself in that blanket.'

'I'd rather die.'

He laughed and went to empty the bowl, returning a moment later. 'And die you will if you stay in those sodden clothes.' He undressed himself, pulling on dry clothes from the bag he had brought.

'I never agreed to this, Robbie Malloy,' she said, turning away, weak from the vomiting. 'You shouldn't have brought me here.'

'I'm thinking the same. Should've left you for McGrath. Now shift, girl, no false modesty. Out of those clothes.'

'Leave me.'

'Very well.'

When he had gone she was able to stir herself enough to slip out of her skirt and hang it against the bulkhead, the hems well below the level of the bunk and out of sight, her head still reeling. Was this to be her punishment then? Deservedly so, perhaps, but whatever happened she must hang on to Will's gold, everything was pinned on that. She pulled her blouse over her head, draped it over her skirt then wrapped herself in her spare shawl, although that too was damp, and then she pulled the filthy blanket over her, trying not to imagine what inhabited it. As the ship eventually settled onto a reach, the pitching became less violent and, exhausted, she slept.

She was woken sometime later by Robbie, who came in bearing a tin cup. 'I looked in earlier but you were asleep,' he said, and sat on the edge of the bunk. 'Feeling better? Tea'll help.'

She pulled herself upright, clutching the blanket, took the cup and scowled at him. 'We agreed Dunedin.'

He was unmoved. 'There's nothing happening in Dunedin. A bunch of long-nosed Presbyterians and drunken miners hurling insults at each other. Why would you want to go there? Melbourne's the place.'

'We agreed Dunedin.'

'Aye, but then I got thinking. Getting rid of that lump of gold of ours,' he paused, 'we agreed it's *ours* now, didn't we?' She said nothing and he continued, his eyes mocking her. 'Getting rid of it in a place like Dunedin was asking for trouble. Word would get out, questions get asked and all we needed was for the authorities to get tipped off.'

'You should have given me the choice.'

'But you saw for yourself that the wind was shifting, macushla – there was no time.'

She drank from the mug, her eyes meeting his over the rim, recognising that Robbie had no intention to play by any rules other than of his own making, and that she would have to be sharp to survive. Recognising that fact gave her strength, so she said nothing more as the ship rose and fell on the waves, and he went on watching her, in no particular hurry, awaiting her next move. Swiftly she considered her options. The voyage to Melbourne would last several days – it had taken her a week on her first voyage across, and the wrecked ship had been a larger vessel, it had an engine and carried more sail – and so she was trapped here in this boatload of smugglers. With Robbie.

She looked around her at the cramped cabin, at the salt-stained timbers oozing damp from the seams, the captain's filthy clothes lying on the floor amidst bottles which rolled across it with every pitch of the vessel. Dear God, this was where her folly had brought her; and now there was no Will to come to her rescue . . . She had no arguments that would alter her situation, no way to resist Robbie, and she knew that further protest was pointless, so she stayed silent. Her eyes met his again and she saw that he was reading her mind, watching her arrive, stage by stage, at this conclusion, and a little smile hovered on his lips.

She had no options at all, no cards to play.

And yet, she was determined to survive.

So, she said nothing more. And after a moment, he put out his hand to take the empty cup from her and he set it aside. And then, with quite another sort of smile, he bent down to pull off his boots.

Chapter 26

After several days of hard sailing the smuggler's schooner put into Hobart Town and Rose came up on deck, gulping at the fresh air, desperate to rid her nostrils of the fetid stench below. Perhaps her clothes would dry a little too in the sharp sunshine as they were failing to do in the dreadful cabin. 'I'll buy you new stuff in Melbourne,' Robbie had said, when she dressed that morning, pulling on her skirt for the first time having spent the days in her shift, huddled beneath the vile blanket.

'I shall have my own money then, once the gold is sold.'

'And I'll get you the finest, sweetheart,' he continued, ignoring her.

Such words did not bode well for his future intentions, she thought, as she contemplated the busy harbour scene before her. Should she try to escape him here, abandon her share of the nugget in order to get away? Or should she remain with him? But how would it be for her here, she wondered, alone and pregnant, and she quailed at the thought.

It had not been the ship's original intention to put in to Hobart, Robbie told her, but with two unexpected passengers on board, water was running low and the crew were protesting at the short rations. Earlier she had heard the skipper grumbling to Robbie, and seen him dig his hand in his pocket and pay over more money, recognising, no doubt, that it would be easy enough for the man to toss them overboard and have done. Harbour officials came and inspected the vessel but, with its contraband cargo already gone, they left with nothing to report. To her dismay Robbie then announced that they would not be going ashore. 'But I *must*! If I have to stay on this stinking ship for another moment, I shall die.'

He was unimpressed. 'Loading water and supplies won't take them long and, given the chance, they'll go without us.'

And so the opportunity vanished anyway and she hung over the rails, watching the comings and goings on the docks, ignoring the whistles and coarse remarks, and thought of how her grandmother had been brought here years ago, transported from the backstreets of Glasgow, condemned as an obdurate thief, barely older than herself; it made her own situation seem bearable. She glanced along the rail to where Robbie stood filling his pipe, whistling softly to himself. Perhaps he would have tired of her by the time they reached Melbourne, she thought, perhaps he would abandon her, disappear with the gold and set himself up in style.

Good luck to him if he did – and good riddance.

Becoming aware of her scrutiny, he turned his head and gave her a nod. She acknowledged it briefly and looked away. He had not treated her badly, choosing to adopt the role of lover rather than captor, but such subjugation she would tolerate only for as long as the voyage lasted, and then she would leave him. For now, though, she had no alternative but to yield to him, and he had no need to remind her of that fact. As part of whatever deal Robbie had struck with the captain, he was working alongside the crew, standing watches in his turn and leaving her alone. And then she would lay in the bunk, hollowed out inside, knowing that there would be no weatherboard house, no fruit trees with hens pecking at the grubs, no cow to milk.

But there would be a child, she was determined of that. There would be no Will, though. Curled up under the unholy blanket, she could sob in solitude until she slept and then, when Robbie's watch finished, he would come down and push her to the edges of the bunk, and he would sleep too, an arm flung across her. She was caught then for if she rose she might wake him and if she went up on deck, she risked lecherous looks – or worse – from the crew, so she stayed where she was and submitted to him when he woke refreshed and lusty. 'I mean to do right by you, Rose,' he assured her, his arms wrapped round her in post-coital possession. 'I owe that much to Will. Nothing will bring him back, God rest the cheating bastard, but I mean to look after you. We'll get that hotel we spoke of once, do you remember? Before you left me for him.' How accommodating was Robbie's memory, she thought through her misery, and forced a little smile.

He lifted his head and looked down at her. 'But what I don't understand is this. If you loved Will like you said, why that photograph? Whatever were you thinking?' She said nothing. 'Had Urquhart got some sort of hold over you?'

Ah, the simplicity of the man. If she had felt unable to explain to Will the curious seduction of Fraser Urquhart's artistry, how much more difficult it would be to make Robbie understand. In Robbie's world, whatever occurred between a man and a woman would only ever lead to one form of transaction, and he would never question where the balance of power resided. In his mind, he had her where he wanted her: dependent on him, penniless but for his promises.

But she still had Will's gold.

And so she smiled her little smile as he reached for her again.

Chapter 27

Will headed back to Hokitika as soon as he was fit. For too many days the fever had kept him low and he had lain in his cot, drifting in and out of a troubled sleep, finding peace in neither dreams nor waking. McGrath had vacated the cabin with ill grace and it was Callum who looked after him, Callum who found someone to examine and treat the infected leg.

And it was Callum who told him that Urquhart had survived.

Will expression must have darkened. 'He's gone, though, taken himself off to Dunedin, I heard,' Callum had said, and he told Will about the other stolen photographs and then went off to the workings with the others, leaving him to digest it all.

As Will lay there he remembered how Urquhart had tried to warn him that day, too cowardly to explain. *Don't think the worst of me*, he had said, and he cursed the man again. What world did Urquhart inhabit where Will would *not* have thought ill of him? Was he telling him that Rose had not been unfaithful? Given what he knew of Urquhart he did not question it, nor care a toss; it was enough that he had used her in that way, exploiting her, indulging whatever whims and fantasies he might have, never considering what might follow. The scale of the damage it might do . . .

It was only gradually that the thought crept into his mind that the worst of the damage he had done himself and, once born, the thought would not leave him. If he had confronted

Urquhart instead of attacking him, demanded that he explain, then things would be different now.

Or better still, if he had spoken to Rose.

He pushed the blanket aside and got to his feet, weak still, but no longer dizzy. He had to find her. He had to get to Hokitika while the trail was still warm, find her and talk to her. Robbie he could deal with. His old partner's brazen move, taking Rose and the gold, was exactly what he would have expected of him, and yet Robbie was no fool. He would never dare try to sell the nugget in Hokitika, too many questions would be asked and McGrath would have come to hear of it. No, Robbie was too cunning for that and he had wider ambitions. Hokitika would not hold him for long, and Will needed to move fast. All that mattered now was that he found them, and that he talked to Rose.

His arrival in Hokitika was greeted with astonishment. The story of the photograph and the fight between Will and Urquhart had provided gossip for several days until it grew stale, but the news of Robbie Malloy's sudden disappearance with Rose had revived it and now here was Will, larger than life, hot on their trail, and the story came alive again. He gave only the vaguest account of his survival to those who asked, inventing rescue by an old hatter, a recluse living of the banks of the Taramakau, and no one had reason to doubt him. His own questions regarding Rose and Robbie, however, produced no results. No one had seen them in town, and even Moll convincingly denied any knowledge of their whereabouts.

She looked at Will with unsympathetic eyes, relishing his misfortune, payback for taking Rose from her. 'They'll have headed straight over the pass, if they'd any sense. Forget the girl, Will Stewart, she was a faithless slut. There's plenty more that's as pretty and they are right here, under your nose.'

Will left.

Over the pass. To Dunedin or to Christchurch? He stood in the middle of the street and considered. If he was in Robbie's shoes, where would he go? Dunedin was bigger but if Robbie was trying to sell the nugget then the anonymity of Christchurch might have attracted him. Putting his fate in the hands of fortune he pulled out a coin, tossed it, and let it land at his feet. Christchurch.

———

He did not stay long there. Money was becoming an increasing problem; Rose and Robbie had taken what little there was along with the gold and that which Chen Lee had given him was gone. Will had 'rented' his cabin to McGrath for a few shillings when he left but most of that went on the stage over the pass. Having toured the bars and hotels of Christchurch, getting nowhere, he then walked the streets of the growing city with an increasing sense of hopelessness. Rocked by earthquakes less than a decade ago, the inhabitants had cleared away the rubble of collapsed buildings and were building more solidly anew, believing that their misfortunes were behind them. He could only admire their resilience, but he found no trace of his quarry.

Then again, he had no photograph of Rose to show folk and asking for information about a dark-haired Irishman and a woman too good to be in his company was never going to get him far.

A railway line linking the city to Dunedin was under construction but until it was complete the fastest route was by sea, and so he arranged to work his passage south on a sturdy coaster, the *Sally Ann*, which plied its trade at small settlements along the broken coastline. But what with repeated loading and unloading at wharves and landings on the way it was several days before they put into Port Chalmers, Dunedin's main port. Dunedin itself lay a few miles further on at the end of the inlet and he stood on the dock chewing his lip. He was down to his last few pennies but just as he had decided that he would have to walk it, he espied an engine getting up steam on the line that linked the two centres. He stole into a railway wagon, emerging from it as they entered Dunedin, outrunning an official who gave chase.

And so, with nothing, he arrived in Dunedin.

Just like last time.

The city had grown in the two years since he and Robbie had arrived there. Founded on piety and good intentions, it had been transformed in the last decade by the relentless stream of gold-seekers heading first for Gabriel's Gully and then south through Otago and latterly to the goldfields on the west coast. And during those ten years many had returned; some flushed with gold and prosperous, building stone houses to flaunt their good fortune, and others hollowed out by failure.

Will looked about him, running his fingers through his hair in despair. However would he find Rose here? As he tramped the unmade streets, dejected and beaten, he realised he could never check each of the hundreds of hotels, boarding houses and bars. And the place oppressed him with its clamour of construction, its crowded streets, and a purposeful energy he no longer shared. He stayed for three days, sleeping in doorways, scrounging for food until he managed to pick the pocket of a drunken swell who had been ejected from one of the bars down a side street, fighting off another scavenger who challenged him for the pickings, wondering all the while at how it had come to this. But with the man's money he bought himself a meal, replaced his worn-out boots with a pair that was little better, and headed back to Port Chalmers.

In a busy port there would always be work, and sure enough he got himself employment on the docks without difficulty. Once he started, he barely had time to do more than notice the great ocean-going vessels that arrived from every part of the globe, bringing a steady stream of immigrants. They disembarked to stand beside their pathetic possessions, pale and thin from voyages that had taken months of fortitude, weary and yet full of hope. He remembered the feeling with bitterness. He heard Scots voices, Irish and English too but others speaking in languages he could not understand – German, perhaps, or Russian.

And he was there, working on the docks, the day the *Otago*, the ship on which he and Robbie had arrived, appeared in the channel, her sails furled as she was towed the last few miles past shifting sand bars where seabirds gathered in the afternoon sun. Glasgow-built, she still held the record of seventy-eight days for the passage from Britain and a great cheer went up as the hawsers were thrown from the deck. He rested on the handle of his cart and watched as the mighty vessel was slowly eased into the dock with orders shouted between harbour officials and crew. And he thought back to his own arrival, Robbie beside him, whooping with excitement, and for a moment he considered trying to get a passage home.

He straightened. Back to work. He needed the money. He needed to eat.

And he needed to find Rose.

It was then that his eye was caught by a figure standing on top of a pile of neatly stacked planks, looking towards the *Otago*. As Will watched him, the man stooped to a tripod he had set up there, his head disappearing under a dark hood. Another of that accursed breed, Will thought as he watched him, a scowl of his face. After a moment the man withdrew his head and bent to a box beside him, took out a plate, and disappeared under the hood again. Will felt himself tensing. There was something about the man's stance, something about the angularity of his movements. He moved closer, abandoning his cart, oblivious to the fact that the ship's gangplank had been lowered and the first-class passengers were descending, deck hands following with their cabin luggage, shouting out for assistance. The photographer re-emerged from under the hood and straightened, his eye sweeping the scene before him, and with a gesture Will knew all too well, framed the shot between the angle of his thumb and forefinger.

Urquhart.

And, as if drawn by Will's malevolent stare, the man shifted his gaze and looked down to where he was standing, and froze.

For a moment neither of them moved, then Urquhart jerked into life and scrambled down off the pile of planks, legs going in all directions, and Will waited, stock still, as he came towards him. 'So there *is* a God!' Urquhart said, as he reached him, breathless and panting.

'Are you sure?'

'There has to be.' And he clasped Will in an embrace as strong as that in which they had fallen to the icy flow of the Taramakau, and yet different in every way, muttering: 'Oh God, thank God. Will! I cannot tell you what this means to me.'

Will extracted himself roughly. 'Have you seen Rose?' he asked, hating that he should have to ask this man.

'Rose? No! I tell you, Will, there was never anything—'

'Or Robbie? She left Kumara with Robbie Malloy.'

'She left?' Urquhart stared at him, open-mouthed. 'With *Robbie*? When?'

Time no longer had meaning and Will was losing all track of it. 'About three weeks ago.' Or a lifetime.

'But why?'

'Because I was dead.'

Then Will's gaffer caught sight of him and ordered him back to work with a shout and a curse. Urquhart looked on, appalled. 'You're working here? On the docks?'

'That or starve,' replied Will, turning as he said it to go and retrieve his cart.

Urquhart followed him, tugging at his sleeve. 'Later then. This evening. Come to the Commercial, on George Street, Will. I've rooms there. You'll come, won't you? Say that you will! Ask for me. I'm going there now and I won't stir until you come.'

———

Urquhart was sitting at the bar beside the door lifting his head each time it opened, and, when Will arrived, he leapt off his stool and came towards him. 'You came. Thank God. Although I'd have haunted the docks until I found you again.' He turned to the man behind the bar and ordered beer and food, and led Will to a table in the corner.

They drew out seats opposite each other, and sat.

'I wonder if this is how it feels to be reborn,' Urquhart said, staring intently across at Will with his clear, open gaze. 'Cleansed in the waters of the Taramakau.'

Will looked back with contempt. 'You still talk bullshit, then,' he said.

Urquhart shrugged in that way he had. 'Forgive me. But you must accept that it's something of a miracle that we both survived that encounter, and now I have you sitting here, alive and apparently sound in limb and wind, I can only rejoice and marvel at the ways of Dame Fortune.'

Will rose in disgust. At first he had told himself that he would not come this evening, but there was just the possibility that Urquhart knew something, had some grain of information that might bring him to Rose. He no longer felt the urge to kill the man but he was damned if he would sit here and listen to his gowk talk.

Urquhart half rose to block his retreat. 'Don't go, Will. I'll only come after you if you do. I want to know how you survived, how you came to be here, about Rose, everything. With *Robbie*! Dear God, poor girl. Look, the food's arriving. Mutton by the looks of it. Stay, and eat. And afterwards, if you aren't done with murdering me, we can go out into the street and finish the matter.'

Will sat heavily and pulled the plate towards him, his stomach growling at the sight of meat, and there was some sort of dumpling floating in the thick gravy, potatoes too. It looked good, and he was not paid enough to eat well. And so, slowly, between mouthfuls, he told Urquhart how Chen Lee had found him, and all that had followed.

'A good man, that! What a lucky chance. But you found Rose gone?' Urquhart said when Will had finished, wiping his mouth and washing the food down with beer.

'Callum said she'd not left the cabin since she thought me drowned,' he said, 'but that he and Robbie had been taking her food, keeping an eye on her, and then suddenly, without warning, she and Robbie were gone. They were seen getting onto a wagon in Kumara the day before I arrived back.' Dame Fortune had been cruel and it seemed they had missed each other by just twenty-four hours. 'When I got there McGrath had already moved into the cabin with his whore.'

Urquhart's sharp brain went straight to the heart of the question. 'But why did they leave so suddenly, so secretly? If you were believed to be dead, they'd no reason to be furtive.'

They had every reason, Will thought grimly.

'And you've no idea where they might have gone?'

Will shook his head. 'Seems they never went to Hokitika, and they'd no reason to head north to Greymouth so I decided they must have come straight over the pass here, to Dunedin. I tried Christchurch first but had no luck. And I can't see that I'll have a better chance in Dunedin. I went into God knows how many hotels before I gave it up as hopeless, and besides, I had to find work.'

Urquhart leant forward. 'It's not hopeless, Will. Far from it! We must advertise. I do occasional work for a newspaper here, it has a big circulation in the area and so we must put in an advertisement asking for information. I can get that done at once.' He pulled the stub of a pencil from his pocket and smoothed out a crumpled piece of paper. 'It's just a matter of deciding on the words. Something like: "Would anyone knowing the where-abouts of Robbie Malloy and Rose . . ." Rose . . .' he stopped. 'She must have another name, I don't think I ever knew it.'

Will's face darkened dangerously. 'Stewart.'

'Oh God, yes, of course—' Urquhart looked stricken.

Will leant across the table and snatched the pencil from his hand as fury surged in him. 'Aye, you overlooked that, didn't you? That Rose is my wife.'

Urquhart lifted his chin and held his look. 'I never once forgot it, Will, and I never laid a finger on her. I treated her with the greatest respect and she trusted me. You, it appears, do not.'

Will stared at him in disbelief. '*Respect*! Rose was naked in that photograph, damn you, flaunting herself, and it was passed around every filthy digger for them to slobber over. And you speak of respect! My God, Urquhart, I'm not sure that I *am* done murdering you.'

'Will—'

'And, in fact, I *did* trust you. I believed you were a decent man, if peculiar, otherwise she'd not have been working for you. My gut instinct was right that night, though, wasn't it? The night I saw those photographs in your studio. There were others, weren't there? Of Rose?' Urquhart nodded, his face strained. 'So much for trust then, you bastard, or respect.'

Urquhart had gone pale but he still held Will's look. 'It was after that night that things went further than they should have.'

'Meaning *what*?' The man's effrontery was astonishing.

Urquhart looked around to ensure no one was listening and lowered his voice. 'The photographs. I took liberties. I took risks. I see that now. But I never touched her, I swear. She understood what we were doing, she was complicit, though I knew that you'd not approve, wouldn't understand.' Will swore again and grabbed at the knife that lay on the table but Urquhart was faster and he gripped Will's wrist, twisting it and forcing him to drop the blade. 'Don't be a bigger fool than you've already been.' Occupants at neighbouring tables looked round and a little hush fell. Urquhart moved the knife out of reach and released Will's arm. 'We're attracting attention and I imagine will soon be required to leave.' He raised a hand and in even tones asked for more drinks to be brought. The waiter looked uncertain, not wholly reassured by Urquhart's bland smile, but returned a moment later with two more beers.

'You have five minutes, Urquhart, to make me understand.'

'I'm not sure that I can.' Urquhart was silent, contemplating Will with a puckered forehead, and then leant forward again. 'What you think depends on the cast of your mind, Will Stewart, but every photograph I took of Rose was taken with her consent, some at her own suggestion. She appreciated and understood what I was trying to do, and she knew she was safe with me, and if you'd asked *her* to explain instead of flying at my throat like a demented hound and causing this Greek tragedy, she might have convinced you.'

Will felt a pang of conscience. 'And what would she have told me?'

'It was never my intention that those photographs left my studio. They were experiments, creative exercises, and it is to my eternal shame that they were stolen. I had promised her that they'd be seen by no one.' Will snorted. 'Rose is a very beautiful young woman, quite exceptional, and to have found such a pearl here, in this rough place, I—'

'Thought you could manipulate her.'

'No! If you'd not married her, I'd have convinced her to come to me, not as my mistress – I'm not that sort of man – but as my muse, my inspiration. I asked her, you know, but she chose your offer, not mine.' He paused while Will absorbed this startling admission.

'If I'd suspected for one moment that you'd had your eye on her, I'd never have consented—'

Fraser scoffed. 'Had my eye on her! How little you understand me. Look, there was nothing inherently wrong, or wicked, in what we did.' Will's fists tightened beneath the table. 'Painters down the ages have depicted women unclothed as objects of beauty or desire, but photography is still trying to decide how to address this challenge. That was what we explored, Rose and I, the space between goddess and harlot.' He hurried on at Will's expression. 'It started with a single photograph that I took of her and then I realised that she was the perfect model, that rakish mole, and . . .' he broke off, his brow furrowed again as he struggled to explain '. . . it seemed somehow to transform her, a strange sort of alchemy and I watched it happen. She began to see that she was beautiful, that she was something more than she had believed herself to be.' He glanced up at Will. 'It was not a one-sided contract, Will, for my lustful gratification. I don't see women as other men do; I think you know that I am made rather differently . . . But I watched her and I saw that the photographs made her *feel* different, made her feel valued in a way she had never imagined. They gave her confidence, she gained a sense of her own worth, and a sort of inner strength. Her upbringing was hard and she had been mistreated and made to feel worth*less*, don't you see? And that began to change.' Something in Urquhart's expression made Will bite back a sharp rejoinder. 'When she married you, she started to feel safe, and from that point of safety she began to explore. That was all we were doing, Will, exploring, she and I, with our different but converging motivations. It would be wrong to say it was not physical as physicality was at the very core of it, but it was never sexual between us, never a personal encounter, and never a threat to you. And if Rose was content to explore, if she was committed to what we were doing, then I was content to go with her and it was not for anyone else, not even you, to tell her that she must cease.'

Will listened, struggling between bafflement and outrage, only glimpsing a part of what the man said. 'Was I even asked?' he demanded.

'Why should you have been?'

Astounded, he said, 'I'm her *husband*, for Christ's sake!'

'And what would you have replied?'

He was silent.

'Exactly, my friend,' Fraser continued. 'For me it was experimentation with tones and exposures, cold science, if you like, and on that level entirely passionless, my only aim being for perfection. For Rose it was an exploration of herself. In my studio she was able to remove herself from her circumstances, see that she was more than just a trull from the backstreets of Melbourne with an undistinguished and dismal story. I watched her unfold before my eyes, I watched the bud that was Rose unfurl and blossom. It was quite remarkable to see! There she was draped in silks and with a growing composure, and I saw the realisation dawning on her that she was no one's creature, no more mine than yours.'

Will sat there, stunned. He was confused, hopelessly so. But he was angry still. 'Never for one moment did I consider Rose to be my *creature*, as you put it,' he said, after a moment. 'She is my *wife*, plain and simple, and I loved her, as a man loves a woman. Sincerely, and honestly.' Not at first, perhaps – the instinct to protect had been strongest then – but physical attraction had grown into love and he had begun to feel that the sentiment was returned. And he remembered then how things had started to change in the weeks following the awkwardness of their wedding night, how timidity had gradually become assurance, and how she had surprised him with a growing sensuality that had been as delightful as it was unexpected. Had *that* been the result of Urquhart's awakening, of her discovery of her own worth? He dropped his eyes to the table, scarred and marked by the many who had sat there before them. 'I wish she had told me,' he said, knowing, even so, that he would have struggled to understand. 'I still hold you accountable, Urquhart. Whatever your crazy head might like to think, you inhabit a world that judges things differently, and that you cannot dodge.'

Urquhart looked stricken again. 'I know. The fault was mine, and I failed you both. She asked me to destroy the photographs but I couldn't bear to.'

'And, as a consequence, Rose is now with a man who sees all women as creatures – *his* creatures – and who can be relied upon to let her down. And I—'

He stopped, unable to continue, and they sat in silence for a while and then Urquhart looked again at Will, a different expression on his face. 'Do you ever wonder who robbed my premises?'

Will looked up. 'You said they were looking for money.'

'There were more rewarding places to rob than mine.'

'What are you saying?'

Urquhart paused, as if considering, and then told him of the knocking on the door one evening, and of the footsteps that had departed and Will's face darkened again. '*Christ*, man! And *still* you never thought to tell me?' Had the man no grain of sense at all?

Urquhart paled but carried on. 'And I later learnt that your partners were in town that night, and the next evening, they took Rose dancing.'

'I know. They told me. *You* told me! And Rose did too. They became wild and rowdy, she said, and Big Sven took her home. What are you saying?' But even as he asked the question he began to understand, and he could well imagine his partners going to Rose's lodgings and not finding her there, and then going to Urquhart's studio and knocking, and the door not being answered. And the men seeing that the room was lit, leaving and drawing their own conclusions. 'So you think it was them, the night before, looking for her?'

Urquhart hesitated. 'I think it was *one* of them. There was only one set of footsteps.' He paused and studied Will's face. 'Did you never realise that there is one man who has watched Rose since the day he carried her off the beach to Moll's, and one man who could not forgive you for marrying her?' A name hung in the silence between them and Will looked back at him. Had he been blind? Surely not . . .

'Who showed you the photograph, Will?'

The question hung between them.

God knows, Will, we wanted to keep this from you. And Will remembered then how a hush had fallen as he bent to pick up the photograph, before the red mist of fury had consumed him.

Robbie Malloy.

Urquhart was right. It had been a set-up. 'And then,' Urquhart was continuing, 'when I survived, I was neatly removed from the scene by those other photographs of mine. Someone must have brought them to the attention of the guardians of our morals. The timing was excellent.'

'And you think Robbie planned it all?' Even as Will asked the question, though, he acknowledged that his partner had cunning enough. And he remembered then Robbie's strange reaction when he had told him of the wedding, his furious energy when he danced with Rose. What he had seen, with complacent pride, as simple admiration of his wife had concealed a dark desire, a coveting that had driven Robbie to make a plan, and act upon it. And the man had ended up winning not only Rose, but gold beyond his wildest dreams. 'It would seem,' Will said, slowly, 'that it was two men needed murdering.'

Before he left the Commercial, he and Urquhart put together the advertisement. Wording was tricky. 'It has to sound worth his while getting in touch,' Will said and in the end they settled on a simple formula: *If Robbie Malloy, lately of Kumara, wishes to hear something to his advantage he should contact this newspaper at his earliest convenience.* 'I can ask them at the newspaper office to forward any enquiries to me,' Fraser said, 'and I daresay we will be swamped by a stream of hopeful Robbie Malloys. And there is one other thing.' He hesitated. 'I left an address with Rose, a point of contact, an old friend in Dunedin, the publican of the Glen Etive Hotel, if ever she should be in need. I slipped a letter under her door, the night before I left. She's not made contact, though.'

Will's expression hardened. 'So you saw her, then, after the fight?'

'She came to see me, just once, at my rooms, demanding to hear my account of what had happened. I'd told everyone it was an accident, you see, that we'd fallen, and she wanted the truth.'

'And when you told her?'

Urquhart gave a sad smile. 'She said she wished you'd succeeded in killing me.'

After that evening Fraser and Will met regularly and, despite everything, Will found that he valued the companionship. Urquhart's main premises were in Dunedin but his current interest was focussed on the docks at Port Chalmers and he had taken rooms there for some weeks, only returning to Dunedin occasionally to keep his business afloat. 'I prefer it here anyway. I'm a chronicler at heart, Will, and I see that our time is passing even as I record it.' It made him little money, he admitted, his earnings coming mainly from the studio portraits. 'The appetite for portraiture amongst the good folk of Dunedin is insatiable,' he said, 'and their vanity infinite. What is it, this conceit that demands a record? You should see them, puffed up with self-importance, the men with waistcoats unbuttoned displaying gold watch chains, canes held just so to ensure that golden knobs are visible. Or they bring wives wearing preposterous hats, fur collars and chamois gloves. Do they send these pictures home, I ask myself, for relatives to admire, or gnash their teeth over? One man actually demanded that I pick out his wife's jewellery on the print, using gold leaf paint that he had thoughtfully supplied.'

'And did you?'

'Of course. But they pay a high price for their vanity even as I fawn, and yet still they return to me for more, or send their fellows. Whiskers groomed, striking the noble pose, all to convey the same message: Behold! I am successful. Envy me, you lesser mortals! These sons and daughters of Narcissus have no shame.' And Will had shrugged, thinking he would never understand half of what the man said. 'But you know what, I want to go back to Kumara, to what is raw and vital, and now that I know you're alive, I can. I couldn't have endured it otherwise. And I must find Harry and make sure that he is all right. I imagine the worthies will have found a new reason for outrage so I can risk a short visit.'

'Why return?'

'For the reason that I went in the first place: to observe and record, to preserve the madness of it for all time in a language that will endure.'

He would be gone for two weeks and insisted that Will took over his rooms in Port Chalmers while he was away. 'I'd paid for them in advance, not expecting to have this opportunity.' Will doubted this was entirely true but the room he shared with the other dock hands near the harbour was cold and damp, and Fraser owed him that much. 'Charge any necessities to my slate, food too, and we can settle up when I return.'

Fraser had rented two rooms. He slept in one and in the other he carried out his processes and Will lingered there, examining the various glass-stoppered bottles, the shallow dishes, the slatted boxes with hinged lids, the drying lines slung from wall to wall, and wondered at Rose knowing the purpose of each. While Fraser assembled his gear Will looked through his portfolios, privately hoping for a photograph of Rose but finding none. But he saw the goldfield as Fraser had meant it to be seen, a great raw scar extending as far as the eye could see with the encampment of tents below the ridge. Here too, in Port Chalmers and Dunedin, Fraser was busy recording the seamier side of life, the ragged souls asleep in doorways, drunks lying outside hotel bars, a forlorn immigrant standing beside a single crushed basket of pitiful possessions. 'Who will want to look at these?' he asked.

Fraser glanced across. 'These are facts, my friend, the realities. Photographs that startle stay with you.'

The man was taking with him only what he said was essential but even that seemed a huge amount when Will helped him carry it to the stage. And when he had gone Will shamelessly went through the rest of his possessions, opening his wardrobe, checking his pockets and leafing through the paperwork in his drawers. He found nothing. If the man had kept photographs of Rose then they were at his studio in Dunedin and Will stood a moment contemplating whether or not he should attempt to break in there and search.

His motives were confused, though, and he had to ask himself if he was still trying to assess the level of their intimacy, or to better understand what Fraser had attempted to explain.

Or did he simply crave the sight of Rose?

Chapter 28

Rose stood at the rail of the schooner as it passed through the Rip and into the vast expanse of Port Phillip Bay on which Melbourne lay. They had had to wait for slack tide to take them through the treacherous narrows and Rose had spent the time looking up at the low limestone cliffs of Point Nepean, remembering the last time she had sailed past them, just three short months ago. A lifetime. And in what a strange mirroring of circumstances she now found herself . . . On the outward trip she had hunkered down behind a ship's boat, quite terrified of what lay ahead, sewing five gold sovereigns into her skirt hem, and now it was raw gold that knocked around her ankles, and she was in no better place. A lost child had been replaced in her womb by a child that she wanted so badly that even the protection of a man of Robbie's stamp was worth enduring.

But for no longer than she must.

How swiftly it had all happened. In just a few short weeks: from wife to widow and now this man's whore. She turned her face into the wind to give her tears another cause. Survival depended now on strength, and she pushed the grief away.

She had expected that they would head north towards Melbourne itself but as they sailed across the bay she realised that their course was set north-easterly and they were now approaching a little staithe some way south of the city. As they drew closer to the land she could see small holdings and paddocks behind a row of buildings along the shore, with tall gum trees etched against the skyline. Here was nothing at all of the city she had known.

Robbie came up close behind her. He took her arm, tightening his grip as she tried to pull away, and bent to speak in a low voice. 'Trouble coming, darlin'. Take this,' he slipped a purse into her hand, 'while I nip back to the cabin. Hide it on you somewhere, and if there's a fight hold your nerve and stay clear.'

Her mind snapped back to confront a new fear. 'A fight?'

'I imagine so.' He squeezed her arm. 'Stay sharp. Be ready to run if I tell you.' And he disappeared down the companionway.

They had already assembled their few possessions on the deck ready to disembark and she stood nervously beside them at the rail as the ship drew close to the staithe. Robbie reappeared, clasping his coat to him, and gave her a nod. The moment the gangplank was lowered he pushed her forward, staying close and urging her swiftly off the ship and down onto the jetty. In his haste he stumbled close to the shore and half fell but recovered fast.

The captain's roar followed them. 'Oi! Where's my money?'

'I gave you half the agreed sum in Hobart,' Robbie called back over his shoulder. Two of the sailors joined their captain and stood either side of him, looking dangerous, and Rose tensed. Robbie turned to face them, seemingly unconcerned. 'I was simply getting the lady onto dry land. She's been very sick on the voyage. I've the rest of your money right here.'

The captain threw a glance at Rose. 'Lady,' he sneered, and then looked down at the coins in Robbie's hand. 'And what of the hire of my cabin? And the food?'

'Included in the sum we agreed.'

'The hell it was!'

Rose looked about her and saw that boat builders at a nearby slipway had stopped to watch, anticipating sport as the argument grew. If it did come to a fight Robbie had no chance, outnumbered three to one and the rest of the crew were standing by on deck, ready to join in. But just as the captain began squaring up to Robbie, one of the men said something and gestured to where an official-looking individual was striding along the beach towards them, flanked by two others. The captain grabbed the coins from Robbie's hand, threw a curse at him and went swiftly back up the gangplank, his men following.

'Trouble?' the official asked, as he reached them.

Robbie watched as the schooner cast off and turned back with a satisfied smile. 'It was brewing, sir,' he said. 'A timely arrival. Thank you.'

'He's notorious, that one, and he's been told many times not to put in here. Not welcome.' He glanced at Rose, taking in her bedraggled state. 'How did you come to be sailing with the likes of him?'

'We've come across from Hobart. My wife's mother is ill and we boarded the first ship we could. He said he'd take us to Melbourne but he's stranded us here, and was demanding more money.' He looked around him at the bend of the creek, at the boat yards along it and the newly built houses with open land beyond. 'Where exactly are we?'

'Mordialloc. Melbourne's some twelve miles round the bay.' He gestured to the north. 'You'll not get a boat there this evening but there's the Bridge Hotel just up the creek, which your wife will find acceptable.'

Robbie put his arm around her. 'She'll be glad of that, won't you, darlin'?' The two men spoke for a moment longer then the official tipped his hat and moved off. Robbie watched him go, then grinned broadly. 'God bless the strong arm of the law.' He swung around to look at the schooner, which was now well away, sails set, heading south, and grunted in satisfaction. 'Wait here.' He left her beside the bags and went rapidly back towards the jetty, peered over the side and then lay full length along it. He reached his arm into the water, stretched and pulled out a boot, which he brought to Rose, smiling at her expression as he shook the water from his sleeve. She frowned, recognising it from the cabin floor where it had lain with its pair amongst the squalor. 'Skipper'll drive himself mad looking for this,' Robbie said, and extracted from it the nugget. 'Didn't want to be losing that in a fight, now did we?' He slipped it into his bag before hurling the boot out to sea; and then Rose understood the return to the cabin and the stumble on the jetty. 'Said you were well off with me, didn't I?' Robbie said, and he planted a kiss on her mouth.

The Bridge Hotel was a two-storey, bluestone building with double verandas and a small annexe on one side. It had recently replaced an earlier structure in anticipation of the new railway planned to link sleepy Mordialloc with the expanding city of Melbourne, the official had explained, and offered rooms at reasonable rates. As they walked towards it, Robbie asked for the return of his purse and laughed when she retrieved it from inside the front of her blouse. 'Oh, darlin'! One way or another they'd have found it there.' Still chuckling, he picked up their bags and headed for the hotel, leaving her to follow, despising him.

He had no trouble securing a room. The landlord said business was slow at this time of the year and offered them one with access to the balcony. Rose went in ahead of Robbie and out onto it, looking back along the winding creek to where fishing boats were pulled up and nets spread to dry. What would Robbie's next move be, she wondered, now that there were just the two of them? Should she try and escape him, or would he simply abandon her here?

As if in answer Robbie came up behind her and slid his arms around her waist, pulling her against him. He kissed the back of her neck.

'So I'm your wife now, am I?' she asked, not troubling to resist.

'You're wearing a ring.'

'Not yours.'

'No, but I've me reputation to think of, girl.' His hand cupped her breast and she sensed the all-too-familiar smirk. 'Or have you had a better offer?'

No, but she would make a plan. Just as soon as she had recovered from that nightmare of a voyage. He would be unlikely to tell her what his intentions were, or at least not the truth of them, and she had no expectation that he would deal fairly with her in any way, so she must bide her time, be watchful and wait. His insufferable conceit she could ignore, or maybe use to gain advantage, and his physical attentions must somehow be endured. So for now, she would be his creature, and place herself under his dubious protection. He could call her what he wanted. She had nothing to lose that was not already lost.

Except the child. Fear clutched at her again. At all costs she must conceal her pregnancy until she could escape him. Every day of the dreadful voyage she had been ill, sickened by the rank odour of the cabin and the relentless pitching of the vessel, and that had sufficed to explain her daily vomiting. Even on calm days she had woken and reached for the bowl that Robbie had placed beside the bunk. 'Will you never grow your sea legs, girl?' he had asked, exasperated. But the nausea was passing now, and she would not begin to show for a few more weeks; she had a little time.

'I've ordered hot water for a bath,' he said, 'so you can get out of those clothes and get clean.'

'I have no other clothes.' Desperate as she was to wash away the filth of the cabin, she had no intention of letting her skirt out of her sight.

'We'll go into town and get some for you. Tomorrow, for sure.'

'So you'll sell the gold?' she asked, and at once he looked sly. 'Perhaps.'

'How will I buy clothes if I've no money?' It was pointless to challenge him but what would he say?

He flicked a knuckle under her chin. 'I've enough for clothes, sweetheart.'

'I prefer to buy my own, with my own money.'

'And so you shall, but for now I'll make you a loan.' And then his expression changed, the mockery gone. 'You'll find me a generous man, Rose, and I'll treat you well, you've no worries on that score as long as we deal well together. I've money enough for the moment and I'm sometimes lucky with the cards.' Rose suppressed a snort. Lucky? It was widely held that he cheated. Will had refused to play with him for stakes higher than pennies. 'He's a cheat, sure enough,' he once said, 'but he's a smart one.' Robbie's words suggested that he had no intention of abandoning her, although the implied threat within them chilled her.

'I need a little time to work out the best way to sell that great lump,' he continued. 'You worry too much, young Rose.' The mockery was back but then came a knock on the door and the maid arrived carrying a tin bath which she set before the fireplace, and a child behind her poured in the first jug of water, followed by a succession of others.

'Shall I stay and help?' the girl asked, addressing Rose, who nodded gratefully but Robbie waved her away, taking from her the soap and towel. 'If a man can't soap his own wife's back then what's the world coming to?' The girl left and Rose smiled her little smile, already stripped of any dignity.

And what more harm could he do to her, she thought, as she

leant back against the warm tin, shutting her eyes and submitting to his lascivious attentions; she would not give him the satisfaction of protest. He was a passionate and demanding lover (although what part could love play in such a transaction?) but so far he had offered her no other violence. *As long as we deal well together* . . . the threat hung there in the steam.

'Right then. You're clean, but by God you're not a lot of fun, are you?' He rose, tossed the soap into the water, and went and stretched out on the bed, leaning against the brass bed head, and watched as she rinsed herself. 'Still sulking, eh?'

'The towel?' she requested.

'Come and get it.' He tucked it behind his head. 'It's time I'd a proper look at you.' She sat there, hating him, and then something Fraser had said came back to her. *Why is it that the body, unclothed, makes us feel defenceless? There's no reason on earth why it should. Strength lays in composure.* Could she *be* composed, she wondered, under the very different gaze of this man? Somehow she must and so, without an outward tremble, she stepped out of the bath, quite poised, refusing to shield herself. And as she went to him she saw how he looked at her, with admiration, yes, but with the smugness of one who is in possession. And as she reached to take the towel, he pulled her down beside him and proved that he was.

Chapter 29

Later that evening, as she lay beside a snoring Robbie, she vowed she would never let what he did to her touch her soul. If she resisted him, she was in no doubt that he would force her, and would relish making clear his hold over her. By submitting she would maintain a measure of control; being passive would be her defence.

A brittle shield, perhaps, but it was all she had.

She rolled over onto her side, facing the open window of the balcony where the cool air blew in the promise of escape. Once he had sold the nugget he might give her some of the money, but she doubted it; keeping her dependent on him was clearly how he preferred things – and for now, perhaps the greater risk was that he would abandon her. She would bide her time.

And as long as she had Will's gold her freedom was there to be grasped.

In the morning she woke to sounds of Robbie moving about and saw that he was up already, dressed and about to go out. 'I've been thinking,' he said, an opening she was learning to dread. 'You'd be better staying here today while I go and scout out the place.'

'But I know Melbourne very well. I grew up there. I can show you—'

'The landlord tells me there's boat setting off soon and she'll be coming back tonight. If I'm quick, they'll take me.'

He was standing in front of the mirror, running his fingers through his hair, frowning at his reflection as he rubbed at a mark on his coat.

She pushed the covers off the bed. 'I can be ready in five minutes.'

He laughed. 'Oh, you've surely had enough of boats and the sea for a while, darlin'. No, you stay and rest yourself. I've told the landlord you'll be staying here and to mark up your food on my slate. You need to get some flesh back on you.'

'But I want to come.'

'Looking like that? Or are you thinking I'll not be back? Is that it?' He bent to her and his voice changed. 'I'd hardly desert you, sweetheart, after wanting you so long.' His eyes were a clear blue, and unreadable. 'So, don't you be worrying.' And with a pat on her cheek he was gone.

She lay there listening to his steps descending the wooden stairs and then jumped out of bed. Wrapping a blanket around herself, she went and stood on the balcony and watched him striding down the path to the jetty, looking neither right nor left, so very sure of himself. *Would* he be back, she wondered as she watched him, or was this a chance she should take. Could she too find a boat and leave, disappear into the chaos of Melbourne and—

And do what?

She stood there a moment, watching two small boys throwing stones into the creek, and then slowly she turned back to their room and sat, looking out across the balcony to the bay. This sudden opportunity threw the question into stark relief: where would she go? Running her fingers along the edge of her shabby skirt, she counted the little lumps again. She had no idea of their value nor how she would even make a start at selling them. Perhaps she should wait, let events play out a little more. Perhaps, she thought, watching a small sloop raise its sail and pull away from the jetty, she too could play a sharp game.

And to leave now might not be the smartest move.

If Robbie did not come back then the decision would be made for her, and she would have to cope. But if he returned with the nugget sold, then he would surely give her at least *some* of the money – or she could take some when the opportunity arose – and so it was perhaps better to wait.

Having reached that conclusion, she was content to let the day take its course, grateful for solitude and rest after the rigours of the voyage and what went before. It gave her too much time to think, though, and too much thinking brought on waves of grief and fear. She must focus, remember what she could of Melbourne, where she might go. In truth her days there had been circumscribed first by the institution where her mother had placed her and latterly by the Gilberts' household routine. Her knowledge of the city was, therefore, very limited. It occurred to her that she had lived within a frame as boxed-in and two dimensional as Fraser's photographs and, if she was to survive, she must step out of the frame and be bold.

Perhaps, after all, she had something to learn from Robbie Malloy.

As the afternoon drifted into evening and he did not come she found herself going out onto the little balcony and looking across the bay, trying to identify the sloop on which he had left, but there was so much coastal traffic it was impossible to be sure. And as boats took their moorings in the fading light and still he did not come, the fear that he had abandoned her began to grow. He had the gold and there were girls aplenty in Melbourne, so what was there for him to come back for? She had been a fool ever to think that he would . . .

It was fully dark now so she undressed beside the fireplace

and crawled into bed, forcing herself to accept this latest betrayal. But then she heard footsteps on the stairs and rolled over to listen. The door was flung open and he stood there, grinning across at her, a man transformed. Hair trimmed, clean-shaven and wearing smart new clothes, a watch chain stretched across his chest. 'Did you think I'd deserted you, darlin'?'

She yawned and stretched, denying him the satisfaction of seeing her relief. 'You told me you were coming back, and you have.' He narrowed his eyes, perhaps fleetingly annoyed. 'And just look at you, Robbie Malloy,' she added, and he grinned again. Then he reached behind him for parcels wrapped in brown paper and came into the room. 'You sold the nugget, I see.'

He came over and cupped her chin in his hand, his face close to hers and she smelt whisky on his breath. 'You see nothing, sweet Rose.' He released her and sat down, placing the parcels in front of her on the bed. 'Melbourne's as grand a place as I thought and every stitch on my back was paid for by the cards and the dice, and the same goes for what's in there. There's a great many simpletons come in from the goldfields with their filthy drawers full of gold just asking to have them pulled down. Sit up, sweetheart, and take a look.'

She pulled herself up and undid the string on the parcel as he watched her, clearly very pleased with himself, and she pulled out a skirt, two blouses, a little jacket and a shawl, all in bright colours and the blouses were fancy, lacy garments. 'I told you I was a generous man, didn't I?' he said, when she said nothing. 'And I'm sick of the sight of you in those shabby clothes.'

'Half that nugget is mine, so deduct the cost from my share, and in future I'll buy my own clothes.'

He scowled at her. 'Now there's an ungrateful girl! And how you do sulk.' He slid his hand under the blanket and pinched her thigh. 'Consider it a gift to make up for me leaving you on your own today, but you couldn't expect me to take you looking like a slag.' She had better humour him, she decided, pulling one of the blouses towards her and holding it up. 'The lass who sold them to me was your height and shape, though not half as pretty.' He leant towards her for a kiss, which was taken not bestowed, and his hand explored higher. 'Have you missed me?'

She moved to avoid him. 'I rested, like you told me.'

He straightened up. 'You're a cool one, make no mistake,' he said, considering her. 'And what would you've done if I'd not come back?'

'Thrown myself on the mercy of the landlord.'

He laughed. 'And slipped in between him and his fat wife? Good luck to you, girl! Admit it, you're better off with me.'

She smiled a little as he took the blouse from her and set it aside.

'Perhaps I am,' she said.

Chapter 30

Will continued to go into Dunedin at every opportunity while Fraser was away and did the rounds of gambling saloons, hotels and bars – but few had time for him and his enquiries got him nowhere. He continued to work on the docks at Port Chalmers, hoping he might spot them if they were heading off somewhere, but these days he seemed to spend more time in the stores and warehouses than seeing who came and went, which only served to fuel his frustration.

So when Fraser returned from Kumara two weeks later and dumped his bag in their rooms, he had an interrogation to endure. 'Not a word, Will, I'm sorry,' he said, shaking his head. 'I made what enquiries I could, but no one has heard from either of them, nor do they expect to. Everyone had an opinion as to where they might have gone, though – here to Dunedin seemed the popular choice, or north to Nelson, or to Thames or even Melbourne. All just speculation, of course.'

'Did you ask in both Hokitika and in Kumara?'

'I did.'

'And did you go and see McGrath and the lads?'

'I did that too. McGrath's daft brother had just been found dead at the bottom of the shaft they'd sunk, poor soul, so McGrath himself was drunk and insensible, inconsolable by all accounts, but I spoke to Callum.'

He felt a fleeting regret for young Ted's fate. 'And nothing?'

Fraser looked back at him with sympathy and shook his head.

Will's cabin had become a squalid hole, he reported, where the men drank or smoked opium, and where they took whatever women they could coax in there, and the men themselves looked worn and beaten. 'I'm not sure Robbie's the type to keep in touch,' he remarked, drily. 'Especially as they say he took a skim off the common pot before he left so he's now *persona non grata*. Not liked,' he added hastily.

Will turned away. He had not really expected that there would be news, but with his own searching so fruitless he had clung to the hope.

'Why Nelson?' he asked, standing at the window and looking down on the passers-by, watching a couple, arms linked and laughing.

'There's talk of a new goldfield opening up, same at a place called Thames.'

Will continued his study of the street as another couple passed. Robbie had no need of gold, but he was not intending to explain this to Fraser. 'And why Melbourne?'

'It was speculation, I tell you, nothing more, but folk said Robbie spoke of going there when he got rich.'

This was true. Robbie would sit and describe the hotel he would one day run: gambling rooms, flashy girls and the whisky flowing free. 'Let the miners sweat it out in Ballarat and Bendigo,' he would say, 'and then pass their takings on to me. Simple! Better than this fool's game, grubbing in the dirt like pigs in shite. Look at Moll, now there's a smart woman, growing fat and rich from dumb mules like us.'

So had Robbie taken Rose to Melbourne? Will continued to stare out of the window and scowled as he considered the possibility. By all accounts, shiploads of immigrants arrived there daily, swelling numbers in a city that was already bursting at its seams with suburbs sprawling wide to accommodate them. He had overheard bar talk marvelling at how the price of property would soon match that of London.

A quarter of a million souls now lived in Melbourne, they said, and so how would Will find Rose there?

He sighed and gave his attention to the photographs that Fraser had begun laying out on the table. In the weeks he had been away from Kumara, more buildings had sprung up along the main thoroughfare and flumes were beginning to appear above the roof lines. Urquhart had created a tableau of a baker leaning on his cart beside a man carrying a side of meat over his shoulder, and in the background was a Chinaman with baskets on a pole slung across his shoulders; a stagecoach stood outside a hotel. There were women too, collecting their stores, just as Rose had done. And but for this man and his damned photographs she would be with him now and they would have left Kumara behind them and be set up for life.

'I'm told there're ten licensed premises there now, and more planned,' Fraser remarked. 'Digging is clearly a thirsty business. And the place is becoming riddled with shafts and tunnels, although men are winning no more than half an ounce to the load for their efforts, and the piles of tailings are growing. Tailings are what come out of the—'

'I know what tailings are,' said Will, stony-faced.

'Of course you do.' And there were other pictures too, taken from a distance, which showed the ravaged landscape, torn and ugly, devoid of vegetation, with great stretches of timber flumes being raised on trestles, snaking their way from the river, oversailing the cramped shanties, carrying water to feed the sluices which would soon blast away at the ancient terraces, creating a sludge from which the gold was won. 'It's a world gone mad,' he continued. 'A raped land, a truly dystopic scene, dehumanised, all for the yellow metal that men crave. Artists have painted Sodom and Gomorrah for centuries and this is our equivalent, and my plates are my canvas.' Will studied the photographs, then glanced at Fraser. Where now the wild romance?

Fraser changed his tone, taking in Will's expression. 'Callum says the claim is not doing well. It seems the land undulates and test shafts suggest that the lode lies very deep there. They talk of false bottoms and are rather discouraged.'

'Is that supposed to make me feel better?'

Fraser shrugged. 'I heard from the start that this was not a poor man's goldfield, few easy pickings.' Unless you built a cabin on an old water course and the devil gave you the luck that dreams were made of, thought Will. 'More land is being pegged out and Dillmanstown is becoming a separate entity—'

Will pushed back his chair and rose. 'I'm heading out.'

Fraser followed him to the door. 'I thought to eat?'

'Then eat.'

Somewhere, Will thought as he strode down to the docks, somewhere Robbie Malloy was enjoying the benefits of what should have been *his* ill-gotten good fortune, and doubtless misusing his wife. Was this some form of divine punishment for the theft at Kinnloss and punching young Armstrong? They seemed such petty offences now. And if there was a God, what of Robbie's sins, why had they been overlooked? Murder had been done that night in Dublin, he had more or less said as much, and yet it was Robbie who was the winner here. And but for Fraser Urquhart he himself would be away with Rose, buying land, buying stock, starting a farm, a new life, his transgressions put behind him. The man was a self-indulgent dabbler who looked at the world through a lens, rendering himself incapable of seeing reality for what it was, neither a wild romance nor a wasted landscape, just lives being lived as best men could. What place had art in this world of sweat and greed? He should never have tolerated the man, never have indulged Rose, never let her work for him. He cursed him aloud, startling a drunk who was picking through a pile of rubbish – and then cursed himself again that by his own rash action he had wrecked the best chance he would ever get.

He leant against the railings at the dockside and stared down into the water, at the bottles bobbing on the tide, the bloated carcass of a rat returned to the shore by the waves. If only he had gone to Rose, and spoken to her . . . Christ what fool he had been! But what now? Should he stay here and continue to hunt, or head off to Melbourne and take his chances there?

Or should he go back to Kumara and get a job with one of the companies sinking shafts or building the water races or adding stones to the piles of tailings like an ant toiling up an anthill, except with less purpose? He spat into the water and watched a fish rise to examine the spittle, and disdain it. No. He would not go back. That would be to admit defeat. He would give it until the end of the month, continue to look for Rose, save what money he could and then work his passage to Melbourne.

———

Two weeks later Will was packing his meagre belongings while Fraser stood watching, aghast. 'To Melbourne? But Will, you never said.'

Will made no reply. He had continued living at Fraser's rooms at Port Chalmers, and at Fraser's expense, thinking that if this served to salve Fraser's conscience then so be it. He also ruthlessly continued to mark food and drink onto Fraser's slate, saving every penny of his own, and Fraser had never murmured a protest. But now the man looked deeply shocked.

'Why stay? There's not a trace of them,' Will said, having reasoned that if Robbie had sold the nugget he would now be a rich man, and the rich like to make themselves visible, for what is the point of riches if not to flaunt them? And still he had found no trace. 'They simply aren't here.'

'But how will you find them in Melbourne? Will, it's a hopeless task.'

'And what hope have I here?'

Fraser looked back at him, his expression bleak. 'When will you go?'

'There's a coaster needing hands round to Nelson. Leaves this afternoon. I'll get to there and then work my passage across on whatever's heading out.'

'But it could take you weeks!'

'Probably will.' He tightened the strap on his bag and lifted it onto his shoulder.

'Wait.' Fraser held up his hand. 'Wait just a moment. Let me think.'

Will brushed him aside. 'Ship sails on the tide. I'm late as it is.'

'I'll come with you.'

'The hell you will.'

'You're not going without me. I swore I'd find Rose for you so you cannot deny me my redemption – my conscience is too heavy. Two can look twice as hard as one. We can advertise again, circulate pamphlets.' Will made for the door but Fraser blocked it. 'I just need a few days to settle my affairs, here and in Dunedin, but then we can get passage direct to Melbourne. I've enough to pay for us both and we'd be there long before your beastly coaster.'

'How did you suddenly get so rich?'

Urquhart looked apologetic. 'My father died. I received word from my mother when I got back from Kumara and it means I now have funds on which I can draw.'

'I'm delighted for you. Now shift, or I'll knock your teeth down your throat.'

Fraser folded his arms and leant against the door. 'An improvement on last time then.'

'I'm serious, let me pass.'

'You'll not leave without me.' Will flung the bag from his shoulder in exasperation and prepared to make good his threat but had only a moment to be astonished before Fraser's fist connected with his jaw.

Chapter 31

'That business at Kinnloss estate,' Fraser said as he stood beside Will, holding onto the rigging of the ship as she cut through the seas, taking advantage of a northerly twist in the roaring forties. She was making good speed, and above them white sails were spread wide.

'What about it?'

Will was still aggrieved at his treatment. When he had come to, he had been furious to find himself locked in Fraser's rooms, missing both the tide and his ship. When Fraser returned and released him, there had been a brief and angry scuffle in which only furniture had been broken, and then Fraser had waved two tickets in his face for a ship sailing to Melbourne leaving in three days' time. The continued resentment had all been on Will's side, however, as Fraser had calmly set about settling his affairs and making plans for departure.

'I'll ditch you as soon as we reach Melbourne,' Will had assured him grimly, rubbing his hand over the tender part of his jaw.

'By all means, but you'd be a fool. I've funded you for weeks now and will continue to do so until we find Rose, so why abandon the hand that feeds you?'

'I don't want your damned charity.'

'It's been useful, though, hasn't it?' Fraser had picked up a broken chair and looked anxiously over his equipment before carefully dismantling the rack on which he dried his prints, pulling

224

down the black curtains he had rigged up at the tiny window, and Will had been unable to dispute the point.

Fraser turned to him now as they entered Port Phillip Bay, his hair blowing across his face as the bow of the ship plunged into the trough of a wave. 'Because of the *theft*, the houses at Srath an loin were torched and people suffered, some died.' Will glared at him. 'Because of the *photograph*, Kinnloss lost his business, went bankrupt and killed himself and others were put out of work. Neither thought is comfortable, of course, but would you do the same again?'

Will hung over the rail and felt the salt spray on his face and, not for the first time, considered the question. 'What Armstrong and Kinnloss did between them was unforgivable,' he said eventually, 'and I regret any part I played in bringing it about. Kinnloss would have cleared the crofters anyway, though maybe not as viciously as the Armstrongs did it. But I don't regret stealing the money. I had no way out.'

Fraser nodded. 'I feel the same. I was right to expose that eviction, and what followed I could never have anticipated. That guilt I have dealt with now.' He glanced sideways at Will. 'And similarly, I've no regrets about photographing Rose, only for the string of events that followed and brought us here. Cause and effect, action and consequence. None of us can predict it, or escape it. We can only hope to atone.'

Will looked down into the foaming ocean. If only life were that simple.

'So where will we start?' Fraser asked, leaving the subject, and Will shrugged; Melbourne was a complete unknown. 'Robbie's a gambler, you said, which might narrow the field a little, but he's hardly respectable so we can rule out the upmarket clubs and casinos.'

Will went on watching how the hull cleaved the water. 'Not

necessarily.' Perhaps this was the moment to tell him about the gold.

Fraser was shaking his head. 'Stakes would be too high, out of his league. And you'd need some sort of introduction, or sacks of cash. What does he play?'

Anything from two-up to poker, Will thought, and he would spend nights rolling dice with the Chinese storekeepers. But now that he had money, big money – would he gamble it or invest it in his wretched hotel? 'I suppose we go suburb by suburb and make enquiries,' Fraser continued.

Will snorted. 'Like I did in Dunedin? And enquire for a crooked Irishman and pretty woman.'

'I have a photograph.'

Will narrowed his eyes. 'What photograph?'

'I know you went through my possessions, my friend – you left them in a state – but I kept some things at my studio in Dunedin.' Fraser looked back at him. 'I've a copy of your wedding photograph.'

'So, you have Rose – and me. What good is that?'

'I also have the other, outside the church. With Robbie on it.'

The three of them.

Will looked away.

As they neared the mouth of the Yarra River, Fraser raised the question of their strategy again. 'So, shall we advertise?'

Will shook his head. 'It'll spook him.'

'We could say the same as before, that he would learn something to his advantage.'

'He'd smell a rat.'

'I don't see why he should. Who would he imagine was after him? Not his partners, that's for sure. He was smart enough not to take their whole pot, and it wouldn't be worth their while chasing after him for a few ounces of gold. And *I'd* have no reason to come after him.'

Will looked back at him, hesitated, then came to a decision. It was time. 'He has more gold than that, much more,' he said, his voice low. 'He has gold beyond dreams. A single nugget weighing the best part of three, three and a half pounds and some fifteen smaller pieces.'

Fraser's jaw dropped. And so Will told him the story, first about the small nuggets he had secreted away in the root of the tree, and then about the fist-sized one that Rose had found winking up at her from the pool. Fraser pulled a pencil and scrap of paper from his pocket and calculated quickly, muttering, 'Given the price per pennyweight at the moment . . .' He looked up at Will. 'It's worth a small fortune.'

'I know.' How would Fraser judge him now, he wondered, watching him.

'And you know for sure that he took it?'

'I know for sure that it was gone when I got back to the cabin. McGrath and his clan would have strung me up if they had known about it, but it was never even mentioned, so Robbie must have taken it.'

Fraser chewed the end of his pencil, still looking at Will. 'But it wasn't actually found on the claim, you say, any of it?'

'A detail they'd have overlooked.'

Fraser went on considering him. 'So ought you to have declared it?' he asked, frowning.

'If I was dealing straight with them, yes, but I wasn't. And on that score, my conscience troubled me only a little at the time, and now not at all . . .'

He broke off and Fraser turned away, his eyes following the seabirds that were flying out from the shore to greet the ship, anticipating a fishing boat returning with a haul.

'So Robbie stole what was already illicit gold,' Fraser continued after a lengthy silence. 'And because it was found *off* the claim it belonged to no one, legally speaking, but it should have been declared to someone, I suppose. And as a partner in a sort of consortium you might have felt morally obliged to tell the others, but you didn't.' Will watched him wrestle with the issue, amused by the serious expression on the man's face. 'Nor, incidentally, did Robbie, when he got to hear of it.'

Will's amusement vanished. 'Good thing he didn't. I can only imagine what they would have done to Rose.'

Fraser looked across at him and, realising his meaning, blanched. 'Oh God, yes. But you must see, Will, this changes things.' Will shrugged and turned aside. He had no need of this man's company, and if the stiff-arsed fool could no longer stomach the association, then he was well rid of him.

The slap on the back came from nowhere and Will turned and saw to his astonishment that Fraser's face was beaming. 'It's wonderful news! It means that Robbie will have to be a little circumspect in selling the gold as it's illegal but once sold, he'll be a man of substance and very much easier to find. Money opens doors in this world and knowing Robbie Malloy, he'll not be able to resist making a splash. We also have the element of surprise.'

Will stared at him, baffled. 'In what way?'

'*You'd* never coming a-seeking him because you, my friend, are dead.'

Chapter 32

'Why ever not, girl? You sulked when I wouldn't take you yesterday.' Robbie frowned down at her where she sat in a chair beside the fire.

Rose simply smiled back. 'But I've no need to go into Melbourne now I have new clothes. And I must alter them to make them fit.'

'They fit you just fine.'

'The skirt's too long, and I need to turn up the hem. The landlord's wife has lent me her work box.' She gestured to a basket that the servant had brought up while Robbie had been down at the privy. It was essential now to transfer the gold. 'It's so fine a skirt, I'll spoil it if it drags in the dirt.'

He viewed her with suspicion. 'It's nothing special. I said I'd buy you better in town, and you can come today and choose them for yourself.'

'I think not, Robbie.'

His scowl deepened. 'I might be gone two or three days.'

'I'll be fine here. And if you're at the cards again, I'll be in the way, and a distraction.'

'You flatter yourself.' He continued to get ready, watching her speculatively through the mirror as she calmly threaded a needle and pulled the new skirt towards her. It was of a lighter material than her old one, both in weight and colour, and the gold pieces would be more conspicuous but if she doubled the hem over then later, when she slotted in the gold, it would not show. And she had decided that she needed to spread her hoard more widely, although doubtless if he found gold in one garment, he would shred the others looking for more.

'I mean to find us rooms in Melbourne. In one of the suburbs. Fitzroy, perhaps.'

'Not Carlton? It's a better part of town, and we're rich enough.'

He adjusted his collar and frowned at her through the mirror. 'Where were you in service?' Moll had filled him in on her past, back in Hokitika.

'Carlton.'

He snorted. 'So you think it's a good idea to set up in the one part of Melbourne where you'd be recognised as the trull who seduced a rich man's son?'

'Perhaps not.' She smiled back at him, and went on with her sewing. Goading Robbie was satisfying but perhaps unwise and she regretted it once he had left, banging the door shut behind him. She went onto the balcony and watched him head back down to the jetty and waited until she saw that the little sloop was well out to sea, and then she locked the door. Carefully, she unpicked the hem of her old skirt and one by one, like wicked secrets, the gold pieces emerged and she set them on the table beside her.

In these little pebbles lay her future.

Perhaps she should hide some in the jacket seams, she thought. But Robbie liked to put his arm around her or steer her with a hand on the small of the back, and might notice. So where was safe? She selected four of the smaller, flatter pieces and decided to sew them behind the buttons at the front of her jacket. It was a gamble, but at least then she had two chances; if he found the pieces in the skirt he might not find them in the jacket, and the opposite applied. The rest, bar one, she sewed into the double hem of the new skirt, so as long as she wore both skirt and jacket when they did go into Melbourne then, if she had the chance to elude him, she had them with her. The last one she rolled tight inside the coil of a ribbon, which she placed with her new blouses, thinking to keep at least one piece ready at hand.

And then she paused, her hand on the half-closed drawer. But what about the big nugget? Where was that now? She had seen no sign of the weight of it pulling Robbie's smart new clothes out of shape when he left, and yet he said he had not sold it. He could have lied, of course, but then where was the cash? It would be a very considerable amount.

Her pulse quickened as she looked around the room. Would he really have left it here? Taken such a risk? If he had, she thought, scanning the room for hiding places, then somewhere there was either the gold, or the money. There had been plenty of opportunities for him to hide it, after all; when she had gone down to the privy, or when she had been asleep. But where was it? Quickly, she pulled back the rug and looked for loose floor-boards but found none, then she scoured every inch of the walls, the windows and their fittings, went through his bag where he had stuffed his other clothes and frowned when she drew a blank. That left only the fireplace and she paused, remembering how he had refused to have a fire lit, saying the room was warm enough without. Perhaps that was not the real reason . . .

Her excitement grew. The chimney was made of brick, unevenly coursed, and she reached up into it, stretching her arm as far as she could, feeling for ledges inside. She coughed as ash and soot fell in a cloud and her skin was soon blackened as she worked her way around the chimney, feeling for it. And then, at the very back her fingers encountered a loose smooth rock, wedged between two of the bricks, and it came down heavily in another little flurry of ash.

And there it was.

She rocked back on her heels, then sat cross-legged on the hearth rug and stared at it. No more than a man's fist in size and yet it had a power that was staggering. And it changed everything. It meant that she *could* go now, escape from Robbie's control. He would come after her, that was for sure, and that thought was terrifying; he must *never* find her. But she could leave this place at once and lose herself in Melbourne, and then later when she had got her bearings, she could take stock and consider.

She had a future now, and so had Will's child.

She picked up the gold, weighing it in her hand and decided she must sell it as soon as she discovered how to, even if she got only a fraction of its value, and in the meantime she would live on the proceeds of the smaller pieces. Her brain began to come alive. Rooms must be found, someone engaged to help her, and then she could lie low until the child was born. Beyond that point she could not think.

And she might never get this chance again.

But had she the courage to go? She sat there, remembering how Will too had weighed the nugget in his hand, how the excitement had lit his eyes, and the plans they had whispered together in their narrow bed. If they had left straight away, that day, that moment, seized the chance—

She must not make the same mistake.

She dressed quickly in the clothes that Robbie had bought her, stuffing her old ones into a bag, wrapping the nugget inside them and then she sat on the edge of the bed, weak at the prospect of what was ahead and took a moment to school her leaping thoughts. The best way to get to Melbourne was by boat, the landlord had said, otherwise it was a long, slow cart ride along the rutted road and she would be vulnerable, easy to track, so a boat it must be. From her window she had seen plenty of coastal traffic, fishing boats for the most part, and she could surely persuade some boatmen to take her. Uncoiling the ribbon, she retrieved the single gold pebble she had hidden there and slipped it into her pocket. She might have to show it as proof that she could pay, even though that risked it being stolen and leaving her stranded. A woman alone would be considered fair game.

She closed the door behind her and went quickly down the stairs carrying her bag, encountering no one. As she passed the doorway to the bar the potboy looked up and she smiled at him and moved on, out onto the veranda where she paused a moment to regain her balance, and then set off down the rutted track to the road that ran parallel to the shore. Not too fast, she told herself; her heart was thudding and she slowed down. She reached the creek and passed the boat builder's yard where again heads were raised. Would they know of a boatman? She hesitated and then moved on, seeing that fishing boats were pulled up on the sloping riverbank and there were men beside them mending nets.

She approached them nervously. 'I want to get to St Kilda,' she said. Tommy's family had had a summer house there and sometimes she had gone when the family went for short spells, so it was at least a little familiar. From St Kilda she could make her way to one of the other suburbs and find herself rooms. 'Will you take me?'

'When?' one of the men replied, running his eyes up and down her.

'At once?'

The men laughed. 'Tide's all wrong, miss. You'll have to wait until this afternoon.'

She cursed silently, having never considered the tide. 'Would you take me then?'

They looked from one to the other, grinning and muttering

amongst themselves. 'We might,' said one, pushing his hat onto the back of his head.

'I'll pay you well.'

'How?' he asked, and the others laughed.

'How much are you asking?'

'How much've you got?' They had set down their nets, prepared to enjoy themselves.

'I've more than enough.'

The first man lit a pipe and leant back on his elbow. 'We can see that for ourselves, but we're talking hard cash.' Again they laughed and she felt her face flush. Why was every transaction between men and women so loaded? And then their attention was taken by something over her shoulder and she turned to see the landlord of the Bridge Hotel striding towards her, and sensed her opportunity slipping away.

'Mrs Malloy!' he called out. 'What brings you out here?'

Did the sliver of a chance remain? She lifted her chin, and said with all the confidence she could muster: 'I've decided to join my husband after all. I told him that I might. Is there some other way of getting to Melbourne? Otherwise I'll wait until this afternoon, when these men will take me.'

The landlord looked back at her, stony-faced. 'Your husband told me, most particular, that you'd be staying here, and asked that I kept an eye out for you. So best you come back to the hotel and wait for him there.'

He put a hand on her arm but she pulled away. 'Thank you, but if these men will take me, I'll go on the next tide.'

'Then you'll miss him, as he expects to be back this evening.'

'No! He said he might be gone two or three days and I could join him if I wanted. He's looking for rooms and I can—'

The landlord's eyes narrowed in suspicion. 'And who's to pay my bill if you both go off?' The fishermen had been enjoying this exchange but now the man swung back to them and they dropped their heads. 'These fellas don't want to be ferrying you to Melbourne, do you, lads?' His word clearly carried weight here and they took up their nets again, avoiding his eye.

'Just being helpful,' one muttered. 'She never mentioned a husband.'

Humiliated and furious, Rose had no option but to allow the landlord to escort her back along the side of the creek, past the boat builders, across the road and into the hotel. 'You're my surety, my dear,' he chuckled, as he held open the door, but the humour did not reach his eyes. 'Couldn't be letting you *both* leave, now, could I?'

She went back up to her room and stood there, staring at the wall. She had achieved nothing – in fact she had considerably worsened her position as the landlord would doubtless report the incident to Robbie, and Robbie would never believe her story and wonder how she expected to pay the fishermen. Reluctantly she took the small gold piece from her pocket and tucked it into her cleavage, resigned to having to sacrifice it. As for the large nugget, all she could do was put it back where she had found it for if Robbie suspected she had been flitting with that she did not like to think what he might do. She replaced it, washed her hands and then, on a sudden inspiration, rang the bell and requested that a fire be lit in their room.

As she stared into the flames, for the first time she felt frightened.

Robbie returned just as the light was fading over Port Phillip Bay. She heard his slow tread on the wooden stairs and her pulse quickened. A moment later he opened the door, and stood there, and she saw his eyes flick at once to the fire. A frown came and went, and then he smiled at her in a way she did not quite like. 'Such a picture you make, darlin', curled up there beside the fire, waiting for me.' He spun his hat onto the bed, then came and stood over her. 'And I came back! Didn't leave you on your own, after all.'

'So I see.' She attempted a smile.

He bent down and lifted her from the chair, taking her place, and settled there with her on his knee. 'And how did you spend the day, sweet Rose? Were you lonely?' he said, running his knuckles lightly over her cheek. He smelt of liquor and tobacco, harsh male smells, and with his face so close to hers she could not judge his expression.

'A little. I stayed here for a while and slept a bit more, then I took it into my head to come and join you after all.' She tried to relax against him, lest he felt the tension in her. 'Three days suddenly seemed a long time to be alone—'

'Did it, darlin'?'

'—so I tried to persuade some fishermen to take me, but I'd not considered the tides.'

'Had you not?' he raised an eyebrow, his tone confirming that he knew all this.

'And then the landlord came down and said you'd told him you were coming back this evening and that I might miss you, so I gave up on the plan.'

He smiled a wry smile, and ran his thumb over her lips. 'Well, it wasn't really much of a plan, was it, when all's said and done?'

'I suppose not.' It was hard to keep her voice steady. 'He was quite offensive, in fact, suggesting that I was trying to slip off without paying the bill.'

'He'd be confused, poor man, since I'd told him you were stopping here.'

She nodded, avoiding his eyes. 'Yes, he said that. But I was confused too as you'd told *me* you might stay away two or three nights.'

'I did, sure enough. But tell me, Rose, how were you going to find me?'

Her mouth was dry and she swallowed. From here it got tricky. 'You said you were looking for rooms in Fitzroy.'

'Big place, Fitzroy.'

'Is it? I imagined I'd find you.'

He nodded again. 'And you might have done. But how were you planning to pay these fishermen, sweetheart?'

She had her answer ready. 'I told them that you'd pay them on our return.'

He shifted her on his knee and turned her so that she had no option but to look directly into his eyes, which were an icy blue. 'Now that's a lie, Rose. It's the first one, I grant you, and so you've done well up 'til now. But no, you told them that *you'd* pay them and that you'd pay them very well, that you had more than enough to give them. And you asked to be taken to St Kilda, not Melbourne, so in fact's it's two lies.' The slap was swift and deliberate, hard across her face, and she cried out with shock as much as pain. 'Now that was just a taste, darlin', and you'd do well to tell me the truth and avoid worse.' She tried to stand but he tightened his grip. 'You were running off, I think.'

Her cause was lost, but she must not show her fear. 'And if I was? Am I not free to go?' He said nothing, his expression unreadable. 'You've not played straight with me, Robbie Malloy.' Frustration and fear made her suddenly bold. 'You brought me here where I'd no wish to be. You took that nugget which you declared was "ours", and you've not told me whether you've sold it or not.' She saw his eyes slide again towards the fire. 'And you've left me here with no money or any—'

'Which brings us back to the boatman. How were you going to pay him?'

With a show of reluctance, she slipped a hand inside her

blouse and brought out the gold piece she had hidden there and offered it on her palm. His eyebrows shot up and he took it, releasing her as he did. She moved quickly away from him, fearful of another blow. 'Where did that come from?' he demanded.

'Will found it.'

He swore softly, cursing Will. 'Is there more?'

She shook her head, holding his look. 'No.'

'You'd better be very sure of that, Rose.' He got to his feet, and pulled her to him, then ran his hands over her, searching inside her blouse, patting down her hips and legs, but not examining her skirt hem. He then began yanking the drawers from the chest, tipping the contents onto the floor and went through her pockets, shaking each garment and finding nothing. She felt sick. 'It'll not go well for you, Rose, if I find more,' he said as he pulled the bed apart and swept curtains aside, scouring the place. She schooled her face to a blank, not letting her gaze wander to where her jacket hung, unnoticed, on the back of the chair.

Finding nothing he held the gold piece between his finger and thumb in front of her face. 'And you planned to survive on this? For how long?'

She stayed silent, terrified by him, but if she showed weakness now she was done for. 'Give it me back. It's all I have.' She put out her hand. 'And then I'll go.'

'Go by all means, but I'll keep this for your board and lodging, aye and to cover your passage here.' He slipped it into his pocket.

'But I never asked to come!'

'And take off those clothes I bought you, put your old ones back on and walk out of the door. Go on, do as I say! I'm done with you.'

'Then I would have nothing,' she said, standing rigid before him.

'Aye. Nothing. It's all you deserve.' Robbie Malloy was a

handsome man but now his face was dark and ugly. 'I mean it, Rose. Change your clothes.' She did as he demanded, not flinching but giving him back look for look, and stood before him in her old, dirty clothes. If he wanted her to plead, he would be disappointed but without any of the gold her situation was desperate.

Then he took her chin in his hand and she saw a spark in his eye. 'You're a cool one, like I said.' But the spark was not simply anger; he was enjoying himself, playing with her, teaching her a lesson, and she raised her chin again. All right then, she would play along. He was a gambler, after all, and she was almost certain that he was bluffing. 'But being a generous man I'll give you a choice,' he continued. 'You want to flit so fine, go, and if you take a single step towards the door that's it, done, out you go with only the clothes you're wearing, and you're on your own. Sink or swim, Flotsam Rose. Or you step towards me, and you stay, we play on. By my rules.' Still she made no movement, letting him wait. 'Which is it to be?'

By his rules, yes, but if this was a game, more mischief than menace, then she perhaps had played her poor hand well. Had she shown weakness he would have despised her. Escape might not be so easy after all but there would be other opportunities, better ones perhaps. The plan had been a poor one, not well thought through, and she could not survive on nothing.

The step she took, therefore, was away from the door.

Chapter 33

The ship from Dunedin joined others vying for position at the mouth of the Yarra, awaiting entry to the congested waterway and a berth amongst the forest of masts at Queen's Wharf. From the railings Fraser and Will watched the well-ordered chaos as ships were warped into position or turned below the falls while lighters darted to and fro, slipping between the larger vessels like pilot fish. The wharf side itself was crowded with wagons and drays delivering great bales of wool or collecting goods, and with passengers who were flooding in from all parts of the world. Carriages collecting well-dressed individuals cleaved their way through throngs of those disembarking on foot, and everywhere there were shouts and cries, the rattle of chain and hoist, and the grind and groan of timber and iron against unforgiving granite.

'It's absolutely extraordinary!' Fraser exclaimed.

Will was watching too, with despair. 'We'll never find her in all this.'

'*Courage, mon gars,*' Fraser replied, his eyes following the trajectory of a rope thrown by a seaman on the bow. It was caught on shore and hauled in, bringing with it the giant hawser which was then made fast.

They disembarked and Fraser went to give instruction regarding his trunk, which was to be held there until they had secured rooms, and they grabbed the last of the waiting cabs and enquired of the cabby about hotels. Fraser dismissed the first suggestions as outside their means and settled on a more modest establishment on the corner of Queen Street and Little Bourke Street, a few city blocks in from the docks. 'Good, central position,' Fraser said as they pulled up there, leaving Will while he returned with the cab to collect his trunk.

Will went across to the window of the hotel room and looked down at the Harp of Erin public house on the opposite corner with its ornate lantern above the door, and he scowled as he watched its clientele coming and going, chattering and laughing. Another nest of cursed Irishmen, he thought. There were probably hundreds of such establishments throughout the city and its expanding suburbs, and how could they check even a fraction of them? Wagons and carts, some empty, some loaded, passed each other on the rutted street below him, and a carter stood a moment to shout at a child who had dashed in front of him, causing the horse to shy. Another cart paused outside the window and the horse deposited a steaming pile of shit on the road before trotting on.

Will closed the window and turned to examine their own cheerless room. Only now did he realise how much of a challenge Melbourne was going to be.

But the city seemed to feed Fraser's energy and he dragged Will out that evening to explore the grid of streets that marked the main business district. There was construction everywhere and old single-storeyed weatherboard structures were vanishing fast to be replaced with solid two, three and even four-storey edifices built in stone, proclaiming a confidence that the city was destined to prosper. They stopped at a hotel for a meal and Fraser relentlessly interrogated two local businessmen who were sitting at the adjacent table. Where in the city were the clubs and upmarket hotels? The casinos? Was there a social area with theatres? Did the different nationalities favour different suburbs, the Italians, for example, did they settle in one place? Or the Irish . . . ? And where did the low life congregate?

The businessmen were only too ready to talk and so tables were pushed together and they continued the conversation over dinner. Will let Fraser do the talking and sat back as his companion demonstrated that he could blether endlessly on a wide range of subjects, frequently straying from the matter in hand when something sparked his curiosity. And then he would catch Will's eye and steer the subject back to what might, conceivably, be useful. Will grew more and more pessimistic as he listened. 'So are there many Irishmen here or are they all out on the goldfields?' he asked, cutting into one of Fraser's digressions.

The man wiped his mouth and nodded vigorously. 'Place is full of them. As the easy gold runs out some of the diggers are returning and setting themselves up, buying property, mostly bars and hotels in the case of the Irish!' Will and Fraser laughed, as was expected of them. 'But it's the same with the Italians and Germans – and the Chinese too, of course, they're everywhere. It's mostly English and Irish coming over here from Europe to settle and a few Yanks, although a lot of them are heading home now the show's almost over. The Irish, though, they're bedding in to stay.' Will glanced at Fraser: another Irishman with a pot of gold was not going to be easy to spot after all.

In the weeks that followed this concern grew into a certainty. Will saw Rose on every street corner, in every fair-haired woman who walked ahead of him on the crowded thoroughfares, and he would rush to overtake, only to fall back disappointed and apologetic, receiving strange looks and affronted frowns. He saw Robbie too in every dark-haired man who sat drinking, elbows on the bar, until a head turned his way dispelled hope. Fraser was doing what he could, spending considerable amounts of money joining clubs and gaining entry to upmarket casinos and private gambling establishments.

'So they just let you join because you speak as you do, and open your wallet?' Will asked, torn between a grudging acknowledgement that Fraser was laying out a lot of expense and a resentment that life could be so easy for some.

They were in a bar, sitting close to the window, a position they always chose, ever watchful. 'For the most part, yes,' and added, apologetically, 'but I've a small handle to my name which helps.'

'A handle?'

'Officially I'm the Honourable Fraser Urquhart. Pa was in the Lords.'

Will glared across the table at him. '*Honourable*?'

Fraser shrugged. 'Been useful on one or two occasions.'

'Jesus.' Will turned away.

Fraser said nothing for a moment, then: 'Look, Will. You say you don't want to advertise, and I understand why, but what if *I* advertise, as a photographer, I mean. I could set up a studio, appointments only so that I'm not tied to the place, and then advertise in the newspapers. A big advertisement, something eye catching.'

Will eyed him, sourly. 'And wait for Robbie to pay a morning call?'

'No, but if Rose saw it, and if she was in trouble, then she would know I was here. It's a long shot but worth a try.' Fraser too, Will sensed, was running low on ideas.

'She wished you were dead.'

'I know that, yes, I do know that, but if she was in need, or just plain curious or even if she came to tell me how much she hated me, we'd have flushed her out and I'd only need to say "Will's alive" and it would do the trick. What d'you say?'

Will looked aside as the thought that blackened his sleepless nights rose to confront him: what if Rose was not in need, what if she did not want to hear that Will was alive, what if she had found that Robbie was an acceptable, or even a preferred, replacement? Maybe having her husband arrive back from the dead would be the last thing she wanted.

Chapter 34

The rooms that Robbie procured for them in Fitzroy were on the second floor of a brick-built house close to the market and were shaded at the front by a large eucalyptus tree. One room overlooked the market and had an old cooking range and a table and chairs, and the second room, where they would sleep, looked onto an overgrown patch of land and down to the privy at the back, shadowed by two ancient she-oaks. There was a water pump on the street outside.

'It'll do for now,' he said, pushing open the door and ushering her in. He then stood and watched her as she took off her hat, placed it on the table, and looked around her. It was better than she had hoped for, but she would not tell Robbie that.

'I need to get stores,' she said.

'We'll do that now.'

He had not let her out of his sight once they had left Mordialloc; hardly a word had been exchanged since she had made the choice (that was not a choice) to stay with him. He had not struck her again but that night he had been ruthless in his demands, and while subjugating her might be a game for him now, he had frightened her and she recognised that there was a deeper violence within him. Quite what he would do if he suspected her pregnancy she did not dare contemplate.

That night, as he lay beside her, spent and silent, he turned his head on the pillow and looked at her. 'Where did that gold piece come from?'

'The old creek bed beside the cabin, same as the big one.'

He digested this. 'You found that one too?'

'Will did.'

'And it was Will who found the other, wasn't it? Not you.'

She shook her head. 'I found it.'

'But Will knew?'

'Yes.' What reason was there to lie about it now?

Robbie grunted. 'Cheating bastard. You know McGrath would have dangled him from his balls over the fire had he known? Just for starters.' Rose said nothing. 'And only those two pieces? That big nugget and the gold piece you had?'

'Yes.'

Silence again. Then he sighed: 'I hope you're not lying to me, Rose, because it was the lying that made me hit you. I've a temper on me but I don't like to hit a woman unless I have to—'

'You *didn't* have to. You hit me because you could.'

'—and I know that we can deal together better than this.' She kept quiet, waiting for an apology that she doubted would come; in Robbie's world, his behaviour was entirely justified. 'You must never lie to me again.' He paused, perhaps waiting for assurance but, not receiving it, went on. 'You know, Rose, you remind me of a fox cub my young brother once saved after we'd dug out the vixen and the rest of the brood. He took pity on it, see, saved it because it was small and helpless, and he kept it in a pen he'd made for it. He'd feed it, look after it, and eventually it'd let him touch it, but it watched him with the same expression that I see in your eyes.'

'Did it?'

'Then one day, despite all he did for it, it bit him.'

'I expect it was angry. Had he hit it, perhaps? Kept it against its will?'

He rolled over to reach for a bottle that he kept beside the bed, ignoring her sarcasm. 'It was safe, it was fed, and it was looked after. What more did it want? Seamus had saved its life, and it was a lovely creature with its red bush.' He took a swig. 'Me brothers and me warned him it wouldn't work out well, and once it'd bitten him it became a stand-off between them. Each watching the other, suspicious like.' He stopped again and lowered the bottle and Rose regarded him warily. What was he telling her?

'He still wanted to keep it, mind you,' he continued, 'but the trust had gone, and next time it bit him, it bit harder and Seamus kicked it across the yard and then stamped on its head.' He took another swig while she digested what was now a clear message. 'He cried for days because he'd loved the creature.'

She swallowed hard. 'Then he should have let it go.'

'Aye, but if it hadn't been for Seamus it'd have been dead already.'

Did he really believe himself to be her saviour? As Will had been? 'He could hardly expect it to be grateful, when its whole world had been destroyed.'

'Ah, but not by Seamus. That's the point. He was mad wild at what we'd done.'

'So he considered the cub was beholden to him, and that it was his to keep?'

His allegory began to unravel. 'Aye, a bit like Will Stewart thought you were his to keep, because he pulled you out of the sea, yet you never looked at him like that.'

Ah, so that was where this was leading. 'Will never made me feel—'

Robbie cut her off, warming to his theme. 'And I've done you no wrong, Rose. Not like that Urquhart with his dirty pictures! I saved you from McGrath, which would have been far worse than drowning, and I saved you from whoredom which those pictures show is all you're fit for.' He might as well have struck her again. 'And I brought you with me here where we can make our fortunes.'

'You brought me with you because of the gold,' she said, keeping her voice resolutely cool. 'You thought I might tell McGrath and then he'd come after you, and I saw you take some gold from their pot. I was there, remember.'

'True enough.'

'Or I might have told the authorities you had the nugget.'

'Aye. Good reasons, those. But I didn't bring you just because of them.' He propped his head up on his elbow and, in the darkness, he looked down at her. 'You're a lovely woman, Rose. And you'd a choice once before and you chose Will Stewart, and I never understood why. He was a dour soul, was Will, and not a better man than me, despite what you think. He was a thief and a cheat and there's no lower scum on earth than a man who cheats on his mates.' She kept her lips tight shut. 'Did he ever tell you that he killed a man in Scotland before he left, a boy actually, hardly a man.'

'That's not true.'

'It is! He told me himself, on the passage over. He stole money from his fellow crofters, and a lad caught him at it. They had a fight, a grown man against a boy! That's how Will got that scar, and then he killed the lad and ran off with the money.'

'He hit the boy, yes, but he didn't kill him.'

'Is that what he told you?' Robbie's finger started exploring her face, across her lips, over her chin and slowly down her neck. 'Well, I suppose he would.' It was all she could do not to smack his hand away.

'It's true. I know it is. Fraser knew the story too. '

'*Fraser?*' Abruptly the finger stopped. 'What's Urquhart got to do with it?'

'He knew Kinnloss House, and the estate. He took photographs there.'

Robbie sat up, the allegory of the fox cub forgotten. 'And so he knew Will then? Before? In Scotland?'

'No. But . . . but he knew of the robbery, about money being taken, but it was rent money, taken from the factor's house, not from the other tenants. And he knew about the houses burning . . .' She stopped, unwilling to show either man in a poor light though she was not sure why she felt compelled to protect Fraser's reputation, nor why Robbie was so interested.

'Go on. What houses?'

Briefly she outlined what Will and Fraser had told her and he listened like a child being told an adventure story, and he seemed delighted by the outcome. 'So between the two of them they had a community driven off the land, a business go bankrupt, folk put out of work, and they drove a man to blow his own brains out.' He whistled. 'Makes me look like a saint!' She turned her head away, understanding him better now. He was looking for flaws against which to measure himself and wished that she had not told him but he reverted abruptly to his previous theme. 'And yet, my thorny Rose, despite all that, you look at *me* the way that fox cub looked at my brother, wary and stand-offish, like I'm some sort of lesser man than Will Stewart. Which I'm not.'

'So you'll never kick me across the room, and stamp on my head?'

'As long as you don't bite. Or lie to me. And start loving me instead.'

Chapter 35

In the days that followed a pattern emerged. Robbie would sleep late, make whatever demands his mood fancied on waking, then rise, dress and go with Rose to buy provisions, before filling the water jars while she emptied the slops, never letting her out of his sight. Newer houses had water laid on but this house was built in the days when water had been delivered by cart and sewage was still dumped in a foul-smelling gutter behind the house. Improvements were underway but had been slow to reach Fitzroy.

Once Rose had prepared food and they had eaten, Robbie would go out and leave her, locking the door behind him and taking the key. The first time this happened she had been furious but he was adamant. 'I'm uneasy about you, sweetheart. It's not safe for you, out on the streets alone.'

'I grew up on the streets of Melbourne!'

'Aye, as a child. But you're a woman now.'

'And so better able to look after myself. I *won't* be locked in.'

'Just until we're more settled here.'

'You think I'd run off?'

'Would you?' She hesitated just a fraction too long, and his face turned grim. 'Right, I'm answered. But I'll be back in a while, and then I'll take you out, and we'll go dancing. But I've my work to go to now, and you can't come with me.' And he had gone.

Once, she thought, as she slumped onto the bed, vexed

beyond tears, she had asked another man to lock her in and take the key, and now, oh how the tables had turned! Will had seen her vulnerability and given her the choice: lock him out or allow him back in, giving her the time she needed. Robbie had made a prisoner of her, and given her nothing. Always, always this cruel mirroring, she thought, balling a handkerchief in her hand, as if fate was taunting her with what she once had, and had lost.

And this work of his, she thought with contempt, the gambling and the card play, how well it defined him! An opportunist and a cheat. He had got himself into a poker game in one of the nearby hotels and met the other players each afternoon, usually returning with a spring in his step and a smile on his lips, having invariably won enough to cover their expenses and more. 'Just steady,' he would say in answer to her question. 'Not too much to make them envious, but they're a simple bunch. And they never watched Ah Luan play poker.' He laughed and she remember the wily Chinese storeman in Kumara with whom Will had told her Robbie would play for hours, confirming her suspicion that it was more than luck behind his success. Occasionally he would come back with nothing. 'It was about time I put the smiles back on their faces,' and he would laugh then and swing her round and kiss her.

After that first day of confinement when she pounded in fury on the locked door and shouted out of the window at his retreating back, she made no further protest. When he left she tried pushing up the sash only to find that nails had been driven into the frame so that it would only open six or eight inches. The back window opened further, but only at the top. She gave up, defeated, and when he returned three or four hours later he was deaf to her indignation, asking instead why she had no food prepared. 'You're an idle slut, Rose, you've had all afternoon,' he said as he emptied the contents of his pockets onto the table. 'Good thing I can provide for us, eh?'

Protest was futile. But what to do for the best, she asked herself each day that followed. She took some of the gold pieces and hid them in various places through their rooms but left most of them in the hem of her skirt so if the opportunity to leave ever did arise she had them with her. Equally if he were to find those ones, then she would not be destitute. Soon her waist would start to thicken, and even now when he slid his hand over her belly she found herself tensing. Soon he would know . . . At the moment, however, she saw no way to escape him and her latest desperate idea was to gather up the gold, smash a window and call out for help. Surely someone would come? But who . . . ? And would she be able to convince anyone in authority that this was anything other than a domestic dispute in which Robbie's side of the story would be sought? They had rented the room as man and wife, and what protection had a wife in such circumstances? From the window she had seen all manner of people around the market and she ran the risk of falling into worse hands. No, she must wait and simply disappear as quietly as she could, and then find a place of safety. Will's child was all that mattered now . . .

And so she schemed endlessly as she did the daily chores and then she would sit, fretful and restless, and watch the birds amongst the branches of the eucalyptus tree. A magpie, she noticed, was nesting there.

One day, Robbie came home early, in high spirits and smelling of brandy. 'Right, get your hat and coat. I've a surprise for you. A day out, darlin.' We're off to Flemington; there's a filly running in the two o'clock and I've a pile of cash riding on her, ten to one. Quick now, or we'll not get a cab.' Hustling her out and down to the market, he pushed her into the first cab they saw, settling back against the worn leather with satisfaction. 'Time for a treat, eh? Have you been to a horse race before?' Not waiting for an answer, he proceeded to tell her about the races back in Ireland, about the Curragh where his horses always romped home in front and how his winnings had sustained him for weeks. 'Ah, the sight of those creatures straining forward, eyes wide, their breath misting and their hooves a-drumming. It's like a drug, once it gets a hold on you.'

And maybe, she thought with a rising sense of anticipation, he would become so intoxicated there would be an opportunity for her to flee. Quickly she reckoned up that she had five gold pieces still in her skirt hem and four behind the buttons of her jacket, which left just five in the room. There had been no chance to retrieve those as he chafed to be off, and she would have to let them go.

If she escaped, nine would have to be enough.

The thought must have animated her features as he smiled at her and lifted her chin with his forefinger. 'Now that's brought a sparkle in your eyes, girl! Better than the sour looks you're always wearing. I thought the bloom had gone off you.' He bent to give her a long, amorous kiss her and slid his hand beneath her skirts. She stiffened as his hand brushed her hemline, and he pushed her angrily away. 'Ah, for God's *sake*, Rose.'

It was when he was in high spirits like this, especially if he had been drinking, that his mood was at its most volatile, so she slipped her hand into his. 'It's too public, Robbie,' she murmured.

'Spoilsport,' he said, relaxing, and nibbled her ear instead.

The road to Flemington was packed with every conceivable form of transport as this race was a popular one and crowds had turned out to enjoy the September sunshine. Horse-drawn cabs vied with carriages, carts and wagons loaded with excited racegoers and many had come on foot, already tipsy and staggering before they reached the place. 'Drop us here,' Robbie told the cabby. 'We'll walk to the entrance and avoid the crush.'

It seemed to Rose that half of Melbourne had turned out and her spirits soared. Surely there would be a chance here . . . Robbie tucked her arm firmly under his and as they strolled through the holiday crowds like any other couple her brain rapidly assessed her options. Privies had been set up for the ladies and she could claim the need to visit them, but he would doubtless simply wait for her outside. She could try wresting her arm free when they were in a crowded space but would she be able to get away fast enough? Or she could—

'If it's going through your mind to run out on me while we're here,' he said, in a mild tone and with a smile, 'I'd not try it, darlin'. I see the way your eyes are flicking about, don't you think that I don't.' She looked aside, furious to have given herself away, and he chuckled. 'I'd have them catch you and say you're a simpleton, a hysteric, let out for a treat. Mad as a march hare with your stories.' He laughed as he took in her scowl. 'Aye, and dangerous too. Think on it, sweetheart. Who'd believe you're treated badly, you in your fine clothes?' She kept her gaze averted, sickened by the thought that he was probably right. And hers was hardly a believable story. He squeezed her fingers. 'You'll soon realise you're well off, you know, Rose. There's only one way you'd survive without me, and you'd not much fancy for that, had you?'

Ah, but there he was wrong.

Tucking her arm more firmly under his, he forced his way to the front of the enclosure, close to the finishing line, ignoring the protests from those already there, and placed her in front of him, his hands on her shoulders. 'I got us a good spot, didn't I?' he said, and set his hat at a rakish angle, indifferent to the glares.

There were two races before the one on which Robbie had placed his bet and she stood, oblivious to the wild excitement of those around her as the horses pounded past. All she was aware of was Robbie close behind her, a very present menace. He stooped and whispered in her ear. 'Next race, sweetheart. This is it. Watch for the bay filly, jockey in black and gold—' The crowd seemed to crane forward, every neck outstretched, eyes fixed on the distant starting line. 'And they're off!' someone cried. Robbie gripped her shoulders so tightly she winced, and he bellowed encouragement as the crowd pressed forward and in the crush she came close to fainting. The horses thundered towards them and the roar of the crowds was deafening as they tore past, a bay filly several lengths in front. The crowds went crazy as it reached the finish ahead of the others and Robbie threw his hat in the air, whooping with delight, and this would have been the moment to duck and slip away but she was hopelessly hemmed in by the throng. A moment later Robbie grabbed her hand and began to pull her back through the crowds. 'My bet was off course,' he shouted over his shoulder, 'so we'll go back and collect the winnings before the masses start to leave.'

'But can't we stay for the other races?'

'No. We've made enough. We'll go back and eat out somewhere.'

She gestured behind her as he pulled her along like a child. 'We could eat here, Robbie, there are booths set up, I saw them—'

'Aye. But I'm going in to collect my winnings and we'll make a night of it. I'm taking you dancing, girl, and we're going to dance until we're dizzy, and then we'll dance some more.' With his arm tight around her he pushed her ahead of him through the throng, against the flow of people making their way to collect their money or jostle for places before the next race. Never once did he release his grip.

And it was then, as she stood on the dusty road beside Robbie, her hand in his, that one shout from the crowd seemed to rise above the roar and reach her. It was not a cry of jubilation but one of desperate urgency and it sounded like her name, at least she thought it did. She turned her head in response but just then a cab pulled up, stopping between her and the crowd. Its restive horse caused a distraction and Robbie seized the moment to bundle her into it, and when she looked from the window it was into a sea of unknown faces.

'I'm a better provider than Will, eh?' Robbie said, leaning his head on the back of the seat and grinning at her. 'This'll keep us for a good long while. God bless the bay filly!' She looked away, saying nothing. '*And* I still have the nugget. Be madness to sell while the price of gold is rising.' He took her chin and turned her head back, lightly touching the mole on her cheek. 'You made a good decision, young Rose, back in Mordialloc. D'you not see that now?' She managed to smile back at him, just enough to satisfy.

They ate well that night, in an old hotel in Collingwood to which a dance hall had recently been added, and Rose decided she would be wise to put on a show of appreciation. Let him think she was coming round to him – perhaps then he would drop his guard. Somewhat to her surprise it appeared that he was well known here, and they were soon joined by a number of his cronies, pulling dance girls after them, and they sat at big round table in the centre of the room, close to the dance floor. Robbie presided over a convivial party that was very much to his taste, then he rose to dance with her and, having nodded permission, he allowed others to lead her out onto the floor. So she was his to bestow, was she? A creature indeed . . . Between dances he would take her hand and raise it to his lips in a gesture that did not convey homage, but quite the opposite, and she played along, sensing a deference to Robbie amongst the company; his word carried weight here, and she would do well not to shame or anger him. And the men who danced with her treated her with respect, aware as she was that Robbie's eyes followed her every move.

Otherwise it was no different than being back in Hokitika, she decided as another of his smart cronies swung her round, except in scale and ornament. The dancing might be a little less wild and there was no shortage of girls, and these were more flashy and artful, but the essential currencies were the same: money, drink, and sex. The men might be better dressed but they were just as clumsy and she winced as her toes were crushed by her partner's heavy feet. Emboldened by brandy he made the mistake of letting his hand stray from her waist and Robbie was out of his seat in an instant. The man backed away, raising his palms in apology as Robbie pulled her from him. 'That was a bad move,' he muttered, as the man vanished, 'as he'll soon discover.'

'Perhaps I liked it,' she said, to provoke, and gasped as he pinched her arm.

'Careful, Rose,' he muttered, and she recognised that he had reached the stage where he was looking for a fight. If someone offered him one perhaps that would be her chance, and perhaps she should provoke him further, but then again it was now dark outside and a woman alone in these parts was not safe.

'I'm tired, Robbie,' she said. 'And I want to go home.'

He glanced at her and his eyes lit up, interpreting her request in quite another way, and he rose, pulling her to her feet. His good humour was further restored in the cab on the way back to their rooms as he remembered his winnings and patted his pocket. 'I've almost enough,' he said.

'For what?'

He grinned. 'You've surely not forgotten?'

Forgotten what? And then she remembered his drunken boast back in Hokitika. Did he still dream of owning a hotel? 'But with the gold nugget you surely have enough already.'

'Aye, but that's our surety. I'll not be spending that unless I have to. There're better ways of going about things,' he said, and would say no more.

When they arrived back at the house he ushered her up the stairs in front of him. He lit just one lamp and placed it beside the bed, then sat to take off his boots, and she saw with a weary resignation that the night was not yet over. He came back to her and took the jacket off her, tossing it onto the chair, then one by one unfastened the buttons of her blouse. It was what he liked to do, peel the clothes slowly off her while his hands and eyes explored and she had learnt to let it happen. His arms encircled her waist and his lips locked onto hers as he unbuttoned the back of her skirt, letting it fall to her ankles so that she could step out of it. He kicked it away, moved towards the bed—

And stopped.

And lifted a stockinged foot.

It was the largest of the gold pieces that he had trodden on and it now lay on the wooden floorboards, glowing warmly up at them in the lamplight. One of her dancing partners must have torn the stitching on the hem but the treacherous gold had waited until now to escape, and condemn her.

He stared at it for a moment, then bent and picked it up. She went cold and a great wave of fear set her trembling but she managed to hold his look, saying nothing as his face grew dark and dangerous. Then he looked down at the skirt and swept it up with his toe, catching it and feeling along the hem. 'Sit down, Rose,' he said, quietly. 'No, not on the bed, over there, at the table.' He took a folding knife from his pocket, shot the blade out and she froze, terrified.

'You were warned, Rose' he said, but he placed the knife on the table in front of her. 'Unpick that hem.'

She had the wild idea of grabbing it and stabbing him but he was standing over her, tense and prepared for any such folly. And so, with a shaking hand, she cut the thread, and one by one the remaining pieces emerged. He looked down at them for a long time, then he picked up the jacket from where he had tossed it and she watched as he ran his fingers along the hems, then the cuffs and then up the opening at the front, and found what she had hidden there, behind the buttons. She felt sick. 'Jesus *Christ*, Rose.' He threw the jacket at her face, 'And this, damn you,' and then he proceeded to pull the rest of her clothes off hooks and out of drawers, carefully checking each one.

He found nothing more as there was nothing to find; the remaining nuggets were still safe, hidden around the room.

When he had finished his inspection, he came back and jerked her to her feet. Would this be where he stamped on her head? she thought fleetingly. But his fingers had flicked open the buckle of his leather belt and a thought had come to her in a flash, a desperate gamble. 'I'm pregnant,' she blurted, and his hand stayed. 'And I'm very tired.'

'Pregnant?'

'It can hardly be a surprise. I've been with you nearly three months and I've not bled.'

He looked dazed, and stared at her for what seemed an eternity, perhaps calculating for himself. 'And before then?'

'The day Will drowned. That was the last time.' Would the lie hold?

'So it's mine?'

'Of course.' She had to make him believe. 'Whose else?'

'Not Will's?'

'No.'

'Why didn't you tell me?'

'I wasn't sure, but I am now.'

He stood there swaying slightly in his stockinged feet, still half drunk, and his eyes rested on the little pile of gold that no longer offered her a means of escape. 'From the creek as well?' he asked, gesturing to it, and signalled that she should sit again. He refastened his belt and pulled out a chair opposite. 'All of it?'

'Yes.'

'Will, or you?'

'Will.'

He banged his hand hard on the table. '*Christ*! I'd make the man choke on it. *Why* would he cheat on us? Tell me that!'

'Because he loved me, and wanted to make a life with me.'

Robbie looked back at her, saying nothing, his expression unreadable. 'Is that so?' he said at last. 'One day you'll realise you've had a better life with me and you'll thank me then. And I *told* you, girl, that if I found you'd more gold, or if you'd lied to me, things would go badly for you. But . . .' he shook his head, as if still dazed '. . . but I can't belt a pregnant woman.' He paused. 'So I'll ask you one more time: do you have more gold?'

'No.'

'Be very, *very* sure, Rose.'

She had never seen him look like this. 'I'm sure.'

'When is the baby due?'

She rapidly added a month, a halfway point somewhere between truth and reality. 'April – mid-April. You'll have to wait until then to belt me.'

'You've not been sick,' he said, suspicious still.

'I wasn't last time.'

He frowned. 'Last time?'

'I was pregnant when I arrived in Hokitika.'

He nodded, as if remembering and then frowned again. 'And all that time you were with Will, he never knocked you up?'

'No.' And then she saw a way of reinforcing her fiction. 'Will was often tired, building the cabin and working the claim as well.'

He snorted. 'What are you telling me? So busy cheating on his mates he'd no energy left to fuck his wife?' He paused, and sat back, his eyes narrowing. 'I saw him, you know, the night he wed you, out on the street, skulking under the eaves instead of doing what he should on such a night. He'd been down on the shore by the looks of it; I thought it strange at the time.'

She looked away, remembering that night, and how on his return Will had been so sweetly tender, and so loving. Her eyes filled at the memory and she dropped them, hating that Robbie could befoul it. He misconstrued the movement and gave a laugh. 'So did you refuse him, or couldn't he perform? Did he bottle it, then, his big moment?' She kept her eyes down, remembering too that it had been that night she had seen the image of Will coming towards her, upside down on the ceiling of the room, and how astonished she had been. It had been that that had brought her to Fraser.

And begun her downfall.

Robbie laughed again, well pleased with his conclusions, and her thought of Fraser was somehow transmitted to him. 'So was *that* it? Was he not much of a man then, young Rose, a bit of a disappointment in the fucking business? And was that why you went and flaunted yourself in front of Mr Bosthoon Urquhart? Is that how it was? It begins to make sense.'

She looked back at him. Aye, it made the sort of sense that Robbie Malloy could understand, that reflected his view of the world, but Will had given her kindness and Fraser confidence, and the memory of that night now gave her strength.

Chapter 36

'Rose! Over here! *Rose*!' Will elbowed his way through the crowds. He lost her for a moment but caught sight of Robbie's hat and fixed his eyes on it as he cleaved through joyous race-goers surging towards the bookmakers. But he was going against this tide of humanity and he cursed as a big man stopped in front of him. 'Steady on, young man. Where's the fire?' Will pushed him aside, his heart racing. Lost them again! But no, there was Robbie, and he could just make out the top of Rose's head at his shoulder.

'*Rose*!'

It seemed that she half turned and he briefly saw her lovely profile, but she was abruptly blocked from his sight as a cab came between them. The horse was side-stepping, wide-eyed and fractious in the pressing throng, and people backed away, carrying Will with them. When the cab moved on Rose had vanished, Robbie too and Will looked around in despair until he realised that they must be inside the vehicle. He summoned another cab but as it came towards him, he felt the back of his collar seized and the big man he had just assaulted elbowed him away. 'My cab, I think,' he said and climbed aboard, nodding stonily at Will. The next cab was also taken, and the next and, as Will looked back up the road in desperation, he could no longer be certain which of them was carrying Rose.

Frantic now, he began running after the line of retreating vehicles but as they left the throng of people the cabbies applied their whips and the long file of cabs picked up speed. Will stumbled to a halt, gasping and cursing, a roaring stitch in his side. He bent over, his hands on his knees, and wept.

He made his own way home that day, not bothering to try and find Urquhart, and so it was not until later that evening when the photographer returned to their rooms that he was able to tell him.

'You're certain?' Urquhart asked, putting his hat and gloves on the table. 'Absolutely certain?'

'I got so close. I thought she'd heard me calling, she half turned as if she had. I saw her face.' He flung himself into a chair. He had never felt so wretched in all his life.

'But Will, this is tremendous news! It means that they *are* here, that Rose is well and if we've found them once we can find them again.'

'In another six months? A year?' He sank his head in his hands.

'Sooner than that, I promise.' Fraser pulled up a chair and sat down opposite. 'And we've learnt that Robbie's a betting man – we knew that, of course, but now we know that he attends the races, and that he takes Rose with him.' Will only half listened as Fraser stated the bloody obvious while the image of Rose, hand in hand with Robbie, following him through the crush of people twisted in his guts. She had been well dressed, as had Robbie, prosperous-looking, and Robbie had had a huge grin on his face. Had Will imagined it or had Rose been smiling too? He was not sure. He had spotted them only because they were going against the flow of people, and Rose's skirt, light in colour, had stood out. It had taken him a moment to believe the evidence of his own eyes, and in that moment all was lost, and the crowd had closed in. Oh God, their one chance! '. . . and so we must find out when the next race meeting is, and make sure that we are there!' Fraser concluded.

They had only gone to the races that day out of desperation, and Fraser had made for the more expensive enclosure, with the nobs, as he put it, in case Robbie might have decided to try and make a splash. He would not, he reasoned, have been accepted as member, so there was no reason to look for him in the members' space. Will, in the cheap enclosure, had watched him conversing easily with the other racegoers, conscious of the resentment that Fraser often roused in him, imagining him to be as fascinated by the idea of a colonial race meeting as by looking for Rose.

'We're a lot further on, Will, really we are,' Fraser said, reaching a hand towards him.

But in the days and weeks that followed even Fraser's optimism seemed to wane. They attended every race meeting, every dog fight, covert or otherwise, every rat-baiting den and low-life haunt but had never a glimpse of Robbie. Will visited every market, every arcade, every place that a rich woman might go and saw Rose a hundred times, but it was never her, never that sweet fey smile that greeted him but puzzlement, or abuse from affronted escorts. Once, he was certain that he saw her in Fitzroy market, accompanied by another woman but she disappeared almost straight away. It was only a fleeting glimpse and he had lost sight of them under the shadow of an eucalyptus tree.

He had stopped and leant disconsolately against its trunk, staring into the market place. Was he to spend his entire life searching for a woman who now held the hand of another man, and smiled at him? He would have to find work soon, earn some money. Fraser's mind, he knew, was more and more engaged on his return to Scotland; his mother, he had said in passing, was on the decline.

At some point, he would have to give up.

Chapter 37

'This is Mrs O'Shea, Rose – Brigid O'Shea.' It was a few days after the races that Robbie ushered the woman in. 'And she'll be staying with you while I'm out. She knows all about babies.'

The woman chuckled. 'Lost track of how many I've birthed.'

Rose stared at her, then looked across at Robbie but was met by an implacable look in return. He had been tight-lipped and silent since the discovery of Will's gold but they had arrived at a sort of truce, agreeing that if she swore she had no more gold and would not run off, he might consider no longer locking her in. But this was worse. She took an instant dislike to the woman with her large bosom and jowly chin, small eyes disappearing in a fleshy face, forty dressed as twenty. 'You'll have a long wait here. Months in fact,' said Rose.

'Time to get to know each other,' Robbie replied, 'and Brigid can escort you when you go out. I'm too busy these days.'

'And that'll be just lovely.' The woman looked around the room where Rose spent her days. 'Good for the spirits to get out.' Rose's first thought was that her last remaining gold pieces now had a new threat, especially the one at the bottom of the flour jar. Another was hidden in the floorboards, under the hearth rug, where she had worked loose a knot in the timber and pushed it into the hole it had left, disguising the gold with dirt and boot blacking. That should be safe, as were the two pieces she had wedged in between bricks above the window sill where again she had made holes in the pointing, mixing dust with flour and fat to mask them. The other one she kept on her person while Robbie was out, in case an opportunity to leave arose quickly, hiding it amongst the vegetables when he was due back.

'I don't require an escort,' she said, looking back at Robbie who had sat down, pushed the chair back and crossed one leg over the other, clearly prepared for an argument.

'You'll be glad of help as you get bigger,' he said.

'Then we will call on Mrs O'Shea's services nearer the time.'

Rose saw Brigid O'Shea's little eyes darting from one to the other, reading the situation, and recognising who was calling the shots. 'It won't be long before you'll wonder how you'd managed without me,' she said and reached into her bag to pull out an apron. 'And the sooner we get started here, the better, I'm thinking. You've let things slip, my dear.'

'Robbie—' Rose appealed to him but he had got to his feet and was taking money from his pocket. 'This is not what we agreed!'

'Close enough,' he said. 'Here's money to buy what you need, Brigid. Keep an account and I'll give you more when you need it. I'll have no time to take Rose to the market, or the butcher or the baker or all those places as I'm concluding a bit of business these next few weeks. I'll not let Rose into the secret yet,' he glanced over at Brigid O'Shea and she smiled back, clearly complicit, 'but she'll be delighted. Right, I'm away. Enjoy yourselves, ladies.' Rose stared at the shillings on the table with a deep sense of bitterness; he had never left her so much as a penny. And now she had not only a gaol but a gaoler.

When he was gone she went straight over to the flour jar and tipped out the flour, retrieving the gold piece while her back was to the woman. A small victory. 'You can make bannock, I assume?' she said, without turning.

'Of course, my love,' Mrs O'Shea said, moving Rose aside and carefully spooning the flour back into the jar. 'Mr Malloy told me you were inclined to be skittish, but don't you try your tricks on me.'

Rose quickly grew to loathe Brigid O'Shea, a fact that the woman must have recognised and cared nothing for; she was Robbie's creature and he must be paying her well. Every servility was a calculated insult and it was a torment having to share the rooms with such a woman. Quite apart from her continuing watchfulness, she talked incessantly, regaling Rose with stories of her vast family back home in County Kerry and how, one by one, they were coming out here to join her. 'You told me already,' Rose said, and the woman had chuckled.

'There's nothing like family stories, my love, as you'll find out soon enough when you've some of your own. Is Mr Malloy planning a large family?' She had worked in Ballarat, she told Rose, in one of the hotels there and it took no imagination for Rose to guess what sort of work it had been. The only conversation that interested Rose was what she let slip about Robbie's life beyond their rooms. 'You're lucky, Mrs Malloy, having such a man, and him so devoted. He's very well respected round here.'

'I'm not Mrs Malloy.'

The woman tutted at her. 'Well you will be soon enough, I'm sure, dear, and I can hardly call you Mrs Stewart, can I! It was a tragedy, losing your husband, but Robbie Malloy is a fine, handsome man, and once the child's born you'll stop your pining. He tells me you get very low, my love, and have the oddest fancies, a danger to yourself and the child. Would you prefer I call you Rose?' She did not wish to be called anything but it was insufferable to be called Mrs Malloy, and so she agreed on Rose, while stubbornly refusing to call her anything but Mrs O'Shea in return, a fact which caused her adversary amusement.

'We get on famously,' the woman told Robbie, when he returned after the first day. 'She's asked me to call her Rose, which is what I call friendly.'

'I loathe her,' Rose told him when the door closed behind her. 'And I hate you for inflicting her on me.'

'Is it better than a beating?' he asked indifferently, looking down at the newspaper he had brought back with him.

'Worse.'

He laughed and tossed it aside. 'Well, I shan't beat you, Rose, but Brigid O'Shea stays.'

'I'd rather go back to how we were before, you locking me in.'

He shook his head. 'Now I know there's a baby growing in you, you need someone with you while I've business to see to.'

She looked back at him in despair as he took a bottle from the shelf and drank, and asked the question that continued to puzzle her. 'Why will you not just let me go, Robbie? I can see why you took me from Kumara, I might have told—'

He cut her off. 'If I'd let you go off on your own that day,' he said, wiping a hand across his mouth, 'you'd have been robbed, one way or another, and destitute. And if it had been McGrath who found the gold on you, you'd be dead, and glad that you were. I saved you that day, sweetheart, same as Will had done.'

So he was back on that theme. 'But once we'd left, and you had taken the gold from me, why not just let me go? I'd have gone from Mordialloc if you had let me have some money, and given you no further trouble.'

He took another swig, and his eyes glinted at her over the

rim of the bottle. 'I was generous to you there, and you *chose* to stay, remember, you could have gone if you'd wanted to.'

'How could I—'

'And you should be more careful, young Rose, when you're aiming to deceive. That nugget was not in the place where I'd put it, though lighting the fire was a nice touch.' He laughed at her expression. 'Oh, darlin', there's guilt for you!'

She regrouped quickly. 'All right. But after that. Why keep me here?'

'It's obvious, isn't it, girl? You're carrying my child.'

There was no getting a straight answer from him, and yet still she persisted. 'Before then – before we knew? There are plenty of girls who'd have been happy to take up with you, Robbie Malloy, and give you more than I do. Why didn't you throw me out after Mordialloc?'

He stretched and yawned. 'Oh, I thought about it, believe me, I thought about it a lot. And I almost did when I found all that gold sewn into your clothes, and realised you'd lied to me again.' His face darkened and grew ugly. 'And don't you imagine for a minute that there aren't other girls now. I said I was a generous man, but I never said I was a faithful one.' He watched for her reaction and his eyes narrowed when there was none, and he took up the bottle again. 'And you don't care a damn, do you? If I thought I could make you jealous, I'd have made more of it, but I knew that you'd not care.'

'So why, Robbie? It's madness!'

He looked back at her and spoke slowly, in a different tone. 'Aye, it is a sort of madness.' And for a moment she glimpsed something else behind the mockery, some bafflement in his mind. 'You're a thorn that keeps pricking at me and I couldn't let you go then, see, and now I won't.' He stared down at the table for a moment, and then up again, his expression subtly changed. 'I saw what there was between you and Will, and I wanted some of it.' He paused, his eyes exploring her face. 'I wanted you from that first day when I carried you to Moll's, all wet and broken, and that wanting kept growing in me. A pearl you were, and you wouldn't have me.' He paused again, and frowned, as if reliving the rejection. 'After Will drowned, I decided that one day you would look at me the way you looked at him. Your whole face would light up, and I'd see the same look from him, reflected back.' He shook his head and gave a little laugh, as if amused by his own folly. 'And when I saw those pictures of you, all but naked, I was confused. Couldn't make sense of it at all. You could look at Will as you did, and yet you'd strip for another man!'

He stopped as if waiting for her to explain, and she looked aside, remembering the seductive softness of the silk and Fraser's mesmeric voice, that other world she had glimpsed, and then returned his look.

'I was angry after that,' he continued when she said nothing. 'Angry that you'd go to that man's room and behave like just another brazen whore – doing it for the money, I decided – and then I wondered if maybe Will knew, he was friendly enough with Urquhart, and I thought maybe the three of you had something going on. But it wasn't that, was it?' He stopped again and looked at her, as if wrestling with something quite unaccountable, something he simply could not fathom. 'There was a look on your face on those photographs and something in the way you held yourself, so rare a thing . . .' He tailed off, then laughed.

'And now you're in my bed, girl, and that's where you'll stay. One day soon you'll see that I'm no worse than any other man and a deal better than most. And when you realise that and accept the cards that fate has dealt you, you'll start loving me. I'm a patient man and I'll wait, but for now, I don't trust you not to run off with my child, seeking something better that you'll not find in this world or the next. So Brigid stays, and you can learn to love her too.'

Chapter 38

After that things settled into a routine of sorts and Rose, resigned and weary, allowed it to be so. In the days that followed she often thought about what Robbie had said, and considered how many ways there were for men and women to misunderstand each other. Fraser had felt no desire for her as a woman being, as he put it, not that sort of man; his interest had lain only in his art. And Will . . . She could not think of Will without the almost unbearable pain of loss, and shame. In the beginning his instinct had been to protect, hers to be protected, but from there had sprung the beginnings a love that seemed as evenly matched as it was profound.

And then there was Robbie. There was a new boldness to him these days, he always dressed well and held himself with the cool assurance of a man who was prospering. From what Mrs O'Shea said he was admired and well regarded in whatever shady circles he moved, but would he ever move beyond envy, lust and possession when it came to his dealings with her?

His next move took her completely by surprise. She and Brigid O'Shea returned from the market one day and the woman went into the bedroom, leaving Rose to sit beside the window and listen to the discordant carolling of the magpies in the eucalyptus tree. The male bird guarded the nest fiercely, and had become increasingly aggressive, swooping down on anyone who approached. It reminded her of Robbie, with its aggression and its boldness – and its conceit – and, as the weeks had passed, she grew increasingly fearful of what might become of the cuckoo child in his nest.

Then Robbie himself appeared unexpectedly on the path. The bird came screeching down to make a strike, and she smiled a little at Robbie's flailing arms. A moment later, though, he was at the door with a grin on his face, and Mrs O'Shea emerged from the bedroom. 'All set?' he asked, addressing the question to her, not to Rose.

'All set, Mr Malloy. I've laid out the dress.'

'Right. Rose, go and change your clothes, quick as you can.'

'I'll help her,' said Mrs O'Shea, holding open the door.

Rose stayed where she was. 'Why am I changing?'

'Because we're going out and you need to look your finest. I've two surprises for you. Quick, now!'

She went through to the bedroom but stopped at the door. A cream-coloured dress with lacy flounces had been laid out on the bed, new shoes beside it. 'It's lovely, don't you think?' Mrs O'Shea whispered beside her. 'I helped him choose.' The garment was clearly not new but it had once been very fine with a deeply plunging neckline and a nipped-in waist. 'And I let it out a bit so you'll be comfortable.'

'It's a wedding dress.'

Brigid gave an arch smile. 'I'm not saying a word.'

Rose turned and went back into the other room where Robbie was busy polishing his shoes on a sheet of old newspaper. 'It's a wedding dress,' she repeated, hardly able to credit what he had in mind.

'And that's the first surprise,' he said, looking across at her and grinning.

'I won't marry you.'

He continued his polishing, a little frown between his brows.

'I'll not have my child born a bastard, and if we wait any longer, you'll be too big to fit in any dress, so off you go.'

'I won't marry you.'

He looked up, the brush suspended. 'You will.'

'I'm married to Will.'

'Will's dead.'

'His body was never found. There's nothing official about his death. I can't. And I won't.'

He tossed aside the brush. 'Either you get yourself dressed or me and Brigid will dress you between us. I've arranged with a priest and explained the circumstances, and he agreed that no child should be brought into the world a bastard and he'll do the business for us without all the formalities.'

'You mean he's not a priest at all.' Was there no end to the man's tricks?

'He was before he left Ireland, and he's just waiting now for a parish to come free.'

'So he's a fraud and the wedding's a fraud, and the marriage will be a fraud.'

He came over, lifted her chin, and put his face close to hers. 'So why be stubborn?'

'Because you will forge some document which says that we are legally wed and then I'll be tied to you forever.' Her voice ended on a wail.

Tight-lipped he said nothing, confirming for her that that was exactly what he had in mind. Then: 'In God's eyes we'll be married and that's all that matters and my child will be true-born. Now, will you dress yourself or will we do it for you?' Mrs O'Shea was waiting in the doorway, still smiling. And as Rose looked back at Robbie she found there was space in her mind to wonder just a little that he had planned all this, this charade of a wedding, believing it would bring her close.

But she gave no responses an hour later as she stood beside him in the half-built church on a street corner at the edge of Collingwood. The builders had presumably been paid to be elsewhere for an hour but their tools were lying around and there was haze of stone dust hanging in the air. The ceremony was performed before a table covered with a plain cloth. A tarnished cross, a fallen priest and an unfinished church, she thought as she stood there, but good enough to satisfy the man who made his money cheating at cards.

The dubious cleric was fawning but obviously nervous, and gabbled through the service, looking across at Robbie when Rose failed to respond and, at a nod from him, moved quickly on to declare them man and wife. She felt defeated, numb as Robbie kissed her, and Mrs O'Shea, determined to maintain the pretence, dabbed an eye before signing as a witness. Another man who had kept to the shadows also signed and left and, with the matter completed, the faux priest gave them a swift blessing and removed the trappings of priesthood. 'With God's help your wife will soon be cured of her affliction,' he said.

Startled, she thought he must mean the child, but then realised this was part of the charade. 'What affliction is this, Robbie?' she asked, watching the man as he hurried away.

'Pig-headedness,' he replied.

'I'm not your wife,' she said, as the cab pulled away. 'That pantomime did not make me so.' And what if she told him that the child would be no bastard anyway, conceived as it had been in loving wedlock?

'Not another word, Rose,' he said, looking out of the cab window, his face pugnacious, and she saw that his mood had turned dangerous, and remained silent.

He did not take her home as she had expected but they drove on and stopped instead outside the place in Collingwood he had taken her to after the races; Mrs O'Shea, who had been following in another cab, arrived a moment later. The second of Robbie's surprises? He handed Rose down and then stood looking up at the frontage where the name of the hotel was being sanded away, and barked at a workman up a ladder. 'Why's that not finished?' he demanded.

What was happening here? She glanced at Mrs O'Shea for a clue but she simply smirked in response.

'The sign's done, Mr Malloy, and all ready to go up. Just ten minutes, sir. We're just doing the fixings.' He quailed under Robbie's glare.

Robbie took her inside where there were signs of hasty preparations for celebrations of some sort. Bunting had been slung from both ends of the bar and the big long mirror behind it, which had been broken and dusty when they were here last time, had been replaced. An assortment of people were sitting at the tables and a cheer went up as they entered, quickly checked at the sight of Robbie's scowl. Behind the bar the barman was polishing glasses and a piano was being pushed into place.

So he had planned a party, had he? Yet she sensed his anger quickening. 'I said four o'clock, damn you,' he hissed at the man.

'We're all set, Mr Malloy,' the man replied, moving down the bar. 'And there's champagne cooling, like you asked for, on ice from the ice house, almost the last of it. Shall I pour it out?' Without waiting for an answer, he filled two glasses and handed one to Robbie. Rose saw that more and more people were arriving and resigned herself to a long evening. Robbie looked around, appeared satisfied, and raised his glass. The room fell silent.

'My *wife* and I bid you a warm welcome,' he said, and this time the cheer was more confident, and sustained. Rose sat there, feeling like a doll in her flouncy gown, a puppet in some bizarre show where Robbie was puppetmaster. The workman who had been up a ladder appeared at the door and gave a signal, which Robbie acknowledged with a nod. 'Today is not only our wedding day but a private gathering to celebrate the re-opening of this establishment. Grand opening to follow.' He looked down at Rose, and gave her a wry look. 'And I'm happy to say that the stunned look on my wife's face is not at the prospect of marriage to me, but because she knew nothing of this, nothing at all.' A ripple of obedient laughter went through the guests. 'But you see, I promised my lovely Rose, soon after we first met, that one day I'd buy her a hotel and that we'd grow rich and fat together. We've still to grow rich, but . . .' he leant down and put a proprietorial hand on Rose's belly '. . . I can assure you, friends, that my wife is not growing *fat*. I'm a much-blessed man.' He bent again and kissed her long and hard, nipping her lip with his teeth. Again there was a cheer and noisy clapping and Rose gripped the table beside her, sure that she would faint. 'And now, darlin' . . .' He pulled her to her feet, took out a handkerchief and blindfolded her, then turned her around and steered her back outdoors. She heard the assembled company following.

Once outside he put his hands on her shoulders and spun her round. 'Ready?' he asked and again a cheer rose. His fingers untied the knot behind her head and then, with a flourish, he whipped the handkerchief away and tilted her head.

And, where just minutes ago, another name had been scrubbed away, a plank had been raised on which lettering had been hastily painted, announcing that the Rock of Cashel had been renamed The Flotsam Rose.

Chapter 39

Will heard Fraser pounding up the stairs and a moment later he flung open the door. 'Got them!' he cried. 'Will! We've found them!' He thrust a newspaper at him. 'Read!'

Will grabbed it and read:

Grand Opening! The ever-popular ROCK OF CASHEL is to re-open on Saturday November the 4th as THE FLOTSAM ROSE, under the management of Mr and Mrs Malloy. Drinks are half price until eight o'clock and customers are invited to come and raise a glass to help us celebrate.

Will stared at it. '*Mrs* Malloy!'

'He can call her what he likes.'

And he used to call her Flotsam Rose. But he had called her other things too and Will had understood too late why he had looked at her in that way he did, covetous and resentful, dangerous and determined, recognising that she was out of bounds. Will's prize, Will's girl, Will's wife.

Not Mrs Malloy.

A pulse began pounding in his temple. 'That's this Saturday.' He was overwhelmed suddenly, swamped by the possibility that he had, after all, found her too late. 'But she's married him,' he said.

'Only because she thinks you're dead, you fool! Rose is a survivor, and what choice do women have, for God's sake? But she's *your* wife so she can't be his, and when she knows that you're not dead, she'll come back to you. I know she will. She loves you.'

But had she ever said as much?

Fraser pulled up a chair opposite him and sat. 'I've already sent a man out there to look the place over, ask around a bit. We must be properly prepared this time because however pleased Rose might be to see you, Robbie won't be. He's presumably sold that lump of gold to buy the place and if you arrive, out of the blue—'

Will got to his feet. 'He's welcome to the gold. I only want Rose. Nothing more.'

Fraser moved quickly and blocked his way to the door. 'Wait. Wait until my man gets back. Rush your fences now and you'll regret it. Robbie has no idea that we're on his trail so we can pause and be canny, think things through, and then act.'

Will made to push past. 'I'm going up there now. I need to talk to her.'

'No! *Wait*, I tell you.' It was all Fraser could do to persuade Will to stay put until, a little while later, a knock came at the door. 'This'll be Richmond now.'

Fraser had employed two investigators when they had first arrived and they had been going through the motions of searching, in a population of almost a quarter of a million, with only a name, a description and the wedding photograph to go on. But now, with a definite lead to follow, Charlie Richmond had produced results and he strode into the room, puffed out with self-importance.

Fraser offered him a drink. 'Seems the Rock of Cashel had something of a reputation, if you take my meaning,' the man said, pulling out a chair, 'and it was easy to find. There's work going on there ready for the grand opening on Saturday. They'd a bit of a do last week, I was told, for the wedding. Private event. And then it was closed up again.'

Will scowled at him. 'Whose wedding?'

'Malloy's.'

He sat back but Fraser waved the matter aside. 'Did you see the woman?'

'His wife?'

'She's not his wife, but never mind. Did you see her?'

'No, I just spoke to the man fixing the sign.'

'And what did he say? The man?'

He had told Richmond that Robbie bought the place a month ago from some low life who was now in gaol, serving time, and that he had got it cheap. 'Seems to command respect in the area, does Malloy, got one or two rackets going on but he said he'd not want to do business with the mob Malloy bought it from, involved in all sorts, not much of it legal.'

Fraser and Will exchanged glances. That sounded like Robbie.

'But nothing about his wife— the woman?' Fraser corrected himself quickly.

'She was there at the do, of course, it was her wedding.' Will made an angry sound, and the man paused.

'Go on,' said Fraser.

'A slip of a thing, the fellow said, not the brassy type. Expecting too, he said, and Malloy seemed mighty proud of her.'

'*Expecting*—' It was like a punch in the gut.

'Pregnant,' the man explained.

Will sat back, reeling as he absorbed this new blow. She was pregnant, she would bear Robbie a child, not him. Oh God, better that Chen Lee had left him in the Taramakau.

'Did you find out where they lived?' Fraser asked quickly, glancing at Will.

'The man didn't know but it'll be easy enough to find out, I'll just follow him home one night.'

Fraser reached into his pocket and brought out a half-sovereign. 'Do that, and there's the other half when you return with an address. Don't be seen, don't give him any cause at all to be uneasy. Just find an address and report back.'

'I know my job, mister,' Richmond said, pocketing the money. 'Malloy doesn't go up there every day, the man said, or if he does, he just turns up, shouts and swears and leaves again. But I'm a patient man.' He left.

Will rose and went to stand by the window looking out as the clientele of the Harp of Erin came and went on the other side of the road. So was that it, the final nail? For what woman would leave a man when she was carrying his child? Not Rose, he imagined. And Robbie, for all his faults, would surely fight for what he now considered to be his. At best Will would be forcing her to choose, at worst she would simply tell him to go. He became aware of Fraser seated behind him, watching him. 'I should leave her be,' he said at last.

'*No*! Not after all this searching.'

'She thinks I'm dead and so she's married Robbie and they're expecting a child and they've a business to run and a life – and then I appear and it all falls apart for her.'

Fraser rocked back on his chair, tapping his teeth with a pen left lying there. 'I never saw you as a quitter, Will Stewart.'

He continued to stare out of the window. 'I'm thinking of what she would want.'

'And have you asked her what that is, or are you deciding for her?'

'I've nothing to offer her.'

'You'd nothing before.' Except a future, a life. 'I imagine she can make up her own mind; Rose is tougher than you think.' Will said nothing. 'Would you like me to go and talk to her?'

'No.'

'So you'll go yourself, once Richmond gives us an address?' And when Will remained silent, he added: 'Why ever wouldn't you?'

'Because she's carrying his child.'

'Oh Lord, how primitive.' Fraser ran his fingers though his hair. 'For all you know the child could be yours, or at least I presume that's the case.'

Will stiffened. 'What do you mean?'

'Do the sums, dolt. How long have we been chasing them?

Will calculated back. They had gone into the Taramakau, locked in combat, sometime in July and it was now almost November. 'Nearly five months.'

'I'm not saying it *is* yours,' Fraser raised a hand, back-pedalling hastily at the spark that had lit in Will's eye. 'And she might not even be certain herself. On the other hand, we can assume that Robbie didn't wait until after the ceremony before consummating . . .' he broke off.

Another thought struck Will. 'But Robbie would no more tolerate her carrying my child than I can bear the thought of her carrying his, so he must *believe* it to be his.'

Fraser looked back at him and shook his head. 'They say that male lions kill their rival's offspring when they take over a pride. Have we evolved no further than that? Ask Rose what she wants, for God's sake, man, and let her decide.'

It was three days before Richmond returned with an address and by then Will was in torment. He never told Fraser that he had gone up to The Flotsam Rose on each of those days and waited in the shadows hoping for a glimpse of either Rose or Robbie but, other than a few desultory workmen, he had seen no one. One time he had spotted Richmond and had withdrawn before being seen.

But now it appeared that Richmond had produced results. Fraser handed over the second half-sovereign and the man gave him a slip of paper in return. 'But I give you a warning, gentlemen. Your man Malloy's got himself into deep waters, playing with the sharks, if you take my meaning. From what I've learnt, things haven't quite gone to plan.'

Chapter 40

'Bring him into the bedroom, in here.' Rose was shaking, horrified by the sight of him. 'Mrs O'Shea, get water and bring it through.'

The two young men half carried, half dragged Robbie through the door. He was barely conscious, his face bruised and bloodied, and he groaned as they laid him down. One eye was closed and the surrounding skin was turning livid. He had a cut on his cheek and his upper lip was caked in dried blood; his knuckles too were bloodied, the skin broken.

'Whatever happened?' she asked, and saw them exchange furtive glances. She recognised them from her wedding party at The Flotsam Rose, Irish lads, both of them. And now they were deciding how much to tell her.

'There was a card game, see,' said the younger one, a red-haired freckled lad with sharp features and eyes that avoided hers. 'And things got nasty.'

'You mean he cheated,' Rose said, taking the bowl of water from Mrs O'Shea. It was a statement, not a question and the lads exchanged another glance.

'That's what they said, but we don't think he would.'

'No?'

The loyal foot soldiers became expansive. 'They must have planted a marked card on him because he'd been on such a winning streak and they wanted some of it back. But Ah Toon said he'd cheated and some of his men took him out to the back—'

Mrs O'Shea stiffened behind her. 'Ah Toon?' she said. 'He was playing cards with Ah Toon?'

The lads nodded vigorously. 'Who is Ah Toon?' asked Rose, and they all three turned to her in astonishment.

'One of the celestials, the Chinese – a big man, into all sorts,' the dark-haired lad said.

'And not a man to cross.' Mrs O'Shea was taking off her apron. 'I'll be going now, Rose. He'll soon mend, if I'm not mistaken. I've seen worse.' She left and the two young men started edging towards the door.

'But you managed to fight them off? Just you two, and Mr Malloy?' she asked, delaying them. They appeared unharmed and were now clearly anxious to leave.

'We couldn't, Mrs Malloy, there were too many of them.'

'So we went for the constables.'

'They'd have killed him otherwise.' They nodded vigorously again, reinforcing each other's story. 'Three constables came and the celestials scattered.'

'So we dived in there and got him away.'

'There might have been questions asked, see,' the dark-haired one explained.

'About him being at the place . . .'

'Where he was playing cards . . .'

She sensed their exasperation at her stupidity and by this time they had reached the door. 'He'll be all right now, though, I'm sure,' the freckled lad said, reaching for the door handle.

'We brought him home in a cab,' the other added, hopefully.

Rose quickly went through Robbie's pockets but they were empty. 'I've no money,' she said. 'But I'll make sure he pays you.' They shrugged and backed out of the room and Rose returned to Robbie.

What a sight he was – worse than any man she had seen

after fights at Moll's. Carefully she bathed his face, cleaning away dried blood from his mouth, dabbing gently around his battered eye. He had passed out but he stirred at her touch and opened the other eye and looked at her. He tried to speak but she shook her head at him. 'Just lie there. Don't speak. I'll get some water.' She came back with a mug and slipped a hand behind his head to raise it so that he could drink. He took a few sips and closed his eyes again. She continued her ministrations, cleaning away the blood and squeezing out the cloth. She unbuttoned his shirt and saw dreadful bruising on his chest and stomach from where they must have kicked him on the ground, and for the first time she felt afraid. Perhaps the lads had been right and, given the chance, they would have killed him.

And then she saw that he was watching her through eyes that were mere slits in bruised flesh and he tried to speak again. She lowered her ear to his lips. 'Now's your chance,' he said, his voice hoarse but she saw that his eyes were glinting. 'Make a run for it.' She straightened and looked down at him. The ghost of a smile hovered on his lips, but he was right. She could take her gold from its hiding places and go and he could do nothing to prevent her.

She returned to the kitchen and came back with a knife. His eyes widened at the sight of it, and then followed her to the window where she pushed up the sash as far as it would go and scraped away the fat and dust that covered two of the gold pieces. She came back to the bed and held them up so that he could see them. Leaving the door ajar, she then pulled back the hearth rug and dug the nugget out of the knot hole in the floorboard and brought that to show him, too.

Three.

Then she went back over to the bed and reached into her

blouse and placed one of the remaining two with the others, and showed them to him again.

Four.

Something made her keep the fifth piece to herself.

His eyes followed her every move and as he looked at the gold in the palm of her hand she was alarmed to see his body convulsing. He moaned a little and put a hand to his stomach as if in pain but continued to shake. And then he beckoned her close so that she could hear him. 'Cheat,' he whispered, and she saw then that he was laughing.

She straightened. 'I'm showing you this, Robbie Malloy, so that you know that I *can* go, and that I *can* leave you and that I would have been provided for by the rest of Will's gold. You've tried to master me all these weeks but I stay now because I choose to stay. And I choose to stay because I cannot leave you in this state even though you don't deserve that I should stay, and I think it's trouble of your own making.' Her breath came in short gasps but her voice was steady. 'You've cheated me often enough, but for now I *choose* to stay. And when Mrs O'Shea arrives tomorrow you tell her she is no longer wanted here.'

He nodded and then beckoned her down to him again. 'Kiss me,' he said. And briefly, not knowing why she did, she touched his lips with hers.

———

It was not necessary to dismiss Mrs O'Shea because she never appeared again. Either the woman assumed that Robbie would not be leaving the house or she considered her association with him too great a risk, which seemed more likely. The shock on her face when Ah Toon's name was mentioned had told its own story.

So Rose, for the first time in months, was free to do as she wished.

She mixed a little oatmeal and put it on the range while she weighed up what that ought to be. This sudden reversal had sent her certainties into disarray and it was hard to think straight. Last night she had made a bed for herself in front of the fire but had barely slept; the hard floor had offered little comfort, but it was not only that which kept her awake. Why, she asked herself, had she not seized the chance when she had it, as even Robbie had expected her to? Why had she not simply taken the gold and gone?

She let the oatmeal cool and then took it through to him. He was awake, still laying on his back but had pulled himself up onto the pillows and was looking out of the window. He turned his head as she entered and his eyes lit up. 'Rose.' His voice was stronger today. 'Where did you sleep last night?' His bruises were even more lurid now, and the cut on his cheek was puffy.

'On the floor, in there.'

He took the bowl from her. 'I woke in the night and decided that you'd gone.' She said nothing. 'It was hard on the floor?'

'Yes.'

'You should have come to bed.' He took a small mouthful of the oatmeal, watching her from over the spoon. 'But you stayed.'

If he were to ask her why she had, she would not have known what to answer, but he did not ask. 'What really happened, Robbie? Did you cheat?'

'Of course. I always cheat. I live by cheating. It's all I've ever known. But usually I don't get caught. Pity it had to be Ah Toon.'

'The men who brought you said they'd have killed you?'

'That's right. And I'd have felt the same in his shoes. I've had a lot of money off him.'

'Oh, Robbie . . .' She said nothing more as he ate the rest of the oatmeal, continuing to stare down at the blanket, his face unreadable with its bruises and cuts. Was he capable of remorse?

'Will that be the end of it, do you think?' she asked, after a little while.

'We'll have to see.'

'Will we be safe?' He made no reply, and after a moment: 'What'll you do?'

'Ask around.' And that was all he would say. He struggled to get off the bed, needing to relieve himself, and leant heavily on her, obviously in pain. 'Just a couple of ribs, I think,' he said, his voice tight, 'and I've cracked a few in my time. Bastards seemed to enjoy kicking me.'

Later that day he tried walking around the place, holding himself stiffly. She told him she needed to go out to the market and he nodded, and then pulled out a purse from behind the place where he kept his beer and smiled a little at her expression. 'Cat and mouse, we've been playing, haven't we, darlin'. Shillings only, I'm afraid.' He handed her two coins and she wondered what they were going to do for money.

Other than her gold.

And that she had hidden again, waiting to see how things would develop.

She bought what she needed from the market and as she walked back up the path, she looked up and saw him standing by the window, watching for her. A mirroring of roles. 'You didn't think I'd come back, did you?' she said as she put her shopping on the table.

'Why have you?'

She made no reply. And that night in bed she realised that it was the first time she had actually chosen to lay beside him, and how odd it was. Had some strange bond grown between them, despite everything? Or was she simply resigned to being with him, too scared of the alternative? Eventually she slept, her head next to his, his arm around her, grunting in his sleep every now and then as he turned.

Next morning she woke first and looked across at him, seeing beneath the bruises a more dissolute Robbie, perhaps a chastened man. Loose living was taking its toll on the lean and muscled digger of goldfield days, and she wondered how he might look ten years from now. Was this to be her life now, stuck at some halfway point between trust and suspicion, on a knife edge waiting for Robbie to fall foul of the law, or the lawless? And how unaccountable it was, this response in her to his beating; it was almost as if she too had been assaulted. She felt a strange sense of outrage. Of sympathy—

He opened his eyes and looked at her. 'Still here?' he said, softly.

'Still here.'

He lifted a hand, the broken knuckles now scabbed over, and gently he stroked her hair. 'I'll not ask again why that is, but I'm glad.'

It was the closest he had ever come to showing gratitude.

After a while he got up, still moving stiffly and said that he needed to go out, to hear the news on the street. She did not try to stop him, and then it was her turn to sit at the window and wait until she saw him walking back up the path. And this time when the magpie swooped on him, she cursed the bird.

But he was quiet and grim-faced upon his return, and left her questions unanswered until she enquired about the grand opening of The Flotsam Rose, planned for that Saturday night. 'Postponed,' he said, and failed to meet her eye. And that night he lay quiet and wakeful beside her, and she did not dare to ask what he had learnt, and what would now become of them. Had he bought the hotel with the proceeds of the nugget, and gambled the rest of it away? Or had he still got the nugget as surety somewhere? Surely now he would tell her . . . Postponed, he had said, but would they ever be able to open the hotel as planned? For surely, if Ah Toon was still bent on vengeance then he would know where to find him, and Robbie could not lay low forever.

And she found herself wondering who, besides Mrs O'Shea and the two young men, knew where they lived.

———

Next morning, Robbie told her that they would have to leave.

'Where will we go?'

'I'm giving it some thought. Before then, though, I need to go up to The Flotsam Rose.'

'Will you be safe?'

He gave a wry smile and put out a hand, cupping the back of her head and pulling her towards him. He kissed her with something like his old enthusiasm but with a tenderness that was new. 'Have you started loving me at last?' he asked, looking down at her. 'Should have got meself beaten up sooner.' Nobody said anything about love, she thought, as she watched him go slowly down the path, but if he did not come back, she was not sure what she would do.

Last night he had spoken of going to Sydney; it was a smaller place than Melbourne although it too was growing. 'What will we do for money?' she had asked and sensed him smile in the darkness, but he had not replied.

Before he left that morning, he asked her for one of the gold pieces. 'Then I can get us some cash.' With some reluctance she went and fetched them from the hiding place and he selected the smallest. 'Now you'll have to find a new place for the rest,' he said, and grinned. 'And I'll have the fun of finding them.'

He was back sooner than she expected, and his face was grim.

He went straight to the window overlooking the market and stood to one side, peering out. 'What is it?' she asked.

'I think I was followed.'

Fear clutched at her. 'By who?'

'A man. A white man, not Chinese.'

She felt a jolt of fear. 'Is he there still?'

'No.'

He turned swiftly. 'Right, pack what you want to take, what we can carry between us. Gather any gold you've got hidden away and be ready to leave.'

'We're going *now*?'

'Right away. I'll empty the slops.' Bewildered, she saw him go and collect the chamber pot that she had already emptied and disappear back down the stairs. From the bedroom window she watched him go through the motions of emptying it, look around, then lift the stone beside the privy and take something which he put into the empty pot before coming rapidly back up the path, holding the vessel with two hands.

Understanding dawned. 'The nugget?' she asked, incredulous, when he appeared at the door. It had been there all this time!

'The same. Get a move on, girl, if someone was following me they'll be reporting back.'

In a daze she collected what she needed, unable to think straight for fear. They had acquired little, but most would have to be left behind. Quickly she selected the clothes she would take, conscious of a great feeling of relief at the thought that, despite everything, they still had the nugget. If Robbie had somehow managed not to sell it then their future, away from here, was assured.

She stopped.

Their future. What madness was this!

He appeared at the door. 'Quick, girl. Just leave the rest.'

'Do we to tell the landlord?'

'Don't be a fool.'

He carried their bags outside and stood at the end of the path. Rose followed and saw him look rapidly from side to side, then call out to a standing cab. The horse had its head in a nose bag and Robbie shouted to the man to make haste and a moment later it pulled up in front of them. He was already bustling her inside it when she became aware that another cab was drawing up on the opposite side and she heard a shout. '*Malloy!*'

He turned and, from inside the cab, she saw him freeze.

'Robbie!' She put a hand out but he grabbed her bundles and threw them in on top of her.

'Drive on! *Go*, man, go!' and as he leapt onto the moving cab he pulled a pistol from his pocket.

She heard another shout.

And then a shot.

Chapter 41

Fraser went with the doctor to the door. 'A nice clean wound,' the physician said. 'Chipped the bone but missed the femoral artery.' He had removed the bullet, stitched the wound and Will had passed out. He was conscious again, though, when Fraser returned to his bedside a moment later. 'Two minutes,' Will said, his face an ashy grey. 'That's all it needed. Two minutes, and we'd have been in time.'

'And he'd have taken better aim,' Fraser replied.

Will turned his head away.

Fraser left him and when he came back sometime later Will was lying there, a hand behind his head, staring up at the ceiling. 'So now he knows I'm alive, and he knows that we're after him. He looked straight at me, you know, straight into my eyes, and then fired.'

'And missed, more or less.'

'The cab lurched when he jumped aboard, put him off his aim, but he was prepared to shoot me down, in cold blood.' Fraser said nothing. 'And if what Richmond says is true, he'll now be lying very low indeed.' Will had filled Fraser in on who Ah Toon was as they had been driven up to Fitzroy. 'Runs opium dens, brothels and various gambling holes. Big man. Most of his money comes from fake pakapoo tickets.'

'Pakapoo?' Fraser, inevitably, had been intrigued.

'Numbers lottery, races drawn every hour. Men get hooked and go mad playing it, can't stop themselves. Soon as the constables close one racket down another opens. Ah Toon's behind most of it. Nasty piece of work.' Richmond had told them a marked card had been found on Robbie after he had scooped big winnings while playing poker with the man. 'And for Ah Toon to be cheated by an Irishman is an outrage.'

And that was not all that Richmond had told them.

'Rumour has it that Malloy's been stung over the deeds to The Flotsam Rose. Borrowed money to get them and now –' his little eyes had glinted, relishing the telling, '– now there's talk that the low life who sold them to him didn't know he'd sold them, if you take my meaning, and he's due for release soon. Malloy's been taken for a ride! Opening's been postponed, workmen laid off. He's lying low, I gather, nursing his injuries.'

And if they had arrived at Fitzroy market just a few minutes earlier, Will thought as he lay there, they would have had him, weakened and taken unawares.

'Did Rose see you?' Fraser asked Will.

Will shook his head. 'He'd bundled her into the cab. But they're on the run now, and so God knows how we'll find them. With Ah Toon and us both on his tail, he'll decide that Melbourne's too hot for him.'

'Perhaps the constables will follow up the shooting and find them. He never saw me so at least I can go on looking.'

Will snorted. 'Ah Toon would have better chance.'

'Should we perhaps make contact with him?' Will threw him a look of scorn and made no reply. They sat in silence for a while. Then: 'Look, Will, I'll go down to the police station now and see what they reckon to our chances. It's worth a try.'

'If you like.' It would get him nowhere, and Will was in despair, not knowing which was worse: the throbbing pain in his leg or the anguish of getting so close a second time.

'And then . . .' Fraser paused. 'Then I really must think about returning to Scotland.'

Will nodded. 'Your mother.'

'I told her I'd be back by spring, and she's only getting weaker.'

'Of course. You must go.'

'I hate to leave with the job unfinished,' Fraser said. 'I sought redemption by finding Rose for you, and I've failed.'

Will turned his head away. He could do without the man's self-pity. 'We found her, and we lost her. Twice. You've been the worst and the best friend a man could ask for. Consider yourself redeemed.'

As anticipated, Fraser's visit to the police station drew a blank. 'Seems the horse bolted at the sound of the shot,' he said, reporting what the officer had told him, 'and it took a while before the cabby got him under control. He reported the incident sure enough, but Robbie and Rose had got into another cab telling the driver that the first cabby was driving dangerously. He swallowed their story and took them down to St Kilda and then the trail went cold.'

'St Kilda?' Will scowled. 'Did they search there?'

'They did. And they spoke to some of the cabbies who work from there but no one picked them up.'

'The hotels?'

'They asked.'

'Shipping?'

'Boats are coming and going all the time.'

It was hopeless. Will rolled over on his side and Fraser left him.

———

That evening when he returned with food, Fraser pulled a chair up to the end of the bed. 'I've been thinking, Will. Come back to Scotland with me.'

'You know I can't. I'm a wanted man.'

'And I'm a despised one. But Mama won't last long and her estate manager is ripe for retirement. Come back with me and help me with the estate.'

'I know nothing of running an estate.'

'Can't be hard, can it, a few sheep, pasture, tenants? I aim to live quietly with my books and my camera for a while, and you can show me how to be a model landlord.' Will said nothing, but he was listening. 'The estate's in the Borders, a lovely spot, hundreds of miles from Kinnloss, a different world. Who would look for you there? You can change your name.'

'I have. It used to be McAuley.'

Fraser got to his feet, his natural optimism returning. 'Well then, there you are. And if anyone *is* still looking for Will McAuley, renegade tenant from Argyll, they'll have no reason to look at Will Stewart, respectable estate manager (a man I've known for years, I'll assure them) in Roxburghshire. Someone here in Melbourne should be able to produce you some papers.' His cheerfulness raked Will's raw nerves. 'Some very skilled forgers here, I'm told, big business for them with folk who come here, escaping their past. I'll ask Richmond, he's bound to know.'

Will refused to give him an answer, and as soon as he was fit he insisted that they went down to St Kilda themselves, where Will questioned every boatman and skipper he could find, but no one had anything to offer him. He sent Charlie Richmond out one more time to put his ear to the ground but the man came back with nothing. Except, as an aside and at Urquhart's request, the name of an engraver who would oblige with regards to papers.

They went up to The Flotsam Rose, too, but the place appeared to have been abandoned. Its windows had been smashed, and Will stood beside Fraser looking up at the sign that now hung at a drunken angle, the chains that held it creaking in the wind. Perhaps that was all Rose would ever be to him, he thought as he looked up at it: flotsam brought ashore by an angry wave only to be carried away, out of his reach, on the retreating tide.

Chapter 42

The little coaster that took Rose and Robbie from the wharf at St Kilda was a sluggish vessel and the weather was contrary. But slack sails and an erratic breeze did not seem to worry Robbie as long as they were at sea, and the more miles they put between them and Melbourne the more Rose sensed him relaxing. And she too felt some of the tension unwind within her as they passed through the Rip on a falling tide, seeing blue waters ahead of her under a cloudless sky. How different this was from her arrival in that foul schooner all those weeks ago, distraught at the loss of Will, sick and filthy, desperate at what the future would hold. It was a sobering thought that she was now fleeing beside Robbie, here with him through choice. But once again, she thought as she followed the flight of a shag low across the water, what real option had there been? It was November now and in March her child would be born; she could only pray that it arrived late, to give support to her fiction. She watched Robbie as he sat in a patch of shadow cast by the mainsail, leaning back against a bulkhead, his eyes shut, an unlit pipe loose in his hand, and wondered what awaited them in Sydney. The bruises on his face were only just beginning to fade, reminding her, should she need reminding, that life with this man would be precarious at best.

But for now the sound of the water swooshing beneath the bow was restful, and an empty sea behind them showed that they were not being pursued. Looking at Robbie she remembered how he had pushed her into the back of the cab with their baggage, then roared at the cabbie to drive on. The sound of the shot had spooked the horse and, while the cabby struggled to get it back under control, Robbie had sat back against the seat, a stunned expression on his face.

Until then Rose had been too terrified to speak. 'Ah Toon's men?' she had asked and he had grunted in reply. 'Did you . . . did you hit anyone?'

'Yes.' Still he stared ahead, poker-faced.

'Do you think you killed him?' Could things get any worse?

He shook his head. Then: 'Wish I had. The bastard.'

'It was Ah Toon *himself*?' she asked, appalled at the thought of further retribution.

'No.'

Her hand had sought his and he had squeezed her fingers. She had frozen with terror when he pulled the pistol from his pocket that day but having come so close to being caught, she was glad that he had used it. 'You did well to shoot him,' she had said, and seen a look of astonishment cross his face.

He had stared at her for a moment with such a strange, intense expression, and then pulled her to him with a great laugh. 'I'm glad you think so, sweetheart, but I wish to God I'd nailed him. He'll not track us to Sydney.'

———

But Robbie did not like Sydney. And nor did Rose. He had found them rooms behind the old bond houses, above the wharves on Kent Street in a busy area crammed with buildings and yards, a jungle of brick and corrugated iron where the sounds and the smells of the hot city were unescapable. The rooms overlooked the back rather than the harbour and were shadowed by an adjacent warehouse building, and while this sheltered them from the worst of the incessant sunshine, the rooms were gloomy and the air was stale. Smoke blew in from the foundry during working hours and smells from the tannery were overpowering when the wind was from the west. She felt far less safe here than she had done in Melbourne and the streets were filled, night and day, with street hawkers and derelicts, drunken seamen whose shouts and raucous laughter were incessant, and fights seemed to spring up like wildfire.

'We can surely afford better than this!' she said, but Robbie brushed her complaint aside.

'We're invisible here.' Her suspicion that he was still looking over his shoulder was confirmed when he insisted they changed their names, becoming Mr and Mrs McCormick, and the man who forged new documents for them replicated their marriage certificate too, altering the names and moving the ceremony to a church in the centre of Melbourne. Rose had looked the papers over carefully and found no fault with them, ignoring the inner voice aghast at her collaboration.

The heat seemed more intense as December wore on, shimmering off the corrugated iron roofs of neighbouring buildings and sheds and she breathed air that was dry and dusty. As the weeks passed and she grew bigger, she lost interest in doing anything other than staying indoors and trying to shut out the din. Opening the windows let in a stench and once she heard rumours of a cholera outbreak in one part of town, they remained firmly closed. The row of sandstone terraces she could see over the back had been sub-divided many times, extended with lean-tos of rusting iron and timber, and washing lines criss-crossed the yards weighed down with shabby garments hanging limp over chicken coops, barrels and rubbish left to fester. A pair of goats in a neighbour's yard bleated endlessly, adding to the cacophony of barking dogs, shouts and cries. It was a terrible place and here, like it or not, Robbie was all that stood between her and destitution.

She made no further complaint.

He was often out though, and she dared not ask him where he went. Sometimes he returned with little treats, pastries from a bakery down the street and once a caged songbird. 'I told you we could deal better together,' he said, his hand sliding onto her belly, grinning as he felt the child stir beneath his palm.

'How long will we stay here, Robbie?' she asked.

He stretched out beside her and locked his hands behind his head. 'Not long.'

His mood seemed benign so she tried pressing him. 'If you sold the gold, we could surely live better than this.' He made no reply.

He had pulled up a floorboard under the bed and hidden the gold there and as she had hardly left the room, it must be there still. She could only assume that he was making ends meet in the same way that he had done in Melbourne, although this thought gave her no comfort. The woman who came daily to help her spoke of the wildness of the larrikins and the pushes, or gangs, who roamed the streets, defending their territory and looking for trouble, and she wondered if here, in Sydney, Robbie might have met his match. Simpletons aplenty there might be returning from the goldfields – lambs for the fleecing, he called them – but where there were lambs, there were wolves.

He had taken the remainder of Rose's little cache, all bar the one piece she had kept back, and evaded her questions as to whether he had spent it all, amusing himself by regularly checking in her cleavage for more. This became tiresome as she grew fretful in the heat but at least he had stopped making other demands on her. Often he stayed out all night, and although she hated being left alone, once she had barred the door it was a relief to sleep alone and have him return to her in a sweeter mood.

She cared not that he slaked his lust elsewhere and, in truth, dared not look beyond the birth of her child, now just weeks away. They would surely not stay here after that? Often she would lay awake fretting at the thought that the child should grow to resemble Will and wondered how Robbie might react if it did. Better perhaps if the child was female and then maybe he would see in a girl child only her mother's features. As the time passed, she worried more and more about the disparity of dates, and whether she could convince him that the child had come early. The bump was still neat and small but nonetheless she began preparing the ground, declaring that her mother had told her that she had been an early arrival, a fiction he showed no sign of hearing. In the daytime, or when he was with her, she scolded herself for her fears, telling herself that Robbie had long forgotten that there was ever a question of paternity and that, in his words, they now dealt better together.

After a fashion.

The dreary days passed slowly, the songbird died, and as Christmas approached she wilted, increasing fretful in the heat. And then, without warning, their fragile peace was shattered and things were just as before. He returned early, and suddenly, breathing fast, his eyes wild, and there was a long slash along the sleeve of his jacket and a bloodstain on the cuff. He told her to pack.

'No!' she wailed.

'Then stay,' he said. His face was dark and uncompromising, and the world stood still. 'Stay here alone or leave with me now. Same question, Rose. Same choice.'

His eyes were as cold as in the worst of the Melbourne days.

'But Robbie . . . ! Where will we go?' Where else could they run to?

He tore off the jacket and cast it aside. Then he shifted the bed, wrenched up the floorboard and stuffed the nugget into a duffle bag, along with his own possessions, his jaw set stubborn. 'Ireland. I've had me fill of these shitholes. We're going home.'

'*Ireland*! But *after* the baby—'

'I'm off now to book passage. Pack, I tell you!'

He swung his bag onto his shoulder and left her standing stunned in the middle of the room, a hand resting on her stomach, the child within her leaping as if picking up on her panic. No! He must see reason . . . The passage would take weeks, and she had not got weeks, or not enough of them—

Her eyes fell on the discarded jacket and she picked it up, slowly running her finger down the length of the slit. The blood on the cuff had dried to a dark stain, but there had been enough to have stiffened the fabric. She remembered the wicked switchblade he always carried, and quailed.

Oh God, what had he done!

He returned, still demon-driven. 'No ships to Dublin for two weeks, but we're on one leaving on the morning tide bound for Glasgow, and we can get on board right away. Got you a cabin too, girl, so no use you moaning.'

'But Robbie! I'll die if I give birth on the passage.'

He was looking around in exasperation. 'Holy Mother, Rose. You've done nothing since I left! For Christ's sake get moving.' Then he flicked a sharp glance at her. 'And enough of your dramas, girl, we'll be on dry land long before then.'

Chapter 43

By the dates she had told him, Robbie's calculations would have been right. But eleven weeks later Rose lay spent and exhausted with her newborn son in her arms, listening to the creak of the ship's timbers, and found, as countless women had before her, that the rewards of labour erase the pain and the fear. It had, in the end, been more terrifying in contemplation than in realisation, due in part to Robbie's continuing reassurance that she had almost four months to go. 'Just be grateful I got us away, girl,' he kept telling her. 'All you've to do is lie there and hang on until we land. Where's the hardship in that?'

Perhaps, she thought, looking down at the child with a sort of wonder, the turbulent seas of the mid-Atlantic had done her a favour by masking the child's 'early' arrival. Her pains had started on the tail end of a storm and the ship's surgeon had delivered her somewhere in the region of the Azores where, for a few blessed hours, the ship's violent plunging had been replaced by long deep swells which provided a rhythmic roll for a birth which had been swift and uncomplicated.

Robbie, who had paced the deck, was eventually invited in to view the child. 'Well done, sweetheart! What a business, eh?' and he kissed her.

Then his eyes fixed on the infant in her arms.

'A fine strong boy,' the surgeon said, gathering up the soiled cloths. 'A good size too, for a—'

'His eyes are blue, Robbie,' Rose said. 'Just like yours.'

'They often are at first,' the doctor agreed. 'But that slatey blue sometimes darkens to brown during the first year of—'

Rose bit her lip as Robbie frowned down at the child. 'They're blue,' he said. 'Very obviously blue, and my wife's eyes are grey, so how will they ever be brown?'

The man dissembled rapidly. 'It is, as you say, most unlikely.'

So Robbie had not forgotten after all, she noted with a stab of fear, as she stroked the baby's cheek, thinking that she could find no resemblance to anyone in the puckered red face. They named him Michael, after Robbie's father, and Robbie was invited to dine in the captain's cabin where he became uproariously drunk, and for the remainder of the voyage Rose doubted whether he noticed that she had given birth to a child or a rabbit. A girl, travelling in the lower decks, was summoned to assist her, but she saw little of Robbie. And so she fed the child in peace and only wept for his absent father when alone.

———·———

The ship entered the Clyde estuary exactly a hundred days after leaving Sydney harbour and was brought upriver past the busy shipyards just as the sun was setting against a charcoal and crimson sky, smudged by smoke from countless chimneys. They disembarked and Robbie found them rooms close to the west end of the city. They were fine enough, a great improvement on Sydney, but they looked out over the grey, wet roofs of a grey, wet city and Rose found little comfort there. She stood at the window and shivered, thinking that in Melbourne early April was a soft month, still warm and mellow with the heat of summer fading whereas here there was nothing yet to see of the spring that Robbie had promised her. During the voyage he had painted her a picture of Ireland, green and lovely with fields of sweet grasses strewn with daisies, of soft rolling hills that swept down to the sea. But here the reality was different; it was cold and it was wet with not a scrap of green to be seen from the window. Yet she dared not complain.

Arrangements were made for a girl to come in daily and, having seen Rose settled, Robbie had gone out on the town. 'Will we stay long here?' she asked, when he returned.

'Not long, no.'

'And then Ireland?' She felt vulnerable here. Nothing was familiar. The girl spoke in a way that was almost unintelligible and from the window the people passing were hunched against the ceaseless rain, their faces pinched and hungry-looking as if they had never known a summer.

'Aye. Leave it to me, Rose.'

'I'll be glad to go there,' she said, coming to sit beside him, hoping he might say more. 'This is a grey place.' Even the cold seemed different here, it penetrated the solid walls and the wind blew soot back down the chimney. She feared for her boy, for he was all that mattered now. 'We'll leave when we've somewhere to go to,' he said, giving her a cursory pat. 'I heard a cry. Go to him, Rose.'

When he was around, Robbie seemed besotted by the child and Rose would find him watching over him as he lay sleeping and wondered a little anxiously at what thoughts went through his mind. And when he woke Robbie would pick him up, carry him to the window and stand there holding him, pointing out the passers-by, making absurd comments on their dress or gait, instructing the infant in what to look for when buying a horse. Rose smiled at his foolishness but watched him warily. Would such devotion last?

But generally he spent little time with them. More often he was out in the city, preoccupied with matters he did not discuss with Rose. He would dress each morning with great care, wearing new clothes he had bought upon arrival, checking his collar in front of the mirror, straightening his shoulders, practising the part he would present to the world: a handsome, confident man of means.

She could only hope that he played the role convincingly, as they were running out of places to flee to.

Rose's own days passed calmly, with just Michael and Kirsty, the girl employed to help her, and slowly her strength returned. As it did, she grew weary of staying indoors and persuaded Robbie that she should get some exercise, and that there was no danger in leaving Michael with the girl watching over him. A seamstress was summoned and a walking-out dress commissioned and, when it was finished, the two of them would stroll together, down the main shopping streets, arm in arm, and she would glance down the smaller side streets and remember the photographs in Fraser's book. And she saw reflected in the bleak tenement buildings the back streets of Melbourne where she had been born. Poverty seemed more ingrained here, though, and the smoke from the chimneys seemed to hang in the air, soiling their clothing and skin. If Robbie were to leave her now, if she gave him any reason to abandon them, then the wheel would have come full circle and she would be here with her child, in no better state than her own mother had been, alone in the city from where her destitute grandmother had been transported.

It was a sobering thought.

But Robbie seemed driven by a new energy and two days later he returned to find her shivering in front of the fire, and threw himself into the chair. 'Still cold, girl? Well, here's news to warm you.' He paused, and then sat forward, his eyes dancing. 'I've sold it, Rose, that great old lump, and the money's in the bank.' She said nothing, remembering for a moment what very different dreams it had once held. 'In the *bank*, for God's sake!'

He gave a great laugh. 'I'm respectable at last, darlin', a man of means.'

'In the bank *here*?' She looked back him, bewildered. 'But what about Ireland?'

'Change of plan.' A smile she knew all too well flickered across his face.

'Robbie . . .'

He rose and poured himself a drink. 'I decided it would be better if we established a past for ourselves before we go back to Ireland and settle. Make some connections here. Respectable ones.' She remembered the bloodied cuff and shuddered. Was he still a hunted man? 'And I think the stars are aligned for once, and I've a surprise for you.'

'Tell me,' she demanded, Robbie's surprises being what they were.

But he shook his head. 'Now what would be the point in that? All in good time.' He patted his pocket. 'But I've money to spend too so I can buy you something fancy. A fur collar maybe, to stop you shivering, or we could stay here and get stuck back into the business of breeding, that'll warm you up.' She opted at once for going out, and he laughed at her. 'Later, then. I want twenty sons, I tell you.'

The offer of a fur collar seemed to be forgotten once they were out in the street but she was content to walk along beside him, a woollen stole wrapped around her shoulders, a stylish hat set at an angle. He had repeated the claim that he was a generous man when they had fitted her out with more new clothes a few days ago, and insisted on accompanying her, recommending more flashy styles than she liked, examining her own choices critically before approving them, and she managed to avoid the worst of his selection.

Today, however, there was no urgency to make further

purchases and she could sense him assuming his new persona: man of substance, his wife on his arm, a child at home with its nurse. His complacent expression indicated that he was well satisfied with his performance, and by the way he squeezed her fingers perhaps he was with hers, but she wondered again what his plans might be. They stopped at one of the street corners while he read a newspaper placard describing a dog race to be run that Saturday, and Rose turned away, smiling a little to herself. The veneer was thin . . . Glancing around she saw that the shop in the corner was advertising photographic supplies and there were cameras on display in the window, and she stepped across to look. They were smaller, more compact cameras than the one Fraser had used and—

'Are you a photographer, miss?' A man had drawn up beside her, a gawky young man with a large Adam's apple and scarf tied too tightly around his neck.

'Oh, no—' and then she stopped. 'At least, yes, in a way. I've done a little.' How fine to be able to say that!

'New stuff here every time I look,' he said, his hands thrust into his pockets. 'Takes all ma wages, you know.' She smiled at him, seeing out of the corner of her eye that Robbie was occupied talking to a man who had also stopped to read the placard. 'More and more of the ladies are taking an interest, you know.'

'Are they?'

'These new cameras are lighter, you see, easier to handle and processes are getting—'

'Rose!' Robbie's voice was a command but she simply turned and smiled at him, before returning her attention to the youth.

'Go on,' she said, but he had seen the scowl on Robbie's face and lifted a respectful finger to his hat brim and moved off. 'I'm going in,' she called to Robbie and pushed open the door.

At once the smell transported her back to Fraser's backroom studio in Hokitika and at the sight of the drying racks and the plates, the bottles and developing dishes, the mounts and the frames she felt a pang, but also a resurgence of the old excitement. Alchemy, Fraser had called it: . . . *a sort of magic . . . a mystical transformation . . .* And there it all was, the elements of that magic: nitrate of silver, collodion . . . she walked slowly past the labelled drawers and bottles . . . glacial acetic acid, photosulphate of iron . . . her lips forming the words as if it was poetry.

And she *had* been transformed by it, if only briefly.

A wave of sadness swamped her. It did not seem so very dreadful now, what she and Fraser had done, and if only Will had come to find her, had asked her to explain. For the first time she found she was blaming someone other than herself . . . The elderly shopkeeper interrupted her thoughts, offering assistance. 'I'm told there are newer, lighter cameras, perhaps suitable for women,' she replied, coming back to the moment, and he showed her what he had.

Some were little more than boxes, with clever devices for opening and closing the shutter. 'I sold one of these to a man last month for his wife to use, and he tells me that she is very pleased with it. And now, with the new dry plates from America becoming popular, processes are altogether more straightfor-ward—' he broke off as Robbie came through the door.

'Please go on,' she said, and he continued with one eye on Robbie who propped himself up against the wall and listened, arms folded, as the man described the various new developments. 'Things are progressing very quickly, sir . . .' he said, now addressing Robbie rather than Rose, as if it were he who had expressed an interest, and as he continued to speak an idea came to her, a sort of defiance, and with it an echo of an assurance she had lost in Robbie's company '. . . especially in America. Gelatin, it has been demonstrated, can be every bit as sensitive as silver nitrate and allows plates to be prepared in advance, which—'

'Do you really know what to do with all this stuff?' Robbie asked Rose, interrupting the man's flow.

'Yes, I do,' she replied. The shopkeeper beamed at her and her resolve grew. The young man outside the shop had seen nothing strange in her being interested. So why should she not?

'Are you not a photographer, sir?' he asked Robbie.

'No.' He glanced at Rose. 'Lands you in a whole heap of trouble,' he drawled.

She ignored him and asked to see the first camera he had shown her again. It was little more than a leather-covered box into which small glass plates would slot. Very neat, quite manageable. 'Apparently someone bought one just like this for his wife,' she said to Robbie, playing the coquette, 'and she is very well pleased with it.'

He raised an eyebrow. 'Is that so?'

'And I would rather have this than a fur collar.'

'Would you now.'

'And all the chemicals and equipment I need to process the pictures, of course.'

The shopkeeper took off his glasses and polished them. 'I could put together a nice little kit for the lady at a very reasonable price, sir, if you wish it, and I would be prepared to offer continuing advice should that be required, at no further cost—'

'We're leaving Glasgow shortly,' Robbie replied and Rose looked at him. This was news. 'How much for such a kit?' After only a little discussion, the two men agreed a price and Robbie produced the money and, with a flourish, wrote down an address. 'Have it all sent up there, if you will.'

The man studied the paper and gave a little bow. 'I would be delighted to do that, sir.'

'So you're not done with photography, after all the trouble it brought,' Robbie said, pulling the door closed behind them.

'It's the first thing I have ever asked for.'

'Other than a thrashing,' he replied, but with a smile.

'I can photograph Michael. Record him through the years, from babyhood to manhood. And all the other twenty sons you're wanting. Where are we going, Robbie? You never said.'

He gave a different sort of smile, more like the old Robbie. 'You think to trick me, do you? It's a surprise, I said. But there'll be plenty of room for you to mess about with your potions. Will you set up something like Urquhart's mad place with all those racks and bottles?' She frowned. Had he ever been into the back room of the Hokitika studio? She could not remember. 'And you'll have time to fill as it's in the back of beyond. Until I've knocked you up again, that is.'

A thin veneer indeed, she thought, turning her head away, appalled at the thought of another pregnancy. 'Why the back of beyond?' she asked. Were they to be in hiding there?

He grinned again. 'I'll tell you this much since you're nagging. It's north of here, on the coast, got it cheap on a two-year lease, part furnished and with two staff, and we can take on more if we need them . . .' She listened in astonishment as he continued. Staff! Would there be anything left to live off? '. . . The owner never leaves Edinburgh and I got good terms because it's stood empty a while. The land's managed separately, which suits me well as I've no mind to do any work.'

'And where is it?'

An odd look crept into his eyes, half sly and half amused,

and he shook his head at her. 'You'll not get it out of me, macushla! But you'll have your camera and I'm told there's fishing in the streams, hunting on the moor and some neighbours we can get to know and, at the end of two years, it'll be safe for me to go to Ireland.'

Chapter 44

It was hard to imagine a greater contrast than that between the soft loveliness of Scotland's Cheviot range and the raw, jagged beauty of New Zealand's Southern Alps, and to Will's battered spirits the landscape offered a balm. Rounded hills, as green and as smooth as felt, sloped down to gentle valleys and, on days like this when he had ridden out early, it was hard to believe that the dense rainforest and ravaged terrain of New Zealand's west coast was part of the same world. It was good to be home.

And yet.

And yet for all the benign mellowness of Fraser's estate, every morning Will woke to the bitter taste of failure. He had left Scotland with such high ambition, and at such a cost, and here he was, three years later, back again, working at another man's bidding, living under a false name in a house that did not belong to him. Alone. This was not how he had planned it. Often, when he was riding out through the estate, he would think back to those west coast days and wonder whether the gold had run out in Kumara. Had the dream there faded, the quest moved on? Or had McGrath and his cronies made their fortunes?

And Rose.

What of Rose?

That was a pain that never left him. They had stayed on for just a few more weeks in Melbourne, following up every pitiful line of enquiry until it became clear that Richmond was stringing them along, milking them, and Will had to accept that Robbie and Rose had vanished. In the end he was forced to agree with Fraser that they had most likely left on some small coastal vessel and could have gone in either direction. West towards Adelaide or east towards Sydney. Or they were holed up in a small settlement along the coast. Or they might even have made their way out to the goldfields to the north. And in the end, no longer caring that Scotland might hold danger, not caring about very much at all, Will had allowed Fraser to persuade him to return with him.

And since then, during these last couple of months here on Fraser's land, the sharp pain of loss had gradually faded to a dull, persistent ache.

But it had never gone.

Fraser had convinced him that he would be safe. 'Why ever would they look for you here?' he said. 'They'll have forgotten all about you. It was theft, after all, not murder.' He did his best working as Fraser's estate manager, his own bitter experiences as a tenant ever in his mind. Things would be different here, they had agreed and, as both landlord and master, Fraser was more than benign. In fact, he was positively foolhardy and Will spent much of his time persuading him that his generosity would bring eventual ruin, and would not produce the benefits he imagined. Fraser had no understanding at all of livestock or land, no appreciation of the seasonal cycle and no real interest in any of it, and the tenants would be quick to exploit his good nature if Will allowed them to.

Fraser had provided him with a cottage on the estate and treated him as a friend, his equal in every way. 'You should marry again, Will,' he often urged him. 'Rose has, and if you can bring yourself to accept that, then you are surely free to wed.'

Will made no reply.

But lately he found that he craved the company of a woman and the closeness that had begun to grow between him and Rose. They had had so little time! Had her child been his? He wondered endlessly, tormenting himself with the thought. He had always imagined that he would have sons, but to have had a daughter born of Rose would have been such a joy and the thought that he would never know twisted in his guts. Could he ever bring himself to marry again? He doubted it. It had nothing to do with God or the Church with its rules and constraints, but bigamy was a crime and even if he was prepared to risk it, could he ask that of another woman? Rose would forever be his wife and he knew full well that, somehow in this world, she still lived, haunting his dreams and leaving his days without purpose.

He dismounted and stood, looking out towards the Great Cheviot, one side of the hill in shadow, the other lit by the soft glow of the low sun. An ancient volcano, Fraser had told him – impotent now, its days of fiery spectacle long passed. Perhaps he too was a spent force; it often felt that way. He had lived his life with such intensity these last years, with such a mad passion, and perhaps that was enough for one man's lifetime. Sometimes it felt as if the drive and energy of the new world had sapped his strength and that he should resign himself to seeing out his days here, back in the old.

And yet.

And yet he could feel a restlessness growing within him. He was surely not done with life. But where next, and what quest should he follow? People spoke of Canada, of vast forests where land could be had for a song, of fertile prairies stretching to the horizon. He could follow that trail like so many Scots had done before him, start afresh. A buzzard soared overhead and he stood and watched as it circled slowly on wings outstretched and powerful, searching for prey. He ought to shoot it – they had lost too many lambs to its talons this year – but he hated to do it; it too sought survival in the only way it knew.

He left his horse to graze and went and sat on a grassy knoll and pulled out his pipe. So should he simply settle for this? The yearly cycle of sheep and lambs, winter, spring, summer, wool and butchery, work and sleep, year after year. Safe, secure and unchanging.

He did not feel able to discuss with Fraser his horror at the thought.

Fraser himself had other outlets for his energies. He frequently took the train up to Edinburgh where he belonged to various learned societies, and there he would attend lectures, go to the theatre and participate in other social gatherings. Photography was still his passion and, he told Will, it was moving so fast it was hard to keep up. It appeared that his earlier social transgressions had been put aside, at least in the circles where he now moved, and his raw photographs of the goldfields were attracting considerable attention. Through no effort of his own, Fraser had inherited considerable wealth, and this allowed him to become a patron of this emerging form of art. He put on exhibitions of his own work, encouraged the work of others and invited contributions to books he intended to publish.

But Will had no place in Fraser's world. He had nothing to gain from it and nothing to offer, and deep down he resented the amount of time and energy these men of substance gave to such frivolous activities, holding them in contempt.

These views he readily shared.

'You're too hard on your fellow creatures, Will,' Fraser replied, defending himself. 'The world needs men of intellect and reason, as well as men of action. Culture is an essential part of our humanity, a counterbalance to commerce and industry. The arts feed the soul and, as I used to say to Rose, the exploration of the . . .' he faltered at the expression on Will's face and veered away. 'As for the landed gentry, it's a matter of educating them, which is what you're doing so admirably here: leading by example. And if High Edenvale is less profitable than other estates, then so be it; the tenants are more content and thanks to you, the land is in good order. How is the new building coming on at Clent Mains, by the way? You must take me to see.'

And so Will's strictures were deflected, as they always were, for Fraser was content here and it was evident that he meant to stay put, his days of adventure over for now. Will doubted that he would ever marry, even for appearance's sake, but he liked to entertain his Edinburgh friends: artists, writers and scholars from a world in which Will wanted no part. Invariably Fraser included him in invitations to dine when he had visitors, but following one or two disastrous occasions, Will had consistently refused. 'I've nothing to say to these men, Fraser,' he had said when the next invitation came. 'We speak another language.'

He lay back on the soft grass, letting the sun warm his face, closed his eyes and listened to the sound of the rooks in a distant clump of trees. He still limped a bit, and an occasional pain in his left leg served to remind him how close he had got to reclaiming Rose. It took only a thought to rekindle the bitterness and anger – and the remorse. But perhaps it *was* time now to put it aside, count his blessings and be content with his lot. What hardship was there, after all, to stand beside Fraser waist deep in the river's current and watch the silken line uncoil from his rod, catching the sun before dropping to the clear water, and for as long as the moment lasted the combat with the salmon brought satisfaction? It was the same when he went out with the keeper, stalking deer over bracken and heath, but these were the pastimes of the gentry and he felt vaguely ashamed of himself. But then again, he had a roof over his head, he need never be hungry, and at very little trouble to himself he could live out his years in this peaceful place, close down those other parts of him—

And die of boredom.

The buzzard had ceased its circling and it now sat perched on the branch of a dead oak, its head swivelling as it scanned the terrain and Will admired for a moment its intense concentration, waiting and watchful. Had he been impatient, he asked himself, given up on Rose too soon? Should he have stayed out there and sought her with the same fixed determination? It was only now after these weeks of calm that he realised how physically broken he had been when he arrived. First the near-drowning, the infected leg and then Robbie's bullet, and to cap it all there had been an outbreak of dysentery on the voyage home. It was not only the physical toll, he now realised, but also the emotional damage, which had been incalculable. Even so, he would probably ask himself for the rest of his days if he had given up the search too soon.

He woke some nights in such an agony of self-loathing that he should be here, taking employment from the man who was, after all, the author of his misfortune and that Rose, his wife, was lying at that very moment beside Robbie Malloy, whose mischief had brought their world crashing down. Did Rose ever think of him, he wondered? Did she curse him, as he cursed himself, that he had not the sense to talk to her, to ask her to explain? What Fraser had said to him back in Port Chalmers had stayed with him.

He saw then that the buzzard had grown still and tense, its attention focussed on the coarse grasses that grew long beside the broken wall, its neck slowly stretching forward, eyes sharp.

Then, in a smooth and practised movement, it took silent flight, rising high. It banked sharply, hovered a moment, balancing on feathered wing tips.

Before dropping like a stone.

Chapter 45

Beyond the rocks the great sea loch spread out in front of her, a blue-black plain flecked with white. Calm now but with an undercurrent of swell, waves breaking near the shore, and behind them the ocean stretched clear out to the horizon to meet a cloudless sky. Exactly as Will had described it.

And as lovely.

She stood on the terrace at Kinnloss House, watching the shags spreading their wings to dry just as they did on the other side of the world, still trying to absorb the reality of being here, still stunned that Robbie had chosen to bring them to this one place. To her right she could see the long slope of The Saddle, with its shadowed folds and gullies, rising from the shore of the loch just as she had pictured it in her mind's eye. To her left the wide-open bay. Will had promised that one day he would bring her here. 'Even if we have to wait until we're old and spent. And, you know, it's strange,' he had said, holding her close in the narrow bed as rain drummed on the cabin roof. 'I was so desperate to leave, so angry with Armstrong, and so frustrated and humiliated – and I would do the same again, make no mistake – but you forget just how deep the roots go.'

Rose, who had no roots, had listened and tried to understand.

And yet fate had so twisted events that it was Robbie, not Will, who had brought her here, and she remembered how he had watched, half wary, half amused after they boarded the train when he had finally told her where they were going. 'I was looking at the possibilities,' he said, 'and the name leapt out at me, seemed like it was meant.' She had turned her head away, hardly able to breathe, aghast at his insensitivity. 'I told you it would be a surprise, and you'd never have guessed, would you?'

'No.' Whatever had gone through the man's mind?

'Come full circle, eh girl?'

She made no reply. Did he see this as his final triumph over Will, to come here as master where Will had been in servitude, from where he had fled, a wanted man? Could he not see the pain that it brought her? But no, Robbie Malloy would only ever be able to see the world through the narrow lens of his own self-interest.

But, she had thought, looking back at him, he never acted without reason. 'Full circle, Robbie,' she agreed.

She had continued to puzzle over it as they travelled north, holding Michael close, her old anxieties re-awoken by this move. To her mind it seemed that Will's features became more and more marked on her child's tiny face, and she was haunted by the thought that some animal instinct would tell Robbie that he was not of his begetting. Perhaps it was her imagination, but he seemed more irritable with the child these days, or was he simply resenting the attention she gave to him? For one as selfish as Robbie, that alone could account for it and now that his physical demands of her had resumed, she was careful never to refuse him.

From a newly built railway station they had taken a coach and then a small coastal vessel, completing the last part of the journey on poor, unfinished roads, and as they travelled further and further, she had been struck by the remoteness of their surroundings. How long would Robbie tolerate such isolation, she wondered. The man she knew was a creature of bars and dance halls, of gambling dens and the noisy haunts of like-minded men and this would surely not appeal to him for long.

And yet upon arrival he had seemed satisfied. The house was grand enough to suit his current aspirations, although a long period of neglect had left it damp and unwelcoming. Some effort had been made to prepare for their arrival but nothing could disguise where the gutters had leaked in previous winters, bringing the plaster down with it, or the fact that the furnishings were tired and shabby, and everywhere there was the fusty smell of emptiness. It had stood untenanted, the housekeeper told them, for three years.

'So ever since Lord Kinnloss took his own life,' Robbie remarked, with bland unconcern, glancing towards Rose. 'Which he did in Glasgow, I understand.'

Mrs Sutton, the housekeeper, looked surprised. 'Is that what you were told, sir?'

Later the woman confided in Rose that he had shot himself out on the terrace, overlooking the bay towards where, on the slopes of The Saddle, the sight of smoke from the crofters' houses had given offence. No wonder they been unable to find a tenant! 'He was broken by it all, you know, after his business failed, and Lady Kinnloss won't come back here. She had to sell all the good furniture and paintings, as well as all the silver and the china, to pay off the debts, so there's not a great deal left. When will your own furniture be arriving?'

In confusion, she had referred her to Robbie. 'But the house itself was not sold?'

'She hangs on to it for her son's sake, poor lady, and the estate provides her with a living, though she never leaves Edinburgh.'

The housekeeper, Rose learnt, had been here at the time of the suicide, a local woman and she wondered a little where her sympathies might lie, having not yet got her measure. 'There was a photograph, I understand, of the houses, the tenants' houses, set ablaze?'

'You've heard about that, have you?' The woman pursed her lips. 'A dreadful business.'

Did she condemn the act of destruction, or the photograph? 'Where were they, the houses?'

Mrs Sutton gestured to a point midway along The Saddle. 'See where there's a fold in the hills? That's it. I grew up there myself, before coming into service here. No one goes there now but a track leads onto the headland from behind the stables. Shall you look over the menus, Mrs MacMahon, or leave until later?'

That was another surprise that Robbie had dropped on her during their journey north. She was now Mrs MacMahon, not Malloy or McCormick. Another transformation; base metal re-gilded. 'Keep 'em guessing, eh, darlin?' There was something he was holding back from her, she was sure of it. Someone was still looking for them . . .

Perhaps it was better not to know. 'But why have we come *here*, Robbie? To Kinnloss?' she had persisted.

'I thought you'd like it.'

'Because of Will?'

'Because it amuses me.'

The amusement was of short duration, however, and Robbie's mood soured as the weeks passed. He soon discovered that prejudices in gentry society were as ingrained as the soot had been in Glasgow, and that money alone did not open the doors. His visits to neighbouring families were not returned and no invitations were received. Privately, Rose was not surprised and she imagined that, for all Robbie's conceit, it was easy to see through the gentleman to the adventurer beneath. For herself it was a relief that she would not have to attend social gatherings, having no idea how she should behave here, where she felt so out of place. Managing a household was demanding enough although, thankfully, Mrs Sutton seemed to sense this and gave orders to the cook and maid, leaving Rose to instruct Kirsty, who had accompanied them from Glasgow. More staff were needed to run the house properly, the housekeeper suggested, but when Rose broached the subject, Robbie bluntly refused. Half the rooms were unused and empty, he said. 'How many women do you need to look after you? Or are you getting grand, darlin'?'

Although strictly speaking he was not part of the household, they saw a good deal of the young man who managed the estate and Rose had had to hide her astonishment when Robbie first introduced him: 'This is Mr Armstrong, my love, Mr *James* Armstrong.' A thick-set individual with powerful shoulders and a belligerent jaw, he had nodded briefly to her.

Afterwards she remarked: 'Is he not the young man you said that Will had killed?'

Robbie grinned. 'He looks well on it, doesn't he? Aye, but he's an angry young man just the same. Told me all about your Will setting the hillside ablaze, then stealing the money and beating him up to get away.' She bit her lip, refusing to be drawn. 'His father drank himself to oblivion, you know, after Kinnloss sacked him. Said Kinnloss tried to shift the blame to save himself.' He paused and looked at her. 'His widow took on young Armstrong by way of compensation, I believe, even though he's over young for the role. There's not much land left to manage now, so I don't think it taxes him too greatly.'

It taxed him so little that Robbie was regularly able to persuade Armstrong to accompany him to Fort William, which seemed to offer the only entertainment in the area, and Robbie would return after a day or two, heavy-eyed but with his spirits briefly revived, and the young man was no doubt flattered by the attention. From what Mrs Sutton let slip the young factor was not well liked on the estate. 'Same mould as his father,' she said, tight-lipped, perhaps sharing these sentiments, 'what with his threats and his demands.' And the destruction of Srath an loin, Rose learnt, was far from being forgiven. 'It was his hand that set the first house alight, you know, and no one's forgotten that.'

'So how did you spend your time, Rose?' Robbie asked upon his return one time, stretching his legs in front of the fire that had been lit in the morning room. The drawing room was too large to heat and Rose had given instruction that the dust sheets be replaced on the furniture. 'Playing with your camera?' He lit his pipe and in the enclosed space the smell of it was overpowering.

'I have been, yes, I—'

'And you've all the kit you need?'

'Yes. I've tried to—'

'And it's what you wanted?'

'Yes, Mr Deuchar sent some instructions describing processes that—'

Robbie took his pipe from his mouth. 'I told you I was a generous man.' Beyond that he showed no interest, but Rose had no need of his encouragement. Immersing herself again in the mysteries of Fraser's alchemy was giving her much pleasure and while Michael slept she experimented with composition and light in the way that she had seen Fraser do, hearing his voice in her ear. 'Decide first *why* you're taking the photograph, what it is you strive to show, and only then see how best to achieve it.' Her early attempts were disappointing, and combined with the challenge of mastering new processes, she began to think that she had forgotten the little that she had known, but slowly she improved. Mr Deuchar had slipped a note into the box he had sent up to Kinnloss respectfully inviting her to write to him for guidance should she need it, and so they corresponded erratically, and recently she had started sending him prints and asking for his comments on aspects she was struggling to master. This connection with another person became precious and so she kept her correspondence from Robbie, using Mrs Sutton to take her letters to where post was collected. With an intuition born of experience she sensed that Robbie's mood was darkening, and this link with the wider world she valued too much to risk losing.

Being here meant that Will was never far from her mind, especially when she stood on the terrace and looked across to that fold in the hills where the old houses were, and she tried to imagine him, reckless and desperate, setting the hillside ablaze to cover his escape. She thought of Fraser too, and how he had been drawn by the smoke of another fire. The rediscovery of the skills he had taught her gave her a renewed confidence and one evening, as she stood watching the sun disappear over a cloudy horizon, an idea came into her mind. If she ever had a clear day, a day when Robbie was away . . . It would be an homage, she decided, a connection, however flimsy – a link.

Full circle, Robbie had said.

Eventually her patience was rewarded. She watched with satisfaction as Robbie and Armstrong rode off for a day's shooting, waiting a little in case they returned and then assembled her equipment before going upstairs to tell Kirsty that she was going for a walk and would be out for several hours, leaving Michael in her care.

Earlier she had identified the start of the track to Srath an loin behind the stables, just as Mrs Sutton had said, and for the first half-mile it was clearly defined. After that it plunged into woodland where its course was overgrown by brambles and nettles, but she picked it up again when it crossed a stream. Soon the woodland was behind her and the track continued uphill onto rough pasture where sheep grazed the coarse grasses, and where ruts left by cartwheels had cut deep into the undulating land. She stopped, shifting her load to her other arm, and rested for a moment, taking in the wide expanse of sky where the clouds were driven by a freshening breeze. Skylarks rose on the soft air and there was a humic scent of wet turf and clover, while beside the rocky outcrop the gorse was a yellow flame. Continuing up the rise she glimpsed the ocean, inky blue and studded with the white crests of waves, and she paused again before dropping down to the valley. How lovely it was, this place that Will had once called home.

On top of the final ridge she stood, panting a little now, and looked down at Srath an loin and saw the lochan just as Will had described it, surrounded in a haphazard ring by the burnt-out shells of dwellings.

Will's home.

And she could almost see him there: a boy and then a youth, dreaming of another life, of land of his own. He felt so painfully close, and as she passed between half-tumbled walls, blackened and scarred, she could see in her mind's eye the children who had once run in and out of the houses, the lazy beds well tended and clothes spread on gorse bushes to dry, just as he had described it.

She withdrew a little, searching for the place she needed to be. Her memory of Fraser's photograph was faint but she reckoned that he must have stood close to where she was now, to one side of the track, an unseen witness to the tragedy. More of his words came back to her: *Am I only to photograph the palatable, then, Rose, and the lovely? Only offer to posterity an acceptable past, cleansed of suffering?* Very well, she answered him. His image had recorded the very moment of destruction, but hers would show the aftermath, the crumbling walls, mellowed a little by time, over-sailed by brambles and bindweed, but still stark in their brutal message.

Perhaps he would have approved . . . And perhaps her photography could convey something else. Beyond the outrage, she would show a place not cleansed of suffering but a scene that offered a ray of hope that time, and the land itself, would begin to heal the scars.

She set her camera on a low wall and framed the shot in the angle between finger and thumb, as Fraser had taught her. And, as if in approval, the sun chose that moment to emerge from the clouds and, when she opened the shutter, it flooded the valley with light.

Chapter 46

She had, with Robbie's agreement, taken over the old dairy for her processes and she pulled her smock over her head and prepared to develop the plates as soon as she returned from Srath an loin. Bending over the developing dish she had placed on the stone settling bench, she watched the images appear with the same sense of wonder this had always given her. Alchemy indeed . . . By and large she was satisfied with the results: the view from the ridge was suitably stark, the charred roof timbers stood etched against the sky while the photographs she had taken inside the old houses showed wildflowers sprouting from the blackened turf, perfectly conveying a message of renewal. That sudden burst of sunlight had been very timely, although the contrast between light and shade was perhaps a little extreme and she would have welcomed Fraser's advice on how to improve on that; perhaps Mr Deuchar could give her guidance. She held the best of her results at arm's length to admire and, on a whim, added the little cipher Fraser had designed for her to the bottom right-hand corner.

She heard hooves on the cobbled courtyard and a moment later Robbie appeared at the door. 'So you're in your lair, are you?' He came in and let his gaze wander over the spread of bottles and dishes. 'It's a strange business for a woman, to be sure,' he said, taking in the stained smock. Then he took hold of her hands, turning them to inspect them. 'No marks, good – see it stays that way. Now, show me the pictures you've done of Michael.'

She slipped the new prints away and pulled out the ones she had taken of the child. 'They're not very good, really, too much shadow.'

He took them from her and went to the open door where the light was better. He dwelt for a moment on one, then handed them back. 'All babies look the same,' he said, and gave her a sideways glance. 'But I'm watching how he progresses.'

She remained where she was after he had left, a little frisson of fear going through her. The one he had studied was one where a crampy grimace had given the child Will's lopsided smile. Was it that that had caught his attention? Provoked that sharp look? Slowly she put the photographs away and pulled off her smock. He had too few distractions, that was the problem, she thought as she crossed the cobbles back to the house. Daily he grew more quarrelsome and she kept out of his way as much as she could, taking Michael into the garden with her on fine days or spending time in the old dairy while he slept. Having failed to make inroads into local society, and for want of any better company, Robbie regularly invited the young factor to dine with them. He would often stay late playing cards or rolling dice and Rose watched with contempt as the young man flattered Robbie and fawned, and her dislike of him increased at every encounter.

On one such evening she came downstairs to find that Robbie and Armstrong had begun drinking early and, as the meal progressed, Rose realised that Robbie was bent on mischief. Halfway through it he glanced across at her before addressing Armstrong. 'That photograph you told me about,' he said, 'the one that caused all the furore here. Remind me what the photographer was called.'

She stiffened and saw Armstrong scowl. 'Urquhart, Fraser Urquhart. It's not a name I'd forget.'

Robbie snapped his fingers. 'I knew it was familiar. You remember Urquhart, don't you, my dear.'

'Do I?' she replied, playing with the lamb on her plate, having appetite for neither food nor Robbie's games.

'Sure you do.' His eyes glinted at her. 'Set himself up as a photographer in Hokitika, and later came out to the Kumara goldfield.'

James Armstrong sat forward. 'You *know* the man?'

'If it's the same Fraser Urquhart, then yes, I do. And so does my wife.' And he described Fraser's features, his aquiline nose, his manner of speaking. Rose's attention sharpened. Whatever was he up to?

'That's surely him!' Armstrong exclaimed. 'But in *New Zealand*! God damn the man, if you will pardon me, Mrs MacMahon. He was entirely responsible for my father losing his job, you know, and driving him to his death.'

Rose looked across the table at him. 'I thought it was because your father set fire to the houses at Srath an loin that he lost his job,' she remarked, contempt turning to anger. 'You were there yourself, I heard.'

Armstrong flushed a deep red and opened his mouth to answer, but Robbie put up his hand. 'Rose, darlin', you've been listening to gossip! And that's unfair. James and his father were simply carrying out Kinnloss's instructions. The tenants knew the houses were to be cleared, but refused to leave.' He turned back to their guest. 'New houses were built for them, I'm told – better houses.'

The young man gave Rose a dark, pugnacious look. 'Aye, much better houses, but they were a stubborn lot. Still are, impossible to manage, they need a firm hand.' This, she had heard, involved a ruthlessness every bit as bad as his father's and, prompted by Mrs Sutton, she had raised the matter once with Robbie, but he had shrugged and replied that it was none of his business, he did not employ the man. 'And anyway,' Armstrong continued, 'it was Lord Kinnloss's land, not theirs. His right to move them if he chose.'

'People died on the hills that night, I heard.'

Her adversary glared at her. 'That photograph of Urquhart's misrepresented the entire affair!' He seized his glass and took a gulp of his wine. 'If we'd not have fired the roofs they'd have tried to come back, they always do. It went to court, you know, and Kinnloss won his case, which just goes to show.'

Rose frowned at him. 'To show what? The court case was not about the evictions, it was—'

'You seem well informed, Mrs—'

Robbie raised his voice and spoke over both of them. 'Say what you like, Rose, my love, it was Urquhart's photograph that drove Kinnloss to suicide.' He flicked at some spilt salt on the tablecloth, clearly well pleased with his mischief.

Armstrong nodded, tight-lipped, his face still dark with indignation. 'And once Kinnloss's business was gone, the estate was ruined, and then everybody suffered.'

'But the fault was not the photographer's,' she insisted, 'it lay entirely—'

'You're defending the man! Now that does surprise me.' Robbie smirked at her expression, then picked up his glass, swirling the claret in it and she shut her mouth, determined to say no more. 'He caused another man's death out there too, Armstrong, with one of his photographs, perhaps you're forgetting that, Rose?' She refused to look at him, hating him, the old Robbie. Whatever was the purpose of this wretched charade? 'He'd been taking photographs of another man's wife,' he continued, lifting his glass and watching her as he took a sip. 'She'd been posing for him, you see, naked as a babe, and

I daresay he was taking more than photographs, if you get my meaning.' Rose sensed Armstrong glance at her, gauging her reaction to the story before urging Robbie to continue. 'The cuckolded husband was one Will Stewart and he got himself drowned soon after, leaving his erring wife to the charity of his partners.'

Furious now, Rose raised her own glass, willing her hand not to shake, goaded out of silence. 'And one of them robbed her of everything she had, as I recall.'

She regretted her words at once for Robbie laughed, and the spark of combat lit his eye. 'So you do remember! But you're forgetting, darlin', her husband had been thieving from his partners, which she knew full well, so she was lucky not to be lynched.' He turned back to Armstrong. 'To return to the eviction, though, had there not been rent money stolen just a few days before?' Rose dug her nails into her palm and wondered if she could leave, pleading a headache that was fast becoming real. 'You told me the man's name, I think. That was Will too was it not? Will . . . ?'

'McAuley. Aye, Will McAuley. Set fire to the hillside first, then—'

'McAuley, you say.' Robbie cut him off and turned back to Rose. 'Now would that be a name you remember, darlin'?'

Armstrong looked confused, as well he might, and Rose stood. 'Why ever would I? And if you'll excuse me, Mr Armstrong, I will leave you and my husband to rake over the past. I have a headache.'

Both men stood and Robbie seized her hand as she passed. 'I'm sorry for that, Rose,' he said. 'Now what can have brought it on? Too much time in the sun with your child? Sleep well, sweetheart.' As he raised her hand to his lips, his eyes met hers, then he released her.

She closed the door behind her and stood a moment, feeling faint.

Your child. He had said it quite deliberately. *Your* child. She went rapidly across the hall and up the stairs, her heart beating fast. Your child . . . She went into the room they used as a nursery to find Michael fast asleep and she stood looking down at him. Kirsty came through from the adjoining room. 'Is anything amiss, madam?'

'No. I just came to see Michael. The gentlemen are at their tobacco and their port. Is he well? Did he settle quickly?'

'Yes, madam.' The girl looked puzzled.

And then, as she went to the door, a thought struck her and she turned back. 'And my husband. Has he been to see him this evening?'

The girl nodded. 'He came in earlier, while you were changing, while I was getting Michael ready for bed.'

'And what did he do?'

Her face flushed. 'Do? Whatever do you mean?'

Rose wondered a little at her reaction but had no time to care. 'With Michael.'

The girl relaxed. 'Why, he simply picked him up as he always does and held him, and took him over to the window and remarked how he was growing.' She smiled a little. 'And asked if I thought Michael resembled you or himself.'

Rose felt a panic growing in her. 'And you said?'

'That I thought it was too early to be sure.' She looked down at the sleeping child. 'I think he has your high forehead but the cast around the eyes is different and . . .'

'And . . . ?'

'I said I thought his eyes were darkening, and would probably be brown. Do either of your parents have brown eyes, madam?'

'My mother,' she said, grasping at a lifeline. 'My mother's eyes were brown.'

'That must be it then; the master said both his parents had clear blue eyes, just like his.'

Chapter 47

Will returned from his round of the tenant farmers to find a messenger on his doorstep. 'Mr Urquhart said to tell you that he's back, and asks if you'll join him for dinner.' The lad paused a moment and gave a shy smile. 'He said to tell you it would be just you and him, and then you'll come.'

Will grinned back at the boy. His antipathy to Urquhart's house guests was well known in Fraser's household. 'Tell him I'll make myself respectable and come at the usual time.'

Fraser was getting restless too, Will had noticed. He was going more and more frequently to Edinburgh and practically begging Will to go with him, quickly bored with country life. As he washed and changed his clothes he thought again that the parting of the ways was coming ever closer, but quite how he would broach the subject he was not sure. It took only a word or a look to send Fraser off into agonies of remorse that Will's misfortune was his doing which, while true enough, left him feeling trapped by his friend's determination to make amends.

He would have to tell him soon, he thought, as he took the little path which led to a side door, once the front entrance to a house much modified over the centuries. He let himself in, crossed the stone-flagged hall and tapped on the door of the untidy room that served Fraser as study, library, card room and on these occasions, an informal dining room. Fraser greeted him with his usual enthusiasm and handed him a drink. 'Take a seat – no, there, in

front of the fire. Warm yourself. How are you, Will? Fill me in
with the rural happenings. Everything I've missed.'

'Everything? Very little changes in two weeks, my friend.'

Fraser looked concerned. 'I know. Which is why I have to get
away. You really must come with me one time, Will. I wish you
would.'

'You ask me very often, and what do I always say?'

'You say you won't, which is very mean-spirited of you.'

Will took a drink and settled back into the worn leather chair.
'So what shall I tell you? Likely yields from the lower fields? Hog
prices last week? Or plans for the tupping?'

'Whichever you like, if you feel you must.'

Will laughed and took pity on him. 'Why don't you tell me
about Edinburgh instead?'

And through their simple meal Fraser regaled Will with
how he had spent his time in the capital – the concerts and
the plays, the lectures and the exhibitions, and Will nodded
and listened with half his attention, the other half savouring
the good food and wine, watching how the firelight bounced
off the mellow oak panelling. It would be hard to give all this
up, this life of ease and plenty, but he knew that he must. It
was just a matter of finding the right moment to open the
matter.

'. . . and we're to have another exhibition of our own, you
know.' Fraser was saying. 'I've been asked to contribute two or
three, though choosing will be a challenge. I still like that one
of all the diggers in Hokitika, the day we learnt about Kumara,
best of all the ones I did. You are in it yourself . . .' Will's expression must have hardened as Fraser went on hastily. 'Must mean
I'm officially off the blacklist to be asked – in Edinburgh at least,
if not in Glasgow – the wolves still await me there. I suppose in
time I'll be forgiven. I hope so, as I should like to go back. There's

a grittiness that draws me there, and I've good friends who stuck by me and are kind enough to stay in touch.'

They had finished eating and Fraser rose to fetch the port and then wandered over to his desk and began rifling through his post. 'Read your letters by all means,' Will said, picking up a newspaper. 'I'll just drink your port and look at this.' It would give him refuge from the man's incessant babble. Did he talk in his sleep, he wondered? He leafed through the pages, although neither politics nor society interested him very much. More and more it seemed that his and Fraser's lives ran parallel, rarely converging except on occasions like this, and even these were becoming a strain lately, conversation soon exhausted. That which had brought them together belonged to a different life, another world. He continued turning the pages, doing little more than glancing at the contents, until he came to where the shipping lines placed their advertisements. Halifax, Montreal, Boston . . .

Fraser, meanwhile, was going through his letters, muttering as he read some, smiling at others; invitations he put to one side. He held up a photograph of a horse and cart crossing a stream to show Will. 'Hardly innovative, but well presented. What do you think?'

'It's a horse,' Will said. 'And a cart.'

'Philistine. Mark the fluidity of the water and the reflections. That's really rather good.'

Will returned to his paper and Fraser continued to work his way through his post, commenting as he went, and Will let him ramble. Whatever would the man be like in forty years – twenty, even? 'Ronald McDonald from Rowan Hall can certainly *request* my presence, but he'll not get it. I'm sure to be indisposed that day. Hello, though – aha, that's more like it. Now what does the old boy have to say . . .' He muttered on, reading another letter, half to himself, and then he fell silent.

Will looked up from his paper. Something had shifted in the atmosphere. 'What is it?'

Fraser was peering intently at the image, a magnifying glass in his hand, then sat back, staring ahead. 'What? Nothing,' he said, jerking to attention. 'No, nothing. Quite a good shot, that's all.' He reached for another letter and Will saw that he had gone pale.

'Of what?' Will asked.

'A landscape. Shows promise.' Fraser gave a tight little smile, and waved the letter aside.

Will lowered his paper. 'Something wrong?'

'Nothing at all, absolutely nothing. I came over a bit queer, that's all. Overdoing things, I imagine. Too much dashing about.'

Will left soon after, wishing him a speedy recovery, and thought no more about it. Next morning, however, when he went over with documents requiring Fraser's signature, he was told that the master had departed early, on horseback, alone. 'A sudden family matter,' the man said, but Will could see that he too was puzzled. 'Something in the post, I imagine. Said he might be gone two or three days.'

'Did he say where he was going?'

'No, Mr Stewart.'

Will stood in the hall, frowning at the floor. Something rang false. Fraser had no family, he frequently lamented the fact. No, it was whatever he had opened in the post last night, something he had not shared. That in itself was odd as Fraser invariably rambled on about matters he would have been wise to keep to himself.

Will looked back at Fraser's man. 'Right, but I need to get some papers we were looking at last night.'

Such was the relationship between the two men that no questions were asked and Will went into Fraser's study and saw the pile of letters he had been going through. It was an abuse of trust to go through it, of course, but something was clearly wrong. Rapidly he sifted through the papers. There was the horse and cart, it had not been that, and there was the despised dinner invitation, a bill from his tailors, Christ, what the man spent on shirts, and then a package with a Glasgow postmark, the corner of a photograph sticking out. Was it that?

He pulled out the accompanying letter and glanced at the signature; the name meant nothing to him. Then he looked at the photograph.

Abruptly he sat, seeing at once what had caused Fraser to blanch. The place was instantly recognisable and he stared at it, knocked off balance. The walls of the low houses were lit in a blaze of light which served to heighten the contrast between the shadows cast by the ruined gables and green shoots sprouting from the fallen roof turves. It was a very striking image, and it tore at his heart. Oh God, how raw it still felt! Off to one side was his aunt's house, a wasted shell with half the roof still intact. Remorse and grief flooded him again . . .

But where had the man gone? And why?

He took up the accompanying letter and read:

I thought I would send you this, my dear friend, although I know it will stir painful memories. You will, I know, forgive me for saying that I am nonetheless delighted with it, if only vicariously. A protégé of mine, a charming young lady who appeared in my shop one day and whom I have since been guiding a little, offering advice when asked. She is not entirely new to photography . . .

Will felt his pulse begin to thud . . .

. . . and she has a talent for composition, a flare for the unusual
and with only a little guidance and encouragement she has
come on a great deal. Such a delight to see young ladies taking
an interest . . .

He let the letter fall and stared ahead and then, with a hand that
shook, he picked up the magnifying glass and, as Fraser had done,
he went over the image, inch by inch, searching for what he had
seen, and found it in the bottom right-hand corner.

———

By the time he had saddled up and was on his way Will reckoned
that Urquhart had at least half a day's lead on him. He fumed
as he wasted time working out how to make the journey to
Kinnloss and then endured the frustration of waiting for slow
trains at small stations, missing coaches that connected to others
and did the last leg of the journey seated beside a wagoner whose
slow progress gave him ample time to fret – and to wonder why
Fraser had not confided in him.

The cipher was unmistakable. But could Rose possibly have
been there, at Kinnloss?

And Robbie too?

Did Fraser think they might *still* be there? Was that where
he was heading, or had he gone to Glasgow to speak to the
letter-writer? But why, for God's sake, had he said nothing? Two
can search better than one, he had told Will . . . Was he still
seeking his redemption? 'Damn the man!' he cursed out loud,
startling the wagoner. 'Not you, my friend,' he said, and then
engaged him in conversation, asking if he was local.

'Born and raised in Lochailort, but always on the road.'

'So you know the area well?'

'As well as any.'

How to frame the question? 'And you deliver to the inns, and all the big houses?'

'Aye, backwards and forwards, railway stations to ports and back. Busier every year.'

'Do you know Kinnloss House?'

'Aye.'

'Does it stand empty?'

He shook his head and spat. 'It's been let, I'm told, just recently. An Irish family, by all accounts, who like to keep themselves to themselves.'

Chapter 48

Rose hung over the bowl, retching horribly, and Mrs Sutton bustled in, sent by Kirsty. 'I'm unwell,' Rose gasped. 'The lamb last night was greasy.'

The housekeeper smiled an indulgent smile. 'Bless you, my dear. And you a mother already!'

Rose lifted her head to stare at her. 'No . . . *No*! It can't be so. I've not bled since Michael's birth and I'm still feeding him, off and on.'

'Tell that to women with fourteen children!' The woman smiled again. 'You've a puffy look around the eyes, my dear. I'm the eldest of nine, and that's a look I know! Ma was pregnant for best part of ten years and I was only thinking to myself the other day that it wouldn't be long—'

'Say nothing,' Rose said, sharply. 'To anyone. Not a hint.'

The woman stiffened. 'It would not have occurred to me, madam.'

'I must pick the right time,' Rose smiled, making amends. 'The best time! Until then it can be a secret, just between the two of us,' and the housekeeper, mollified, smiled a little in return.

Rose made her way downstairs and out onto the terrace. Mrs Sutton brought her tea and cushions for the back of the chair, and she sat there gripping its arms as she tried to absorb what this might mean. Could it really be so? How could she have been so foolish not to have realised? The headaches, the fatigue . . . And now she had Robbie's renewed hostility to deal with. Had this sprung simply from mischief, or from something more? Last night's conversation with Kirsty made her stomach churn with fear. There could be no question of paternity this time, but if he was now questioning Michael's—

And another child. So soon.

'You're up, then.' Robbie appeared at the end of the terrace. He came towards her and dragged over a chair. 'I thought you'd sleep all morning.'

'I felt unwell last night, if you remember.'

'Ah yes, the head.' He stretched out his legs and said nothing more, offering no sympathy, making no enquiry. If he was waiting for her to challenge him over last night's dinner conversation then he would be disappointed. But she grew tense as they sat there in silence.

The attack, when it came, came from an unexpected angle. 'How old were you when your mother gave you up in Melbourne?' he asked, crossing one leg over the other and looking enquiringly at her.

'Why, I was eight, but—'

'And what do you remember of your life up until then?' His top leg began to bounce.

'Very little. A vague memory only, of a poor dirty place and of other people living there, other women, other children. And of being hungry, I remember that. It was always—'

'And your father,' he interrupted. 'What do you know of him?'

'Nothing at all.'

'So was your mother a whore?'

Rose lifted her chin. 'I expect she had little choice, being destitute. But I recall kindness, and she was sad when she handed me over.' Having sewn pennies into the hem of her skirt – a lesson that had served Rose well.

The silence lengthened, and then he spoke quietly. 'And yet of those few vague memories you were able to tell Kirsty that she had brown eyes, and from a coupling she probably couldn't remember herself, your mother was able to tell you that you were born early.' She felt a hot flush creep up her neck and suffuse her face. 'And you, an eight-year-old child, understood what she meant and remembered.'

There was nothing she could say.

'You're blushing, Rose, darlin',' he remarked, his gaze fixed out to the loch. 'You do that when you lie.'

So it had come at last. Indirect and unanswerable, but a clear accusation. They went on sitting in silence and she resolved that he must be the one to break it. After a time, he continued. 'The ship's doctor remarked that Michael was a good size and I thought nothing of it, being just relieved that you were both safe. And you had, after all, sworn that he was mine.' He sighed then and stretched his legs out again. 'You gave yourself away, Rose, over time, so watchful when I held him, so tense and so quick to take him back. I wanted to believe you, you know, I really did. But the cards kept stacking against you.' Still she said nothing, holding her panic in check. 'You should not have lied to me.'

She could see only his profile and his calmness was terrifying.

Then he turned to look at her. 'And what will James Armstrong make of that, do you think, should he get to know? Will Stewart's child – no Will *McAuley's* child – living here, at Kinnloss House, masquerading as the son of the master. What irony is that, eh, girl?' Last night's dinner conversation was now explained; he had been laying the foundations, setting the scene. But for what? A chill spread through her. 'Will McAuley and Fraser Urquhart,' he continued, 'the two men who ruined his family and wrecked the estate, and if he should learn of your association, your very *close* association, with the both of them, I don't think he'd ever look on you, or Michael, the same—'

She sat forward in her seat, the cushion falling to the ground. 'If any harm should come to Michael—'

He raised an eyebrow. 'Go on.'

Should she play her last card, tell him she was pregnant, or keep it in reserve? It had helped her once, would it do so again? 'There are other people here besides Armstrong. There's Mrs Sutton, Cook, Kirsty – they would know—'

'Know what, Rose?' He gave her a wide-eyed, questioning look that was no less menacing for all its guile.

'If Michael came to harm. But I will go. Give me enough to live on and I'll take Michael and go.'

He smiled, a twisted smile. 'Are we back there again, Rose? I thought we were past that. You should've gone when you'd the chance, darlin', back in Melbourne and then you could have set yourself up with your little stash of stolen gold, had your child and we'd have been done with each other.' He shook his head. 'But it's too late now, isn't it? Kirsty's a good lass, an obliging one in many ways, and keeps her eyes open for me, and she says you were sick this morning, and then the old Sutton trout went all pursed-lipped and prim when she asked. You're pregnant, aren't you, Rose?'

She looked back at him. She had nowhere to hide. Her last card, not played, was rendered worthless. She nodded.

'And so you're staying right here with me, m'dear, because this one at least *is* mine.' He sat looking at her, tapping the tips of his fingers together. 'But where does this leave us?'

The rooks that haunted the trees down by the loch chose that moment to lift in a raucous cloud as the wind gusted and they circled the top branches like dark rags, their cries mocking her while she and Robbie continued to sit in silence. 'You're not an easy woman to be with, Rose,' Robbie said, raising his eyes to watch them. 'With your cheating and lying.'

She could only gasp at him. 'This from *you*, Robbie Malloy!'

'Aye, but I've always had our best interests at heart, protecting you from things you didn't need to know, looking to the future for us both, but you never see that, do you? You just keep on resisting me, always pulling away. I thought we'd got well beyond that.'

'I don't trust you.'

He gave a short laugh. 'Well, there's honesty at least! And that's what I'm saying. Will we never move on from that point—' He broke off and turned his head as hoof beats sounded on the gravelled drive and a rider went past their field of view to the front door. 'Now who's this come a-visiting?'

A moment later the housemaid appeared at the door which led out onto the terrace. 'A visitor, sir. A Mr Fraser. Shall I bring him out here or—'

'He's found his own way, I'm afraid.' Rose's eyes widened as she heard a familiar voice. 'No need for formality, we're old friends after all.' She watched, in disbelief, as Fraser Urquhart strolled across the gravel towards them, waving the maid inside with astonishing nonchalance. Robbie gripped the arm of his seat and half rose. 'Don't get up, Robbie. No need.' The photographer bent over Rose's hand, squeezing her fingers. 'Rose, my dear. How splendid. I'll join you, if I may.'

He pulled up a chair and sat while Rose, stunned, continued to stare.

'Fraser—'

'Forgive the little subterfuge with the name.' He gave an apologetic half-smile, which included Robbie. 'I wanted to be sure you'd receive me – and then I find you out here, enjoying the sunshine, just the two of you. How splendid,' he repeated, looking around him and then up at the walls of Kinnloss House. 'And how extraordinary to find you *here* of all places!'

Robbie's face had blanched but it now suffused with colour. 'And how did you? Find us.'

'Through a mutual acquaintance, and the oddest coincidence.' Robbie leant forward. 'What acquaintance?'

'My old friend Deuchar. Remember him? He sells cameras and photographic supplies in Glasgow. Can you imagine my amazement?' He looked from one to the other with his wide-open smile. Then, over his shoulder to the maid who had reappeared. 'No, no refreshments for me,' he said, before he was offered any. 'I've just finished an enormous breakfast, and I shan't stay long.' He turned back to Robbie. 'I'm visiting at Connel Castle, with the Abercrombies – I daresay you know them – and I said I'd pop over here this morning, before luncheon, and see if I could possibly be right, and that it really was you. And it is! How absolutely *extraordinary*.' Robbie sat, rigid and watchful, his eyes not leaving Fraser's face. 'You both look well,' Fraser added, still smiling. 'Prospering, too, I see.'

Rose was recovering and sensed a false note. He was being too genial, trying too hard. 'Yes,' she said, smiling back at him. 'We're doing fine.' A thought came to her and she grasped at it. 'And we have a child! A boy. Michael. He's almost four months old, such a big healthy boy.' She made to rise. 'I'll fetch him down—'

Robbie raised a hand. 'Stay there, Rose. Mr Urquhart has no wish to see a baby—'

'But I should love to—'

'The oddest coincidence, you were saying.'

'Ah yes! A photograph.' He gave Rose a rueful look. 'But first, Rose, let me tell you how deeply I still regret what happened in Kumara. Not a day goes by but that I think of my part in that tragedy. The guilt of it plagues me . . .' Robbie made a sound somewhere between a growl and a snort but Fraser pressed on, '. . . and I'm only glad that you have put the whole wretched business behind you.' He included Robbie in his smile, ignoring the scowl. 'I went back to Kumara, you know, once I was able to bring myself to do so, to see how Rose was faring, but you'd both already left—'

'A photograph, you said.' Robbie's tone was steely.

'One that Rose took, one you sent to Deuchar, my dear, he showed it me. We are old friends, you see, but how were you to know!' He gave Rose a reassuring smile. 'It was really rather good, I thought. A little too much contrast, perhaps, sometimes it's better—'

'A photograph of what?' Robbie demanded.

'Why the house, of course. I recognised it at once. Another reason for the subterfuge with the name,' he looked about him. 'Memories are long in such places. And you too have found that a name change was in order,' he added, giving Robbie a conspiratorial smile. 'I shan't ask why.'

'D'ye think I'd tell you?' Robbie scoffed, looking more comfortable now. 'But it's a poor sort of story you're telling me, mister whatever you choose to call yourself. You see a picture of Kinnloss House and you think: I bet Rose took that, so I'll just drop by and ask her about it. D'ye take me for a fool?'

'Oh. Didn't I say? I once showed Rose how to make a little design to mark her work and it was there, on the print.' Robbie flashed her a dark look. 'And then there was Deuchar's description of you both when I made enquiries, and when I showed him the photograph he recognised you at once. And so I told him I'd come and see you, surprise you—'

'*Another* fucking photograph!'

Fraser gave him a disdainful look and pulled a card from his jacket, passing it to Rose. And there they were, she and Robbie and Will, outside the little Free Church in Hokitika, on her wedding day, in another life. Wordless and wary, she handed it to Robbie.

'And you carry this round with you?' Robbie's eyes were now a glacial blue.

'I confess that I do. It reminds me of the great wrong I did to Rose, and to Will. I valued him very much as a friend, you know.' He turned sorrowful eyes to Robbie. 'Nothing more was ever heard, I suppose? No body found?'

Robbie sat there, considering him, scraping the edge of the photograph against his chin. 'No,' he said, at last.

Fraser turned back to Rose. 'My dear girl, if I can make amends in any way—'

Robbie cut him off. 'Where did you go after Hokitika? You were on the run, as I recall. More dirty photographs.'

Fraser looked down his nose at him. 'I had a business in Dunedin for a while, and then received word that my father was dead and came back to Scotland. I have a place in the Borders, not far from—'

'When? When did you come back?' Robbie asked and Rose looked at him, wondering at his persistence.

'Oh Lord,' Fraser scratched his ear. 'I wasn't long in Dunedin. Must have been August when I left there, home before Christmas.' Robbie leant back in his chair and Fraser turned to Rose. 'As I say, if there is any way I can be of service—'

'Enough!' Robbie's hand came down hard on the chair arm. 'My wife has no need of your services, and it's time for you to leave. Like you said, we're prospering, and have no wish to drag up the past. We'll not expect to see you again. That's right, isn't it, Rose?'

Fraser made no move to go but looked at Rose. And this time

the look he gave her was direct and sharp. She answered carefully: 'It is good to see you, of course. And how extraordinary that we should both know Mr Deuchar. He's been very helpful, such a support, if only through correspondence.' She paused. 'I just wish that I could let you see Michael,' she went on, speaking fast. 'He was born on the crossing back from Australia, and since then he has thrived—'

Robbie got to his feet. 'Time to go, Mr Portrait Man. And I'll be keeping this, I think, for old time's sake.' He put the photograph in his pocket and Fraser shrugged his agreement. 'It's a pity James Armstrong isn't here as he'd have been glad to see you too.'

'Another neighbour?' Fraser asked, also rising.

'Estate manager. His father drank himself to death because of another of your damned photographs.'

'Oh Lord, that man. Then I had better go!' He turned back to Rose, took her hand and raised it to his lips. 'My dear, take care of yourself. And of your son.' She tried to communicate her fear in her eyes and believed she saw an acknowledgement in his smile. 'Another time—' he said.

'No, Urquhart. *No* other time.' Robbie took a step towards him. 'I'll be sure Armstrong knows you're in these parts.'

Fraser straightened and looked back at him. 'Understood.' The charade was dropped for an instant and Rose watched as he strode purposefully back across the terrace, and a few moments later she saw him ride away.

And then Robbie came and stood behind her.

Chapter 49

Will had slept under the trees for two nights and could safely assume that he looked sufficiently like a vagrant to be ignored by anyone he might encounter along the familiar road from Fort William to Kinnloss. He still took care, nevertheless, to slope off the track whenever he saw someone ahead of him, so at the sound of an approaching horse, he stepped into the shadow of the trees and waited for the rider to pass. It was only as it did that he recognised Fraser Urquhart and then he leapt out behind him, waving his hands and shouting. Fraser looked back, reined in, and wheeled the horse round.

'Will, for God's sake!' He dismounted, looking up and down the track and pulling the horse into the trees. 'Have you no sense at all! How did you—? Ach, you went through my papers, damn you.'

Will glared back at him. 'You should have told me.'

'And this is exactly why I didn't. Dear God, I thought you were safe at home.' They went deeper into the woods.

'You've been to Kinnloss House?' Will asked.

Fraser nodded. 'Just come from it.'

'Is Rose there?'

'Yes.' Will's heart gave a great leap. 'Robbie too. I spoke to them both.'

'And you told her?'

'No. Because, unlike you, I'm not a fool.'

Will scowled. 'How did she seem?' How did she look? Did she appear well? Happy? Questions pressed hard.

Fraser lay an arm across the saddle and stared into the trees. 'She looked . . . anxious. Malloy is clearly a bully and my sudden appearance shook him, but I'd no chance to speak to Rose alone. All I could do was let her know that I know Deuchar – the man who sent the photograph. I gave her a lifeline, spun a story about going to see him, and she grasped the idea that she could reach me through him.'

Will snorted. 'And so now what? We go home and wait for her to get in touch?'

But Fraser was frowning, and shook his head, speaking slowly. 'No. She was fretting about the child, telling me what a healthy boy he was, and I think she was trying to tell me something else, but I don't know what.' Will glanced across at him, arrested, and his pulse began to thud. 'Malloy kept cutting her off, wouldn't let her fetch the boy. I think she wanted me to see him.' Why would that be important? Unless . . . 'Told Malloy I'd returned some time ago, made no mention of Melbourne so he'd not associate me with you. Couldn't risk it. Malloy's a nasty piece of work. He threatened me.'

'With what?'

Fraser pulled a face. 'Armstrong the younger. Old Jock Armstrong's son would like to meet me on a dark deserted track, or so he implied.' He squinted out through the trees to the road beyond.

'And not only you,' said Will. So Jamie Armstrong was still around, was he? This was unwelcome news, the lad had a score to settle and had promised to see him hang. The horse bent its head and began cropping at a clump of grass at the edge of the clearing.

'I told Malloy I was staying with the Abercrombies at Connel

Castle,' Fraser continued, 'and that I was expected back for lunch. Not that I am, of course – they were friends of old Kinnloss and would've liked to see me skewered at the time – but I doubt Robbie will ask them. Frightful snobs, they'll not have received him.'

'So where are you staying?'

'At a little inn at a fishing harbour a couple of miles north. I borrowed this nag from them. And you?' Will gestured to the trees. 'I see. Probably safest. So what happens now? We need to get Rose on her own somehow, talk to her. We need a plan, Will.'

'Aye.' Will looked across at him. The horse lifted its head, ears pricked as if it too was suddenly on the alert. A plan. Will stood there, running his fingers through its knotted mane, thinking hard as he stared into the dark shade of the trees, and then his hand grew still. He raised his own head, turned his cheek to the wind and grinned at Fraser.

It was blowing from the west.

Chapter 50

Robbie still stood behind her on the terrace watching the dust thrown up by the hooves of Fraser's horse. 'Go up to your room, Rose. And stay there.'

She did not argue but went quickly, her mind in a whirl, across the hall and upstairs to her room where she closed the door and leant against it, shaking from relief as much as fear. *Fraser*! However had he found her . . . ? Never had she expected to be pleased to see him. And now she could reach him via Mr Deuchar, send a message, explain her situation, and he would help her, she knew he would; that little smile he had given her had said as much. Fraser was a fool in many ways but his brain was sharp.

But, oh God, things were happening too fast.

She went over to the window and looked down onto the terrace. Robbie was still standing there but was now in close conversation with James Armstrong, and she felt a lurch of fear. She had dropped her guard these last weeks, forgotten that Robbie Malloy was, at heart, a dangerous man and now that he knew that Michael was not his, and that they were discovered, there was no knowing what he might do.

A tray was brought up to her for lunch. 'Master said you were resting,' Kirsty said, setting it beside her. 'But to come down when you've eaten. Or should he come up?'

'I'll come down.'

She had no appetite but delayed as long as she could, pacing the floor, her thoughts all in a jumble. The world was shifting around her and she needed time to absorb the implications of it all, to think things through. If she appealed to Fraser for help, and if she were to leave Robbie, would he let her go, or would he come after her? And would she spend her life looking over her shoulder, always fearful? Could she ever be truly free of him?

She could delay no longer and went down to find him standing beside the fireplace in the morning room, staring down into the flames. He looked up as she entered and gestured to a chair. 'Sit Rose, we must talk,' he said, but remained standing, kicking lightly at the hearth guard as he contemplated the fire. 'It was a mistake, coming here,' he said, at last, looking across at her. 'We need to leave. Go to Ireland now.'

'What has changed?' she asked, as calmly as she could.

'Mr Portrait Man, of course. I've done my best to cover our tracks and build us a past, but now he knows where to find us.' He flung himself into the chair opposite her, his eyes still on her.

She felt that familiar sick sense of dread. There *was* no way out . . . Stay or leave him, she would always be fearful. 'Is someone still looking for you, Robbie?' she asked.

'I can't be sure . . .' there was a strange look on his face, '. . . but if he finds us, that'll be the end of it, darlin'. We need to leave at once.'

As bad as that? And yet . . . 'But . . . but, Robbie, surely whatever happened in Melbourne, or in Sydney, Fraser can have no connection to—'

He raised a hand. 'We must go, I tell you, and leave now. Trust me for once! I'm sick of this God-forsaken place anyway, no wonder Will robbed his way to freedom, I'd have done the same.' He carried on looking at her in a way that was different, devoid for once of guile and mischief. 'And it matters now, between you and me, Rose, what happens next.' He rose abruptly and went to pour himself a drink.

'You threatened Michael.'

He shrugged. 'Only to make you behave. I'd not hurt the boy.' But could she ever be sure of that? He took his drink and sat, searching her face with an odd intensity. 'We've seen how well we *can* deal together, Rose, but I need to be sure of you, not always wondering if I'll wake up one day and find you've run off. I'm all done with making you stay.' She looked back at him in astonishment. After all this time, after all they had been through, he was asking her. Giving her a choice . . . In all her thinking she had never once considered he would do this. 'I'll treat you well, make a life for us – which is what I've been trying to do all this time, though you could never see it. You've got Will's child to remember him by and I'll raise him, and soon you'll have mine and to my way of thinking that's a beginning. In Ireland we can start afresh, no more living on a knife edge.' He paused. 'I love you, Rose, like I've loved no other woman.'

His words robbed her of speech. She had never seen him like this, stripped of the assurance and the conceit that defined him, exposed and vulnerable. But what was he asking of her? And what assurance could she possibly give? He spoke to her of *love*, but what distortion of it was this? Nothing he had shown her so far suggested he was capable of love. Not the sort there had been between her and Will where it was in every glance, every smile, every touch . . . awaiting the moment to be declared. Here, surely, she was being offered only the husk, the brittle shell of a void—

And yet, perhaps this was all there would be for her now. She doubted that the void could ever hold substance but maybe it was a chance she would have to take. He had, after all, achieved what he set out to do and gained wealth and a counterfeit respectability, so perhaps his wild days were done at last. But could she ever be more than a faux wife to him? She searched his face trying to see behind his inscrutable expression. *Trust me for once*, he had said, and he went on looking at her, awaiting her response. This man was a gambler, and something was telling her that this declaration was a sham, the only card he had left.

And he had played it.

She was struggling to frame her response when a sharp knock came at the door, and Armstrong burst, breathless, into the room. 'Have you seen? Out on The Saddle.' He gestured to the window and Robbie strode across. Rose followed and saw that the servants were lined up on the terrace outside gesturing and pointing to where a great cloud of grey smoke was rising from the fold in the land halfway along the ridge. 'It's coming from Srath an loin, from the old houses, half the hillside's alight, and the wind's strengthening, blowing this way.' Robbie swore. 'I've sent word for everyone to go and try to beat it out, but I couldn't find half of the tenants and some refused. Will you come, sir?' Rose watched as the plume of smoke rose higher, a looming dark shadow. 'I think you should. Someone in authority. And we'll need every hand to beat it out.'

'Go, Jamie. I'll follow. And tell those women to get back inside, it's not a spectacle.' But Rose saw that Cook and Mrs Sutton had already vanished. Robbie seemed arrested, considering something beyond the scene before him, and she saw the muscles in his jaw tighten.

Then he swung around. 'All right, Armstrong. I'm coming.' He turned to Rose. 'Stay in the house,' he said, 'and if it spreads take Michael down to the loch side. You'll be safe there.'

She nodded and he left, squeezing her arm as he passed her, and she watched as he and Armstrong set off across the drive, then rang the bell for Kirsty. 'I want Michael here with me,' she said. Turning back to the window, she saw that the fire was moving fast down the hillside. It had been hot these last few days and the bracken was dry, and if the flames got beyond the area of rough pasture it would reach the trees in no time and the stables would be in danger. And then the house.

Kirsty returned with Michael and Rose settled the child in a deep chair at the far end of the room, framed with cushions. 'There's no need for you to stay. Go and give whatever help you can.' The girl left and Rose watched through the window as she too set off down the drive, pulling her shawl over her head.

Rose went on standing there, watching, not fearful but somehow detached from it all. Bewildered. It was all too much. This fire now, on top of Fraser's appearance and Robbie's extraordinary turn-about . . .

The smoke had spread right across The Saddle, a dark smudge against the soft green. And so it must have looked on the day that Will had made his desperate escape. Behind her she heard the door open but she did not turn.

Then something shifted in the air behind her.

'Rose.'

That voice. The floor seemed to tip beneath her. She turned then, and stared in stunned disbelief at the doorway where he stood, his clothes blackened, his face unshaven, a phantom summoned by her thought.

She gripped the window frame as her head spun and in two strides he covered the distance between them and took her in his arms, crushing her hard against him and she smelt smoke on him, and the earthiness of woodland. He was real.

Will.

'How can this be . . . ?' It was hard to speak, hard to stand as he kissed her.

He released her, his eyes consuming her. 'By the luck of the gods, my love.' She saw then that Fraser had followed him into the room, his eyes dancing. 'Sit a minute, then we must go.' He led her to a chair and looked around. 'Some water . . .'

Fraser handed him Robbie's abandoned brandy glass. 'Need to move, Will,' he said, but his eyes shone at Rose.

'But how . . . ?' The brandy seared her throat.

Will crouched beside her, taking her other hand. 'Been chasing you since Kumara,' he said, with a twisted smile. 'Saw you once at Melbourne races, and got so close that day at Fitzroy market. Then we lost you—'

'Fitzroy?' The brandy was clearing her head. '*Fitzroy*. It was *you*!'

'Aye.'

'And . . . and you that Robbie shot?' Her eyes widened as she absorbed this and she sat upright. 'So he knew? He *saw* you?'

Will nodded, grimly.

Fraser had gone across to the window. 'This'll keep, Will—'

But Rose was frozen. 'All this time, Robbie has *known*!' A fury was building in her, and with it came a stab of panic. 'He's out there now, and Armstrong. Will, we must leave!' But Will too had grown still, for a different reason. He was looking beyond her to where Michael lay sleeping, sunlight from the window dappling his cheek. He looked back at her, the question unspoken, and she nodded. 'Yours,' she said.

His eyes blazed and he rose then and went and stood looking down at the sleeping child.

Fraser was still at the window. 'Right, Will, take up your son—'

But even as Will bent to do this a sound came from the hall. The door flew open and Robbie stood there, a pistol in his hand, levelled at them. 'I'd my suspicions this morning,' he said.

With a cry of rage Rose sprang at him but Fraser caught her, pulling her back and holding her to him, and she saw then that in Robbie's other hand was his knife, the long blade glinting. In a flash he moved so that his back was to the fireplace, putting distance between them, his eyes and the pistol now fixed on Will.

And Rose saw that glint of wild recklessness she knew so well. He threw a glance at Fraser. 'Connel Castle's been closed up for weeks, Armstrong tells me. And then the fire made sense.' His eyes went back to Will. 'Setting the old houses ablaze was poetic, and it could only have been one man.'

They stood there, the four of them, still as waxworks, and through the window Rose saw the smoke had reached them.

Robbie saw it too. 'Not much time, Will.'

Will straightened, leaving Michael asleep.

Fraser's grip on Rose tightened as she struggled. 'You *knew* he was alive!' she spat. 'All this time—'

'Aye, darlin',' said Robbie, his eyes still fixed on Will who was trapped at the end of the room with a chair and a table between them, 'but you didn't, which was all that mattered.'

'And he stole that photograph,' Fraser said, 'and made sure Will saw it.'

Rose stared across at Robbie. 'But . . . but *why*?' The air was so charged she could hardly breathe.

'I told you this morning, little fox cub.' He gave a short laugh. 'Though in truth, I'd not expected such spectacular results when I did.'

'So will you shoot us all, Robbie?' Step by step, Will was advancing on him.

'Stay where you are!'

'You could hardly miss this time.'

'Aye, but I'm waiting for Armstrong. The man's set his heart on you hanging.'

'I don't see that happening.' Will took another step.

Robbie's eyes narrowed. 'No? So how will this play out?'

'You'll put the gun down.' Will reached the back of the chair where Rose had been seated, but they all knew that a bullet would find him well before he could get past it.

'Now why would I do that?'

'Or better still you'll turn it on yourself, like old Kinnloss did, and have done.'

Robbie scoffed. 'That'll not be happening either.'

'You're beaten just the same.' Will's eyebrow was hooded in a scowl and Rose held her breath.

No one moved.

Her eyes fixed themselves on Robbie's trigger finger and she saw it tighten. 'Robbie—'

His eyes flickered to her, back to Will and then, with the bark of a laugh, he snapped his knife closed and pocketed it, keeping the pistol levelled. 'You'll not stay with me now, will you, sweetheart? Just for a moment this morning, though, you were considering it . . .' And, with another deft movement, he broke open the pistol and removed the bullets, taking in their astonished faces. 'The game's played out, sure enough, though I'm not sure who won.' He put the pistol down and flung himself into a chair. 'So here's an ending, eh? I thought this was the one place you'd never come looking, Will McAuley.'

It was as if the room itself exhaled.

Will moved the chair aside but came no closer. Rose felt Fraser relax, releasing her, and she went to Will. He put an arm out to her, still watching Robbie, still wary.

'You've the devil's own luck, it seems.' Robbie glanced towards the window then tossed back his drink. 'But you'd best be on your way, I'm thinking, before young Armstrong arrives.'

Fraser went to the window. 'He's right, Will. It's that or the fire.'

Will went on watching Robbie. 'Take Rose and the child. I'll follow.'

Fraser took a step towards Rose but she raised her hand to halt him. 'Not without Will,' she said, the bloodied cuff not forgotten. 'He still has the knife.'

Robbie laughed. 'I'll not harm your precious Will, darlin'. And Mr Portrait Man has as good a hand to play, if any of this gets out.' He gave Will a considering look. 'Why stay, partner? Whatever reckoning was due is paid and I say we're even. That brat's yours,' he added, gesturing to where Michael slept on behind a wall of cushions, 'but she's carrying mine – which balances that score too, and you'll have to make the best of it.' He rose and filled a glass with brandy. 'I took Rose, thinking you were dead, but you kept that nugget, you bastard, knowing that you cheated.' He took a drink and gave his old grin. 'Though I'd have done the same meself.'

'You did.'

Robbie nodded, acknowledging the hit. 'Aye, true enough, and I'll be keeping the money.' He glanced towards Rose. 'So go, and take Rose with you. She's more trouble than she was worth.' But something in his eyes belied the words. He rose and took his glass to the window, turning his back to them. 'And I'm leaving meself, very shortly, unless the fire reaches me first.'

'A fitting end,' Will said. Fraser looked across at him, an eyebrow raised in query. They could easily jump Robbie, wrest the knife from him – it was almost as if he was inviting them to try.

Will stood a moment, then shook his head, bent and swept up the sleeping child and handed him to Rose. He went across to the door and held it open, still watching Robbie and, as Rose passed through, she too turned to look across at him. Still he did not move but then, as if aware of her scrutiny, he raised his glass in salute.

Epilogue

Rose stood beside Will on the cobbles beside the jetty, still barely able to believe that he was there, holding Michael in his arms, looking down at the son who stared back at him, gripping his finger. He looked older, leaner, and she wondered a little how she appeared to him; did the scars show? There had been no time yet for words but she sensed he was building up to something, awaiting the right moment.

She saw him glance across to where Fraser was negotiating with the ferry man, and turned to her. 'I'm going to Canada, Rose. I'd decided this even before Fraser saw the photograph and we realised that you were here, in Scotland. He's been a good friend to me, but I need to be my own man. Start afresh.'

He stopped abruptly, as if unable to continue, and she looked back at him, quelling a sudden fear. Would he leave her, after all . . .?

'I've nothing to offer you,' he said, 'and I don't imagine life will be easy.'

Was it only that? 'No field of gold?'

'No.' She would have said more but he held up his hand. 'Fraser says that he'll provide a home for you, and for Michael and for Robbie's child when it arrives.'

Fraser? What was he telling her? 'So he is to be my good friend too?' she asked, as calmly as she could.

Will nodded. 'He will be if you ask it of him.' He took a breath and seemed to distance himself from her. 'It must be your choice, Rose. Your decision. If you can forgive me . . . This mess is as much of my making as his.'

She regarded him steadily. 'And am I to choose between you and Fraser?'

'No, *no*. I didn't mean that.' He switched Michael to his other arm, a frown pulling at the well-remembered scar. 'Fraser, it turns out, is a rich man and he says that he will set you up independently, if you wish, and give you an allowance. But once I've made good in Canada, I'll provide for you, and the children. Both of them.' He looked down at his sleeping son and she sensed his grip tighten.

'From Canada?'

He nodded. 'Aye, I'll send money over. You are, after all, still my wife if you choose to remain so, but you must decide what you do. That much, at least, I have learnt.' He smiled a little, but she sensed he was holding himself back as tightly as he had on their wedding night.

I'll not touch you, Rose, except that you want me to.

Full circle, Robbie had said.

'You promised me nothing once before.'

They stood there, in the chill morning air, and neither spoke. A pair of shelducks rose from beside the jetty and flew low over the water, heading west. Then she remembered. 'I have something of yours.' She reached into her pocket and brought out the remaining piece of gold. 'Robbie took the rest.'

Will looked at it, not taking it, and the moment seemed suspended in the soft mist of evening. 'But I'd go with you anywhere,' Rose said. 'For us, Will McAuley, the quest was never about the gold.'

Historical note

Alchemy and Rose is a work of fiction with imaginary characters and plot, hung loosely on a framework of historical fact. Kumara, where part of the story is set, lies on the Taramakau River, some seventeen miles to the northeast of Hokitika on New Zealand's South Island. It is possible to walk along Gibson's Quay in Hokitika today and still see old capstans and moorings and imagine the hundreds of vessels that once crossed the sand bar and tied up there, bringing hopeful diggers from all over the world to the rich goldfields of New Zealand's west coast. In his book *New Zealand's Last Gold Rush* (1997) Heinz gives a fascinating account of the Kumara goldfield which includes the romantic, and possibly apocryphal, tale of its discovery. As early as 1874 two disillusioned diggers, Dick Cashman and James Connor, are said to have found coarse nuggety gold in the water course of a creek emptying into the Taramakau river whilst setting up an illegal whisky still. They kept this discovery to themselves, working away quietly until their muddy outwash in the river attracted attention. By April 1876 suspicions were growing and a subsequent dispute over claims confirmed that a rich new field had been discovered. In the course of that year there were reported to be 6000 diggers on the goldfield creating a sprawling camp of tents, calico stores and grog shanties. Once it was found to be 'no duffer' more solid buildings were erected and a grid of streets was laid out, and by June 1877 Heinz reports that there were forty licensed premises and applications for another nine. Just one hotel now remains on the main thoroughfare of this small town along with one or two other buildings which survive from those early days. It is, however, still possible to walk along the route of a railed track and see the huge piles of boulders, tailings from the miners' shafts and tunnels that were later dug there.

Fiction permits a little licence and a nugget the size of the one that Rose found would have been an exceptional find. I allowed myself the liberty of its invention on the grounds that New Zealand's largest nugget (twice the size of Rose's) was found at Ross (14 miles south of Hokitika) in 1909. Weighing in at just over six pounds this nugget was christened the Hon. Roddy Nugget and was given to George V as a Coronation gift, after which time, so the story goes, it was melted down to produce a royal tea service. As recently as 2019 a nugget weighing almost half a pound was discovered with a metal detector near Hokitika, so there is still gold to be found in Westland.

Fitzroy market in Melbourne is no longer there, its site now occupied by a school, but in the 1880s an adventurous forebear of mine, having emigrated from Manchester, was a meat salesman operating from there and from Collingwood, which is why I chose these suburbs for that part of the story. This same individual then established a hotel and coffee house at Mordialloc where, in the 1870s, there was already a hotel called the Bridge Hotel. Sydney was growing fast in the 1870s, but had rough lawless areas, especially around the docks and wharves.

Kinnloss House is fictional, as are all the associated characters, but the remains of cleared croft houses can be seen disappearing into the gorse and heather in many places along the west coast of Scotland. Tales of ruthless evictions abound through the highlands and islands during the 19th century making the events that took place at Srath an loin at least a possibility, and set in train the story of *Alchemy and Rose*.

Acknowledgements

My family has long-standing connections with both New Zealand and Australia and I am lucky enough to have helpful friends and connections in both places. There are many good books written about the New Zealand gold rushes and I particularly enjoyed the engrossing *Diggers, Hatters and Whores* written by Stevan Eldred-Grigg (2008) who was also kind enough to answer some of my questions. Books specifically about the west coast rushes include *The Romance of Westland* by A. J. Harrop (1923), *Westland's Golden Sixties* by J. Halket Millar (1959) and *The West Coast Gold Rushes* by Philip Ross May (1967) but there are many others. For my purposes *New Zealand's Last Gold Rush* by William F. Heinz (1977) gave valuable insights into the Kumara goldrush and I would recommend Hokitika museum's excellent publication '*The Diggers' Story*', edited by Julia Bradshaw (2014). I enjoyed conversations with Cliff Samson regarding developments in early photography and if there are mistakes in the book they are my own. I am also grateful to Suzanne Collinge and Margaret Fairhurst for their hospitality and for showing me new parts of New Zealand, and discussing the flora and fauna of Westland. Research for another project took me to Melbourne and the book *Building Jerusalem: The Rise and Fall of the Victorian City* by T. Hunt (2004) sets the growth of Melbourne beside other great 19th century cities while *Rising Damp: Sydney 1870–90* by Shirley Fitzgerald (1987) looks closely at this formative period in Sydney's history.

My agent, Jenny Brown (Jenny Brown Associates), has been

a tremendous support throughout the writing process and I am very grateful to the wonderful team at Hodder & Stoughton led by Kimberley Atkins, and especially to Thorne Ryan whose editorial input was so very helpful and thanks too to Will Speed for the gorgeous cover design. My family has, as ever, been right behind me and bravely bear with my obsessions.

The book is dedicated to my great-uncle, Edwin Rowland, who went out to Australia and New Zealand looking for adventure in 1907. He came back to England with the Canterbury Rifles (New Zealand Expeditionary Force) in 1917, and was killed on October 12 at Bellevue Spur, in the first battle of Passchendaele, four days after arriving at the front.

I'm proud to have Scottish blood, even if it isn't a full measure. My grandfather was from Dumfriesshire and was brought up by his redoubtable grandmother, known to all as 'The Granny'. She was a baker in Old Cumnock but she claimed descent from McLeods of Skye and, twice married and having raised her own family, went on to raise the five children of one of her daughters, my great-grandmother, who had died in childbirth – as well as a number of other family strays. A tiny woman, my grandfather told me, who would stand on a chair to box his ears – all six foot two of him – and he was utterly devoted to her. She died just short of her 100th birthday and I wish I'd known her.

Scotland, therefore, is part of my make-up. Visits were a regular feature of my childhood, especially to the islands, a tradition I kept up for many years with my own family.

When I was a child, my family emigrated to Canada and we encountered many different nationalities in the small lumber town where my father was the doctor. Amongst them, inevitably, were several Scots. It was a Scot and his wife who ran The Hudson Bay Company store, following a practice that went back centuries to when the Company recruited Scots because they were tough, resourceful and dependable. I well remember the soft-spoken Mr Gordon taking us into the basement to see beaver and muskrat pelts brought in by trappers, surely amongst the last in a tradition going back to the very foundation of the Company (chartered in 1670). My grandparents would come out to Canada to stay and my grandfather was soon on close terms with the Gordons, and every other Scot he could find amongst the small population. He had a fine tenor voice and I can remember him, one convivial evening, singing Scottish ballads to a mixed company of Swedes, Finns, Italians and Ukrainians, and watching them fall under his spell.

The Scots' wide diaspora has been much written about and is something I enjoy researching to include in my writing. The role of Scots in exploring and settling Canada is something of which both Scots and Canadians are rightly proud. It was common when I was a teenager in Canada to hear both Scotland and England referred to as the 'old country' with the ties still meaningful two or three generations after initial emigration. 'I'm Scottish,' they would state, having grown up with the stories, but perhaps never having set foot on Scottish soil. My father later worked in the high Arctic, flying out from Inuvik hospital to far-flung nursing stations which were staffed by extraordinary nurses, a good number of them Scottish, exhibiting the same characteristics that The Hudson's Bay Company had admired. I visited my parents when he was working briefly at the hospital at Moose Factory, a former Hudson Bay Company post on James Bay. John Rae, the intrepid Orcadian, had been doctor there a century or so before him, before setting off to explore, more or less single-handed, huge unmapped areas of the eastern Arctic, surviving by adopting the ways of native Inuit and, unintentionally, discovered the fate of the doomed Franklin expedition who had gone in search of the North-West Passage. My parents eventually retired back to Britain, initially to a small community in the Scottish Borders where I married my husband, himself a hybrid Anglo-Scot, his mother's forebears having left the Montrose area in the late 19th century to work as lighter-men and Trinity House pilots on the Thames.

Canada was a land of opportunity, a magnet for Scots through the various hardships of the 19th century when so many left Scotland, continuing a pattern of emigration which began after the Jacobite rebellions in the previous century. They took their music and their dances, their stories and their songs and nowhere, perhaps, is the connection with Scotland stronger than in Canada's maritime provinces where, for a brief period, there were more Gaelic speakers than in Scotland, a situation which has now thankfully been reversed. I have worked sporadically in that area, the first landfall for many migrating Scots and Irish settlers arriving in leaking ships, and often getting no further.

The United States too, drew many Scots. My grandfather, as a teenager, had the chance to go and live there, encouraged by an aunt who had already settled in New Jersey and who was trying to help the spread the load for The Granny. He chose to stay in Scotland, however, where he joined the London Scottish Regiment in the final year of WW1. One of his younger sisters took up the offer instead and left for New York where she lived for the rest of her life. Mysterious, and often glamorous, presents used to arrive from 'Oor Lizzie' and the brother and sister kept in touch, long before the internet made it so much easier.

North America was not, of course, the only place that drew Scots away from their homeland. They were dispersed widely throughout the former British Empire, and at one time were actively encouraged to go to New Zealand. In the middle of the 19th century agents would appear amongst struggling communities disillusioned by the lack of social mobility and opportunity at home, offering free land and cheap passage. Dunedin (the Gaelic for Edinburgh is Dùn Èideann) was established as a Free

Church of Scotland colony in 1848 and emigrants were promised a new way of life, amongst their own kith and kin. Gaelic and Caledonian Societies were formed, reinforcing bonds and strong networks of support for those who might never see Scotland again. Maps of New Zealand, especially in Otago in the South Island, are littered with Scottish names for towns, rivers and other landmarks in the same way that swathes of the New Zealand countryside are clothed in broom and gorse brought by these resolute settlers. New Zealand is working hard to eradicate invasive plant and animal species, but the Scots ancestry of many New Zealanders is deep rooted – and valued.

I have past and present family connections in New Zealand (through the English side of my family) and I go there when I can. It was during one of these visits that I became fascinated by the late 19th century gold rush which is the setting for *Alchemy and Rose*. News of gold being found in the 1860s brought not only more Scots but hopefuls from all over the world, an onslaught which soon swamped the young colony. Dunedin, in consequence, grew very rapidly, with several civic buildings adopting versions of the Scottish baronial style. The Irish too flocked to New Zealand, together with other Europeans and a great many Chinese, all drawn by the gold. The same had happened in British Columbia, Canada where I have family of many generations. My parents lived for a while in Victoria B.C., where the colony's first governor was another Scot, James Douglas and the story goes that he came out of Sunday service to find the place invaded by prospectors as news of gold finds in the Fraser Canyon brought hoards steaming up from the dwindling California goldfields. Many of these same individuals would later head to Australia, New Zealand or South Africa in the ever-frenzied quest for riches. A great-great uncle of mine met his end in the Queensland goldfields, under suspicious circumstances, and that family story is an extraordinary one. A little gold nugget that he sent home in the early 1920s still survives, adorning a hatpin worn by a daring great-aunt.

Many of the fictional characters in my books have followed these adventurous souls. At one point Cameron Forbes in *The House between Tides* leaves his Hebridean island home for Canada, in *Beyond the Wild River* James Douglas flees injustice in the Borders and heads for the Canadian wilderness, while in *Women of the Dunes* archaeologist Libby Snow, returns to Scotland from Newfoundland to trace her mysterious ancestry. For the first time, in *Alchemy and Rose,* my characters head for New Zealand, seeking gold, adventure and a new beginning, and finding that life was demanding there, and dangerous. Rose, the impoverished grand-daughter of a Glaswegian convict, washes up on the inhospitable west coast of New Zealand's South Island, with little hope of a future, while Will Stewart, a disaffected crofter, represents that determined breed who were willing to risk all to improve his life chances, craving nothing than more than land he could call his own. Fraser Urquhart is from a different class entirely but, having offended polite society back in Scotland, is also seeking new freedoms. Robbie Malloy, an Irishman, another fugitive from justice, is a man who will stop at nothing to get himself where he wants to be and, in the melting pot of gold rush Hokitika, their fortunes become entwined. Each of them, in their own different ways, is seeking to break free of the strictures of their previous lives and find independence, economic gain, creative expression or, in Rose's case, the ability to determine her own future. The gold in the foothills of the Southern Alps drew them together but they find, for each of them, that the quest undergoes a metamorphosis.

Many families, past and present, have, for whatever reason, a restless gene – my own family included. The exploits of adventurous

Scots have a particular fascination for me, and their stories and family lore passed down, provide a rich well for my fiction to draw upon. And, much as I enjoy discovering more about their lives in the places they went to, I also frequently stop a moment and look around, and contemplate the rich history and beautiful landscapes they left behind.